Richard Pike

Quaker Anecdotes

Richard Pike

Quaker Anecdotes

ISBN/EAN: 9783337399528

Printed in Europe, USA, Canada, Australia, Japan

Cover: Foto ©Andreas Hilbeck / pixelio.de

More available books at **www.hansebooks.com**

QUAKER ANECDOTES.

EDITED BY

RICHARD PIKE.

SECOND EDITION.

LONDON:
HAMILTON, ADAMS, & CO., PATERNOSTER ROW,
NOTTINGHAM:
J. DERRY, ALBERT STREET.
1881.

PREFACE.

The history of the Society of Friends from Fox's time to the present day, has been a remarkable one. No class of men have lived more unselfish lives. Many beautiful characters have graced their annals, persons whose sympathies were broad—whose activities embraced the varied fields of benevolent enterprise; whilst for shrewdness, business capacity, and readiness of reply, they have had no superiors. The influence and achievements of the Quakers have been out of all proportion to their numbers. In the last Parliament there were sixteen members who had been born and educated in the Society, and it is very remarkable, two of that number were Cabinet Ministers, viz., Mr. Bright and Mr. Forster.

Several years ago, being much interested in some quaint and striking anecdotes of members of the Society of Friends, the thought occurred to me—I have never met with any considerable collection of such anecdotes, and it is pretty certain from my reading it would not be difficult to make such an unique collection. To this end, for some years, my leisure has been frequently devoted to researches which, I fain would believe, have not been barren of results.

There is no doubt a change going on among the Quakers, which will interfere greatly with that racy individuality which has so long characterised them as a distinct community. According to appearances, it seems very unlikely that the future will be so prolific in this respect as has been the past.

My share in the production of the book has been mainly that of a collector of anecdotes. Those relating to I. T. Hopper are taken from his "Life," written by L. M. Child, of New York. The anecdotes collected, for the most part redound highly to the credit, shrewdness, and benevolence of the Quakers.

N.B.—Should this collection of "Quaker Anecdotes" meet with public favour, from materials at hand and which are to be obtained from outside assistance, it will give me much pleasure to publish a second series of "Quaker Anecdotes." Many interesting ones exist. I would therefore ask my readers who may be able to furnish them, to be so kind as to enclose them to me, addressed to the Editor of "Quaker Anecdotes," care of Mr. J. Derry, Bookseller, Albert Street, Nottingham.

CONTENTS

4   CONTENTS.

CONTENTS.

QUAKER ANECDOTES.

THE FOUNDER OF THE QUAKERS.

IN the Year 1643, a rude, gaunt, illiterate lad of nineteen, a shoemaker by trade, affected with the religious fervour of that age, being at a country fair in his native Leicestershire, met with his cousin and another friend there, and the three youths agreed to have a stoup of ale together. They accordingly adjourned to a tavern in the neighbourhood, and called for drink. When the first supply was exhausted, the cousin and his friend called for more, began to drink healths, and said that he who would not drink should pay for the entire ale-score. The young shoemaker was alarmed at this proposal, and as he explained the circumstances afterwards, he put his hand into his pocket and took out a groat, laid it down on the table, and said, if it be so, I will leave you, and so he went home. The village ale-house incident was an important event in the history of the Anglo-Saxon race; for through it where to come Quakerism, the writings and teachings of Penn and Barclay, the colony and constitution of Pennsylvania, the republics of the west, and in no very remote degree the vast movement of liberal ideas in Great Britain and America, in more modern times. The illiterate and upright shoemaker who would drink no more was George Fox, "I went away," he afterwards wrote in his journal, "and when I had done my business, returned home. But I did not go to bed that night, nor did I sleep, but sometimes walked up and down, and sometimes prayed, and called to the Lord."

Dixon's *Life of Penn.*

ORIGIN OF THE TERM QUAKERS.

On the 30th of October, 1650, the celebrated George Fox being at a Lecture delivered in Derby by a Colonel of the parliamentary Army, after the service was over addressd the congregation till there came an officer who took him by the hand, and said, that he, and the other two that were with him, must go before the Magistrates. They were examined for a long time, and then George Fox, and one John Fretwell of Staniesby, a husbandman, were committed to the house of correction for six months upon pretence of blasphemous expressions. Gervase Bennett, one of the justices who signed their mittimus, hearing that Fox bade him, and those about him "*tremble* at the word of the Lord," regarded this admonition so lightmindedly, that from that time, he called Fox and his friends *Quakers*. This new and unusual demonstration was taken up so eagerly, that it soon ran over all England, and from thence to foreign countries. It has since remained their distinctive name, insomuch, that to the present time, they are so termed in acts of parliament, and in their own declarations on certain public occasions, they designate themselves "the people called Quakers." The community in its rules and minutes, for government and discipline, denominates itself "The Society of Friends."

Hone's "Table Book."

GEORGE FOX AND CROMWELL.

In 1654, there was a rumour of a plot formed against the Protector, in which it was thought the Quakers had a hand, and in consequence of this Fox was seized at one of his meetings, and carried a prisoner to London   Captain Dury, who had charge of him, reported his arrival to Cromwell, who asked him to subscribe a paper to the effect that he would never use a carnal weapon against him or his government. Fox, who abjured the sword even in self-defence, readily did so. Next morning he was taken to Whitehall, that the Protector might see him and judge of him for himself. When he arrived Cromwell was still undressed, but it did not matter, he was at once admitted to his presence, which he entered with the priestly words, "Peace be on this house," and with his hat firmly fixed on his head. An interesting peep behind the scenes—the meeting of these two immortals. The great Protector in his shirt receiving the humble Quaker—a man half-crazed, but destined by the earnestness of his convictions, to found a sect which has lasted for centuries, and done some good in the world! The conversation was about religion, and the Quaker exhorted the Protector to live in the fear of God, and order all things for his glory. The Protector remarked that the Quakers quarrelled with the Ministers of religion. The Quaker replied that the prophets and apostles preached not for hire, whereas the priests of that day divined for money, and bartered the free Gospel for filthy lucre. He declared that the Spirit was necessary to illuminate the mind, and that without it the Scriptures were useless. As he proceeded, Oliver frequently interjected, "It is good," "It is truth." When the poor Quaker was ready to leave, the absolute master of three Kingdoms took him warmly by the hand, and with tears in eyes, said, "Come again to my house, for if thou and I were but an hour of a day together, we should be nearer one another." As he was returning a servant followed him, and invited him to remain and dine with the Protector's attendants, but, though pleased with his reception, he, in rather a surly way, told the servant to say to his master that he would not eat of his bread nor drink of his drink. Was it pride or an outburst of independence—a foolish protest that he would not sell his birthright for a mess of pottage, though served in a silver plate in the hall of a court?

The "Quakers." by Dr. Cunningham.

Fox's Adventures.

In 1655, Dr. Cunningham writes "Fox was now master of a horse, on which he performed his journeys. In his wandering life he necessarily met with strange adventures. On one occasion there was a hue and cry that two men who had been seen on the road clad in grey clothes and riding on grey horses were highwaymen, and that they had broken into a house. They were pursued, overtaken, and carried before a justice of the peace. "Take off your hats," cried the justice, when the supposed highwaymen were brought into his presence. "I kept on my hat in the presence of the Protector," said Fox, who, with a brother Quaker, were the supected housebreakers, "and he was not offended, and why should you who are but his servant." The magistrate was convinced there had been a mistake, and set them at liberty. On another occasion, being in a tavern, he began to speak to the men who were enjoying their pot of ale, of the light which lighteneth every man who cometh into the world. The landlord being a facetious fellow, and seeing that this kind of discourse was likely to spoil his custom, snatched up a candle, and said, "Come, here is a light to light you to your bed," and so marched him off to his chamber.

Marriage of George Fox.

About the latter end of 1669 he went to Bristol, at which place, he entered into matrimonial alliance with his old friend and fellow-sufferer, Margaret Fell. The particulars of this event afford a pleasing trait of the integrity and simplicity of his dealings.

"I had seen from the Lord a considerable time before, that I should take Margaret Fell to be my wife; and when I first mentioned it to her, she felt the answer of life from God thereto. But though the Lord had opened this thing to me, yet I had not received a command from Him for the accomplishing of it at this time. Wherefore I let the affair rest, and went on in the work and service of the Lord, according as he had led me, travelling in this nation and through Ireland.

But being now at Bristol, and finding Margaret Fell there, it opened to me from the Lord, the thing should be accomplished. After we had discoursed the matter together, I told her, if she was also satisfied with the accomplishing of it now, sho should first send for her children, which she did. When her daughters were come, I asked both of them and her sons-in-law, 'if they had anything against it, or for it?' and they all severally expressed their satisfaction therewith. Then I asked Margaret Fell, ''if she had fulfilled her husband's will to her children?' She replied, ' the children knew sho had.' Whereupon I asked them, whether, if their mother married, they should not lose by it? I asked Margaret, ' whether she had done anything in lieu of their claims, which might answer it to the children? They replied, ' she had answered it to them, and desired me to say no more about it.' 'I told them that I was plain, and would have all things done plainly : for I sought not any outward advantage to myself.' So our intention of marriage was laid before Friends both privately and publicly, to their full satisfaction, many of whom gave testimony that it was of God. Afterwards a meeting being appointed on purpose for the accomplishing thereof, we took each other in marriage, in the meeting-house at Broad Mead, in Bristol; the Lord joining us together in honourable marriage, in the everlasting covenant and immortal Seed of Life In the sense whereof, living and weighty testimonies were borne thereunto by Friends in the movings of the heavenly power which united us together. Then was a certificate, relating both the proceedings and the marriage,

openly read, and signed by the relations, and by most of
the ancient Friends of the city; besides many others from
divers parts of the nation.

"We stayed about a week at Bristol, and then went together to Oldstone : where, taking leave of each other in
the Lord, we parted, betaking ourselves each to our several service; Margaret returning homewards to the North,
and I passing on in the work of the Lord as before. I
travelled through Wiltshire, Berkshire, Oxfordshire, Buck-
inghamshire, and so on to London, visiting Friends : in all
which counties I had many large and precious meetings."

RUSTIC QUAKER.

Cunningham remarks, " Penn was always a welcome
visitor at the palace, and was known to have a large share
of the royal confidence. Great nobles were kept waiting in
the ante-room while he was closeted with the King. Other
Friends were also admitted into the royal presence with
their hats undisturbed, and that was always the point of honour with them. On this matter the grim, monkish monarch,
even ventured a joke. A rustic Quaker had been admitted to
an audience with his majesty, and of course kept his
hat on his head, but the king pulled off his own beaver and
held it under his arm while the Quaker spoke. The man,
in his simplicity, thought this was doing him too much
honour, and ventured to say, "The king need not keep off
his hat for me." "You don't know the custom," replied
his majesty, no doubt with a hardly repressed smile, "for
that requires that but one hat must be on here."

COMPARATIVE EXCELLENCE OF GOVERNMENT.

"Locke" says Clarkson in his Life of Penn, " drew up
at the request of Lord Shaftesbury, a form of government
for Carolina, which then comprehended both the northern

and southern districts of that name. It happened that he
and William Penn, and Mr. (afterwards Sir Isaac) Newton,
and others were in company, and that the conversation
turned upon the comparative excellence of the new American governments, but particularly those of Carolina and
Pennsylvania. The matter was argued at length in the
presence of the two legislators, when Locke ingenuously
yielded the palm to Penn." The two constitutions were
diametrically opposed. Locke's was feudal and aristocratic,
Penn's was purely democratic.

PENN AND THE INDIANS

King Charles II., in consideration of a considerable sum
due from the crown for the services of Admiral Sir William
Penn, granted to his son, the ever-memorable William Penn,
and his heirs, in perpetuity a great tract of land on the
river Deleware in America; with full power to erect a new
colony there, to sell lands, to create magistrates, and to
pardon crimes.

In August, 1682, Penn, after having written to his wife and
children a letter eminently remarkable for its simplicity and
patriarchal spirit, took an affectionate leave of them, and
accompanied by several friends embarked at Deal, on board
the Welcome, a ship of three hundred tons burthen. The
passengers, including himself, were not more than a hundred.
They were chiefly Quakers, and most of them from Sussex,
in which county his house at Warminghurst was seated.
They sailed about the first of September, but had not proceeded far to sea, when the small pox broke out so virulently,
that thirty of their number died. In about six weeks from
the time of their leaving the Downs they came in sight of the
American coast, and shortly afterwards landed at Newcastle,
in the Delaware river.

William Penn's first business was to explain to the settlers

of Dutch and Swedish extraction the object of his coming,
and the nature of the government he designed to establish.
The next great movement was to Upland, where he called
the first general assembly, consisting of an equal number, for
the provinces and for the territories, of all such freemen as
chose to attend. In this assembly the frame of government,
and many important regulations, were settled; and subsequently he endeavoured to settle the boundaries of his territory
with Charles Lord Baltimore, a Catholic nobleman, who was
governor and proprietor of the adjoining province of Maryland, which had been settled with persons of his own
persuasion.

Penn wished to live in friendship with the Indians; he was
assured that this was possible. The Quakers already settled
in New Jersey had solved this problem—"Ye are our
brothers," said the Sachems to them, "and we will live like
brothers with you. We will have a broad path for you and
us to walk in. If an Englishman falls asleep in this path,
we will pass him by and say it is an Englishman, he is asleep,
let him alone. The path shall be plain; there shall be no
stump in it to hurt the feet."

Penn's religious principles which led him to the practise of
the most scrupulous morality, did not permit him to look upon
the King's patent, or legal possession according to the laws of
England, as sufficient to establish his right to the Country
without purchasing it by fair and open bargain of the natives
to whom, only, it properly belonged. He had therefore instructed commissioners, who had arrived in America before
him, to buy it of the latter, and to make with them at the
same time a treaty of eternal friendship, This the commissioners had done; and this was the time when, by mutual
agreement between him and the Indian chiefs, it was to be
publicly ratified. He proceeded, therefore, accompanied by
his friends, consisting of men, women, and young person of

oth sexes to Coaquannoc, the Indian name of the place where Philadelphia now stands. On his arrival there he found the Sachems and their tribes assembling. They were seen in the woods as far as the eye could carry, and looked frightful both on account of their number and their arms. The Quakers are reported to have been but a handful in comparison, and these without any weapons, so that dismay and terror had come upon then, had they not confided to the righteousness of their cause.

It is much to be regretted when we have accounts of minor treaties between William Penn and the Indians, that there is not in any historian an account of this. though so many mention it, and though all concur in considering it as the most glorious of any in the annals of the world. There are, however, relations in Indian speeches, and traditions in Quaker families, descended from those who were present on the occasion, from which we may learn something concerning it. It appears that, though the parties were to assemble at Coaquannoc, the treaty was made a little higher up at Shackamaxon Upon this Kensington now stands; the houses of which may be considered as the suburbs of Philadelphia. There was at Shakamaxon an elm tree of a prodigious size. To this the leaders on both sides repaired, approaching each other under its widely-spreading branches. William Penn appeared in his usual clothes. He had no crown, sceptre, mace, sword, halberd, or any insignia of eminence. He was distinguished only by wearing a sky blue sash round his waist, which was made of silk, net-work, and which was of no larger apparent dimensions than an officer's military sash, and much like it except in colour On his right hand was Colonel Markham. his relation and Secretary, and on his left his friend Pearson, after whom followed a train of Quakers. Before him were carried various articles of merchandise which, when they came near the Sachems, were spread upon the ground.

He held a roll of parchment, containing the confirmation of the treaty of purchase and amity, in his hand. One of the Sachems, who was the chief of them, then put upon his own head a kind of chaplet, in which appeared a small horn. This, as among the primitive eastern nations, and according to scripture language, was an emblem of kingly power, and whenever the chief, who had a right to wear it, put it on, it was understood that the place was made sacred, and the persons of all present inviolable. Upon putting on this horn the Indians threw down their bows and arrows, and seated themselves round their chiefs in the form of a half-moon upon the ground. The chief Sachem then announced to William Penn, by means of an interpreter, that the natives were ready to hear him.

Having been thus called upon, he began. The Great Spirit, he said, who made him and them, who ruled the heaven and the earth, and who knew the innermost thoughts of man, knew that he and his friends had a hearty desire to live in peace and friendship with them, and to serve them to the utmost of their power. It was not their custom to use hostile weapons against their fellow creatures, for which reason they had come unarmed. Their object was not to do injury, and thus provoke the Great Spirit, but to do good. They were then met on the broad pathway of good faith and good will, so that no advantage was to be taken on either side, but all was to be openness, brotherhood, and love. After these and other words, he unrolled the parchment, and by means of the said interpreter, conveyed to them, article by article, the conditions of the purchase, and the words of the compact then made for their eternal union. Among other things they were not to be molested in their lawful pursuits even in the territory they had alienated, for it was to be common for them and the English. They were to have the same liberty to do all things therein relating to the improvement of their grounds, and providing sustenance for their families, which the English had. If any disputes should arise between the two, they should be settled by twelve persons, half of whom should be English and half Indians. He then paid them for the land, and made them many presents besides from the merchandise which had been spread before them. Having done this, he laid the roll of parchment on the ground ; observing again, that the ground should be common for both people. He then added that he would not do as the Marylanders did ; that is, call them children or brothers only, for often parents were apt to whip theirchildren too severely, and brothers sometimes would differ: neither would he compare the friendship between him and them to a chain, for the rain might sometimes rust it, or a tree might fall and break it ; but he should consider them as the same flesh and blood with the Christians, and the same as if one man's body were to be divided into two parts. He then took up the parchment, and presented it to the Sachem who wore the horn in the chaplet, and desired him and the other Sachems to preserve it carefully for three generations, that their children might know what had passed between them, just as if he had remained himself with them to repeat it. The Indians on their part solemnly pledged themselves, according to their country manner, to live in love with William Penn and his children as long as the sun and moon should endure.

Thus ended this famous treaty of which more has been said in the way of praise than of any other ever transmitted to posterity. "This," said Voltaire, "was the only treaty between those people and the Christians that was not ratified by an oath, and that was never broken." Noble, in his continuation of Granger, says, "He occupied his domains by actual barguin and sale with the Indians. This fact does him infinite honour, as no blood was shed and the Christian and barbarian met as brothers. Penn has thus taught us to

respect the lives and properties of the most unenlightened
nations." "Being now returned," says Robert Proud, in his
history of Pennsylvania, "from Maryland to Coaquannoc, he
purchased lands of the Indians, whom he treated with great
justice and sincere kindness. It was at this time when he
first entered personally into that friendship with them, which
ever afterwards continued between them, and which for the
space of more than seventy years was never interrupted, or
so long as the Quakers retained power in the government."

The great elm-tree, under which this treaty was made,
became celebrated from that day. When in the American
war the British general Simcoe was quartered at Kensington,
he so respected it, that when his soldiers were cutting down
every tree for fire-wood, he placed a sentinel under it, that
not a branch of it might be touched. In 1812 it was blown
down, when its trunk was split into wood, and cups and
other articles were made of it, to be kept as memorials of it.
The identical roll of parchment given by William Penn to
the Indians was shown by their descendents to some English
officers some years ago.

What shows the scrupulous adherence of the Indians to
their engagements in the most surprising light is, that long
after the descendents of Penn ceased to possess political influ-
ance in the State, in comparatively recent times, when the
Indian character was confessedly lowered by their intercourse
with the whites, and they were instigated by their own
injuries and the arts of the French to make incursions into
Pennsylvania, the 'Friends' were still to them a sacred and
inviolable people, while the tomahawk and the scalping knife
were nightly doing their dreadful work in every surrounding
dwelling—theirs were untouched ; while the rest of the inhabitants abandoned their houses and fled to forts for security,
they found more perfect security in that friendship which
the wisdom and virtue of Penn had conciliated, and which
their own disinterested principles made permanent.

It has been well observed that "It is William Penn's peculiar honour to stand alone as a statesman, in opposing principle to expedience, in public as well as in private life. Even Aristides, the very beau-ideal of virtuous integrity, failed in this point. The success of the experiment has been as splendid as the most philosophic worshipper of abstract morals could have hoped for or imagined. "These sentences exemplify an expression elsewhere.—"Politics are Morals."
Hone's "*Table Book.*"

LORD PETERBOROUGH AND WILLIAM PENN.

One morning I went to hear Penn preach, for 'tis my way to be civil to all religions.

I took a trip once with Penn to his colony of Pennsylvania. The laws there are contained in a small volume; and are so extremely good. that there has been no alteration wanted in any one of them. They have no lawyers. Every one is to tell his own case, or some friend for him; they have four persons, as judges, on the bench; and after the case has been fully laid down, on both sides, all the four draw lots, and he on whom the lot falls decides the question.—'Tis a fine country, and the people are neither oppressed by poor's-rates, tythes, nor taxes.—LORD PETERBOROUGH.

PENN'S DISLIKE TO TOBACCO.

William Penn disliked tobacco. Clarkson, in his *Life* of him, records this, and says, that while in America he was often annoyed by it, but here submitted in good humour. Once, on his way to Pensburg, he stopped at Burlington to see old friends, who happened to be smoking, and discovering that the pipes had been hid, he said pleasantly, "Well, friends, I am glad that you are ashamed of your old practice." "Not entirely so," replied Samuel Jennings, one of the company; "but we preferred laying down our pipes to the danger of offending a weak brother."

The old colonists who planted tobacco were equally severe against the Quakers. Thus, in what are termed the "Blue Laws" of old Virginia, 1663, we find it enacted: every master of a ship or vessel, that shall bring in any Quaker to reside here after the 1st of July next, shall be fined 5000 pounds of tobacco." This is followed by another:—"Any person inhabiting this country and entertaining any Quaker in or near his house, to preach or teach, shall, for every time of such entertainment, be fined 5000 pounds of tobacco." It was the custom in the colony at this period to pay invariably all fines for crimes in pounds of tobacco.—F. W. FAIRHOLT, F.S.A.

QUAKERS AND THE JUSTICE OF THE PEACE.

William Penn and Thomas Story once sheltered themselves from a shower of rain in a tobacconist's shop, the cross-grained owner of which said to them, "You enter here without leave. Do you know who I am? I am a Justice of the Peace." To which Story replied, "My friend makes such things as thee—he is governor of Pennsylvania."

JOHN THE QUAKER.

In the reign of Charles II., John Kesley, popularly known as "John the Quaker," went to Constantinople, upon no less a design than of converting the sultan. He preached at the corner of one of the streets of that city with all the vehemence of a fanatic; but as he spoke in his own language, the people stared at him, but could not so much as guess the drift of his harangue. They soon concluded him to be out of his senses, and carried him to a madhouse, where he was confined for six months. One of the keepers happening to hear him utter the word *English*, informed Lord Winchelsea, who was then ambassador to the Porte, that a mad countryman of his was under confinement. His Lordship sent for John who appeared before him in a torn and dirty hat, which he could not by any means be persuaded to take off. The ambassador thought that a little of the Turkish dicipline would be of service to him, and presently ordered him to be drubbed upon the feet. This occasioned a total change in his behaviour, and he acknowledged that the drubbing had " a good effect upon his spirit." Upon searching his pockets a letter was found, addressed to the sultan, in which he told him he was a seourge in the hand of God to chastise the wicked; and that He had sent him, not only to dencunce, but to exeeute vengeance. He was put on board a ship bound for England, but found means to escape in his passage, and returned to Constantinople. He was soon after put on board another ship, and so effectually seeured that he could not escape a second time.

[There can be no doubt that this poor fellow was simply a lunatic; and the conduct of the British ambassador in causing him to be bastinadoed, as above related, was cruel in the extreme, however much it may have been in accordance with the barbarous methods employed at that period, and long afterwards, in dealing with persons suffering from that most awful of human afflictions, the loss of reason.]

ANECDOTE OF CROMWELL.

During the Proteetorate of Oliver Cromwell, an English merehant ship was taken in the chops of the Channel, carried into St. Maloe's, and there confiscated on some groundless pretenee. As soon as the master of the ship, who was an honest Quaker, got home, he presented a petition to the Proteetor in Couneil, setting forth his ease, and praying for redress. Upon hearing the petition, the Proteetor told his couneil he would take that affair upon himself, and ordered the man to attend him the next morning. He examined him strictly as to all the cireumstanees of his case, and finding by his answers, that he was a plain, honest man, and that he had been eoncerned in no unlawful trade, he asked him if he eould go to Paris with a letter. The man answered he could. "Well, then," said the Proteetor, "pre-

pare for your journey, and come to me to-morrow morning."
Next morning he gave him a letter to Cardinal Mazarin
and told him he must stay but three days for an answer. "The
answer I mean," said Cromwell, "is the full value of what
you might have made of your ship and cargo; and tell the
Cardinal that if it be not paid in three days, you have express orders from me to return home." The honest blunt
Quaker, we may suppose, followed his instructions to a tittle;
but the Cardinal, according to the manner of ministers when
they are in any way pressed, began to shuffle; therefore, the
Quaker returned as he was bid .As soon as the Protector saw
him, he asked, "Well friend, have you got your money?"
And upon the man answering he had not, the Protector told
him "Then leave your direction with my secretary, and you
shall soon hear from me." Upon this occasion that great
man did not stay to negotiate, or to explain, by long, tedious
memorials, the reasonableness of his demand. No; though
there was a French minister residing here, he did not so much
as acquaint him with the story, but immediately sent out a
man-of-war or two, with orders to seize every French ship
they could meet with. Accordingly they returned in a few
days with two or three French prizes, which the Protector
ordered to be immediately sold; and out of the produce he
paid the Quaker what he demanded for the ship and cargo.
He then sent for the French minister, gave him an account
of what had happened, and told him there was a balance,
which, if he pleased, should be paid to him, to the end that
he might deliver it to those of his countrymen who were the
owners of the French ships that had been so taken and
sold.—*Providence of God Illustrated.*

PHONOGRAPHY ANTICIPATED.

Dr. Cunningham remarks—"We have already seen the
Quakers endeavouring to reform our grammar, and making a
due observance of the singular number a point of piety.

A member of the sect proceeded still further in the same direction, and attempted to remodel our spelling, and though his system of orthography never received the sanction of religion, he has the undoubted merit of having anticipated phonography. The author of this invention subscribes himself "John" the servant of the most high God, the former and upholder of all things, (who weigheth the mountains in scales and the hills in a balance, and taketh up the isles as a very little thing.)" He tells us that he wrote from a place called "Great Gomara, on a certain island in Hungary," when he was a prisoner, and his pamphlet, which is entitled "The Arraignment of Christendom," is declared on the title-page, with a sublime generality, to have been printed in Europe in the year 1677." In the preface to this production, we are told that the author had endeavoured to spell as people speak, and three advantages are pointed out as likely to be the result of this improved orthography—children would learn to read more readily; all would learn to write more correctly; and foreigners would acquire our pronunciation more certainly; the very arguments which are used by phonographers of the present day. As an example of his meaning, he points out that "righteousness" has four superfluous letters, which, after all, do not represent the sound, and therefore he strikes them out, and spells it "ryteosues." The man and his pamphlet are full of extravagance, but here there is a gleam of sense. Had the Quakers consecrated the idea, and made it a matter of concience to spell as they spoke, they might have relieved overburdened memories from the "letter which killeth."

JAMES NAYLOR.

But of all the disciples of Fox, male and female, none was more famous than James Naylor, and no one brought upon the sect a deeper reproach. He had unfortunately kindled the admiration of some crazy woman, who persuaded him that he

was nothing less than divine; and his judgment, already dis-
ordered by fanaticism, was unable to resist the intoxication of
female flattery. One admirer wrote him, " Thou shalt no
longer be called James Naylor, but Jesus." Others addressed
him as *The Everlasting Son of Righteousness— The Prince of
Peace—The only begotten Son of God—The fairest among ten
thousand.* It was famed abroad that he had raised a woman
from the dead. When lying in Exeter jail into which he had
been cast, some female devotees got admittance to his presence,
they knelt before him; they kissed his feet; and malicious
tongues whispered that their too ardent devotion had
melted into love. Released at Exeter, it was arranged that
he should enter Bristol in triumph, as Christ had entered
Jerusalem. A man walked before him bare-headed. A
woman led his horse by the reins. Three others ran before
and spread their scarfs and handkerchiefs in the way; and a
company followed singing, "Holy, holy, holy, is the Lord
God of Hosts; Hosannah in the highest, Holy, holy, holy, is
the Lord God of Israel." So they entered the city; but they
were quickly laid hold of and marched to the jail. From
Bristol he was sent to London, where he was charged before
the parliament with blasphemy, for assuming the name and
attributes of Christ, and a parliamentary committee was appointed to examine witnesses in the cause. That divine
honours were rendered in his presence he confessed, but he
pleaded that they were not paid to him but to Christ who
dwelt in him. For ten days was the great council of the
nation employed in deliberations as to whether Naylor
was an imposter, a maniac, or a man divinely inspired. At
last they found him guilty of blasphemy, and if slow in coming
to judgment, when they did come to it, they forgot mercy.
The unhappy man was sentenced to be placed in the pillory
at Westminster for two hours, thereafter to be whipped at a
cart's tail, from Westminster to the Old Exchange: two days

afterwards he was to be put in the pillory again, with a pla-
card over his head stating his crime, and then to have his
tongue bored through with a hot iron, and his forehead bran-
ded with the letter B; and, as if this were not enough, he
was to be sent the following week to Bristol, carried through
the city on horseback, with his face to the tail, whipped
again, and finally to be brought back to London, confined in Bridewell, and kept at hard labour during the parli-
ment's pleasure. A most barbarous sentence! When he had
undergone one-half of it there was an effort made—and many
who were not Quakers joined in it—to have the remainder
cancelled; but the parliament through zeal for religion, was
unrelenting, and the whole of the terrible punishment was
endured An unflinching Friend stood by him at the pillory,
gently held his head while his tongue was being bored, and
licked his wonds to assuage the pain. The spectators through
pity uncovered their heads when he was in his agony The
Quakers in general were far from approving these insane and
blasphemous pretensions, but they commiserated him in his
cruel sufferings; and as he repented in prison and acknowledged his errors, they received him, on his liberation, back
into their body.

"*The Quakers*," by Dr. Cunningham.

JAMES NAYLOR AT BRISTOL.

Preachers of the Quaker sect first came to Bristol in the
year 1653, and the 13th of November 1656, James Naylor and
Dorcas Erbury, were summoned to appear before the parliament
in London. James Naylor was sentenced by the parliament
to a severe punishment, which was executed in Bristol on the
17th of January, 1657, according to the following order:—

Cause James Naylor to ride in at Lawford's gate upon a
horse bare ridged, with his face backward; from thence along
Wine-street to the Tolzey; thence down High-street over

the bridge, and out of Rackley-gate; there let him alight and
bring him into Saint Thomas-street, and cause him to be stript
and made fast to the cart-horse; and there in the market first
whipped; from thence to the foot of the bridge, there whipped;
thence to the end of the bridge, there whipped; thence to the
middle of High-street, there whipped; thence to the Tolzey,
there whipped; thence to the middle of Broad-street, there
whipped, and then turn into Taylor's hall, thence release him
from the cart-horse, and let him put on his clothes, and carry
him from there to Newgate by Tower-lane the back way.

There did ride before him, bare headed, Michael Stamper,
singing most part of the way, and several other friends, men
and women, the men went bare-headed by him, and Robert
Rich, (late merchant of London) rode by him bare-headed,
and singing, till he came to Redcliff-gate, and there the
magistrates sent their officers and brought him back on horseback to the Tolzey, all which way he rode singing very loud,
where the magistrates met. It seems James Naylor is not
noticed in the sufferings of the Quakers, being justly censured
by the generality of them, till he had passed the bitter pangs
of a sincere repentance. Howbeit it was very observable,
that he endured his extreme punishment with a patience and
magnanimity astonishing to the beholders; and many were of
opinion, that had not the blindness of their zeal who condemmed him, been at least equal to the blackness of his
guilt, a punishment much more moderate might have sufficed.
This rigourus punishment was inflicted according to the
sentence of a bigoted parliament, and not by the desire of
Cromwell, who was naturally brave, and no persecutor.

Corry's History of Bristol.

QUAKERESS MISSIONARY.

But this religious knight-errantry was surpassed by a
young woman who travelled to Turkey to make a Quaker of
the Grand Sultan. Mary Fisher was the first Quakeress who

visited America, and we have already seen her suspected to be a witch; but as she happily had no spots upon her person which were insensible to pain when pricked with a pin, she was saved from the stake, and sent back to England. She now directed her steps towards the Orient. When she arrived at Smyrna, the English Consul thought it an act of kindness to his countrywoman to stop her from proceeding further, and sent her back to Venice, from which she had come. But she was not thus to be baulked of her purpose, and managed to make her way, by another route, to Adrianople, in the neighbourhood of which Mahomet IV. was then encamped with his army. All alone she entered the Turkish camp, and got a message delivered to the Vizier that she had something from the Great God to declare to the Sultan. Surprised at the arrival of an ambassador so strange the Sultan agreed to receive her on the following day: which he did, surrounded by his great officers. "Is is true," said his Majesty through an interpreter, "that you have a message to me from the Lord God ? "Yea," said the Quakeress. "Then speak on without fear," replied the Sultan; and the young woman, after a little natural hesitation, poured out what she conceived to be her commission from on high. The Turks sat and listened, with their usual gravity, and when she was done, Mahomet remarked that they could not but respect one who had come so far with a message from the Lord; and offered her a guard to conduct her to Constantinople, where she now wished to proceed, as it was scarcely safe for one like her to travel alone. She declined the guard, adroitly eluded expressing any opinion of the Prophet, reached Constantinople in safety, and from thence returned to England; having shown that a Quaker could be more quixotic than Cervantes could conceive.

" The Quakers," by Dr. Cunningham.

PEPY'S DIARY.

In the Diary of this gossipping chronicler of events that occured during the reign of Charles II., are several references to the Quakers.

January 11, 1663-4. This morning I stood by the King arguing with a pretty Quaker woman, that delivered to him a desire of hers in writing. The King shewed her Sir J. Minnes, as a man the fittest for her quaking religion, she modestly saying nothing till he began seriously to discourse with her, arguing the truth of his spirit against hers; she replying still with these words, "Oh King!" and thou'd all along.

February 7, 1665-6. To the Hall, where in the Palace I saw Monk's soldiers abuse Billing and all the Quakers, that were, at a meeting-place there, and indeed the soldiers did use them very roughly, and were to blame.

July 29, 1667. One thing extraordinray was this day: a man, a Quaker came naked through the Hall, only very civilly tied about the loins to avoid scandal, and with a chafing-dish of fired brimstone, burning upon his head, did pass through the Hall, crying, "Repent, repent!"

QUAKER TAVERN.

Pepy's, on the 3rd of August, 1660, informs us that he dined at an ordinary called the Quaker, a somewhat unusual godfather for a sinful tavern. The house was situated in the Great Sanctuary, Westminster, and was only pulled down in the beginning of the present century to make way for a market place, which in its turn has made room for a new sessions house. Tull the last landlord, opened a new public-house in Thieving Lane, and adorned the doorway of his house with twisted pillars decorated with vine-leaves, brought from the old Quaker tavern.

History of Signboards.

FANATICISM.

The conduct of some of the early Quakers in the New England States, was characterized by indecent fanaticism. Grahame in his History remarks, "In public assemblies, and in crowded streets, it was the practice of some of the Quakers to denounce the most tremendous manifestations of the divine wrath on the people, unless they forsook their carnal system. One of them, named Faubord, conceiving that he experienced a celestial eucouragment to rival the faith and imitate the sacrifice of Abraham, was proceeding with his own hands, to shed the blood of his son, when his neighbours, alarmed by the cries of the lad, broke into the house, and prevented the consummation of this blasphemous atrocity.

Others interrupted divine service in the churches, by loudly protesting that these were not the sacrifices that God would accept.

The female preachers far exceeded their male associates in folly, phrensy, and indecency. One of them presented herself to a congregation, with her face begrimed with coaldust, announcing it is a pictorial illustration of the black pox, which heaven had commissioned her to predict as an approaching judgment against all carnal worshippers. Some of them, in rueful attire. perambulated the streets, proclaiming the immediate coming of an angel with a drawn sword, to plead with the people ; and some attempted feats that may seem to verify the legend of Godiva of Coventry. One woman, in particular, entered stark-naked into a church in the middle of divine service, and desired the people to take heed of her as a sign of the times, and an emblem of the unclothed state of their own souls; and her associates highly extolled her submission to the inward light, that had revealed to her the duty of illustrating the spiritual nakedness of her neighbours by the indecent exhibition of her own person. Another Quakeress was arrested as she was making a similar display in the *streets of Salem.*

Buckingham remarks "If the records of these extravagancies were from the pens of writers opposed to the Quakers generally, they might well be discredited ; but two authors of their own sect, Bishop, the writer of a work entitled "New England Judged," and Besse, the author of a work entitled "Collection of the Sufferings of the People called Quakers," relate similar instances, and either defend or excuse them. Both these writers mention the case of Deborah Wilson, whom they describe as "a modest woman, of retired life and conversation; but bearing a great burden for the hardness and cruelty of the people. She went through the town of Salem naked as a sign ; which, having in part performed, she was laid hold on, and bound over to appear at the next court of Salem, where the wicked rulers sentenced her to be whipped. And Besse records the instance of Lydia Wardle, a Quakeress, who "found herself inwardly prompted to appear in a public assembly in a very unusual manner, and such as was exceeding hard and self-denying to her natural disposition, she being a woman of exemplary modesty in all her behaviour. The duty and concern she lay under was that of going into the church at Newbury naked, as a token of the miserable condition in which she conceived the people to be. But they (the people,) instead of religously reflecting on their own condition, which she came in that manner to represent to them, fell into a rage, and presently laid hands on her.",

This is the language in which Quaker writers themselves speak of these transactions, and one can hardly wonder that the magistrates of the places named should have endeavoured to put a stop to such proceedings.

EDWARD BURROUGH.

Among the most famous of the early Quaker preachers, was Edward Burrough. Educated as an episcopalian, he had become a presbyterian when the tide set in that way; but, still disappointed of peace, he went over from the presbyterians to the Quakers. For this he was turned out of doors by his father, for Quakerism was enough to bring disgrace upon any family. Being possesed of considerable fluency he soon became distinguished as a preacher among the new sect. And a forward man was he.

It was usual in those days for the London tradesmen, when their day's work was done, to meet in the fields, of a summer's evening to try their skill in wrestling.

Burrough once on a time came upon a crowd where such athletic exercises were going on. A stout fellow had already thrown three antagonists, and now waited to see if any other would challenge his skill, when Burrough stepped into the ring. Everybody gazed, for he had not the appearance of a mighty man, and the champion himself was not a little disconcerted; but Burrough soon shewed what was the nature of the encounter he sought, for instead of casting his coat and coming to gripes with his antagonist, he opened his mouth and thundered against spiritual wickedness in high places. He was as ready with his pen as his tongue, and almost rivalled Fox in the abundance of his epistolary writings. He assailed the Protector with letters about his pride, his forgetfulness of his vows, and the judgments which would come upon him and his house if he did not repent. He favoured in a similar way his wife and favourite daughter, the Lady Claypole; for the Quakers had often been very successful in gaining a hold upon the female heart. Thus forward in the cause of the Friends, he had his share of the horse-whippings and imprisonments to which they were exposed.

"*The Quakers*," by Dr. Cunningham.

WILLIAM STOUT.

We insert a few entries from the autobiography of William Stout, of Lancaster, wholesale and retail grocer and ironmonger, a member of the Society of Friends—A.D. 1665-1752. The autobiography is most interesting as affording information respecting the manners and customs of the people of his day, and gives perhaps as clear an insight into the mode in which trade was then carried on as is to be obtained from any source. The substance of it appeared many years ago in the *Manchester Guardian*, and subsequently the autobiography was published in a seperate form, edited from the original manuscript by J. Harland.

In 1690, William Stout went on horseback to London on business, and to attend the yearly meeting of the Friends. He writes, this being Whit Sunday, so-called, at which time yearly and every year my friends called Quakers have a general meeting of representatives from all parts of our king's dominions, where any of them have meetings, where accounts are brought of their sufferings for tithes, and for refusing an oath in several courts, and other testimonies, and the necessities of the sufferers, and the relief of the poor, and many other occurrences incident among them respecting to good order and a truly Christian department in life and conversation. Which meeting continued some days, and was much to my information and satisfaction and observation of condescention and piety.

And after the said meeting was over, I had time to settle my accounts with all I dealt with, and bought and ordered what goods I had occasion for, and ordered most of them by waggon carriage to Standish, at 3s. 6d. or 4s. a cwt. There were some shipping and [convoys appointed, but they were tedious; one perhaps to Portsmouth, another from thence to Plymouth, and another about the land to Bristol or Dublin, which often was six months, and hazard from

Dublin ; for the French privateers cruised off Holyhead and the Isle of Man ; and this tediousness did wholly discourage the sending cheese by sea, which would all be spoiled in a long passage, or many other goods besides the loss of time and a market; the land carriage being quick, if dear.

Having dispatched my business in London in a week, I came back the Yorkshire road, with my neighbour, John Bryer, to Leeds, and I to Sheffield with what money I had to spare at London, and bought what goods I had occasion for and got home at that week end, and finding all well, and that my sister, under whose care I had left my trade, had been diligent, and taken near £20, for goods in my three weeks absence. My expenses in my former and this journey to London were very near £3 each.

1690.—I was boarded at Alderman Thomas Bayne's house two years at the rate of £5 a year, and then, he being disappointed of a housekeeper, upon the 5th day of the third month of this year, I removed to be boarded with Richard Sterzaker, a butcher, very near my shop, at the same price, with several others, and very good entertainment, to our good liking and satisfaction.

I went to Sheffield in the 1st month of 1691-2 to settle accounts with Obadiah Barlow, who I employed to buy goods for me in my absence, and also then bought some packs of the makers of the goods, I also went to Preston fair, principally to buy cheese, the market for cheese then being mostly at Garstang and Preston fairs, which afterward came to Lancaster, mostly at Michaelmas fair. At this time we sold much cheese to funerals in the country, from 30lb. to 100lb. weight, as the deceased was of ability: which was shived into two or three (slices or pieces) in the lb., and one with a penny manchet (loaf) given to all the attendants. And then it was customary, at Lancaster, to give one or two long, called Naples, biscuits, to each attending the funeral; by which from 20lb. to near 100lb. was given, according to the deceased's ability; I think they were near 1s. a pound.

William Stout being a man of great repute for probity and wisdom, was not unfrequently wished to discharge the duties of executor for various families. He was appointed executor under the will of John Johnson, (a Churchman) who left a widow, two sons, and one daughter. After the mother's second marriage, William Stout, referring to the daughter, remarks in his diary—she was with me about two years, and was kept at school to write, sew, knit, and other necessary employ, till about a year after her brother's death, when she was about 16 years of age; and then was desirous to go and see her father's mother, an ancient woman and her daughters, poor people, near Warrington, which was granted, and decently fitted out and sent from hence. Her aunts had been nurses to Charles Owen, a noted Presbyterian preacher in Warrington, into whose acquaintance they introduced her; who, upon inquiry or information that she was under my tuition, a Quaker, expressed himself with much pretended surprise that any Christian should leave his child under the tuition of a Quaker; and soon after she writ to me that I might not expect her return, and that she had chosen Mr. Owen for her tutor, which expression of his, and her slighting my care for her, gave me some trouble; and having some business in Liverpool, I went from thence to Warrington, and had an opportunity with the said Owen, and before several persons of good repute, reproved him for his uncharitable reflection against the Quakers in general and me in particular, before he knew any occasion, and for which he was reproved of all my neighbours of his religious persuasion. But as is customary with priests and preachers of all professions, not to confess themselves in an error, he persisted in what he had done, and expected to have the management of her effects; which we refused, but only to allow the yearly profits of the same, which was about £15 a-year for her maintenance. But he employed a lawyer to compel us to more, which we slighted. But he entertained her as a gentlewoman, and got her a fiddle, and learned her to play and dance. She remained with him until she attained to 21 years of age, and then we accounted with her and paid her what was due. The said Owen got a good part more than we allowed for education, and got her a husband, Peter Heys, an indolent man, a joiner, who had built some houses at the utmost N.W. end of Liverpool, the year before the dock was made, upon which the north end was of no value—by which, and his indolence they became poor. They continued married four years, when he became consumptive and died, and left her four or five small children; upon which she was forced to industry to maintain them, to the discredit of the aforesaid tutor.

Important Trial.

A cause of great importance to the Quakers, was tried in 1661, at Nottingham assizes, upon the decision of which depended the legality of all the marriages hitherto contracted among this people. A Quaker died leaving his wife with child, together with a copyhold estate in lands; after the widow's delivery, a kinsman of the deceased husband endeavoured to prove the child illegitimate, and his council to make good his case, pleaded that the Quakers did not legally marry, but went together like brute beasts.

Judge Archer, in summing up the case, told the jury "that there was a marriage in Paradise, when Adam took Eve, and Eve took Adam; and that it was the consent of the parties that made a marriage. He did not know the opinion of the Quakers, but he did not believe they went together, as had been so unbecomingly asserted, 'like brute beasts,' but as Christians, and therefore he did believe the marriage was lawful, and the child a lawful heir." And further to satisfy the jury, he related the following case, ·· A man that was of weak body, and kept his bed, had a desire, in that condition to marry, and declare before witnesses, that he did take such a woman to be his wife ; and the woman declared, that she took that man to be her husband. The marriage was afterwards called in question, but all the bishops did at that time conclude it to be a lawful marriage." The jury having received this instruction, gave their verdict for the child, and declared it legitimate.

Life of G. Fox, by J. Marsh.

SELF-CONTROL.

A merchant in London had a dispute with a Quaker respecting the settlememt of an account. The merchant was determined to bring the account into court, a proceeding which the Quaker earnestly deprecated, using every argument in his power to convince the merchant of his error; but the latter was inflexible. Desirous to make a last effort, the Quaker called at his house one morning, and inquired of the servant if his master was at home. The merchant hearing the inquiry and knowing his voice, called out from the top of the stairs, "Tell the rascal I am not at home." The Quaker looking up to him, calmly said, "Well, friend, God put thee in a better mind." The merchant, struck afterwards with the meekness of the reply, and having more deliberately investigated the matter, became convinced that the Quaker was right, and that he was wrong. He requested to see him, and after acknowledging his error, he said, " I have one question to ask you. How were you able, with such patience, on various occasions, to bear my abuse?" " Friend," replied the Quaker, " I will tell thee. I was naturally as hot and violent as thou art. I knew that to indulge this temper was sinful; and I found it was imprudent. I observed that men in a passion always spoke loud; and I thought if I could control my voice, I should repress my passion. I have, therefore, made it a rule never to let my voice rise above a certain key; and by a careful observance of this rule I have, by the blessing of. God, entirely mastered my natural temper." The Quaker reasoned philosophically, and the merchrnt as every one else may do, benefited by his example.

ROBERT BARCLAY AND THE ROBBERS.

Robert Barclay, the celebrated apologist of the Quakers, and Leonard Fell, a member of the same Society, were severally attacked by highwaymen in England, at different times. Both faithfully adhered to their non-resistance principles, and both signally triumphed. The pistol was levelled at Barclay, and a determined demand was made for his purse. Calm and self-possessed, he looked the robber in the face, with a firm but meek benignity, assured him he was *his* and every man's friend, that he was willing and ready to relieve his wants, that he was free from the fear of death through a divine hope in immortality, and, therefore, was not to be intimidated by a deadly weapon; and then appealed to him, whether he could have the heart to shed the blood of one who had no other feeling or purpose but to do him good. The robber was confounded; his eye melted, his brawny arm trembled, his pistol fell to his side, and he fled from the presence of the non-resistant hero whom he could no longer confront.

NOBLE DISINTERESTEDNESS.

The Quakers as a community in the United States were the first that protested against the injustice of slavery and passed a resolution disowning any of their members that bought or sold negroes or kept them in bondage. Many Quakers voluntarily manumitted their slaves. They had many difficulties to encounter, as the legislation of the States had been framed in the interests of the masters.

In Pennsylvania a man who liberated a slave had to give a bond for the payment of £30 should the liberated slave ever become a burden to the State. In New Jersey the law was stricter, entailing responsibility for the misconduct of the liberated slave and likewise of his posterity. The Quakers in spite of many obstacles were determined that their negroes should have freedom. One Quaker, William Mifflin deserves to have his name specially remembered, he not only liberated his slaves, but paid their wages which were due to them from the first day of their servitude. So that strict justice might be awarded, arbiters were mutually chosen by the master and his freed slaves whose decision as to the amount of compensation was to be final.

Peter the Great and William Penn.

Penn became acquainted with the young Czar, Peter of Russia, then working in the dockyard at Deptford as a carpenter and ship-builder. With that passion for converting the great, which had led their brethren to Rome, to Adrianople, and to Versailles, in search of royal proselytes, Thomas Story and another friend, hearing that the ruler of Muscovey could be easily approached, went to him for the purpose of delivering what they believed to be the new gospel. They found to their suprise that the Czar could speak no Latin; and as they were ignorant of German, it was impossible to converse without the aid of an interpreter. Peter was interested though not much edified by their discourse, but the Friends were greatly charmed with their reception, and immediately reported to Penn, who spoke German with great fluency, that a new field was opening in the imperial mind for the spread of truth. On this hint Penn went down to York Buildings, where the Czar resided, when not at the docks, with Prince Menzikoff, and there saw the object of his visit. As a man who had lived in courts and seen the world, as the son also of the renowned

Admiral, Penn got on much better with the young and sagacious prince than the simple-hearted Story. With the practical turn of mind which distinguished him through life, Peter had at once gone to what appeared to him the heart of the matter. You say you are a new people, will you fight better than the rest? Story had told him they could not bear arms against their neighbour. Then tell me, said Peter, of what use you would be to any kingdom, if you will not fight? The fact of their wearing their hats in his presence rather amused than offended him; but he could not be made to comprehend the reason of it. Eager for knowledge of every kind, he listened with courtesy and interest to the discourses of Penn; he wished, he said, to learn in a few words what the Quakers taught and practised, that he might be able to distinguish them from other men; whereupon his visitor wrote. "They teach that men must be holy, or they cannot be happy, that they should be few in words, peaceable in life, suffer wrongs, love enemies, deny themselves—without which faith is false, worship formality, and religion hypocrisy." Peter was not converted, but he was interested; as he knew a little English he began to attend occasionally at the meetings of Friends at Deptford, where he behaved very politely and socially, standing up or sitting down as it suited the convenience and comfort of others. Some of the Quaker preachers evidently regarded their imperial listener as a convert to the faith; they were probably not aware that, as an acute observer of human manners, it was his humour to attend the religious services of all sects and denominations.—Hepworth Dixon.

QUAKERESSES AT MALTA.

Dr. Cunningham in his history of "The Quakers," observes. So early as 1658 two Quaker women had "drawings in their minds" to proceed to Alexandria, that they might in the city where Neo-Platonism had been so

c

eloquently taught by Hypatia twelve hundred years before, promulgate their Neo-Christianity, and, if need were, die for their mystic faith, as she had. They had husbands and children, but the divine "drawings" overcame all conjugal and parental instincts. The ship in which they sailed touched at Malta, which was then held by the Knights of St. John. The Quakeresses landed, and were kindly entertained by the English Consul, who, at the same time, warned them of the danger they ran if they offended the religious prejudices of the people. The governor also visited them, and told them he had a sister in the nunnery who greatly desired to see them. They went, but refused to bow before the high altar of the convent chapel, and for this no one will blame them. On another occasion they went into a church—or mass-house as they called it—while service was going on, and one of them knelt down with her back to the altar, as a testimony against it, and prayed aloud. A priest, probably struck with her fervour, came up to her, and offered to slip something into her hand, but she thought it must be the mark of the beast, and refused it with loathing. Yet another time they entered a church while high mass was being celebrated; they saw the lighted tapers, the embroidered draperies, the carved crucifixes, the bowings and the kneelings; and horrified at the idolatrous spectacle, they stood in the midst of the people, weeping and trembling violently, and even afterwards when they came into the street they reeled and staggered as if they had been drunken, at which the poor Maltese marvelled greatly. It was probably felt that such exhibitions could no longer be permitted, for the two Quakeresses were now removed from the Consul's house and lodged in the prison of the Inquisition. While there they were sometimes treated with kindness, and sometimes with severity; threats, promises, and arguments were in turn employed to induce them to become catholics, but they continued steadfast, and after four years incarceration they were set at liberty, and sent back to England.

When they had been about four years in the prison of the Inquisition, a Friend, named Baker, who had been travelling in the East, came to Malta, in order, if possible, to procure their release.

The inquisitors at once offered to set them at liberty if they would find bail never to return to Malta again. But this they refused even to endeavour to procure, as they knew not what the Lord might require them to do. Baker now offered to be imprisoned for them, or even to die for them; but such vicarious suffering did not seem good to the Roman inquisitors. Foiled in his endeavours to procure their release, this devoted Friend could do nothing more than take his station near their prison, where he and the captives could catch a glimpse of each other, and exchange a few words, and by this their souls were exceedingly refreshed. But at last he must leave Malta, and on his return home he was wind-bound for some weeks at Gibraltar. When its towering rock first loomed upon his view, he remembered he had seen such a crag in the visions of the night, and therefore inferred that the Lord had work for him there.

He accordingly went ashore on a Maunday Thursday, and repaired to the mass-house. He found the priest in his surplice kneeling before the high altar, adoring the host. A divine indignation instantly took hold on him. He therefore turned his back upon the priest and his dead God, and his face toward the people who were down upon their knees; and taking off his his coat he rent it from top to bottom and cast it from him, and then lifting his hat from his head, where it had hitherto remained, he threw it to the ground, and stamped upon it, and thrice he cried out— "The life of Christ and his saints is risen from the dead!" The priest and the people no doubt concluded that a furious

madman had found his way into the church, and instead of
laying hold of him, they felt relieved when he had made his
escape and returned to the ship."

Mr. Hull and his man Charles.

In King William's war, Mr. Hull, a Quaker of Rhode
Island, who commanded a vessel of which he was the owner,
was met at sea by a French privateer, which coming up
with him, the captain ordered him to strike. The Quaker
made answer that he could not resolve to part with either
his ship or cargo, which were his property, and of considerable value: neither could he by the laws of his religion,
fight, but he would speak to his man Charles, who was of
another persuasion, and in case he was inclined to fight, he
should not hinder him. Accordingly Charles was called,
who accepted the encounter, and falling to work with the
Frenchman, soon obliged him to sheer off.

This Charles was no other than the late Sir Charles Wager
who then served that honest Quaker; and the report which
Mr. Hull made, when he arrived at London of this gallant
action, was the first rise of that worthy Admiral

John Bunyan and the Quaker.

A Quaker called on Bunyan one day with a "message
from the Lord," saying he had been to half the gaols in
England, and was glad at last to have found him To
which Bunyan replied; "If the Lord sent thee, you would
not have needed to take so much trouble to find me out for
He knew that I have been in Bedford Gaol these seven
years past."

Compelling a Quaker to Swear.

In a paper contributed to the meeting of a county historical society—the following amusing anecdote is told of a
Quaker named Fitz Randolph, who once lived in the neighbourhood. This Fitz Randolph is said to have been a

devoted Friend, and to have had in his employ a man who was a singular character, and allowed by his master almost as many liberties as the " King's fool."

On a certain Sunday morning, Mr. Fitz Randolph wished to go to the Quaker Meeting House on the opposite hill, but the brook was so swollen with the rain as not to be easily crossed. The man offered to carry him across on his back. When in the midst of the stream he stopped, and said to Mr. Fitz Randolph " Will thee give me a quart of apple-jack if I take thee safe over ? " " No, I will not ; go on," said Mr. Fitz Rondolph. " But say, will thee give it to me ? for if thee does not, I will let thee down into the water !" " I must not give thee that will do thee harm ! " " But I say thee must give it me, or I will let thee down into the water quickly !" was the reply of the impudent fellow, whose motions indicated that he meant what he said " Well I promise to give thee the apple-jack ! now go on,". said the Quaker. " But swear that thee will give it me," persisted the man. " Thee knows that I must not swear ! " " But I say thee must swear that thee will give me the apple-jack, or I swear I will put thee quickly into the water !" " Well, well," said Mr. Fitz Randolph, " thee is very unreasonable, but thee has me in thy power, and so I swear I will give thee the rum ! " There, now, Mr. Fitz Randolph, thee hast done it ! exclaimed the man with an ill-concealed chuckle, ' thee hast done it now,' for thee always said that a man who will swear will die, and so I will let thee down into the water at any rate !" and he at once suited the action to the word, leaving his employer in no good plight physically or spiritually for the service he was designing to attend

SCRIPTURE AUTHORITY.

A Quaker married a woman of the Church of England. After the ceremony. the Vicar asked for the fees, which he said were a crown. The Quaker, astonished at the demand, said if he would show him any text in the Scriptures which proved his fees were a crown, he would give it unto him; upon which the Vicar directly turned to the 12th chapter of Proverbs, verse the 4th, where it said, " A virtuous woman is a crown to her husband." "Thou art right, friend, in thy assertion." said the Quaker, "here are thy twelve penny-pieces and something besides, to buy thee a pair of gloves with."

A Plan to Discover the True Religion.

Solomon Eccles, who died about the end of the seventeenth century, was an English musician much admired for many years for his remarkable skill on several instruments, but while in the zenith of his fame became a Quaker, and practised so many foibles in his new profession that he was the ridicule of all London. He burnt his lute and his violins, and by meditation found out a new expedient for ascertaining the true religion. This was to collect under one roof the most virtuous men of the several sects that divide Christianity, who should unanimously fall to prayer for seven days without taking any nourishment. "Then," said he " those on whom the spirit of God shall manifest itself in a sensible manner— that is to say, by the trembling of the limbs, and interior illuminations--may oblige the rest to subscribe to their decisions." He found, however, that none would put this strange conceit to the trial, and his persistence in propagating his folly, his prophecies, his invectives, and his pretended miracles only served to pass him from one prison to another, till at length by this sort of discipline he was brought to confess the vanity of his prophecies, and finish his life in tranquility, but without religion.

Strong Language.

Some of the early Quakers manifested a fierce and vindic-tive spirit, and were not particular as to the language they addressed to their opponents. Humphrey Norton, who was sentenced to be removed from Plymouth colony, thus address-ed the Governor, Thomas Prince on the bench. . "Prince, thou lyest; Thomas, thou art a malicious man ; thy clamorous tongue I regard no more than the dust under my feet ; and thou art like a scolding woman, as thou pratest and deri-dest me! Norton afterwards addressed the Governor by letter in such language as, Thomas Prince, thou hast bent thy heart to work wickedness, and with thy tongue has set forth deceit ; thou imaginest mischief upon thy bed, and hatchest thy hatred in thy secret chamber ; the strength of darkness is over thee, and a malicious mouth hast thou opened against God and his annointed ; and with thy tongue and lips hast thou uttered peverse things ; thou hast slandered the innocent, by railing, lying, and false accusations, and with thy barbar-ous heart hast thou caused their blood to be shed, &c., &c. ' John Alden is to thee like unto a pack-horse, whereupon thou layest thy beastly bag; cursed are all they that have a hand therein ; the cry of vengeance will pursue thee day and night.' After continuing in this strain at great length, he closes with " The anguish and pain that will enter thy veins will be like gnawing worms lodging betwixt thy heart and liver. When these things come upon thee, and thy back is bowed down with pain, in that day and hour thou shalt know to thy grief that prophets of the Lord God we are, and the God of vengeance is our God."

THE QUAKERESS AND THE OFFICER.

Somewhere about the year 1740, there lived at Stourbridge a respectable family of the Society of Friends of the name of Winter. They occupied a house contiguous to the principal inn of the town, and their windows overlooked the yard. Mrs. Winter was a clever, amiable woman, and the lady at the inn generally consulted her in any case of domestic difficulty It happened that there were a number of soldiers quartered in the town, and the officers' head-quarters were at this inn One of these officers was given to the habits of intemperance; and sometimes, after hard drinking, he became quarrelsome and irrational, approaching even to madness. One afternoon, having sat long over the bottle, a difference arose between him and a brother officer, when he became so furious, through intoxication, that he drew his sword, and dared his opponent to single combat, at the same time rushing into the yard ready for the bloody purpose. There he continued raving and reeling for some time, with his naked sword flourishing about, making very ludicrous gesticulations, and shouting forth most amusing pot-valiant defiances, when a number of thoughtless people gathered around him to enjoy the fun. At this juncture, the landlady, observing the scene, concluded that murder would most assuredly follow, and that for which her husband, who was then absent, might be seriously brought into trouble; and she was so affected at the sight that she fainted. In this dilemma, Mrs. Winter was hastily applied to for advice and assistance; and having surveyed the ground, she immediately perceived the danger the people were in of being wounded or killed. through some eccentric lunge of the drunken warrior; and she paused a few moments to consider if she could do anything to avert such a catastrophe. Confiding in the purity of her motives she now put on her bonnet, and proceeded to the scene of action. Having quietly made her way through the crowd, she placed herself directly before the vaunting soldier, at the same time looking him placidly in the face. His countenance quickly fell and he ceased his boasting, gazing on his unexpected visitant, with awe and reverence, as though she had been an angel. Mrs. Winte · now very gently put her hand on the hilt of his sword, when he unconciously relaxed his grasp, and she drew it away from him. Having secured the dangerous weapon, she carried it home to her own apartment, to the no small amusement of those who witnessed the hazardous deed. The drunken man having stared vacantly about him for some time, staggered off to his quarters, and slept away the fumes of his potations. On awakening, a few hours afterwards, his recollection returned, and he inquired anxiously for his sword, as his appearance without it on parade next morning might lead to some very awkard inquiries. He therefore sent his servant with Major ——'s compliments to Mrs. Winter, and begged that she would return the weapon. Her answer was, that she had it safely locked up in her closet, and if he himself would call in the morning she would deliver it to him. These were hard terms for a British officer to submit to, but he very prudently considered, under present circumstances, it was the best policy to yield. In the morning the major arose fully sensible of the folly he had been guilty of, and the dilemma in which he had placed himself. He, however, determined now to pursue the only right course before him (mortifying as it was to his feelings), and he accordingly sought an interview with Mrs. Winter, to whom he apologized very amply, and acknowledged himself under the greatest obligation for her kind and timely interference. Mrs. Winter then restored his sword, desiring him to replace it in the scabbard ; after which she delivered him a short lecture on the benefits arising from temperance and peace. Promising to be more circumspect in his future conduct, and again thanking her for her kindness, he departed, let us hope, a somewhat wiser and better man.—

Paxton Hood's Representative Women.

A Speculation

At a business meeting among certain Quakers about a proposed canal ; one of the most influential men present opposed the project on the ground of its being a speculation.

This was, of course, unanswerable, but, among other objections, he went on to say:—" When God created the world, if he had wished canals, he would have made them." Upon this, "a weighty friend," (one of their terms) rose up, and said, slowly, in the intoning voice in which they always speak in meeting, "And Jacob digged a well," and sat down. The influential man immediately retired into private life ; but he bought some shares in the canal for all that.

QUAKER PREACHING.

Sewel, who is more generally known by his Dutch and English Dictionary, than as an English writer, relates the following anecdote of his mother, Judith Zinspenning, who visited England, and was much esteemed there among the Quakers Being at a meeting in London, and finding herself stirred up to speak of the loving-kindness of the Lord to those who feared him, she desired one Peter Sybrands to be her interpreter, but he, though an honest man, being not very fit for that service, one or more friends told her they were so sensible of the power by which she spoke, that though they did not understand her words, yet they were edified by the life and power that accompanied her speech ; and, therefore, they little regretted the want of interpretation. And so she went on without any interpreter !

QUAKERS ADDRESS.

An address of the Quakers to James II. on his accession, preserved in Wanley's Common-place Book, is highly characteristic of that shrewd sect. "We come to condole the death of four friend ;Charles; and we are glad that thou art come to be our ruler. We hear that thou art a dissenter from the Church of England, and so are we. We beg that thou wouldst grant us the same liberty that thou takest thyself, and so we wish thee well Farewell." [Harl. MS. 6030.]

INDIANS AND THE QUAKER MEETING.

A little before the revolutionary war, there were a few families of Friends, who had removed from Duchess county and settled at Easton, then in Saratoga county, New York. These requested the favour of holding a religious meeting, which was granted. The section of country proved to be one which was so much distressed by scouting parties from both the British and American armies, that the American government, unable to protect the inhabitants, issued a proclamation, directing them to leave their country: and they did generally go.

The Friends requested to be permitted to exercise their own judgment, (saying, "You are clear of us in that you have warned us,") remained at their homes, and kept up their meeting.

Robert Nisbet, who lived at that time at East Hoosack, about thirty miles distant, felt a desire to walk through the then wilderness country, and sit with the Friends at their week-day meeting. As they were sitting in meeting, with their door open, they discovered an Indian peeping round the door post. When he saw the Friends sitting without word or deed, he stepped forward and took a full view of what was in the house: then he and his company, placing their arms in a corner of the room, took seats with the Friends, and so remained till the meeting closed.

Zebulon Hoxie, one of the Friends present, then invited them to his house, put a cheese and what bread he had on the table, and invited them to help themselves: they did so, and went quietly and harmlessly away.

Before their departure, however, Robert Nisbet, who could speak and understand the French language, had a conversation with their leaders in French. He told Robert that they surrounded the house, intending to destroy all that were in it; 'but," said he, " when we saw you sitting with your door open, and without weapons of defence, we had no disposition to hurt you—we would have fought for you." This party had human scalps with them.

QUAKER'S OPINION OF TITLES.

A Quaker vindicating the pertinacity of his sect in refusing to give titles to men, gave this whimsical account. "I had the honour," said he, "one day to be in company with an excellency and an highness. His excellency was the most ignorant and brutal of his species, and his highness measured just four feet eight inches without his shoes."

WITTY REPLY.

A Quaker having bought a horse which proved unsound, of a gentleman named Bacon, he wrote to inform him of it, but received no answer. Shortly after, meeting the seller, he requested him to take back the horse, which the other positively refused to do. Finding his remonstrances of no avail, the Quaker, calmly said, "Friend, thou hast doubtless heard of the devil entering the herd of swine. and I find that he still sticks fast to the *bacon* Good morning to thee, friend."

THE QUAKER AND THE INFIDEL

A gay young spark, of a deistical turn, travelling in a stage coach to London, forced his sentiments on the company by attempting to ridicule the Scriptures, and among other topics, made himself merry with the story of David and Goliah, strongly urging the impossibility of a youth like David being able to throw a stone with sufficient force to sink into a giant's forehead. On this he appealed to the company, and in particular to a grave gentleman of the denomination called Quakers, who sat in one corner of the carriage. "Indeed, friend," replied he, I do not think it at all impossible. if the Philistine's head *was as soft as thine*

FREDERIC PRINCE OF WALES.

A clause in the Tithing Bill, relative to the Quakers, being in agitation in the House of Commons, in the year 1735, a deputation from the Quakers waited on his royal highness to solicit his interest in favour of that clause. His answer was every way worthy of his high character: "that as a friend to liberty in general, and, toleration in particular, he wished that they might meet with all proper favour; but for himself, he never gave his vote in Parliament, and it did not become his station to influence his friends, or direct his servants; to leave them entirely to their own conscience and understanding, was a rule he had hitherto prescribed to himself, and purposed through his whole life to observe."

The reply from Andrew Pitt, the person who spoke in the name of the body, was not less remarkable: "May it please the Prince of Wales, I am greatly affected with thy excellent notions of liberty; and am more pleased with thy answer, than if thou hadst granted to us our request."

JOHN WESLEY AND THE YOUNG QUAKER.

In 1740, Mr. Wesley had an interview with a young Quaker named Joseph Chandler, who had frequently spoken in the meetings. Mr. Wesley had never seen him, and did not know there was such a person. Some one had carried a formal challenge to him from Mr. Wesley to dispute with him, and afterwards told Mr. Chandler that he heard Mr. Wesley declare in open Society, "I challenge Joseph Chandler to dispute, and he promised to come, but broke his word." Joseph immediately sent to Mr. Wesley to know from his own mouth if these things were so. Mr. Wesley adds, "If those who count themselves better Christians had but done like this honest Quaker, how many idle tales which they now believe would, like this, have vanished into air!"

JOHN WESLEY AND THE QUAKER'S DREAM.

The work of God had greatly revived at Newcastle, but the people had no house of worship. Mr. Wesley purchased a site; the building was to cost seven hundred pounds, many were sceptical concerning its ever being finished. Mr. Wesley says 'I was of another mind; not doubting but as it was begun, for God's sake he would provide what was needful for finishing it.'

Mr. Wesley had only one pound and six shillings when he commenced. Soon after he began he received a letter from a pious Quaker which read thus:—" Friend Wesley, I have had a dream concerning thee. I thought I saw thee surrounded by a large flock of sheep, which thou didst not know what to do with. My first thought after I awoke was that it was thy flock at Newcastle, and that thou hadst no house of worship for them; I have enclosed a note for one hundred pounds, which may help thee to provide a house." Money came from various quarters, and the building was completed, and Mr. Wesley called it "The Orphan House."

THE QUAKER TO HIS WATCHMAKER.

I herewith send thee my pocket clock, which standeth in need of thy friendly correction. The last time it was at thy friendly school he was in no way reformed nor in the least benefited thereby; for I perceive by the index of his mind that he is a liar and the truth is not in him; that hi- put e is sometimes slow, which betokeneth not an even temper; at other times it waxeth sluggish, notwithstanding I frequently urge him; when he should be on duty as thou knoweth his hand denoteth, I find him slumbering, or, as the vanity of the human reason phrases it, I caught him napping. Examine him, therefore, and prove him. I beseech thee, thoroughly, that thou mayest, being well acquainted with his inward frame and disposition, draw him from the error of his way, and show him the path wherein he should go. It grieves me to think, and when I ponder therein I am verily of the opinion that his body is foul, and the whole mass is corrupted. Clense him, therefore, with thy charming physic, from all pollution, that he may vibrate and circulate according to the truth. I will place him for a few days under thy care, and pay for his board as thou requirest. I entreat thee, friend John, to demean thyself on this occasion with judgment, according to the gift which is in thee, and prove thyself a workman; and when thou layest thy correcting hand upon him, let it be without passion, lest thou shouldest drive him to destruction. Do thou regulate his motion for a time to come by the motion of the light that ruleth the day, and when thou findest him converted from the error of his ways, and more conformable to the above-mentioned rules, then thou send him home with a just bill of the charges drawn out in the spirit of moderation, and it shall be sent thee in the root of all evil."

The Choice.

A Quaker residing at Paris, was waited on by four of his workmen in order to make their compliments, and ask for their usual new year's gifts. 'Well, my friends,' said the Quaker. 'here are your gifts; choose fifteen francs or the bible.' 'I don't know how to read,' said the first, 'so I take the fifteen francs.' 'I can read,' said the second, ' but I have pressing wants.' He ook the fifteen francs. The third also made the same choice. He now came to the fourth, a young lad of about thirteen or fourteen. The Quaker looked at him with an air of goodness. 'Will you too take these three pieces, which you may obtain at any time by your labour and industry?' 'As you say the book is good, I will take it, and read from it to my mother,' replied the boy. He took the bible, opened it, and found between the leaves a gold piece of forty francs. The others hung down their heads, and the Quaker told them he was sorry they had not made a better choice.

QUAKER RESPONSIBILITY.

A young man desirous of entering into business on his own account, applied to a wholesale linendraper, to give him credit for goods to the amount of £500. Being asked for a reference as to character, he mentioned Mr. B., a Quaker, who, upon being applied to, gave the young man such a character, as induced the tradesman immediately to let him have the goods he wished for. After being some time in business, and by his conduct justifying the trust reposed in him, he fell into habits of dissipation, neglected his shop, and, as a natural consequence, became insolvent. The injured creditor meeting Mr. B., complained that he had been deceived as to the character of the young man, by which he had lost £500. The honest Quaker replied, that he had spoken to the best of his knowledge, and had been deceived. As, however, it was on his representation the credit had been given to the insolvent, he would pay the debt; which he did immediately, by a cheque on his banker.

THE QUAKER AND HIS VISITOR.

A gentleman of indolent habits made a business of visiting his friends extensively. He was once cordially received by a Quaker, who treated his visitor with great attention and politeness for several days. At last he said, "My friend, I am afraid thee will never visit me again."—"Oh, yes, I shall," said the visitor; "I have enjoyed my visit very much; I shall certainly come again."—"Nay," said the Quaker, "I think thee will not visit me again."—"What makes you think I shall not come again?" asked the visitor. "If thee does never leave," said the Quaker, "how canst thee come again?"

WHITFIELD AND THE QUAKER.

Whitfield, having preached at Edinburgh to a large and attentive audience, from "The Kingdom of God is not meat and drink, but righteousness and peace and joy in the Holy Ghost," was after the sermon called upon by a large company, including some of the nobility, who bade him God-speed. Among the rest a portly Quaker, who, taking him by the hand, said, "Friend George, I am as thou art; I am for bringing all to the life and power of the ever-living God, and therefore if thou wilt not quarrel with me about my hat, I will not quarrel with thee about thy gown."

WASTING OTHERS' TIME.

A committee of eight ladies, in the neighbourhood of London, was appointed to meet on a certain day at twelve o'clock. Seven of them were punctual; but the eighth came hurrying in, with many apologies for being a quarter of an hour behind time. The time had passed away without her being aware of it; she had no idea of its being so late, &c. A Quaker lady present, said, "Friend, I am not clear that we should admit thine apology. It were matter of regret that thou shouldst have wasted thine own quarter of an hour; but here are seven besides thyself, whose time thou hast also consumed, amounting in the whole to two hours, and seven-eighths of it was not thine own property."

CONVERSATION.

Once I happened to overhear a dialogue somewhat similar to that which Charles Lamb, perhaps, only feigned to hear. I was travelling in a railway carriage with a most precise-looking, formal person,—the Arch-Quaker, if there be such a person. His countenance was very noble, or had been so before it was frozen up. He said nothing. I felt

D

a great respect for him. At last his mouth opened. I listened with attention. I had hitherto lived with foolish, gad-about, dinner-eating, dancing people; now I was going to hear the words of retired wisdom; when he thus addressed his young daughter sitting opposite: "Hast thee heard how Southamptons went lately?" (in those days South Western Railway shares were called Southamptons); and she replied with like gravity, giving him some information that she had picked up about Southamptons yesterday evening I leant back rather sickened, as I thought what was probably the daily talk and daily thoughts in that family, from which I conjectured all amusement was banished save that connected with intense money-getting.—

Helps' Friends in Council.

THE SKATING QUAKER ARTIST.

The following anecdote of West is given by his biographer, Allan Cunningham:—"West was a skilful skater, and in America had formed an acquaintance on the ice with Colonel, afterwards too well known in the Colonial war, as General Howe. This friendship had dissolved with the thaw, and was forgotten, till one day the painter, having tied on his skates at the Serpentine, was astonishing the timid practitioners of London by the rapidity of his motions, and the graceful figure which he cut. Some one cried out, 'West! West!' it was Colonel Howe. 'I am glad to see you,' said he, 'and not the less so that you come in good time to vindicate my praise of American skating.' He called to him Lord Spencer Hamilton, and some of the Cavendishes, to whom he introduced West as one of the Philadelphia prodigies, and requested him to show them 'the salute.' He performed so much to their satisfaction, that they went away spreading the praise of the American skater over London. Nor was the considerate Quaker insensible to the value of such commendations: he continued to frequent the Serpentine, and to gratify large crowds by cutting the Philadelphia salute. Many, to their praise of his skating, added panegyrics on his professional skill; and not a few, to vindicate their applause, followed him to the easel, and sat for their portraits."

Benjamin West's Subjects.

The Quaker artist as he advanced in his profession, not only executed various works upon classical and historical subjects, but suggested a series of pictures to illustrate the progress of revealed religion. "No subtle divine," says Mr. Cunningham, "ever laboured more diligently on controversial texts than did our painter in evolving his pictures out of this grand and awful subject. He divided it into four dispensations,—the Antediluvian, the Patriarchal, the Mosaical, and the Prophetical. They contained in all thirty-six subjects, eighteen of which belonged to the Old Testament, the rest to the New. They were all sketched, and twenty-eight were executed, for which West received in all twenty-one thousand seven hundred and five pounds. A work so varied, so extensive, and so noble in its nature, was never before undertaken by any painter."

Leigh Hunt's Description of Benjamin West.

I need not enter into the merits of an artist who is so known, and has been so often criticised. He was a man with regular, mild features ; and though of Quaker origin, had the look of what he was, a painter to a court. His appearance was so gentlemanly, that, the moment he changed his gown for a coat, he seemed to be full-dressed. The simplicity and self-possession of the young Quaker, not having time enough to grow stiff, (for he went early to study at Rome), took up, I suppose, with more ease than most would have done, the urbanities of his new position.

And what simplicity helped him to, favour would retain, yet this man, so well bred, and so indisputably clever in his art (whatever might be the amount of his genius), had received so careless, or so homely an education when a boy, that he could hardly read. He pronounced also some of his words, in reading, with a puritanical barbarism, such as *haive* for *have*, as some people pronounce when they sing psalms. But this was perhaps an American custom. My mother who read and spoke remarkably well, would say *haive*, and *shaul* for *shall*, when she sung her hymns. But it was not so well in reading lectures at the Academy. Mr. West would talk of his art all day long, painting all the while. On other subjects he was not so fluent; and on political or religious matters he tried hard to maintain the reserve common with those about a court. He succeeded ill in both. There were always strong suspicions of his leaning to his native side in politics; and during Bonaparte's triumph, he could not contain his enthusiasm for the Republican chief, going even to Paris to pay him his homage, when First Consul. The admiration of high colours and powerful effects, natural to a painter, was too strong for him. How he managed this matter with the higher powers in England, I cannot say. Probably he was the less heedful, inasmuch as he was not very carefully paid. I believe he did a great deal for George the Third, with little profit. Mr. West certainly kept his love for Bonaparte no secret; and it was no wonder, for the latter expressed admiration of his pictures. The artist thought the conqueror's smile enchanting, and that he had the handsomest leg he had ever seen. He was present when the "Venus de Medicis" was talked of, the French having just taken possession of her. Bonaparte, Mr. West said, turned round to those about him, and said, with his eyes lit up, "She's coming!" as if he had been talking of a living person I believe he retained for the Emperor the love that he had for the First Consul, a wedded, love, "for better, for worse." However, I believe also that he retained it after the Emperor's downfal; which is not what every painter did.

FINE DISTINCTION.

Henry Crabb Robinson, in his diary. 1820, writes, "I left London on the 1st of August, and reached Lyons on the 9th. On the journey I had an agreeable companion in a young Quaker, Walduck, then in the employ of the great Quaker chemist, Bell, in Oxford-street. It was his first journey out of England. He had a pleasing physiognomy, and was staunch to his principles, but discriminating. Walking together in one of the principal streets of Lyons, we met the Host, with an accompanying crowd. "You must pull off your hat, Walduck."—"I will die first!" he exclaimed. As I saw some low fellows scowling, and did not wish to behold an act of martrydom, I pulled off his hat. Afterwards passing by the cathedral, I said to him, "I must leave you here, for I wont go in to be insulted." He followed me with his hat off. "I thought you would die first!"—"Oh, no; here I have no business or right to be. If the owners of this building choose to make a foolish rule that no one shall enter with his hat, they do what they have a legal right to do, and I must submit to their terms. Not so in the broad highway." The reasoning was not good, but one is not critical when the conclusion is the right one practically.

HAT VERSUS HEAD.

A deputation of Quakers was waiting in an anteroom at Carlton Palace, to present an address of congratulation to the Prince Regent, when one of the pages advanced to take off the hats of the Quakers. Dr. Waugh, the Nonconformist, who was standing by, and who loved a joke, said to the foremost Quaker, in an audible whisper, "Persecution, Brother;" to which the brother significantly replied, while pointing upwards (to the portrait of Charles I.), "not so bad to take off the hat as the head."

STEPHEN GRELLET AND THOMAS PAINE.

Stephen Grellet thus writes about the closing scenes in the life of Paine. "I may not omit recording here the death of Thomas Paine. A few days previous to my leaving home on my last religious visit on hearing that he was ill, and in a very destitute condition, I went to see him, and found him in a wretched state : for he had been so neglected and forsaken by his pretended friends, that the common attention to a sick man had been withheld from him. The skin of his body was in some places worn off, which greatly increased his sufferings. A nurse was provided for him, and some needful comforts were supplied. He was mostly in a state of stupor, but something that had passed between us had made such an impression upon him, that a few days after my departure, he sent for me, and, on being told that I was gone from home, he sent for another Friend. This induced a valuable young Friend, (Mary Roscoe), whe resided with my family, and continued at Greenwich during part of my absence, frequently to go and take him some little refreshment suitable for an invalid, furnished by a neighbour. Once when she was there, three of his deistical associates came to the door, and in a loud unfeeling manner said, Tom Paine, it is said you are turning Christian, but we hope you will die as you have lived, and then went away. On which, turning to Mary Roscoe, the said, "You see what miserable comforters they are."

Once he asked her if she had ever read any of his writings, and on being told that she had read but little of them, he inquired what she thought of them, adding, "from such

a one as you I expect a correct answer." She told him
that when very young, his "Age of Reason" was put into
her hands, but that the more she read it, the more dark
and distressed she felt, and she threw the book into the
fire. "I wish all had done as you," he replied : "for if the
Devil has ever had any agency in any work, he had it in my
writing that book." When going to carry him some refreshment, she repeatedly heard him uttering the language,
"O Lord! Lord God! or, Lord Jesus, have mercy upon
me!"

It is well known that during some weeks of his illness,
when a little free from bodily pain, he wrote a great deal;
this his nurse told me ; and Mary Roscoe repeatedly saw
him writing. If his companions in infidelity had found
anything to support the idea that he continued on his death-
bed to espouse their cause, would they not have eagerly
published it. But not a word is said: there is a total
secrecy as to what has become of these writings.

THE COUNTESS OF HUNTINGDON AND THE QUAKERESS.

As my mother grew better, she frequently took me with
her to the Pump Room, and she sometimes told me anecdotes of those she had seen there when a child. On one
occasion, when the room was thronged with company—and
at that time the visitors of Bath were equally distinguished
for rank and fashion,—a simple, humble woman, dressed
in the severest garb of the Society of Friends, walked in
the midst of the assembly, and began an address to them
on the vanity and follies of the world, and the insufficiency
of dogmatic without spiritual religion. The company
seemed taken by surprise, and their attention was arrested
for a few moments. As the speaker proceeded, and spoke
more and more against the customs of the world, signs of
disapprobation appeared. Amongst those present was one

lady with a stern yet high-toned expression of conntenance; her air was distinguished; she sat erect, and listened intently to the speaker. The impatience of the hearers soon became unrestrained; as the Quakeress spoke of giving up the world and its pleasures, hisses, groans, beating of sticks, and cries of "Down, down!" burst from every quarter. Then the lady I have described arose with dignity, and slowly passing through the crowd, where a passage was involuntarily opened to her, she went up to the speaker and thanked her, in her own name and in that of all present, for the faithfullness with which she had borne testimony to the truth. The lady added, "I am not of your persuasion, nor has it been my belief that our sex are generally deputed to be public teachers; but God who gives the will can make the exception, and He has indeed put it in the hearts of all His children to honour and venerate fidelity to His commission. Again I gratefully thank you." Side by side with the Quakeress she walked to the door of the Pump Room, and then resumed her seat. This lady was the celebrated Countess of Huntingdon.—*Life of Mary Anne Shimmelpenninck.*

QUAKERS.

"There is something, in the very aspect of a "Friend," suggestive of peace and good-will. Verily, if it were not for the broad-brimmed hat, and the straight coat, which the world's people call "shad," I would be a Quaker. But for the life of me I cannot resist the effect of the grotesque and the odd. I must smile, oftenest at myself. I could not keep within drab garments and the bounds of propriety. Incongruity would read me out of meeting. To be reined under a plain hat, would be impossible. Besides, I doubt whether any one accustomed to the world's pleasures could be a Quaker. Who, once familiar with Shakespeare and the opera, could resist a favourite air on a hand organ, or pass, undisturbed, 'Hamlet!' in capital letters on a play-bill? To be a Quaker, one must be a Quaker born. In spite of Sydney Smith, there is such a thing as a Quaker baby. In fact, I have seen it—a diminutive demurity, a stiff-plait in the bud. It had round blue eyes, and a face that expressed resignation in spite of the stomach-ache. It had no lace on its baby-cap, no embroidered nonsense on its petticoat. It had no beads, no ribands, no rattle, no bells, no corals. Its plain garments were innocent of inserting and edging; its socks were not of the colour of the world's people's baby. It was as punctiliously silent as a silent meeting, and sat up rigidly in its mother's lap, twirling its thumbs and cutting its teeth without a gum-ring. It never cried nor clapped its hands, and would not have said " papa " if it had been tied to the stake. When it went to sleep, it was hushed without a song, and they laid it in a drab-coloured cradle without a rocker.

Something I have observed, too, remarkably, strikingly Quakeristic. The young maidens and the young men never seem inclined to be fat. Such a thing as a maiden lady, nineteen years of age, with a pound of superfluous flesh, is not known among Friends. The young men sometimes grow outside the limits of a straight coat, and when they do, they quietly change into the habits of ordinary men. Either they are read out of meeting, or else they lose their hold when they get too round and too ripe, and just drop off. Remarkably Quakeristic, too, is an exemption the Friends appear to enjoy from diseases and complaints peculiar to other people. Who ever saw a Quaker marked with the small-pox, or a Quaker with the face-ache? Who ever saw a cross-eyed Quaker, or a decided case of mumps under a broad-brimmed hat? Doubtless much of this is owing to their cleanliness, duplex cleanliness, purity of

body and soul. I saw a face in the cars, not long since—
a face that had calmly endured the storms of seventy yearly
meetings. It was a hot, dry day; the windows were all
open; dust was pouring into the cars; eyebrows, eyelashes,
ends of hair, moustaches,, wigs, coat-collars, sleeves, waistcoats, and trousers of the world's people, were touched with
a fine tawny colour. Their faces had a general appearance
of humidity in streaks, now and then tattooed with a black
cinder; but there, within a satin bonnet (Turk's satin)—a
bonnet made after the fashion of Professor Espy's patent
ventilator—was a face of seventy years, calm as a summer
morning, smooth as an infant's, without one speck or stain
of dust, without one touch of perspiration or exasperation.
No, nor was there, on the cross-pinned 'kerchief,
nor on the elaboratory plain dress, one atom of earthly contact; the very air did seem to respect that aged Quakeress.
    And Thomas Lurting, too; his adventures are well worth
reading to the children. A Quaker Sailor, the mate of a
Quaker ship, manned with a Quaker crew, every one of
which had a straight collar to his pea-jacket, and a tarpau-
lin with at least three feet diameter of brim. Thomas
Lurting, whose ship was captured by Algerine pirates after
a hard chase, and who welcomed them on board as if they
had been brothers. Then, when the Quaker vessel and the
Algerine were seprated by a storm, how friendly those salt-
water nonresistants were to their captors on board their
own vessel; with what alacrity did they go aloft to take in
sail, or to shake out the reef, until those heathen pirates left
the handling of the ship entirely to their broad-brimmed
brethren, and went to sleep in the cabin; and then, what did the
Quakers do but first shut the cabin-doors, and fasten them,
so that the Turks could not get out again? And then,
fearless of danger, they steered for the Barbary coast, and
made those fierce, moustached pirates get into a small boat

(they had been for ever locked up else), and rowed them to
the shore; and when the Turks found themselves in a small
boat with but a small crew of broad-brims, and gave signs
of mutiny, what did the brave Thomas Lurting? Lay violent hands on them? Draw a cutlass, or cock a pistol?
No; he merely struck the leader "a pretty heavy blow with
a boat-hook, telling him to sit still and be quiet," as he
says himself, "thinking it was better to stun a man than
to kill him." And so he got the pirates on shore and in
their own country. .

The most singular spectacle I ever witnessed was the
burial service over a Quaker, in a Catholic cathedral. He
had formerly been the rigidest of his sect—a man who had
believed the mitre and crosier to be little better than the
horns and tail of the evil one—a man who had looked upon
church music and polygamy with equal abhorrence, and
who would rather have been burned himself than burn a
Roman candle on the anniversary of the national jubilee.
Yet, by one of those inexplicable inconsistencies, peculiar
to mere men, but rare among Quakers, he had seceded from
the faith of his fathers, and become one of the most zealous
of Papists.

The grand altar was radiant with wax tapers; the priests
on either side, in glittering dresses, were chanting respon-
ses; the censer boys, in red and white garments, swung the
smoke of myrrh and frankincense into the air, and as the
fragrant mist rolled up and hung in rosy clouds under the
lofty, stained-glass windows, the great organ panted forth
the requiem. Marvellously contrasted with this pomp and
display appeared the crowd of broad-brims and stiff-plaits,
the friends and relatives of the deceased. Never perhaps
had such an audience been gathered in such a place in the
world before. The scene, to the priests themselves, must
have been novel and striking. Instead of the usual display

of reverence, instead of the customary show of bare heads
and bended knees, every Quaker stood stoutly on his legs,
with his broad-brimmed hat clinging to his head as strongly
as his faith to his heart. Disciplined as they had been in
many a silent meeting, during the entire mass not one of
the broad-brims moved an inch until the service was over.
Then the coffin was opened, and solemnly, silently, decorously, the brethren and sisters moved towards it to look, for
the last time, upon the face of the seceder. Then silently,
solemnly, decorously, they moved from the Popish temple.
"I saw," said one of the sisters, "that he" (meaning the
departed ex-Quaker) "had on worked slippers with silver
soles; what does thee think that was for"? The person
spoken to wore a hat with a goodly brim. Without moving
his head, he rolled around, sideways, two Quakeristic eyes,
large blue eyes, with little inky dots of pupils, like small
black islands in oceans of buttermilk, and said, awfully, "I
suppose they was to walk through Purgatory with."

Titan.

George IV. Frustrated Attempt to Penetrate the Mysteries of the Women's Meeting.

I was shewn in the Women's Meeting-room, the seat
on which his Majesty, King George IV. when Prince
Regent, had for a moment placed himself, when led
by the spirit of adventure, and as my informant stated, a
most unbecoming curiosity, he had disguised as a Woman
Friend, made his way into the secret conclave. His dress
was all right: a grey silk gown, a brown cloth shawl, a
little white handkerchief, with hemmed edge, round his neck,
and a very well-poked Friend's bonnet with the pretty crimped
border of his clean muslin cap tied under the chin, completed
the disguise, in which he might have escaped detection very
well, were it not for the tell-tale boots, and the unfeminine
position in which the arms and legs bestowed themselves.

The young woman who sat behind him, and saw the heel protruding from its silken robe, slipt quitely out of Meeting, and gave the alarm. Two men Friends were speedily summoned, and the royal intruder felt himself gently tapped on the shoulder, and requested to walk into another room. He made no resistance, but quitely went away ; and receiving the usual notice, that the rules of the Society would not allow any but members to be present, he retired, and calling a hackney coach, drove off, perhaps flattering himself that his *incognito* had not been penetrated, for although his countenance had been instantly recognised, still nothing was said to intimate that it had been so. Resolute that none but the initiated should be present, they were yet careful to treat with courtesy their most unexpected visitant, and even deferentially to respect his assumed character.

" *Quakerism,*" by Mrs. J. R. Greer.

Sabbath Observance.

The following actual fact concerning a Quaker occurred some years ago in the West of England. The late Sir Knowle Wellman, well-known to the inhabitants of Taunton, was one Sunday morning in his carriage on his way to Church, when, in passing through the crescent, he observed the bar across the carriage-way was padlocked. The coachman drew up and waited for instructions as to what should be done. Sir Knowle was in the act of telling his man to turn back, when an old townsman, a Quaker, observing how the case stood came from his house hard by, and, handing the coachman a saw, said, "There, friend—I cannot help thee, because to-day is the Sabbath, but I can lend thee this saw, whereby thou canst cut thy way through."

Self-Composure.

Charles Lamb, in illustrating the " astonishing composure" of some members of the Society of " Friends " relates the following anecdote. "I was travelling in a stage-coach with three male Quakers, buttoned up in the straitest non-conformity of their sect. We stopped to bait at Andover, where a meal, partly tea apparatus, partly supper, was set before us. My friends confined themselves to the tea-table. I in my way took supper. When the landlady brought in the bill, the eldest of my companions discovered that she had charged for two meals. This was resisted. Mine hostess was very clamorous and positive. Some mild arguments were used on the part of the Quakers, for which the heated mind of the good lady seemed by no means a fit recipient. The guard come in with his usual peremptory notice. The Quakers pulled out their money, and formally tendered it—so much for tea—I, in humble imitation, tendering mine—for the supper which I had taken. She would not relax in her demand. So they all three quietly put up their silver, as did myself, and marched out of the room, the eldest and gravest going first, with myself closing up the rear, who thought I could not do better than follow the example of such grave and warrantable personages. We got in. The steps went up. The coach drove off. The murmurs of mine hostess, not very indistinctly or ambiguously pronounced, became after a time inaudible— and now my conscience, which the whimsical scene had for a while suspended, beginning to give some twitches, I waited, in the hope that some justification would be offered by these serious persons for the seeming injustice of their conduct. To my great surprise, not a syllable was dropped on the subject. They sat as mute as at a meeting. At length the eldest of them broke silence, by enquiring of his next neighbour, "Hast thee heard how indigos go at the India house?" and the question operated as a soporific on my moral feeling as far as Exeter."

INDIRECT REPLY.

There are some persons who insensibly acquire the habit of never giving a *direct answer*. A Quaker in the West of

England (a most respectable man) was so remarkable for this, as to occasion a wager, that a direct reply could not be obtained from him to *any question whatever*. Upon which one of the parties, to put it totally out of his power to evade the point, watched the opportunity of the *arrival of the mail;* actually saw him reading his dispatches, and accosted him with "your servant, Mr. —, pray is the post come in ? But alas! all that he could extort from the honest Quaker, was " Why, friend, dost thou expect letters ? "

A CHALLENGE.

Early in the present century an actor said to a Quaker, " Do you think I am a good Actor?" " Certainly, thou be'est," answered the Friend. He was at once requested to choose his weapons.

FRIENDS AND THE IRISH REBELLION.

The condition of the peace-loving members of the Society of Friends during the Irish rebellion, was an interesting exemplification of moral heroism sustaining a people in peace in the midst of conflicting parties, and while under the apprehension of impending violence and death.

As early as the years 1795-6, their attenion was called to the threatening aspect of affairs, and their course determined on. In the county of Wexford, many friends resided, and it is remarkable that, though they aided the martial operations in no particular, yet in seasons of distress they succoured the wounded and wretched of each party.

· This mode of conduct, at the time subjected the Friends to the animadversions of both parties. The military accused them of disloyalty—the rebels of apathy ; and yet they carried out their principles in the minutest particular.

A worthy man at Ferns, in the county of Wicklow, on the breaking out of the rebellion, to show his neighbours the part he meant to act, took out his fowling-piece, the only weapon that would find a place in the dwelling of a Friend, and broke it to pieces before his door, in the open street; thus showing to all that his house was entirely without weapon of offence or defence.   Another individual, who kept a shop where ropes and hardware were sold, had his dwelling surrounded by the military, who came and demanded ropes to hang the rebels they had taken.   Though his life was imperilled by the refusal, as it might be construed into rebellion, the Friend refused to supply a rope for taking away the life of a fellow-creature.   At another time, a night attack on a town in possesion of the rebels was intended by the military, and all persons not in league with the rebels were commanded to put lights in their windows; but, as Friends chose to put confidence in the protection of God rather than man, they declined to do this, particularly as such lights would aid the combatants in their murderous warfare.

In all these instances, though sternly threatened and in imminent peril, the moral heroism of the Friends triumphed, and their lives were preserved.

Scarcely any one who, in that dreadful time, resided in Ireland, dared to attempt going out on their usual pursuits, for all subordination was at an end; and yet Friends, unarmed, went constantly to their religious meetings, through the most disturbed districts of the country, and though commanded on peril of their lives, to desist.   Conscience commanded them to go, and they went, leaving the issue in the hands of the Almighty, who wonderfully preserved them.

Throughout the whole of that fearful time, it is a remarkable fact, that only one member of the Society of Friends perished, and he was led to trust in the power of earthly weapons to preserve him rather than in the care of the Almighty, and the exercise of his own moral heroism.

"Moral Heroism," by C. L. Balfour.

QUICK RETORT.

Some time ago, a Quaker, and a hotheaded youth had a disagreement in the street. The Friend, kept his temper most equably, which seemed but to increase the anger of the other. "Fellow," said the latter, "I dont know a bigger fool than you are," finishing the sentence with an oath. "Stop, friend," replied the Quaker, "thee forgetest thyself."

AMUSING ENCOUNTER AT A SUPPER PARTY.

Edmund Ward, who lived in the early part of the last century, gives an amusing account of a supper at which he was present. He writes as follows, "From thence I went to a Coffee House were I had appointed my' acquaintance to meet with me at certain hours in the day; and there I found a letter from my friend, to request my company to supper at a private house in the city; where a gentleman had provided a commodious entertainment for us and some other of his friends that evening. Amongst them were two Country Parsons, and a notable sharp Town Quaker, who I had reasonable foresight would produce some good diversion as soon as our cups, and the season of the night, had made us fit instruments for each others felicity.

I shall not tire you with a Bill of Fare; but in short, a plentiful supper we had, to the great content of the Founder, (it being served up in such admirable order) as to the satisfaction of the guests.

When we had tired cur hands with stopping our mouths, to assuage the fury of our appetites, and one of the Parsons had put a spiritual padlock upon the mouths of the company, and gave a holy period to our fleshly sustenance for that evening; a magnificent bowl of punch, and some bottles of right Gallick Juice were handed to the table, which received, as the glasses went round, a circular approbation. Our stomachs craving a hearty supply of wine for the digestion of our Fish, made us at first pour down our liquor in such

E

plentiful streams, that it soon put our engines of verbosity to
work, and made us as merry as so many school-boys at a
breaking-up, o'er a batch of cakes, or a dishful of stewed
prunes. At last we came to a good-looking soldier's bottle of
Claret, which at least held half a pint extraordinary; but
the cork was drove in so far, that there was no opening o'nt
without a bottle-screw; several attempted with their thumbs
and fingers to remove the stubborn obstacle, but none could
effect the difficult undertaking; upon which says the donor
of the feast, What is no body amongst us so provident a toper,
as to carry a bottle-screw about him?   One cried No.
Another No, Poize o'nt he had left his at home. A third never
carry'd one, and so 'twas concluded no screw was to be had:
the Parsons being all this time silent, at last says the Lord of
the banquet to his men, Here take it away; tho' I protest,
says he, 'tis a fine bottle, and I'll warrant the wine's better
than ordinary, it's so well cork'd, but what shall we do with it?
We cannot open it, you must take it down I think; tho' I
vow, 'tis a great deal of pity; but prithee bring us some
more bottles that may not puzzle us so. The oldest and
wisest of the Parsons having observed the copious dimensions
of the bottle, and well knowing by experience that sound
corking is always an advantage to liquor.   Hold, hold,
friend, says he to the servant who was going out with the
bottle, I believe I have a little engine in my pocket that may
unlock the difficulty; and fumbling in his pockets, after he
had pluck'd out a Common Prayer Book, an old comb-case
full of notes, a two-penny nut-grater, and made a remove of
such kind of wordly necessaries, at last he came to the
matter, and out he brings a Bottle-Screw which provok'd not
a little laughter thro' the whole company. Methinks, friend,
says the Quaker, a Common Prayer Book and a Bottle-Screw,
are improper companions, not fit to lodge in one pocket together.
Why dost thou not make thy breeches afford 'em different

apartments? To which the Parson made this answer, Since devotion gives comfort to the soul, and wine in moderation, preserves the health of the body, why may not a Book that instructs us in the one, and an Instrument that makes way for the other, be allowed, as well as the Soul and Body, for whose good they were intended to bear one another company? But, methinks, friend, says the Quaker, a Bottle-Screw in a Minister's pocket, is like the practice of piety in the hand of a Harlot; the one no more becomes thy profession than the other does hers. To which the Parson replied, a good book in the hand of a sinner, and an instrument that does good to a whole society, in the hand of a Clergyman, I think both are very commendable: and I wonder why a good man should object against either. I am very glad, says the Quaker, thou takest me to be a good man; then, I hope, thou hast no reason to take anything ill that I have spoken? Nay, hold, says the Parson, I did not design it as a compliment to thee; for to tell thee the truth, I do not think thee near so good as those who, I believe, thou hast a bad opinion of; meaning, as I suppose the Church Clergy. To which replied the Quaker. Thou may'st see the Government has a better opinion of us, than it has of those people whom I imagine thou meanest, or else they would never have made our words, of equal validity with your oaths. Therefore, I think, we have reason to be look'd upon as the most honest people in the Kingdom. In answer to this, says the Parson, I remember a Fable, which, with as much brevity as I can, I will repeat to the Company in answer to thee.

Once upon a time, when the lion found there were many divisions amongst his four-footed subjects, insomuch that he could not, without some difficulty, preserve peace in his dominions, and allay the grumblings of each dissatisfied party. But amongst all the factious beasts of the forest, the asses were most obstinate and would never change their

pace in obedience to those wholesome laws provided against
their humdrum sloathfulness.   The Lion, considering they
were a serviceable creature, notwithstanding their formality,
and would bear any burden without complaining, let them
have but their own ways and go their own pace, thought it
very necessary to make a law that every ass should have
his own will, which they would always have before, in spite
of all the laws against it :   and in answer to their petition
that they should not be obliged to go shod like horses, but
with this proviso, That if ever they trip'd or stumbled,
they should be soundly whipt for their fault.   A little time
after the commencement of this law, an ass meeting with
a horse could not forbear boasting what great favourites
the asses were at court, upbrading the horse with being
iron-shod, and how they, by the law, were made free to
travel upon their own natural hoof, which is much more
easy; you are mistaken, says the horse, shoeing makes us
walk more upright and tread with more security, and pray
Friend Ass, remember this amidst your benefit, that you
must be whip'd if you stumble as well as we.

Upon the application of this Fable, the whole company
burst into laughter, to the great discountenance of our
merry Ananias, who had nothing left but blushes for a reply.
But having a great desire to be level with his antagonist,
lay so very close upon the Catch, that the Parson was forced
to put a guard upon his tongue, lest he should give him an
advantage to recover his credit.   Till at last, in a silent
interval, the glass coming two or three times quick about,
made the Parson neglect to take off his wine with his usual
expedition, and set it down before him; which the Quaker
observing, ask'd him what countryman he was?   The
Priest returned him a satisfactory answer.   Did'st thou not
lately hear of a great Living that was vacant in thy country,
computed to be worth about four hundred pounds a year?

Upon this the Parson began to prick his ears, and enquired where abouts it was, never minding his glass. Truly, says the Quaker, I cannot tell directly where it lies, but I can tell thee 'tis in vain to enquire after it, for it is already disposed of to an eminent person of thy function, who is now in this town, and of whom I have some knowledge. At a coffee house where he uses, I happened to hear him highly commending the good hospitality of the late Incumbent. It being, says he, indeed so plentiful a benefice, that he might well afford it. And I hope says he, that I shall not be backward in following his example. The Parson showing great dissatisfation in his looks that such a living should fall, and be disposed of without so much as his knowledge, not knowing but his own interest might have been sufficient to have carried it. The Quaker, he proceeds all the while in praising the Orchards, Gardens, Barns, Stables, fine rooms, large kitchens, noble parlour, convenient buttery, &c., which set the Parson so on gog, that he listened and gap'd as if he would have it catch in his mouth. But, at last, says the Quaker, I heard him very much complain of one great inconvenience indeed, and that was the mis-placing his wine-cellar, for which reason he would have it removed. Why where did the cellar stand, says the Parson? Just under the pulpit, says the Quaker, and he look'd upon it to be a great fault to preach over his liquor. The Parson, who had let his glass stand charged all the time of the story, readily took the application. I confess says the Parson, I very unadvisedly left a blot in my tables, and you by chance have it, and now you have done, it serves only to verify the old proverb, That fools have fortune. This unexpected retort of the Parson's quite dumb-founded the Quaker, and added a great deal of pleasure to the company. Our merry dispos'd Friend taking breath after this sparring blow a considerable time, sitting as silent as a young swearer before his father, endeavouring as much to hide his failings, as the other does his vices.

By this time the stock of wine upon the tables being exhausted, we began to apply ourselves to the Punch, which upon the wine we had already drank, soon put our spirits into a fresh ferment; and made us now as noisy as gamesters in a cock-pit, all bawling and betting on the one side or to'ther. Insomuch that with one impertinent question or other they had almost put the Parson into a passion, during which uneasiness his Yea and Nay adversary ask'd him what he thought a Quaker to be? The Parson, a little angry they had began to teaze him, made this response, a Quaker, says he, is some of old nick's venom, spit in the face of God's Church, which her clergy cannot lick out with their tongues, or rub; off with their lawn sleeves: Therefore the Church makes a virtue of necessity, and uses them as Ladies do their black patches, for foils to magnify their beauty. Indeed, Friend, says the Quaker, thou talkest as if the liquor had disturbed thy inward man. Prithee tell me who thou think-est was the first Quaker, that thou talkest with such prophaness against so good a profession? The first Quaker, says the Parson, who after a very short deliberation, answered Balaam. Balaam, says the Quaker, how didst thou make that out? It's plainly so, says the Parson, because he was the first that ever gave his attention to hear an ass hold forth. The whole company expressed by their laughter an approba-tion of the jest, and it was agreed on all hands, that it might reasonably pass for a good punch-bowl answer.

The potency of the liquor, and the weakness of our brains, had now drawn our mirth to the dregs, that we were more in danger of falling into disorder than we were of recovering our almost stupified souls to their pitch of felicity; several of the company having wisely submitted their distempered heads to that great physician sleep, who alone can recover the patient's giddy brains of his epidemical fever. At last down dropt the body of Divinity, in the condition of a weaker Brother, and left the Quaker one of the survivors, who, with great joy, brandish'd a triumphant brimmer round his head, as a trophy of the inebrious victory he had obtained over a Father of the Church."

A RECKLESS SPECULATOR.

Mr. Fordyce a reckless speculator of the last century, wishing to procure assistance to enable him to tide over his difficulties, amongst others, applied to a shrewd Quaker for help. "Friend Fordyce," was the reply of the latter, "I have known many men ruined by two dice, but I will not be ruined by Four-dice."

THE KING AND THE QUAKER.

On the occasion of the state visit of George III. to the City on the first Lord Mayor's Day after his accession to the throne, and when the cavalcade had reached Cheapside, the acclamations of the people were so great "as to pierce the air with their shouts;" added to which, the dismal noise made by the creaking of the various signs which hung across the streets caused one of the horses attached to the king's carriage to become very restive and unmanageable when oppossite Bow Church, causing considerable confusion to the procession, and alarm to their Majesties.

A certain Quaker, named David Barclay, a linendraper in Cheapside, who was viewing the procession from the balcony of his first-floor window, perceiving the embarrassed situation of the king and queen, descended to the street. At this moment the procession halted, and our friend approaching the carriage, addressed the king, saying, "Wilt thee alight, George, and thy wife Charlotte, and come into my house and view the Mayor's show?" The king, who had on many occasions before he came to the throne evinced a strong partiality for Quakers, and who, from the plainness of his manners, would no doubt have been one himself, had he not been born to a throne, condescended to accept the invitation of the worthy linendraper, and in the balcony of the first floor of the house, exactly opposite Bow Church, the king and queen stood during the remainder of the procession.

Our friend David introduced to their Majesties the whole of his family. His eldest son, Robert, who was then a young man about twenty years of age, received especial notice from their Majesties. On their taking their leave to proceed to Guildhall, his Majesty said, "David let me see thee at St. James's next Wednesday, and bring thy son Robert with thee." Accordingly, David Barclay and his son Robert attended the levee, and on approaching the royal presence, the king, throwing aside all 'regal restraint, descended from the throne, and giving the Friend a hearty shake of the hand, welcomed him to St. James's. He said many kind things both to the father and to the son : among the rest, he asked David what he intended to do with Robert; and without waiting for a reply, said, "Let him come here, and I will provide him with honourable and profitable employment."

The strict and cautious Quaker, with many apologies, and with much humility, requested permission to reject the proposal, adding, "I fear the air of the court of your Majesty would not agree with my son."

The king, who had seldom witnessed a similar rejection of intended royal favour, said, "Well, David, well, well; you know best; but you must not omit to let me see you occasionally at St. James's."

Soon after this David Barclay saw his son Robert established as a banker in Lombard Street; who, instead of becoming a courtier, a position for which Nature never intended him, became the founder of one of the most eminent banking firms of the present day.—*Lawson's History of Banking.*

George III., visit to Worcester, 1780.

An attempt was made to *move* the *spirit* in the Quakers of Worcester to address his majesty; but these people kept in their old dull track of life, and were rather concerned that such a thing as a royal visit had happened to break in upon their quietude. About a dozen of the more curious among them got leave to step into the court-yard where his majesty's coach left the palace, but they stood unmoved, with their hats on their heads. The king saw they were Quakers, and taking off his hat, bowed to them. They, in return, moved their hands, and the eldest of them said, "*Fare thee well, friend George!*" The king and queen laughed heartily at this systematic affection.

Odd Decision.

Two Quakers resident in Philadelphia, applied to their society, as they do not go to law to decide the following difficulty:—*A*, uneasy about a ship that ought to have arrived; meets *B*, an insurer, and expresses a wish to have the vessel insured. The matter is agreed upon. *A* returns home, and receives a letter informing him of the loss of his ship. What shall he do? He is afraid that the policy is not filled up, and should *B* hear of the matter soon, it is all over with him. He therefore writes to *B* thus:—"Friend *B*, if thee hasn't filled up the policy, thee needn't, for *I've heard of the ship.*" "Oh! oh!" thinks *B* to himself— "cunning fellow—he wants to do me out of the premium." So he writes thus to *A*:—"Friend *A*, thee bee'st too late by half an hour— the policy is filled." *A* rubs his hands with delight. Yet *B* refuses to pay. Well, what is the decision? The loss is divided between them. This may be even-handed justice, though unquestionably it is an odd decision.

Quakers' Meeting.

I accompanied Mrs. Drummond to their meeting; she behaved with the greatest steadiness and seriousness. No whining when she spoke, and scarce any action. Very good language; particularly full of metaphors, but pretty and well managed ones; rather a general discourse, than any one subject pursued : and accordingly the proposition was made, not at the beginning, but at the conclusion.—"That we may all endeavour to amend our lives, and to be always ready for this great change; is the earnest desire of my heart, and the design of my present exhortation."—Then another preached; and then she made a prayer (at which they all stood up, with their hats off) with good language, and with a good deal of devotion: and, among other things, begged, " that God would enlighten the eyes of those who were at all inclined to see the truth; and bring them fully and heartily to embrace' it."—She sat at the head of the elders in the highest line: there was a row, under all, of women preachers : (three only spoke while I was there; and these all women.) There was above half an hour's silence in the beginning; for that deep attention, &c., which she spoke of. The people on the speaking benches seemed more particularly moved, both then and afterwards. Some of them had a great deal of the tranquility in their looks, some were quite impassioned, some looked sullen, but the more general air, especially in the congregation, was that of drowsiness. One of the women in the preacher's seat, had a constant gentle agitation of the head. Another, who seemed extremely pretty when she came in, grew quite ugly before I came out. Her colour, which was very fresh at first, sunk gradually till she was quite pale; her lips grew lurid, her look wan, and somewhat ghostly; her eyes lost all their lustre; and the air of her face all its pleasingness. So that Quakerism is by no means a proper religion for the pretty women of this world; at least if they think of sitting on the bench of the preachers; or should affect to appear strongly moved, with the supposed influences which they sit to receive in their congregations.—*Spence's Anecdotes.*

UNEQUAL SALARIES.

A poor parson complaining of the unequal salaries which were paid to bishops and curates, a Quaker who was present, observed that it was just the same in ancient time; " For," added he, " thou knowest we are told, that while the *oxen were ploughing in the field, the asses were feeding in the field by the side of them.*"

PRACTICAL JOKE.

The only practical joke in which Richard Harris Barham —better known by his *nom de plume* of Thomas Ingoldsby —ever personally engaged was enacted when he was a boy, in company with a schoolfellow. Entering a Quaker's meeting-house and looking around at the grave assembly, Barham's companion held up a penny tart and said solemnly, "Whoever speaks first shall have this pie." · " Go thy way, boy, and ———— " " The pie's yours sir ! " exclaimed the lad, placing it before the astonished speaker, and he and Barham hastily made their escape.

ADVICE TO MONEY-HUNTERS.

A prudent and well-disposed member of the Society of Friends once gave the following friendly advice:—"John," said he, " I hear thou art going to be married." " Yes," replied John, " I am." " Well," replied the Quaker, " I have one little piece of advice to give thee, and that is, never marry a woman worth more than thou art. When I married my wife, I was worth fifty shillings, and she was worth sixty-two; and, whenever any difference has occurred between us since, she has always thrown up the odd shillings."

THE QUAKER AND THE PARSON.

A Quaker, that was a barber, being sued by the parson for tithes, Yea and Nay went to him, and demanded the

the reason why he troubled him, as he had never any dealing with him in his whole life.

"Why," says the parson, "for preaching in church."

"For tithes!" says the Quaker; "I pr'ythee, friend, upon what account?"

"Why," says the parson, "for preaching in church."

"Alas! then," replied the Quaker, "I have nothing to pay thee; for I come not there."

"Oh, but you might," says the parson; "for the doors are always open at convenient times;" and thereupon said he would be paid, seeing it was his due. Yea and Nay hereupon shook his head, and, making several wry faces, departed, and immediately entered his action (it being a corporation town) against the parson for forty shillings. The parson, upon notice of this, came to him, and very hotly demanded why he had put such a disgrace upon him, and for what he owed him the money.

"Truly, friend," replied the Quaker, "for trimming."

"For trimming!" says the parson; "why I was never trimmed by you in my life."

"Oh, but thou mightst have come in and been trimmed, if thou hadst pleased; for my doors are always open at convenient times, as well as thine."

A VEHEMENT TIMEPIECE.

A clock pedlar was tramping along, hot, dusty, and tired, when he came to a Meeting-house wherin sundry Friends were engaged in silent devotion. The peripatetic tradesman thought he would walk in and rest himself. He took a seat upon a bench, doffed his hat, and placed his clocks on the floor. Thare was a painful stillness in the Meeting-house, which was broken by one of the clocks, which commenced striking furiously. The pedlar was in agony, but he hoped every minute the clock would stop. Instead of that, it struck just four hundred and thirty times, by the actual count of every Friend in the Meeting, for even the best-displined of them couldn't help numbering the strokes. Then rose one of the elder Friends, at the end of the four hundred and thirtieth stroke, and said,--"Friend, as it is so very late, perhaps thee had better proceed on thy journey, or thee will not reach thy destination, unless thee art as energetic as thy vehement timepiece."

THE QUAKER AND THE VICAR.

A Nobleman was in the habit once-a-year of inviting his tenants, among whom was a conscientious Quaker, to dine with him. The Quaker, not anxious to brave the senseless ridicule to which members of the Society of Friends were at that time exposed, invariably declined the honour. At length his lordship pressed him, as a personal favour, to attend. On the right of the host sat the Vicar, and on the left his Curate. After dinner the Vicar, who stuttered painfully, attempted to put a question, by way of banter, to the Quaker. The Quaker made no reply. The clergyman repeated in the same incomprehensible manner, the query. Still the Quaker made no answer, and the Curate, who was of a glib and ready tongue, interfered and said, "I do not think you understand what the Vicar says." "I do not see how I should, friend," quietly replied the Quaker. "Oh," replied the Curate, "he simply asks you whether you can tell him how it was that Balaam's ass spoke?"—"Balaam had an impediment in his speech, and his ass spoke for him," was the Quaker's rejoinder.

SEASONABLE KINDNESS.

Notwithstanding that the principle of the Quakers will not allow them to sanction war, much less contribute to its support, unless when compelled, yet in the rebellion of 1745, a deputation of this society waited on Sir William Yonge and Lord Ligonier, with an offer to furnish, at their own

expense, to the troops employed in his majesty's service during the winter in the north, a supply of woollen waistcoats,
to be worn under their other clothing. The offer was
accepted.

QUAKER AND JUSTICE.

A Quaker, having been cited as an evidence at a Quarter
Sessions, one of the magistrates, who had been a blacksmith,
desired to know why he would not take off his hat? 'It is
a privilege,' said the Quaker, 'that the laws and liberty of
my country indulge people of our religious mode of thinking
in.' 'If I had it in my power,' replied the justice, I would
have your hat *nailed* to your head. 'I thought,' said
Obadiah, drily, 'that thou hadst given over the trade of
driving nails."

LORD DERBY AND THE QUAKER.

In the days when Preston was considered "fashionable,"
ere the requirements of trade had swallowed up nearly every
vestige of green park and spacious gardens formerly connected
with many town residences, there were in Stoneygate several
neat villas, surrounded by shady trees and luxuriant orchards.
One of these was occupied by a rather eccentric Quaker,
named John Danson. The house which John occupied was
owned by the Earl of Derby, of Sporting notoriety. In their
early days the embryo earl and the Quaker boy had been
schoolfellows at the Preston Grammar School, which was
then in Stoneygate. The Quaker had been for some time
very tardy in paying up his rent, and Mr. Baines, the earl's
agent, had on sundry occasions threatened him with a descent
of the "Philistines," in the shape of bailiffs. One morning
he started off on foot to Knowsley, and gaining admission to
the park, walked up to the hall-door and rang. On the
footman answering the bell, John put the simple question,
"Is Edward in?"—"Edward!" exclaimed the astonished

lackey; "what Edward do you mean?"—"Edward Stanley. He lives here, doesn't he? Is he in? I want to see him," replied the Quaker. "Go away, you impertinent fellow!" was the indignant rejoinder, and the footman slammed the door in the Quaker's face. But John was not to be discouraged by this ungracious reception; he had come to see the earl, and did see him. The lackey eventually took in his name, and John was immediately ushered into the presence of the noble earl, whom he saluted with—"Well, Edward, how art thou getting on?"—"Very well, thank you, John," replied his Lordship, extending his hand and warmly shaking that of his visitor. "It's a long time since thou and I went to Preston Grammar School together," added the blunt Quaker. "It is indeed, John, a very long time," replied his lordship. "I am very glad to see you. How are you getting along? And what has brought you over here to Knowsley?"—"I am sorry to say," responded John, "that I have been getting on but very badly lately. I cannot raise brass to pay my rent, and that man of thine at Preston— Baines—he's a vast saucy fellow—says if I don't pay up before next Thursday he'll send th' bums. So, I've come to to a-k thee to give me a bit longer time."—"Well, John," said his lordship, "I suppose you've been rather unfortunate lately; so I'll forgive you the rent altogether. And," added his lordship, "I'll tell you what I'll do further. You may live in the house rent free as long as you do live." John's protestations of gratitude for this act of generosity were unbounded. He took his departure from Knowsley with a much lighter heart than when approaching it. Some time after John's visit to Knowsley, during one of the race weeks, Lord Derby, when proceeding to the Cock Pit, to join in his favourite sport, met John in Stoneygate, when, after a friendly salute, the latter said, "I see, Edward, thou hasn't given up thy silly, sinful practices yet!"—"No, John, replied the earl, "I have not. But if all my tenants paid their rents as you do, I should very soon have to give up altogether;" and with this rebuke his lordship walked on.

A FRIEND'S REBUKE.

Some years ago the attention of people passing near the drawbridge at Hull was attracted by hearing a man on a barge swearing in a most awful manner. A Weslyan minister spoke to him, but without effect, and the bystanders waiting till the bridge went down had to submit to the painful sounds. Presently a Quaker came up, and with a loud voice called out, "Swear on, man, swear on." The Wesleyan minister expressed surprise that he should tell a man who was blaspheming so dreadfully to swear on. The Quaker said he could hear there was a great deal of bad within the man, and he wanted it to come out. Whether it was the oddness of the advice, or whether the conscience of the man was touched, he was silent from that moment, instead of replying with abuse, as might have been expected. Many months afterwards one of the bystanders met the same boatman in Hull, and asked him if he remembered when he was swearing so under the drawbridge when the Quaker spoke to him. "Yes, I do," he said; "and an oath has never passed my lips since." He learned afterwards that the boatman had become an altered man, and the beginning of his change dated from the time when the pious Quaker's strange advice arrested his attention.—J. F.

A SHREWD BROKER.

A Quaker broker in New York having had a bag of golden eagles (coins) stolen from his counter while he stepped into his back room for a moment, never mentioned the loss to anybody, but quietly bided his time. Several months afterwards, a neighbour being in his office, carelessly asked him, "Have you ever heard anything about that bag of eagles that you lost ?" "Ah, John!" exclaimed the Quaker, "thou art the thief, or thou couldst not have known anything about it!" The shrewd old Quaker was right, and the gold was restored, with interest.

CLEARING THE LAW.

Tho forbearance of the Quakers was once the subject of a wager, a bully claiming that the Quakers were the quint-essence of meekness, and that he would prove it; which he proceeded to do by finding out a Friend, whom he smote upon the right cheek. The Quaker immediately turned the left cheek, which the bully struck also, and the Friend quietly rolled up his sleeves, and quaintly remarked, "I have cleared the law, and now I will give thee a beating for thy brutality," which he forthwith proceeded to do very vigoursly, to the evident delight of the bystanders.

A MYSTERY EXPLAINED.

A Quaker grocer in a country village became notorious for selling small eggs. The village gossips were ready to testify that he bought large and fine-looking eggs, and where could he find so many small-sized eggs as he daily sent out to his customers was a mystery they could not fathom. There were two mysterious-looking holes in his counter about the size of an egg, and curiosity was excited to the highest pitch to ascertain what use they were put to. The only answer anybody could get from the old man, when questioned concerning the use of the holes, was, "My friend, if I tell thee the truth, it would not benefit me nor thee, and I don't wish to tell a lie. It is a pity that lying is a sin, for it comes so easy in trade." At last it was resolved by some of the spinsters to watch his actions through the cracks of the shutters after he had closed his shop for the night, and thus endeavour to find out their use. This reso-lution was put into execution, and the ladies caught the grocer passing eggs through the holes, by the light of a penny dip. All those that passed through the smaller hole he placed in one basket; and those that passed through the larger one he put in another; and all that would not pass through either he placed in a tin pan and took them to his house. On his way thither he heard the rustling of the women's dresses, and saw he was caught; so he called them to him, and in the blandest manner said, "Sisters, ye have given yourselves much trouble to appease this curiosity, and I will therefore explain all to ye. Ye see, I sort my eggs into three sizes by means of those holes. The largest I use in my own family; the next size I sell a halfpenny cheaper on a dozen than any of my neighbours, for *cash;* the smallest I send to those who will buy no other way than *on credit.*" The ladies were satisfied with the lesson in trade, and spread the news abroad until we heard it.

LORD ELLENBOROUGH.

A Quaker coming into the witness box at Guildhall without a broad brim or dittoes, and rather smartly dressed, the crier put the book into his hand, and was about to administer the oath, when he required to be examined on his affirmation. Lord Ellenborough, asking if he was really a Quaker, and being answered in the affirmative, exclaimed —" Do you really mean to impose upon the court by appearing here in the disguise of a reasonable being?"

THE QUAKER WHO BOUGHT A STOLEN HORSE.

Charles Carey lived near Philadelphia, in a comfortable house with a few acres of pasture adjoining. A young horse, apparently healthy, though lean, was one day offered him in the market for fifty dollars. The cheapness tempted him to purchase; he thought the clover of his pasture would soon put the animal in good condition, and enable him to sell him at an advanced price. He was too poor to command the required sum himself, but he borrowed it of a friend. The horse, being well fed and lightly worked, soon became a noble-looking animal, and was taken to the City for sale. But scarcely had he entered the market, when a stranger stepped up and claimed him as his property, recently stolen. Charles Carey's son, who had charge of the animal, was taken before a magistrate. Isaac T. Hopper was sent for, and easily proved that the character of the young man and his father was above all suspicion. But the stranger produced satisfactory evidence that he was the rightful owner of the horse, which was accordingly delivered up to him. When Charles Carey heard the unwelcome news, he quietly remarked, " It is hard for me to lose the money ; but I am glad the owner has recovered his property."

About a year afterwards, having occasion to go to a tavern in Philadelphia, he saw a man in the bar-room, whom he at once recognized as the person who had sold him the horse. He walked up to him and inquired whether he remembered the transaction. Being answered in the affirmative, he said, " I am the man who bought that horse. Didst thou know he was stolen ? " With a stupified manner and a faltering voice, the stranger answered, " Yes."

" Come along with me, then," said Charles, "and I will put thee where thou wilt not steal another horse very soon."

The thief resigned himself to his fate with a sort of hopeless indifference. But before they reached the magistrate's office, the voice within began to plead gently with the Quaker, and turned him from the sternness of his purpose. " I am a poor man," said he, " and thou hast greatly injured me. I cannot afford to lose fifty dollars; but to prosecute thee will not compensate me for the loss. Go thy way, and conduct thyself honestly in future."

The man seemed amazed. He stood for a moment, hesitating and confused; then walked slowly away. But after taking a few steps, he turned back and said, "Where shall I find you, if I should ever be able to make restitution for the wrong I have done?"

Charles replied, "I trust thou dost not intend to jest with me, after all the trouble thou hast caused me?"

"No, indeed, I do not," answered the stranger, "1 hope to repay you some time or other."

"Very well," rejoined the Friend, "If thou ever hast anything for me, thou canst leave it with Isaac T. Hopper, at the corner of Walnut and Dock-streets." Thus they parted and never met again.

About a year after, Friend Hopper found a letter on his desk, addressed to Charles Carey. When it was delivered to him, he was surprised to find that it came from the man who had stolen the horse, and contained twenty dollars. A few months later, another letter containing the same sum, was left in the same way. Not long after, a third letter arrived, enclosing twenty dollars; the whole forming a sum sufficient to repay both principal and interest of the money which the kind-hearted Quaker had lost by his dishonesty.

This last letter stated that the writer had no thoughts of stealing the horse ten minutes before he did it. After he had sold him, he was so haunted by remorse and fear of detection, that life became a burden to him, and he cared not. what became of him. But when he was arrested, and so unexpectedly set at liberty, the crushing weight was taken from him. He felt inspired by fresh courage, and sustained by the hope of making some atonement for what he had done. He made strenuous efforts to improve his condition, and succeeded. He was then teaching school, was assessor of the township where he resided, and no one suspected that he had ever committed a dishonest action.

The good man, to whom this epistle was addressed, read it with moistened eyes, and felt that the reward of righteousness is peace.

DIFFERENCE OF DIALECT.

A Quaker of Scarborough appointed a Scotchman to command a West Indiaman, and heard with indignation that Captain C. insisted to have her fitted out with guns. They mutually expostulated on the subject. The respectable, conscientious owner would not permit so flagrant a deviation from his pacific tenets. The brave seaman would not go a voyage in the time of war without means to repel an enemy. At length the Caledonian said, 'There is but one way to end this debate. Suit (pronounced shoot) yourself, and I shall suit myself in half an hour.' The Quaker, shocked by such a measure, hastened to the counting-house of Mr. D. who had recommended Captain C. 'Friend!' said he, 'the person thou hast spoken of so highly, is a savage, a madman. Because I would not consent to equip the *Neptune* with guns, he bade me shoot myself, and he would shoot himself in half-an-hour.. When Mr. D. could suppress his laughing, he explained the pronunciation in frequent use north of the Tweed; and assured Mr.———, that Captain C. had the interest of his employers in view, by making a point of being enabled to defend their property. The difference was thus amicably settled.

PRIVATEERING.

During the war with France, in 1780, Mr. Fox, a merchant of Falmouth, had a share in a ship, which the other owners determined to fit out as a letter of marque, very much against the wishes of Mr. Fox, who was a Quaker. The ship had the good fortune to take two French merchant-men, and the share of the prize money which fell to Mr. Fox, was £1500. At the close of the war, Mr. Fox sent his son (who was soon afterwards elected physician to the Bristol Infirmary), to Paris, with the £1500, which he faithfully refunded to the owners of the vessels captured. The young gentleman, to discover the owners, was obliged to advertise for them in the Paris papers, In consequence of this advertisement, he received a letter from a small village near Nismes, in the province of Languedoc, acquainting him that a society of Quakers was established in that remote part of France, consisting of about one hundred families; that they were so much struck with this rare instance of generosity in one of their sect, that they were desirous to open a correspondence with him in England; which immediately commenced.

This society is supposed to be a remnant of the Ancient Albigenses against whom several persecuting crusades were instituted in the reign of Philip the Second, towards the close of the twelfth century. They were known to have continued in the same place for upwards of a century, without maintaining a correspondence with any other society.

GRELLET'S INTERVIEW WITH THE POPE.

Stephen Grellet having for some time been engaged in a benevolent mission at Rome, presented his letters of introduction to the Cardinal Consalvi, the Pope's prime minister. Dr. Cunningham remarks " Consalvi requested him to call at his own palace the next morning. The Quaker accordingly called on the Cardinal and was kindly received. Who the Quakers were was a mystery to the Italians, and therefore Consalvi asked Grellet particulars about the principles of his sect. In giving the information desired, Grellet did not hesitate to state some truths not generally agreeable to Roman ears. Notwithstanding this the Cardinal parted with him in a very friendly manner, and promised to send him orders of admittance to the different institutions which he wished to visit.

Notwithstanding the friendship he had received from men in power, and the ready entrance which he obtained to every public institution, Grellet's mind was often oppressed

by indescribable suffering while he remained in Rome.
These painful thoughts reappeared in the night-time, and
in his dreams he felt as he were among lions and serpents,
and treading upon scorpions. Albeit he was thus distressed, he resolved to make an effort to get admission to
the Inquisition, and thus to thrust himself into the very
lion's den. The necessary orders were, with some difficulty,
procured, and he entered the buidings near the Church of
St. Peter's, where so many heretics like himself, had bid
farewell to liberty and life. He saw the underground cellars in which the Inquisition had sat and questioned, and
tortured and condemmed their victims. He saw the cells in
which the unhappy captives were confined, and had pointed
out the one in which Molinos had lain. He was conducted
to the public library, and then, after some hesitation, led
into the secret one, where, ranged on shelves, he saw the
legions of books which the Inquisition had condemmed.
From this he was taken to the secretary's room, and permitted to inspect the records of this dark and deadly court,
whose buildings he had explored. Then he found, regis-
tered with business-like accuracy, the name and crime of
every one who had suffered, the tortures he had endured,
the death which he died   Everything, however, convinced
Grellet that the prisons of the Inquisition had not been
used for many years   He came out of its dreary portals
thankful he was safe   This was a considerable feat for a
Quaker to perform, but he now hinted to Cardinal Consalvi
that he would not stand acquitted in the Divine sight unless
he attempted to see the Pope. The Cardinal undertook to
arrange a private interview ; and, according to appointment,
he proceeded to the Vatican. After being led through several apartments, he arrived at a private cabinet, and the
Holy Father's Valet, arrayed like a Cardinal, opened the
door, and announced, " The Quaker is come." " Let him

come in," said his Holiness. Upon this the priest who was
to act as interpreter, led him in; but just as he was entering, some one behind deftly whipped off his hat, and before
he had time to look round, the door was closed. Well,
there he was, with his hat off in the presence of the Pope;
but there was no help for it, for the door was closed. The
spare old man, with a serious mild countenance, rose to receive his Quaker visitor, but he appeared feeble, and
immediately resumed his seat. He told Grellet he had
read the reports he had made to Consalvi regarding the
prisons and other public establishments, and said that he
was resolved to make several changes, as he believed that
Christian tenderness was more likely to effect reformation
than harshness. He said he was glad Grellet was convinced of the change which had taken place in Rome in
regard to the Inquisition, and that he wes anxious to bring
about a similar change in Spain and Portugal, but the
popes were not so powerful as was supposed. He even
assented to the proposition that God alone is Lord of the
conscience, and that the weapons of the Christian should
not be carnal, but spiritual. Encouraged by this, Grellet
spoke of the sin of burning Bibles, and of the licentiousness
of many monks, and of the spiritual anointing which alone
could make a man a minister, to all which the Pope politely
agreed. Finally, he felt, as he tells us, the love of Christ
flowing in his heart towards the good old man, and so he
became more special and searching in his address. He
alluded to his sufferings under Napoleon, his deliverance
from all his enemies, and prolongation of his days, and
suggested that if now, in his old age, he would declare that
Jesus Christ alone was Head of the Church, his sun would
set in brightness, and his portion in eternity would be with
the sanctified ones amid the joys of salvation. The Holy
Pontiff had hung down his head while the Quaker spoke,

and now he courteously rose, and addressing Grellett, expressed a desire that, "the Lord would bless and protect him wherever he went." It was the Pope's blessing, but what could the old man think of his plain-spoken friend in drab?

When Grellet returned to the outer appartment, his hat was returned to him. The Valet made many apologies (and no doubt, some secret grimaces), remarking that he understood the same plan was resorted to when Friends were admitted into the presence of the King of England. His mission to the City of Seven Hills was now accomplished, and he felt at liberty to depart."

THE BAILIFF OUTWITTED.

A bailiff who had tried numerous expedients in vain to arrest a Quaker, resolved to adopt the habit and manner of one, in hope of catching the primitive Christian. In this disguise, he knocked at the Quaker's door and inquired if he was at home. The housekeeper replied "Yes." "Can I see him?" "Walk in, friend," she said, "and he shall see thee." The bailiff confident of success walked in, and after waiting nearly an hour, rung a bell, and on the housekeeper appearing, said, "Thou promised me I should see friend Aminadab." "No, friend," answered the housekeeper, "I promised *he* should see *thee*. He hath seen thee, but he doth not like thee." Upon which the bailiff uttering some hearty curses, left the house.

GEORGE THE THIRD AND THE QUAKERS.

The King was remarkable for his free and kindly bearing to men of genius. To Reynolds and West he showed particular favour, and his support of the Royal Academy from its commencement is well known. It is said that the King first suggested to Mr. West the professional study of Scripture history, and desired him to bring his drawings to the palace for inspection. Mr West did so, and came at a time when the Sovereign had with him some dignified clergymen. The company were all gratified with the sketches and with their accuracy to the Scripture text, affording proof of the painter's acquaintance with the Scriptures. "And do you know how that was?" said his Majesty to the prelate who made the remark. "Not exactly, your Majesty." "Why, my lord, I wlll tell you. Mr. West's parents are Quakers, and they teach their children to read the Bible very young. I wish that was more the case with you, my lord·"

TIMELY REPROOF.

Mr. Adams, a worthy Quaker of Philadelphia, on a visit to a lady whom he found sitting on a sofa, six months after the death of her husband, in deep sorrow, approached her with much solemnity, and thus addressed her; "So, friend, I see thou hast not yet forgiven God Almighty." This timely reproof had the intended effect and restored the lady to a becoming submission of God's will.

WHITE FEATHER OF PEACE.

A family of Quakers from Pennsylvania. settled at the west in a remote place, then exposed to savage incursions. They had not been there long before a party of Indians, panting for blood, started on one of their terrible excursions against the whites, and passed in the direction of the Quaker's abode; but, though disposed at first to assail him and his family as enemies, they were received with such open-hearted confidence, and treated with such cordiality and kindness, as completely disarmed them of their purpose. They came forth, not against such persons, but against their enemies. They thirsted for the blood of those who had injured them; but these children of peace, unarmed, and entirely defenceless met them only with accents of love, and deeds of kindness. It was not in the heart even of a savage to harm them; and, on leaving the Quaker's house, the Indians took a white feather and stuck it over the door, to designate the place as a sanctuary not to be harmed by their brethren in arms. Nor was it harmed The war raged all around it; the forest echoed often to the Indian's yell, and many a white man's hearth was drenched in his own blood, but over the Quaker's humble abode gently waved the white feather of peace, and beneath it his family slept without harm or fear.

A Judicious Adviser.

Dr. Franklin when a young man embarked for New York. "At Newport" he writes "we took on board a number of passengers; among them were two young women, and a grave and sensible Quaker lady with her servants. I had shown an obliging forwardness in rendering the Quaker some trifling services, which led her, probably, to feel an interest in my welfare, for when she saw a familiarity take place, and every day increase, between the two young women and me, she took me aside and said: " Young man, I am in pain for thee. Thou hast no parent to watch over thy conduct, and thou seemest to be ignorant of the world, and the snares to which youth is exposed. Rely upon what I tell thee : those are women of bad characters ; I perceive it in all their actions, if thou dost not take care, they will lead thee into danger. They are strangers to thee, and I advise thee, by the friendly interest I take in thy preservation, to form no connection with them." As I appeared at first not to think quite so ill of them as she did, she related many things she had seen and heard, which had escaped my attention, but which convinced me that she was in the right. I thanked her for the obliging advice and promised to follow it.

When we arrived at New York, they informed me where they lodged, and invited me to come and see them, I did not however go, and it is well I did not; for the next day, the captain missing a silver spoon and some other things which had been taken from the cabin, and knowing these women to be prostitutes, procured a search-warrant, found the stolen goods upon them, and had them punished. And thus after being saved from one rock concealed under water, upon which the vessel struck during our passage, I escaped another of a still more dangerous nature.

Dr. Franklin and the Quakers.

The Doctor writes, "My being many years in the assembly, a majority of which where constantly Quakers, gave me frequent opportunities of seeing the embarrassment given them by their principle against war, whenever application was made to them, by order of the crown, to grant aids for military purposes. They were unwilling to offend government on the one hand, by a direct refusal · and their friends (the body of the Quakers) on the other, by a compliance contrary to their principles; using a variety of evasions to avoid compliance, when it became unavoidable. The common mode at last was, to grant money under the phrase "*for the King's use*," and never to enquire how it was applied. But if the demand was not directly from the crown, that phrase was found not so proper, and some other was to be invented. Thus, when powder was wanting (I think it was for the garrison at Louisburg) and the government of New England solicited a grant of some from Pennsylvania which was much urged on the house by Governor Thomas; they would not grant money to buy *powder*, because that was an ingredient of war, but they voted an aid to New England of three thousand pou.ids, to be put into the hands of the Governor, and appropriated it for the purpose of bread, flour, wheat, or *other grain*. Some of the Council, desirous of giving the House still further embarrassment, advised the Governor not to accept that provision, as not being the thing he had demanded; but he replied, 'I shall take the money, for I understand very well their meaning; *other grain* is gunpowder;' which he accordingly bought, and they never objected to it.

"It was in allusion to this fact, that when in our fire company we feared the success of our proposal in favour of the lottery, and I said to a friend of mine, one of our members, 'If we fail, let us move the purchase of a fire engine with the money; the Quakers can have no objection to that: and then, if you nominate me, and I you, as a committee for that purpose, we will buy a great gun, which is certainly a *fire engine:*' 'I see,' said he, 'you have improved by being so long in the Assembly; your equivocal project would be just a match for their wheat or *other grain.*'"

JAMES LOGAN IN FAVOUR OF DEFENSIVE WAR.

Dr. Franklin remarks, The honorable and learned Mr. Logan, who had always been of that sect, wrote an address to them declaring his approbation of defensive war, and supported his opinion by many strong arguments: he put into my hands sixty pounds to be laid out in lottery tickets for the battery, with directions to apply what prizes might be drawn wholly to that service. He told me the following anecdote of his old master, William Penn, respecting defence. He came over from England when a young man with that Proprietary, and as his secretary. It was war time, and their ship was chased by an armed vessel, supposed to be an enemy. Their captain prepared for defence, but told

William Penn and his company of Quakers that he did not expect their assistance, and they might retire into the cabin, which they did, except James Logan, who choose to stay upon the deck, and was quartered to a gun. The supposed enemy proved to be a friend, so there was no fighting; but when the secretary went down to communicate the intelligence, William Penn rebuked him severely for staying upon deck, and undertaking to assist in defending the vessel, contrary to the principles of Friends; especially as it had not been required by the captain. This reprimand, being before all the company, piqued the secretary, who answered, "I being thy servant, why did thee not order me to come down? But thee was willing enough that I should stay and help to fight the ship when thee thought there was danger."

DEFICIENT IN ARRANGEMENT.

A Quaker, by name Benjamin Lay (who was a little cracked in the head, though sound at heart), took one of his compositions to Benjamin Franklin, that it might be printed and published. Franklin looked over the manuscript, observed it was deficient in arrangement: "It is no matter," replied the author; print any part thou pleasest first."

REQUEST DENIED.

Mr. Hopkinson went with Dr. Franklin to hear Whitfield preach, and knowing that a collection was to be taken for an object of which he did not altogether approve, took the precaution to leave his money at home, so that he might be sure not to give anything; but the eloquent appeals of Whitfield so moved and melted him that he tried to borrow some money off a Quaker to put into the collection. The Quaker in declining said, "At any other time, Friend Hopkinson, I would lend thee freely, but not now for thee seems to be out of thy right senses." Franklin says, " The request was *fortunately* made, perhaps, to the only man in the company who had the *firmness* not to be affected by the preacher."

FIGHTING QUAKER.

In the late American war, a New York trader was chased by a small French privateer, and having four guns with plenty of small arms, it was agreed to stand a brush with the enemy rather than be taken prisoners. Among several other passengers was an athletic quaker, who withstood every solicitation to lend a hand, as being contrary to his religious tenets, kept walking backwards and forwards on the deck, without any apparent fear, the enemy all the time pouring in their shot. At length the vessels having approached close to each other, a disposition to board was manifested by the French, which was very soon put in execution; and the Quaker being on the look-out, unexpectedly sprang towards the first man that jumped on board, and grappling him forcibly by the collar, cooly said, "Friend, thou hast no business here," at the same time hoisting him over the ship's side.

THE QUAKER'S CHARITY.

A certain benevolent Quaker in New York was asked by a poor man for money as charity, or for work. The Quaker observed, "Friend, I do not know what I can give thee to do? Let me see; thou mayest take my wood that is in the yard, up stairs, and I will give thee half-a-dollar." This the poor man was glad to do, and the job lasted him till about noon, when he came and told him the work was done, and asked him if he had any more to do. "Why friend, let me consider," said the queer Quaker: "Oh! thou mayest take the wood down again, and I will give thee another half dollar."

A Big Inclination.

Cobbett, who lived for more than a year at Hempstead, Long Island, used sometimes to tell laughable stories at the expense of the Quakers, some of whom lived in his neighbourhood there. The author of "Recollections of Mr. Jay," a Bath clergyman, gives the following as received from Cobbett's own lips :—

" I was acquainted with a well-disposed young gentleman of large fortune whose only fault was the habit of swearing —such a habit that he often declared that he would give half his fortune to get rid of it. This desire came to the ears of a Quaker, who thereupon had an interview with the young gentleman, and said—

"'I can cure thee of that bad habit'

"Whereupon the youth caught hold of the Quaker's hand and gave it a hearty shake, saying—

"'How can you perform the miracle?'

"'I can tell thee. I have heard that thou art just my size; nobody will know thee; thou shalt come to my house, put on the cocked hat, the coat without buttons, the knee-breeches, and the shoe-buckles; and thou wilt find that the strangeness of the dress will have such an effect on thee when thou art going to talk, that it will restrain thee from swearing—as thou perhaps knowest, my friend, that we Quakers never swear.'

"The young man cheerfully assented to the proposal, and accompanied the Quaker to his house, where, after changing his clothes, he took his departure in the garb of a Quaker, and went on his way rejoicing.

" The period of the young gentleman's tour elapsed, and the Quaker, all anxiety, started to meet him. Having met him, he said—

"'Well, friend, how hast thou got on?'

"'Very well,' replied the young man.

"'Hast thou sworn so much with that dress on?'

"'The young man, rubbing the sleeves of his coat, replied—

"'Certainly not; but I felt a great inclination to lie!'"

JOSEPH LANCASTER AND THE DEAN.

This distinguished friend of education, encountered much opposition in carrying out his benevolent projects. Once being at Windsor, and observing a great number of children running about the streets, apparently uncared for, he called upon the Dean, and in a feeling and friendly manner, represented this to him, proposing at the same time, with the Dean's consent, to call a meeting of the inhabitants, to whom, he had no doubt, that he could deliver such an address as would induce them to open a School for the education of these poor neglected children. The Dean, in the place of receiving this friendly overture in the Christian spirit in which it was made, replied, "Pray, Mr. Lancaster, mind your own business we are quite as well qualified to educate our own poor as you are." Lancaster replied, "I know you are, but you don't do it." The Dean then, in a very angry tone, said, "Sir, the countenance you have received from the King, and other exalted characters, has give you a confidence, which you do not know how discreetly to use; my friends, the Archbishops and Bishops, assure me, that you will not much longer be favoured with His Majesty's support." Lancaster replied, "If I do lose the King's countenance I have no doubt, that it will be occasioned by the interference of thy friends, the Archbishops and Bishops. But, as the King is here, I will, before I leave Windsor, ascertain whether he is with me or not." This threw the Dean into a state of alarm, and led

F

him, in severe terms, to deprecate such a proceeding. However, Lancaster went to the castle, and through one of the pages, announced his wish to see the King, (who was in the midst of his family,) which was immediately granted, when he communicated what had passed between him and the Dean. To this, the King replied, "No, Lancaster, you have not lost my countenance; you are a good man, and have done much good to benefit my poor subjects, you may, therefore, count upon my support, but you must not tease these men—let them alone—never mind them—never mind them."

GEORGE III AND JOSEPH LANCASTER.

In 1805, Joseph Lancaster, the educationist, was admitted to an interview with George III at Weymouth. On entering the Royal presence, the King said; "Lancaster, I have sent for you to give me an account of your system of education, which I hear has met with opposition. One master teach five hundred children at the same time! How do you keep them in order Lancaster?" Lancaster replied, "Please thy Majesty, by the same principle that thy Majesty's army is kept in order—by the word of command." His Majesty replied, "Good, good, it does not require an aged general to give the command, one of younger years can do it." Lancaster observed that in his schools the teaching branch was performed by youths, who acted as monitors. The King assented, and said "Good." Lancaster then described his system; the King paid great attention, and was highly delighted; and as soon as he had finished, his Majesty said, "Lancaster, I highly approve of your system, and it is my wish that every poor child in my dominions should be taught to read the Bible; I will do anything you wish to promote this object." "Please thy Majesty," said Lancaster, "if the system meets thy approbation, I can go through the country and lecture on the system, and have no doubt, but in a few months I shall be able to give thy Majesty an account where ten thousand poor children are being educated, and some of my youths instructing them." His Majesty immediately replied, "Lancaster, I will subscribe £100 annually; and," addressing the Queen, "you shall subscribe £50, Charlotte; and the Princesses, £25 each, and then added, "Lancaster, you may have the money directly." Lancaster observed, "Please thy Majesty that will be setting thy Nobles a good example." The Royal party appeared to smile at this observation, but the Queen observed to his Majesty, "How cruel it is that enemies should be found who endeavour to hinder his progress in so good a work." To which the King replied, "Charlotte, a good man seeks his reward in the world to come." Joseph then withdrew.

Lancaster received great encouragment from many persons of the highest rank, which enabled him to travel over the kingdom, delivering lectures, giving instructions, and forming schools. Flattered by splendid patronage, and by unrealized promises of support, he was induced to embark in an extensive school establishment at Tooting, to which his own resources proved unequal, he was thrown upon the mercy of cold calculators, who considered unpaid debts as unpardonable crimes. About this time, we remember to have seen him frequently smoking his pipe, at the door of a small Inn at Dorking. Concessions were made to his merit, which not considering sufficient, he abandoned his old establishment, and left England in disgust; and about the year 1820, went to America, where his fame procured him friends, and his industry rendered him useful. But his life was terminated by an accident: he died October 24th 1840, in his 68th year, at New York, in consequence of being run over by a wagon the day before.—Timbs' *Century of Anecdote.*

THE LAWYER AND THE FRIEND.

A cunning lawyer meeting with a shrewd old Friend, on a white horse, determined to quiz him—Good morning, daddy! Pray what makes your horse look so pale in the face? "Ah, my dear friend," replied the old man, "if thee had looked through a halter so long, thee would look pale, too."

VOLTAIRE AND THE QUAKER.

Voltaire, during his visit to England, paid a visit to Andrew Pitt, a celebrated Quaker of his day, and was much interested in what he heard and saw about the Friends "My dear sir, are you baptized?" was the first question which Friend Pitt was expected to answer, it was the question which good Catholics were accustomed to put to the Huguenots. His reply was, of course, negative. "What? morbleu?" Voltaire asked, "are you not Christians then." "My friend," answered Andrew, "swear not; we are Christians, but we don't think that Christianity consists in throwing water and a little salt on an infant's head." "Have you forgotten that Christ was baptized?" inquired Voltaire. "Christ," replied Andrew, "received baptism from John, but he never administered baptism. We are not disciples of John, but of Christ." "How about the Sacraments?" was the next article of the sceptic's catechism. "We have none," was the Quaker's response; and on this head he referred to Barclay's "Apology" for the sect, which he declared was one of the best books that ever came from the hand of man, and was shown to be excellent by the fact that their enemies agreed that it was dangerous. An allusion to Barclay led Andrew to offer his own apology for the Friends. He excused himself from responding to his polite visitors bows and compliments without taking off his broad brim. He explained the literal and spiritual

significance of the Quaker use of the second personal pro-
noun singular. He had some remarks to make about
Quaker dress. He expounded the objections of the Friends
to the use of oaths and their opposition to war, being careful to state that this latter peculiarity was not due to any
deficiency of courage, but to a becoming recollection of the
fact that "we are neither wolves, nor tigers, nor dogs, but
men, but Christians."

ANTY BRIGNAL AND THE BEGGING QUAKER.

A few years ago a stout old man, with long grey hair,
and dressed in the habit of the Society of Friends, was seen
begging in the streets of Durham. The inhabitants
attracted by the novelty of a "*begging Quaker,*" thronged
about him, and several questioned him as to his residence, &c.
Amongst them was "Anty Brignal," the police-officer,
who told him to go about his business, or he would put him
in the kitty (house of correction) "*for an imposteror!*"
" Who ever heard," said Anthony, " of a begging Quaker ?"
" But," said the mendicant, while tears flowed adown his
face, " thou knowest, friend, there be bad Quakers as well
as good ones ; and, I confess to thee, I have been a bad one.
My name is John Taylor; I was in the hosiery business at
N——, and through drunkenness have become a bankrupt.
The Society have turned me out, my friends have deserted
me. I have no one in the world to help me but my
daughter, who lives in Edinburgh, and I am now on my
way thither. Thou seest, friend, why I beg, it is to get a little
money to help me on my way : be merciful as thou hopest
for mercy." " Come, come," said the officer, " it won't do,
you know; there's not a word of truth in it; 'tis all false.
Did not I see you drunk at Nevill's Cross (a public-house
of that name) the other night?" " No, friend," said the
man of unsteady habits, " thou didst not see *me* drunk

there, but I was there, and saw *thee* drunk; and thou
knowest when a man is drunk he thinks every body else
so!" This was a poser for the police-officer. The crowd
laughed, and Anty Brignal slunk away from their
derision, while money fell plentifully into the extended hat
of the disowned Quaker.—Hone's *Table Book.*

REMARKABLE PROSECUTION.

The Rules of the Discipline of Church Goverment of the
Society of Friends are clearly recognized and allowed by the
laws of England, as appears in the case of *Rex* v *Francis
Hart*, on an indictment for a libel, the rules of their discipline were recognized by the judges, who refused to grant
an information for libel, for which application was made to
them, founded on an act of the Society in the course of
their disciplinary proceedings, and afterwards, when the
defendant was found *guilty,* on an indictment, the court
granted a *rule absolute* for a new trial on the first application.
The prosecutrix, Mary Jerom, was educated among Friends,
at the Town of Nottingham ; her parents who lived there,
being of that persuasion. She having acted in disobedience
to the rules, the usual means by visiting and admonishing,
were taken by the Society, but they proving ineffectual, and
she absenting herself from the meetings and declaring that
she did not look upon herself as one of the body, the Society
proceeded in their usual manner to the sentence of expul-
sion, which was reduced ˙into writing, approved by the
monthly meeting, and afterwards read by the defendant as
clerk of the meeting, at the close of the meeting for worship
at Nottingham, in 1762.

The prosecutrix being acquainted with this proceeding,
sent the maid servant to the defendant for a copy of the
sentence; who transcribed it, and enclosed it in a cover,
directed to Mary Jerom ; who being thus possessed of it,

annexed to it an affidavit, and applied to the Court of King's Bench for an information for a libel. But the court rejected the motion, and refused to grant a rule to show cause. She afterwards, on the 12th of March, 1762, preferred a bill of indictment against the defendant for a libel, before the grand jury at the assizes, held for the Town of Nottingham ; which bill being found by them, was afterwards removed by certiorori into the King's Bench. After the defendant having pleaded *not guilty*, it was tried before. Justice Clive, at the Summer Assizes at Nottingham, July 30, 1762. The evidence on the part of the prosecution was, the prosecutrix and her servant maid who went for the paper ; and the evidence of the publication of it as a libel, was, the direction of it to the prosecutrix, and the defendant's acknowledgment to the servant that he read it at the meeting. The defendant's counsel called no witnesses; being of opinion, that the Quakers, who were the only persons that could give an account of their method of proceeding, were disabled by the statute 7, and 8, Will. c. 34, from being witnesses on a criminal prosecution ; and being restrained from arguing that the paper in question was no libel, by the judge, who said that such a question was more proper to be determined by the court above, could only insist, that the evidence on the part of the prosecution was not sufficient to mantain the indictment. The judge left the case, with its circumstances to the jury ; but rather recommended it to them to acquit the defendant. The jury after withdrawing about three hours, found the defendant guilty.

In the Michaelmas Term following, counsel moved the Court of King's Bench for a new trial ; and after stating the above mentioned facts, and observing upon the circumstances of hardship which would attend the case on a motion in arrest of judgment. when no facts could be relied on but what appeared on the record, and after a verdict, it might

be presumed that a malicious intention to defame the prosecutrix (which was charged in the indictment) was proved.
insisted, that the leaving such   case as this to a jury,
would be enabling a jury to set up judgment in opposition
to the Legislature, and overturn the Toleration Act, and
that therefore the verdict ought to be set aside as a verdict
against law   The Court was clearly of opinion, that the
jury should have been directed to acquit the defendant ;
and, as notice of the motion was given, and counsel
appeared for the prosecution, who did not contradict the
above-mentioned facts, the court said they would not do so
much credit to such a prosecution, as to grant a rule to
show cause and they ordered the verdict to be set aside on
the first motion.—Burns *Ecc. Law*, vol. 2. p. 199.

A QUAKER ON GOOD MANNERS.

Recently a Quaker was travelling in a railway carriage.
After a time, observing certain movements on the part of
a fellow traveller, he accosted him as follows : " Sir, thee
seems well-dressed, and I daresay thee considers thyself
well-bred, and would not demean thyself to any ungentle-
manlike action, wouldst thee ? "   The person addressed
promptly replied, with considerable spirit: " Certainly not;
not if I knew it." The Quaker continued : " And suppose
thee invited me to thy house, thee would not think of offering me thy glass to drink out of after thee had drunk out
of it thyself, wouldst thee ? " The interrogated replied :
"Abominable! No. Such an offer would be most insulting."
The Quaker continued : " Still less would thee think of
offering me thy knife and fork to eat with after putting
them into thy mouth. wouldst thee ? " The interrogated
answered : " To do that would be an outrage on all
decency, and would show such a wretch was out of the pale
of civilised society." " Then," said the Quaker, " with

those impressions upon thee, why shouldst thee wish me to take into my mouth and nostrils the smoke from that cigar which thou art preparing to smoke, after sending the smoke out of thine own mouth?"

A Bellmaker and the Quaker

A bellmaker, endeavouring to sell a large gong to a Quaker gentleman, remarked that it would be very useful in the country, for it would not only serve as a dinner-bell, but would, also, in case of an attempt to break into the house, enable the inmates to give an alarm to the surrounding neighbourhood. "Friend," replied the Quaker gentleman, after listening attentively to these recommendations, I will not purchase thy gong; for if I put it to both these uses, how should my friends distinguish between a late dinner and an early burglary."

Samuel Fox and the Idle Lads.

"Old Sammy Fox," (as he was, and is, commonly called) was a good old Quaker, of whom Nottingham may be proud, and of whom the following story is told:—One day, about the year 1830, a number of lads, somewhat tired with their play, were hanging about St. Mary's gate, Nottingham. Samuel, in his usual brisk manner, walked up to them, and seizing one of them by the arm, said, "What art thou doing?" "Nothing," replied the lad. "Nothing, didst thou say? Nothing! What wast thou made for?" asked Mr. Fox. "I don't know," was the answer. "Don't know," Mr. Fox exclaimed, "don't know?" "Bear in mind, boys, we are all made for some good purpose. Time was when men shutting themselves in monastries, because in ignorance they knew not what to do; but we have now learnt that there is something for everybody to do. Go, boys; let every one think what his mission is, see what he is best qualified for.

Then let him set to work, and work with all his might."{ Then taking another boy by the hand, he added for the bene- fit of all, "Thy duty is to be in the world, and of the world useful in some capacity. Thou must try to leave this world better than thou found it. Some may misjudge thee, many who can do little themselves may misrepresent and malign thee—this is the common weapon of little and mean minds; but heed not, go on, and see how much of that which is good thou canst do."

Briscoe's *"Nottinghamshire Facts and Fictions."*

HAT TESTIMONY.

I was one day greatly amused, by watching a very plain man Friend, who was paying us a morning visit. It was a hot summer's day, and he had walked a long distance. He came into our room, as all orthodox Friends do, with his broad-brim on, shook hands, and sat down. After bearing his testimony thus for a few minutes, he took off the hat, and laid it on the floor beside him. We were chatting away, when a loud rap at the door announced some more visitors. Friend Hugh in a great hurry popped on his hat, lest any one should see him "shirking his testimony." As soon as he had satisfied himself that his orthodoxy was sufficiently manifested, he yielded again to the natural feeling, and laid the hat beside him. But soon came another visitor, and another, and poor hot-headed Hugh replaced the badge of membership again and again. This happened so often, that it at last became very ludicrous.

"Quakerism," by Mrs. J. R. Greer.

A GOOD NAME.

A Friend writes that when he was a youth his father said to him one day,—"Henry, can you make up your mind to live at home an l be a farmer?" "I would rather be a tanner than a farmer," replied Henry. "Very well," responded his father, who was willing to let Henry follow his own tastes, as he was now seventeen years of age—"very well, my son, I will try to find a place for you." Very shortly after a place was found for Master Henry with a good Quaker. When the youth presented himself at the tannery, the honest Quaker said "Henry, if thee will be a good boy I will do well by thee; if not, I will send thee home again. All tho bargain I will make by thee is that thee shall do as well by me as I do by thee." "Very well, sir," said Henry, "I will try what I can do." Henry now went to work with a hearty good-will. He worked hard, read his Bible, was steady, honest, and good-natured. The Quaker liked him He liked the Quaker. Hence the Quaker was satisfied. Henry was happy, and the years of his apprenticeship passed pleasantly away. Just before Henry became of age, his master said to him, "Henry, I think of making thee a nice present when thy time is out." Henry smiled pleasantly at the scrap of news, and said "I shall be very happy to receive any gift you may please to make me, sir." Then the Quaker looked knowingly at Henry, and added, "I cannot tell thee now what the present is to be, but it shall be worth more than a hundred pounds to thee." "More than a hundred pounds!" said Henry to himself, his eyes sparkling at the thought of such a costly gift. "What can it be?" That was the puzzling question which buzzed about like a bee in Henry's brain, from that time until the day before he was of age. On that day the Quaker said to him, "Henry, thy time is out to morrow; I will take thee and thy present home to-day." Henry breathed freely on hearing these words. Dressing himself in his best suit, he soon joined the Quaker, but could see nothing that looked like a gift worth more than a hundred pounds. He puzzled himself about it all the way, and said to himself, "Perhaps the Quaker has forgotten it." At last they reached Henry's home. After he had been greeted by his friends, the Quaker turned to him and said, "I will give thy present to thy father." "As you please, sir," replied Henry, now on the very tiptoe of expectation. "Well," said the Quaker, speaking to Henry's father, "thy son is the best boy I ever had." Then turning to Henry, he added, "This is thy present, Henry—*A Good Name.*" Henry blushed; perhaps he felt a little disappointed because his golden visions were so soon spirited away. But his sensible father was delighted, and said to the Quaker who was smiling a little waggishly, "I would rather hear you say that of my son, sir, than to see you give him all the money you are worth; for "a good name is rather to be chosen than great riches."

REYNOLDS AND THE ORPHAN.

A lady applied to the eminent philanthropist of Bristol, Richard Reynolds, on behalf of a little orphan boy. After he had given liberally, she said, "When he is old enough, I will teach him to name and thank his benefactor." "Stop," said the good man, "Thou art mistaken. We do not thank the clouds for rain. Teach him to look higher, and thank HIM who giveth both the clouds and the rain."

SMART REBUKE.

An English country clergyman was bragging in a large company of the success he had in reforming his parishioners, in whom his labours, he said, had produced a wonderful change for the better. Being asked in what respect, he replied that when he first came among them they were a set of unmannerly clowns, who paid him no more deference than they did to one another; did not so much as pull off their hat when they spoke to him, but bawled out as roughly and familiarly as though he were their equal; whereas now, they never presumed to address him but with cap in hand, and in a submissive voice made him their best bow when they were at ten yards' distance, and styled him "your reverence" at every word. A Quaker who heard the whole patiently, made answer, "And so, friend, the upshot of this information, of which thou hast so much carnal glory, is that thou hast taught thy people to worship thyself!"

DANIEL WEBSTER OUTWITTED.

A Quaker gentleman of Nantucket once called upon the celebrated advocate Daniel Webster, at his office in Boston, for the purpose of securing his services in a suit which was about to be tried on the Island and wound up his appeal by demanding his terms.

"I will attend to your case for one thousand dollars," replied Mr. Webster.

The client demurred but finding that the lawyer would not visit Nantucket for a less amount than the one specified, he promised to pay the proposed fee, provided Mr. Webster would agree to attend to any other matters that he might present during the sitting of the court, to which Mr. Webster consented.

Having thus arranged matters, the Quaker inquired of those persons who had cases to be tried at the Court what they would give him if he would get the great Daniel Webster to plead their cases. One proffered 400 dollars, one 300 dollars, one 200 dollars, and another 200 dollars. Thus the Quaker secured 100 dollars for himself in excess of the amount of his agreement with Mr. Webster.

The appointed time arrived and Mr. Webster was at his post. The leading case of his client was brought forward, argued, and decided in his favour. Another case was taken up, and the Quaker assigned it to the care of Mr. Webster, when it was satisfactorily disposed of; another still, and with the same result; and still another, and another, until Mr. Webster became impatient and demanded an explanation; whereupon the client remarked :—

" I hired thee to attend to all the business of the court, and thou hast done it handsomely; so here is thy money, one thousand dollars."

Dr. Johnson and the Quakers.

Boswell in his life of the Doctor, remarks, "I have always loved the simplicity of manners and the spiritual mindedness of the Quakers; and talking with Mr. Lloyd, I observed, that the essential part of religion was piety, a devout intercourse with the Divinity; and that many a man was a Quaker without knowing it.

As Doctor Johnson had said to me in the morning, while we walked together, that he liked individuals among the Quakers, but not the sect; when we were at Mr. Lloyd's, I kept clear of introducing any questions concerning the peculiarity of their faith. But I having asked to look at Baskerville's edition of "Barclay's Apology," Johnson laid hold of it; and the chapter on baptism happening to open, Johnson remarked, "He says there is neither precept nor practice for baptism, in the Scriptures; that is false." Here he was the aggressor, by no means in a gentle manner; and the good Quakers had the advantage of him; for he had read negligently, and had not observed that Barclay speaks of infant baptism; which they calmly made him perceive. Mr. Lloyd, however, was in a great mistake; for when insisting that the rite of baptism by water was to cease, when the *spiritual* administeration of Christ began, he mantained that John the Baptist said, "*My baptism* shall decrease, but *his* shall increase." Whereas the words are, "*He* must increase, but I must *decrease*."

Sunday, July 31, (1763) I told him I had been that morning at a meeting of the people called Quakers where I had heard a woman preach. Johnson: "Sir, a woman's preaching is like a dog walking on his hind legs. It is not done well; but you are suprised to find it done at all."

I saw little of Dr. Johnson till Monday, April 28, when I spent a considerable part of the day with him, and introduced the subject which then chiefly occupied my mind. Johnson: "I do not see, Sir, that fighting is absolutely forbidden in Scripture; I see revenge forbidden, but not self-defence." Boswell: "The Quakers say it is; 'Unto him that smiteth thee on one cheek, offer him also the other.'" Johnson: "But stay, Sir; the text is meant only to have the effect of moderating passion; it is plain that we are not to take it in a literal sense. We see this from the context, where there are other recommendations, which I warrant you the Quaker will not take literally; as, for instance, 'From him that would borrow of thee, turn thou not away.' Let a man whose credit is bad, come to a Quaker, and say, 'Well, Sir, lend me a hundred pounds;' he'll find him as unwilling as any other man. No, Sir, a man may shoot the man who invades his character, as he may shoot him who attemps to break into his house. So in 1745 my friend Tom Cumming the Quaker, said he would not fight, but he would drive an amunition cart; and we know that the Quakers have sent flannel waistcoats to our soldiers, to enable them to fight better."

DIALOGUE BETWEEN DR. JOHNSON AND MRS. KNOWLES.

Mr. Boswell, for reasons best known to himself, refused to admit into his book, Mrs Knowle's account of her Theological Dialogue with Dr. Johnson, although he had previously applied to her for it, and had frankly acknowledged to the truth of the particulars therein, which he afterwards thought proper to suppress. She therefore permitted her own account to be published in the Gentleman's Magazine for June, 1791.

Mrs. K. Thy friend Jenny H—— desires her kind respects to thee, Doctor.

Dr. J. To *me!* tell me not of her! I hate the odious wench for her apostacy : and it is you, madam, who have seduced her from the Christian Religion.

Mrs. K. This is a heavy charge, indeed, I must beg leave to be heard in my own defence : and I entreat the attention of the present learned and candid company, desiring they will judge how far I am able to clear myself of so cruel an accusation.

Dr. J. (much disturbed at this unexpected challenge) said, You are a woman, and I give you quarter.

Mrs. K. I will not take quarter. There is no sex in souls ; and in the present cause I fear not even Dr. Johnson himself.

("Bravo!" *was repeated by the company, and silence ensued.*)

Dr. J. Well then, Madam, I persist in my charge, that you have seduced Miss H—— from the Christian Religion.

Mr. K. If thou really knewest what were the principles of the Friends, thou would'st not say she had departed from Christianity. But, waving that discussion for the present, I will take the liberty to observe, that she had undoubted right to examine and to change her educational tenets whenever she supposed she had found them erroneous ; as an accountable creature, it was her *duty* so to do.

Dr. J. Pshaw!— an accountable creature —girls accountable creatures !—It was her duty to remain with the Church wherein she was educated ; she had no business to leave it.

Mrs. K. What! not for what she apprehended to be better? According to this rule, Doctor, hadst thou been born in Turkey, it had been thy duty to have remained a Mahometan, notwithstanding, Christian *evidence* might have wrought in thy mind the clearest conviction ! and, if so, then let me ask, how would thy *conscience* have answered for such obstinacy at the great and last tribunal?

Dr. J. My conscience would not have been answerable.

Mrs. K. Whose then would ?

Dr. J. Why the *State*, to be sure. In adhering to the Religion of the State as by law established, our implicit obedience therein becomes our *duty*.

Mrs. K. A Nation, or State, having a conscience, is a doctrine entirely new to me, and, indeed, a very curious piece of intelligence, for I have always understood that a Government, or State, is a creature of time only; beyond which it dissolves, and becomes a non-entity. Now, Gentlemen, *can* your imagination body forth this monstrous individual, or being, called a State, composed of millions of people? Can you behold it stalking forth into the next world, loaded with its mighty conscience, there to be rewarded, or punished, for the faith, opinions, and conduct, of its constituent *machines* called men? Surely the teeming brain of Poetry never held up to the fancy so wondrous a personage!

(When the laugh occasioned by the personification was subsided, the Doctor very angrily replied,)

I regard not what you say as to that matter. I hate the arrogance of the wench, in supposing herself a more competent judge of Religion than those who educated her. She imitated you no doubt; but she ought not to have presumed to determine for herself in so important an affair.

Mrs. K. True, Doctor, I grant it, if, *as* thou seemest to imply, a wench of twenty years be not a moral agent.

Dr J. I doubt it would be difficult to prove those deserve that character who turn Quakers.

Mrs. K. This severe retort, Doctor, induces me charitably to hope thou must be totally unacquainted with the principles of the people against whom thou art so exceedingly prejudiced, and that thou supposest us a set of Infidels or Deists.

Dr. J. Certainly, I do think you little better than Deists.

Mrs. K. This is indeed strange; 'tis passing strange, that a man of such universal reading and research has not thought

it at least *expedient* to look into the cause of dissent of a
society so long established, and so conspicuously singular!

Dr. J. Not I indeed! I have not read your Barclay's
Apology; and for this reason—I never thought it worth my
while. You are upstart Sectaries, perhaps the best subdued
by a silent contempt.

Mrs. K. This reminds me of the language of the Rabbies
of old, when their Heirarchy was alarmed by the increasing
influence, force, and simplicity of dawning Truth, in their
high day of worldly dominion. We meekly trust, our principles stand on the same solid foundation of simple truth;
and we invite the acutest investigation. The reason thou
givest for not having read Barclay's Apology is surely a very
improper one for a man whom the world looks up to as a Moral
Philosopher of the first rank; a Teacher, from whom they
think they have a right to expect much information. To this
expecting, enquiring world, how can Dr. Johnson acquit
himself for remaining unacquainted with a book translated
into five or six different languages, and which has been
admitted into the libraries of every Court and University in
Christendom!

*(Here the Doctor grew very angry, still more so at the space
of time the Gentlemen allowed his antogonist wherein to make
her defence, and his impatience excited* Mr. Boswell *himself, in
a whisper to say,* "I never saw this mighty Lion so chafed
before!"*)*

The Doctor *again repeated, that* he did not think the Quakers
deserved the name of Christians.

Mrs K. Give me leave then to endeavour to convince
thee of thy error, which I will do by making before thee,
and this respectable company, a confession of our faith.
Creeds, or confessions of faith, are admitted by all to be the
standard whereby we judge of every denomination of pro-
fessors.

To this every one present agreed, and even the Doctor *grumbled out his assent.*

Mrs. K. Well then, I take upon me to declare, that the people called Quakers do verily believe in the Holy Scriptures, and rejoice with the most full and reverential acceptance of the divine history of facts, as recorded in the New Testament. That we, consequently, fully believe those historical articles summed up in what is called The Apostle's Creed, with these two exceptions only, to wit, our Saviour's descent into Hell, and the resurrection of the body. These mysteries we humbly leave just as they stand in the holy text, there being, from that ground, no authority for such assertion as is drawn up in the Creed. And now, Doctor, canst thou still deny to us the honourable title of Christians?

Dr. J. Well!—I must own I did not at all suppose you had so much to say for yourselves. However, I cannot forgive that little slut, for presuming to take upon herself as she has done.

Mrs. K. I hope, Doctor, thou wilt not remain unforgiving; and that you will renew your friendship, and joyfully meet at last in those bright regions where Pride and Prejudice can never enter!

Dr. J. Meet *her!* I never desire to meet fools any where.

(This sarcastic turn of wit was so pleasantly received, that the Doctor joined in the laugh; his spleen was dissipated; he took his coffee. and became, for the remainder of the evening, very cheerful and entertaining.)

RIGHT OR LEFT.

Two Quaker girls were ironing on the same table. One asked the other which side she would take, the right or left. She answered promptly. " It will be right for me to take the left, and then it will be left for thee to take the right."

THE WAY TO YORK.

A traveller lost on a Yorkshire moor, after desperately pursuing a rather hopeless track for some time, had the good fortune to meet a member of a shrewd and plain-speaking sect. "This is the way to York, is it not?" said the traveller. To which the other replied, "Friend, first thou tellest me a lie, and then thou askest me a question."

ADDRESS TO GEORGE I.

The Quakers in common with other Christian Communities presented an address to George I. on his accession to the throne in 1714, when the King had made his reply, George Whitehead, the leader of the deputation, an eminent Quaker of his day, stood forward and said—

"Thou art welcome to us, King George; we heartily wish thee health and happiness, and thy son the prince also. King William III was a happy instrument in putting a stop to persecution, by promoting toleration. We desire the King may have further knowledge of us and our innocency, and that to live a peaceable and quiet life, in all godliness and honesty, under the King and his government, is according to our principle and practice."

At the conclusion of this address, the deputation applied for permission to see the Prince of Wales. The application was cheerfully acceded to; they were at once admitted into the prince's apartment, when again George Whitehead, as their spokesman said—

"We take it as a favour that we are thus admitted to see the Prince of Wales, and truly are very glad to see thee, having delivered our address to the King, thy royal father, and being desirous to give thyself a visit in true love, we very heartily wish health and happiness to you both; and that, if it should please God, thou shouldst survive thy father and come to the throne, thou mayest enjoy tranquility and peace. I am persuaded that if the King, thy father, and thyself, do stand for the toleration for liberty of conscience to be kept inviolable, God will stand by you. May King Solomon's choice of wisdom be thy choice, with holy Job,s integrity, and compassion for the distressed.

THE QUAKER PHYSICIAN.

Dr. Fothergill one of the most celebrated medical men of the last century was of Quaker origin. Perhaps assisted in part by the religious community to which he belonged he soon obtained one of the most lucrative practices of the day. He was a most disinterested man, at the outset of his career, he said "My only wish, was to do what little business might fall to my share as well as possible; and to banish all thought of practising physic as a money-getting trade, with the same solicitude as I would the suggestions of vice or intemperance." When in the height of prosperity he writes "I endeavour to follow my business, because it is my duty, rather than my interest; *the last is inseperable from a just discharge of duty;* but I have ever wished to look at the profits in the last place, and this wish has attended me ever since my beginning." Again he says "I wished most fervently, and I endeavour after it still, to do the business that occurred, with all the diligence I could, as *a present duty*, and endeavoured to repress every rising idea of its *consequences*, such a circumscribed, unaspiring temper of mind, doing every thing with diligence, humility, as in the sight of the God of healing, frees the mind from much unavailing distress, and consequential disappointment."

Dr. Fothergill was an enthusiastic student of botany and extensive collector of plants. The late Sir Joseph Banks speaking of him says "At an expense seldom undertaken by an individual, and with an ardour that was visible in the whole of his conduct, he procured from all parts of the world a great number of the rarest plants, and protected them in the amplest buildings which this or any other country has

seen. He liberally propo ed rewards to those whose circumstances and situations in life gave them opportunities of
bringing plants which might be ornamental or probably useful to this country, or her colonies; and as liberally paid
these rewards to all that served him. If the troubles of war
had permitted, we should have had the Cortex Winteranus,
&c. &c., introduced by this means into this country; and also
the Bread-Fruit, Mangasteen, &c., into the West Indies. For
each of these and many others, he had fixed a proper premium. In conjunction with the Earl of Tankerville, Dr.
Pitcairn, and myself, he sent a person over to Africa, who
was employed on the coast of that country, for the purpose
of collecting plants and specimens. Those whose gratitude
for restored health prompted them to do what was acceptable
to their benefactor, were always informed by him, that presents of rare plants chiefly attracted his attention, and would
be more acceptable to him than the most generous fees. How
many unhappy men enervated by the effects of hot climates,
where their connexions had placed them, found health on their
return home at that cheap purchase! What an infinite number of plants he obtained by these means, the large collection
of drawings he left behind will amply testify; and they were
equalled by nothing but royal munificence, at this time
largely bestowed upon the botanic gardens at Kew. In my
opinion, no other garden in Europe, royal or of a subject, had
nearly so many scarce and valuable plants. That science
might not suffer a loss, when a plant he had cultivated should
die, he liberally paid the best artist the country afforded, to
draw the new ones when they came to perfection; and so
numerous were they at last, that he found it necessary to
employ more artists than one, in order to keep pace with their
increase. His garden was known all over Europe, and foreigners of all ranks asked, when they came hither, permission
to see it; of which, Dr. Solander and myself are sufficient

witnesses, from the many applications that have been made through us for that permission."

Dr. John Fothergill, whose attachment to botany was a leading feature in his character, having noticed a spot of land suitable for a garden, on the Surrey side of the Thames, which was to dispose of, agreed for the price. One obstacle alone remained to make it his own. It was let to a tenant at will, whose little family subsisted on its produce, and whose misery was inevitable, had he expelled him from its fruitful soil. The moment Dr. Fothergill was made acquainted with the circumstance, he broke off the bargain, saying, that "nothing could ever afford gratification to him which entailed misery on another;" and when he relinquished this projected Eden, he made the family a present of the intended purchase money, which enabled them to become proprietors, where they had formerly only been tenants at will.

His disposition was very charitable, when at his summer residence, Lea Hall, in Cheshire, he gave advice gratuitously one day in the week to the poor at Middlewich, the nearest market-town. It was common for him to refuse fees from persons who were not in opulent circumstances, once a friend expostulated with him for refusing a fee from a clergyman of high position in the church. He replied. "I had rather return the fee of a gentleman with whose rank I am not perfectly acquainted, than run the risk of taking it from a man who ought, perhaps be the object of my bounty." When calling for the last visit to patients in reduced circumstances whilst apparently feeling the pulse he would frequently put money into their hand, sometimes it would be a bank-note and in one instance the present amounted to one hundred and fifty pounds.

A poor clergyman settled in London on a curacy of fifty pounds per annum, with a wife and numerous family, was known to Dr. Fothergill. An epidemic disease, at that time prevalent, seized upon the curate's wife and five children. In this scene of distress he looked to the Doctor for his assistance, but dared not apply to him. from a consciousness of not being able to pay him for his attendance. A friend, who knew his situation, kindly offered to accompany him to the Doctor's house, and give him his fee. They took the advantage of his hour of audience; and, after a description of the several cases, the fee was offered, and rejected, but a notice was taken of the curate's place of residence. The Doctor called assiduously the next and every succeeding day, until his attendance was no longer necessary. The curate, anxious to return some grateful mark of the sense he entertained of his services, strained every nerve to accomplish it; but his astonishment was not to be described, when, instead of receiving the money he offered, with apologies for his situation, the Doctor put ten guineas into his hand, desiring him to apply without diffidence in future difficulties.

When during the war the prisons were filled with foreign captives, he was one of the most active and influential members of the committee appointed to distribute the funds raised for their relief. To the honour of the Quakers be it stated, they, although forming scarcely the two-hundreth part of the nation, contributed one-fourth of the whole subscriptions raised for the purpose by the country

Without confining his attention to his own profession he was interested in every scheme calculated to promote the general good. We are told he directed his thoughts at one time to the establishment of public baths and of public *cemetries*. He was very instrumental in establishing an excellent school for the children of Quakers, not in affluent circumstances, at Ackworth. Shortly before his death to a friend he expressed the hope "That he had not lived in vain, but in a degree to answer the end of his creation, by sacrificing interested considerations, and his own ease, to the good of his fellow-creatures." The memory of the just is blessed. More than seventy carriages filled with sincere mourners followed the remains of this good man to the grave.

BOOTH THE ACTOR AND THE QUAKER.

The elder Booth—or "Richard III Booth," as he was not improperly designated—was at times the victim of strange fancies. Once he took the fancy to be an absolute vegetarian, and while possessed of this idea he was travelling on a Western steamboat, and happened to be placed at table opposite a solemn Quaker, who had been attracted by the eloquent conversation of the great actor. The benevolent old Quaker, observing the lack of viands on Booth's plate, kindly said—"Friend, shall I not help thee to the breast of this chicken?"—"No, I thank you, friend," replied the actor. "Then shall I not cut thee a slice of the ham?"—"No, friend, not any." "Then thee must take a piece of the mutton; thy plate is empty," persisted the good old Quaker. "Friend," said Booth, in those deep stentorian tones, whose volume and power had so often electrified crowded audiences, "friend, I never eat any flesh but human flesh, and I prefer that raw." The old Quaker was speechless, and his seat was changed to another table at the next meal.

MRS. FRY AT NEWGATE.

When first Mrs. Fry heard of the condition of the female prisoners in Newgate, their profligacy, their conduct, their hardy and determined recklessness, she was deeply moved at the account. Her determination to visit these people, and try by the *might* of gentleness to make some impression on them, received the sanction of her husband, friends, and religious society; but it was considered very hazardous by parties supposed to know the characters

and habits of criminals best. And it must be borne in
mind that, with reference to the female character, while it
is capable of reaching the noblest heights of virtue, yet.
when perverted and degraded, it is equally capable of sinking to the lowest depths of vice. Nothing on earth can be
better than a good, or worse than a bad woman.

Hence when Mrs. Fry determined to visit Newgate, she
was advised to leave her watch and purse behind her; but
she declined doing so, wisely resolving to attempt to win
confidence by reposing it. Accordingly she appeared among
the vilest criminals of our worst metropolitan prisons, and
was locked in with them. The effect of her winning, yet
authoritative demeanour and instructions, were soon apparent. Order was introduced among a set of human
beings supposed to be incapable of acting on any right impulse, and wholly incorrigable. Many was the hard heart
that melted under the influence of Mrs. Fry's teaching;
many the lip that had only known how to curse and scoff,
that learned from her to pray. Meanwhile, to suffering
innocence unjustly condemned—to thoughtless credulity,
heartlessly seduced and betrayed—Mrs. Fry extended, not
merely a comforting, but a rescuing hand. "The cause
that she knew not she searched out."

" Moral Heroism," by C. L. Balfour.

THE KING OF PRUSSIA WITH MRS. FRY AT NEWGATE.

The following report is taken from the *Times* Newspaper,
January 31st, 1842. His Majesty was received by the
Sheriffs, Mrs. Fry * * * * They were conducted to one
of the female wards, in which all the female prisoners at
present in custody were assembled round the table, at the
head of which Mrs. Fry took her seat, the King of Prussia
occupying a chair on her right, and the Lady Mayoress on
her left. Mrs. Fry, then addressing His Majesty,

explained that the unfortunates were untried prisoners. She informed His Majesty that much had been effected in respect of the improvement in the character and morals of the offenders who came under their notice. Mrs. Fry then proceeded to read to the prisoners two chapters, commenting on them as she proceeded, with a view to convey to His Majesty the idea of the mode in which she conducted her charitable visitations. Then followed a Psalm, which being concluded, Mrs. Fry knelt down,—an example which His Majesty instantly followed, and with the most devout attention, listened to a beautiful extemporaneous prayer, to which Mrs. Fry gave utterance. The scene, at this moment was indeed, a strange one,—at one view the beholder witnessed the Monarch of a great nation—a portion of the nobles of the realm—the wealth and authorities of the great metropolis of the commercial kingdom, approaching with prayer their common Creator, in unison with those whom vice and crime had made the occupants of a prison ! The prayer concluded with invoking the Divine blessing upon the Christian Sovereign now present—upon his beloved consort,—and upon the kingdom over which he reigned.

" His Majesty then rose, and again offering his arm to Mrs. Fry, was escorted back to the Governor's apartments. He made many inquiries and expressed himself gratified with the cleanliness and order of the prison."

" His Majesty then leaving Newgate, proceeded to Mrs. Fry's residence, at West House, Essex, about five miles from the city."

The author of " Memoirs of Mrs. Fry " observes " many inquired what good would be likely to result from these visits of this Christian sovereign to the philanthropist, Mrs. Fry. Doubtless much good to many, especially to prisoners in his own kingdom, and to multitudes beyond its limits.

We have it on undoubted authority, that Mrs. Fry improved
the opportunity to appeal most powerfully to the King
against the wickedness and impolicy of persecution on
account of religious opinions, and in favour of complete
religious liberty in his own kingdom. His Majesty's tears
bespoke the deep feeling at this appeal. And both then
and by letter the following day Mrs. Fry entreated His
Majesty to use the best influence with the King of Denmark,
to put a stop to the shameful persecution carried on against
the Baptists in his kingdom. Multitudes yet unborn,
therefore, will be benefitted by this visit of the King of
Prussia, the result of conduct so worthy of the enlightened,
philautrophic, and Christian character of Mrs. Fry.

Quick Retort.

On one occasion, when the father of the "Sherwood
Forester" was passing along a street in the lower part of
Nottingham, and coming to a corner where a number of
gossiping men stood, he was approached by one who meant
to raise a laugh at the Quakers expense. Staring him
impudently in the face, he said, "I say, master, how long
have you worn that big hat?" Pausing for a moment,
and looking at his questioner, he turned the tables by
saying, loud enough to be heard by all, "I cannot remember exactly, but am afraid not so long as thou'st been a
fool." Old Mr. Hall was an excellent pedestrian, and he
seldom allowed any person walking the same way to pass
him. One day a stout man, who came almost up to him
near the seven mile house, between Mansfield and Nottingham, and who had another person upon a pony for a
companion, got so annoyed at his inability to go ahead, as
to get talking at the Friend somewhat offensively. At
length, becoming even more personal than before, he
shouted loudly, "If I had that man's hat, it would make

two for me." "No," quietly retorted **Mr. Hall**, turning round, and looking calmly at the stout quiz, "it would take a larger hat than this to make two for one big head!" while the man on the pony made the forest echo with his laughter, and his shout of "Well done, old Quaker!"

Briscoe's "*Nottinghamshire Facts and Fictions.*"

AT FAULT.

The Duke of Grafton being fox-hunting one day near Newmarket, a Quaker, at some distance upon an eminence, pulled off his hat, and gave a 'Yoicks, tally-ho!' The hounds immediately ran to him, and being drawn off the scent, were consequently at fault, which so enraged the duke, that galloping up to the offender, he asked him in an angry tone, 'Art thou a Quaker?' 'I am, friend,' replied the man. 'Well, then,' rejoined his grace, 'as you never pull off your hat to a Christian, I will thank you in future not to pay that compliment to a fox!'

PUBLIC TESTIMONY IN CHURCH.

Dr. Cunningham remarks "Toward the end of 1745, when England was recovering from its panic, caused by the inroad of Prince Charles and his Highlanders, a young Quakeress, named Risdale, of the humble condition of a servant, felt herself called upon to give a public testimony in church. Such exhibitions were very common in the days of Fox; but, by the strong arm of the law, they had been entirely put down. It is proboble this enthusiastic serving woman had been reading the lives of some of the ancient worthies, and fancied she was commissioned to do like them, and play the part of a prophetess. She, accordingly, persua-ded her mistress and some other Friends to accompany her to the steeple-house, and, when the sermon was ended, she stood up and said—"Neighbours, I am sent with a message from the high priest of our profession to desire you to turn the eye of your mind inward and examine yourselves, and to come to true repentance and amendment of life." Then turning to the officiating Clergyman, she said—"You must come down from your high place, and bow at the footstool of Christ, before you can teach the people the way to the kingdom of heaven." The astonished parson called the churchwarden to put the intruder out, but the churchwarden was as one amazed, and did nothing; whereupon the parson himself descended from the pulpit, and in wrath thrust her to the door. But this was not all. The poor woman was fined £20 for her misdemeanour; and not being able to pay it, was thrust into jail."

MEETING THE DIFFICULTY.

You remind me of a story which I once heard in England, concerning a worthy Quaker who lived in a country town there. The Friend was rich and benevolent, his means were put in frequent requisition, for purposes of local charity or usefulness. The townspeople wanted to rebuild their parish Church, and a committee was appointed to raise the funds. It was agreed that the Quaker could not be asked to subscribe towards an object so contrary to his principles; but then, on the other hand, so true a friend to the town might take it amiss if he was not at least consulted on a matter of such general interest. So one of their number went and explained to him their project; the old church was to be removed, and such and such steps taken towards the construction of a new one.

"Thee was right," said the Quaker, "in supposing that my principles would not allow me to assist in building a church. But did'st thee not say something about pulling down a church. Thee may'st put my name down for a hundred pounds."

Merivale's " Historical Studies."

Feeling in the Right Place.

A gentleman was one day relating to a Quaker a tale of deep distress, and concluded very pathetically by saying, "I could not but feel for him." "Verily, friend," replied the Quaker, "thou didst right in that thou didst feel for thy neighbour; but didst thou feel in the right place—didst thou feel in thy pocket?"

How to Get Warm.

A Quaker gentleman, riding in a carriage with a fashionable lady, decked with a profusion of jewellery, heard her complain of the cold. Shivering in her lace bonnet and shawl, as light as a cobweb, she exclaimed, "What shall I do to get warm?"—"I really don't know," replied the Quaker, solemnly, "unless thee should put on another breast-pin."

Advice on Matrimony.

"John," said a Quaker to a young friend, "I hear thou art going to be married."—"Yes," replied John, "I am."—"Well," replied the Quaker, "I have one little bit of advice to give thee, and that is never marry a woman worth more than thou art. When I married my wife, I was worth just fifty shillings, and she was worth sixty-two, and whenever any difference has occured between us since, she has always thrown the odd shillings in my face."

A Fine Distinction.

A Quaker being examined by a judicious counsel, as he was retiring, another counsel on the same side asked him a question which he did not like to answer. "I have told all

I know to the counsel," said the Quaker. " I am counsel also," answered the barrister. " Thou mayst be counsel also," replied the Quaker, " but thou art not counsel like-wise."

Fox, The Quaker.

This individual, many years deceased, was a most remark-able man in his circle; a great natural genius, which employed itself upon trivial or not generally interesting matters. He deserved to have been known better than he was. The last years of his life he resided at Bristol. He was a great Per-sian scholar, and published some translations of the poets of that nation, which were well worthy of perusal. He was somewhat eccentric, but had the quickest reasoning power, and consequently the greatest coolness of any man of his day, who was able to reason. His house took fire in the night; it was situated near the sea; it was uninsured, and the flames spread so rapidly, nothing could be saved. He saw the consequences instantly, made up his mind to them as rapidly, and ascending a hill at some distance in the rear of his dwelling, watched the picture and the reflection of the flames on the sea, admiring its beauties, as if it were a holi-day bonfire.

Hone's " *Table Talk.*"

Planting Fruit Trees by the Way-side.

.Fruit was unknown in the early days of the settlement of New York State, but orchards of apple-trees were soon planted between the stumps of cleared forest. One rugged farmer passing through a neighbouring settlement at a little later period, picked up an apple from under a tree, and was roughly ordered by the owner to replace it on the ground. Obeying, the Quaker turned to the owner with the remark, " Friend, thou art a very close man with thy fruit. Next year, if I live, I will plant 100 apple-trees by my wayside for the use of travellers," and he fulfilled his promise.—*Times*, 1879.

THE GREAT FIRE OF LONDON.

The great fire of London which followed the pestilence of 1666, broke out the day after George Fox was released from Scarborough Castle, and was a confirmation in his belief, of those judgments of God, of which he had a vision while a prisoner in Lancaster Castle. London was fore-warned of this calamity by a Quaker from Huntingdonshire, by name Thomas Ibbott, who entered London on horseback, the Friday preceding the fire, and turning his horse loose, he unbuttoned his garments, and ran about the streets, scattering his money and crying out "So should they run up and down, scattering their money and goods, half un-dressed like mad people, as he was a sign to them," which prediction though no one believed at the time, was fully verified during the conflagration.—*Life of Fox*, by J. Marsh.

THEE AND THOU.

In 1661 appeared a curious little book, called *The Battle-dore*, compiled by John Stubbs and Benjamin Furley, at the instigation of George Fox, and was written to prove that *Thee* and *Thou* is a proper and usual form of speech to a single person, and *you* to more than one. Examples were taken out of the scriptures, and from books of instruction and grammars of thirty different languages. A copy was presented to the king and his council, to the bishops, and to the universities, which distribution, he says, "had the effect of informing and convincing people, so that few after its publication, were so *rugged* to them for saying, Thou and Thee."

PRINCE FREDERICK OF WALES.

In 1735, a deputation from the Quakers, waited on Frederick, Prince of Wales (father of George the Third), to solicit his interest for the tithing bill. The prince replied, "That as a friend to liberty in general, and toleration in particular, he wished that the Society of Friends might meet with support; but that as for himself, it did not become his station to influence his friends, or direct his servants, he wished to leave them c. ti ely to their own consciences and understandings, which was a rule he had hitherto prescribed to himself, and proposed through his whole life to observe."

Mr. Andrew Pitt, who was one of the deputation, replied in the name of the body, in the following terms; "May it please the Prince of Wales, I am greatly affected with thy excellent notions of liberty, and am still more pleaesd with thy answer, than if thou hadst granted our request."

JOHN BRIGHT AT GLEN URQUHART.

In the visitors' book at Drumnadrochit Inn, Glen Urquhart, the following lines may be seen:—

> In Highland glens 'tis far too much observed
> That man is chased away, and Game preserved:
> Glen Urquhart is to me a lovelier glen—
> Here Deer and Grouse have not supplanted men.

A BRIGHT STORY.

The President of the Board of Trade was dining with a well-known citizen of Cottonopolis, and the conversation turned on the subject of the growth and development of America. "I should like," said the host, who is an enthusiastic admirer of the great Republic, "to come back fifty years after my death to see what a fine country America had become." — "I believe you would be glad of any excuse to come back," said Mr. Bright.

DR. FRANKLIN'S ADVICE.

"Friend Franklin," said Myers Fisher, a celebrated Quaker lawyer of Philadelphia, one day, "thee knows almost everything; can thee tell me how I am to preserve my small-beer in the back-yard? my neighbours are often tapping it of nights."

"Put a barrel of old Madeira by the side of it," replied the doctor; "let them but get a taste of the Madeira, and I'll engage they will never trouble thy small-beer any more."

SOMETHING LIKE A FRIEND.

Many good anecdotes are told of the late Thomas Garrett, whose life was devoted to the liberation of the slaves. He never lost a chance to assist a fugitive, and many times imperilled his life and property in so doing. He once forfeited all his goods to the State of Delaware for having aided a slave to escape. At the close of the auction, the officer turned to Garrett. and said, "Thomas, I hope you'll never be caught at this again." "Friend," was the reply, "I hav'nt a dollar in the world, but if thee knows a fugitive who needs a breakfast, send him to me."

ANTHONY PURVER'S TRANSLATION OF THE BIBLE.

A poor Quaker carpenter, of the above name, conceived that the spirit impelled him to translate the Bible He accordingly learnt Latin, Greek, and Hebrew, and published a literal version of the Old and New Testament in two vols., folio, 1764.

This Book is curious for its Hebrew idioms By adhering to those, Anthony has in some rare instances excelled the common version; but when he alters only for the sake of alteration, he makes miserable work

E. G. *A hind let go may exhibit genteel Naphtali; he gives fine words*—for. "Naphtali is a hind let loose; he giveth goodly words."

I am he who am, is better than *I am that I am*.

He calls the Song of Solomon, the poem of Solomon; " Song, (he says) *being of profane use*."

Southey's " Omniana."

JOSEPH TORREY AND THE DISEASED HORSE.

A Quaker who resided in Dublin, by the name of Joseph Torrey, was one day passing through the streets, when he saw a man leading a horse, which was evidently much diseased. His compassionate heart was pained by the sight, and he asked the man where he was going. He replied, "The horse has the staggers, and I am going to sell him to the carrion-butchers."

"Wilt thou sell him to me for a crown!" inquired Joseph. The man readily assented, and the poor animal was led to the stable of his new friend, where he was most kindly tended. Suitable remedies and careful treatment soon restored him to health and beauty. One day, when Friend Torrey was riding him in Phœnix Park, a gentleman looked very earnestly at the horse, and at last inquired whether his owner would be willing to sell him. "Perhaps I would," replied Joseph, "if I could get a very good master for him."

" He so strongly resembles a favourite horse I once had, that I should think he was the same, if I didn't know he was dead," rejoined the stranger.

"Did he die in the stable?" inquired Joseph.

The gentleman replied " No. He had the staggers very badly, and I sent him to the carrion-butchers."

" I should be very sorry to sell an animal to any man, who would send him to the carrion-butchers because he was deceased," answered Joseph. "If thou wert ill, how wouldst thou like to have thy throat cut, instead of being kindly nursed?"

With some surprise, the gentleman inquired whether he intended to compare him to a horse. "No," replied Joseph, but animals have feelings, as well as human beings; and when they are afflicted with disease, they ought to be carefully attended. If I consent to sell thee this horse, I shall exact a promise that thou wilt have him kindly nursed when he is sick, and not send him to have his throat cut."

The gentleman readily promised all that was required, and said he should consider himself very fortunate to obtain a horse that so much resembled his old favourite. When he called the next day, to complete the bargain, he inquired whether forty guineas would be a satisfactory price. The conscientious Quaker answered, "I have good reason to believe the horse was once thine; and I am willing to restore him to thee on the conditions I have mentioned. I have saved him from the carrion-butchers, but I will charge thee merely what I have expended for his food and medicine. Let it be a lesson to thee to treat animals kindly, when they are diseased. Never again send to the butchers a faithful servant, that cannot plead for himself, and may with proper attention, again become useful to thee."

The Clergyman and his Books.

On board the ship in which Isaac T. Hopper returned from England to America, there was a Clergyman who had brought with him a large quantity of books. When they reached New York, he was in some perplexity as at the custom-house high duties were demanded for the books. "Perhaps I can get them through for thee," said Friend Hopper. "I will try." He went up to the officer, and said, "Isn't it a rule of the custom-house not to charge a man for the tools of his trade ? " He replied that it was. Then thou art bound to let this priest's books pass free," rejoined the Friend. " Preaching is the trade he gets his living by; and these books are the tools he must use." The Clergyman being aware of the Quaker views with regard to a paid ministry, seemed doubtful whether to be pleased or not, with such a mode of helping him out of difficulty. However, he took the joke as good naturedly as it was offered, and the books passed free, on the assurance that they were all for his own library.

ON ARISTOCRATIC PREJUDICES.

How little Friend Hopper was inclined to minister to aristocratic prejudices, may be inferred from the following anecdote. One day, while he was visiting a wealthy family in Dublin, a note was handed to him, inviting him to dine the next day. When he read it aloud, his host remarked, " These people are very respectable, but not of the first circles. They belong to our Church, but not exactly to our set. Their father was a mechanic."

" Well I am a mechanic myself," said Isaac, " Perhaps if thou hadst known that fact, thou wouldst not have invited *me* ? "

" Is it possible," exclaimed his host, " that a man of your information and appearance can be a mechanic? "

" I followed the business of a tailor for many years," rejoined his guest. " Look at my hands! Dost thou not see marks of shears ? Some of the Mayors of Philadelphia have been tailors. When I lived there, I often walked the streets with the Chief Justice. It never occured to me that it was any honour, and I don't think it did to him."

THE AGED SLAVE EMANCIPATED.

At an early period, it became an established rule of discipline for the Society (in America) to disown any Member, who refused to manumit his bondmen. Friend Hopper used to tell an interesting anecdote in connection with a committee appointed to expostulate in private with those who held slaves. In the course of their visits, they concluded to pass by one of their members, who held only one slave, and he was very old. He was too infirm to earn his own living, and as he was very kindly treated, they supposed he would have no wish for freedom. But Isaac Jackson, one of the committee, a very benevolent and conscientious man, had a strong impression on his mind that duty required him not to omit this case. He accordingly went alone to the master and stated how the subject appeared to him, in the inward light of his own soul. The Friend was not easily convinced. He brought forward many reasons for not emancipating his slave; and one of the strongest was that the man was too feeble to labour for his own support and therefore freedom would be of no value to him. Isaac Jackson replied, " He laboured for thee without wages while he had strength. and it is thy duty to support him now. Whether he would value freedom or not is a question he alone is competent to decide."

These friendly remonstrances produced such effect, that the master agreed to manumit his bondman and give a written obligation that he should be comfortably supported during the remainder of his life, by him or his heirs. When the papers were prepared the slave was called into the parlour, and Isaac Jackson inquired, " Would'st thou like to be free?" He promptly answered that he should. The Friend suggested that he was now too feeble to labour much, and inquired how he would manage to obtain a living. The old man meekly replied, " Providence has been kind to me thus far ; and I am willing to trust him the rest of my life."

Isaac Jackson then held up the papers and said, "Thou art a free man. Thy master has emancipated thee, and promised to maintain thee as long as thou mayest live."

This was so unexpected, that the aged bondman was completely overcome. For a few moments he remained in profound silence, then, with a sudden impulse, he fell on his knees, and poured forth a short and fervent prayer of thanksgiving to his Heavenly Father, for prolonging his life till he had the happiness to feel himself a free man.

The master and his adviser were both surprised and affected by this eloquent outburst of grateful feeling. The poor old servant had seemed so comfortable and contented, that no one supposed freedom was of great importance to him   But, as honest Isaac Jackson observed, *he alone* was competent to decide *that* question.

TESTIMONY AGAINST SLAVERY.

Friend Hopper went to Maryland, to visit two sisters who resided there. He was accompanied in this journey by his wife's brother, David Tatum. At an Inn where they stopped for refreshment, the following characteristic incident occurred : a coloured girl brought in a pitcher of water. "Art thou a slave?" said Friend Hopper. When she answered in the affirmative, he started up and exclaimed, "It is against my principles to be waited upon by a slave." His more timid brother-in-law inquired, in a low tone of voice, whether he were aware that the mistress was within hearing?" "To be sure I am," answered Isaac aloud. "What would be the use of saying it, if she were *not* within hearing?" He then emptied the pitcher of water, and went out to the well to re-fill it for himself. Seeing the landlady stare at these proceedings he explained to her that he thought it wrong to avail himself of unpaid labour. In reply, she complained of the ingratitude of slaves and

the hard condition of their mast rs. "It is very inconve-
nient to live so near a free state," said she. "I had sixteen
slaves; but ten of them have run away, and I expect the
rest will soon go."

"I hope they will," said Isaac, "I am sure I would run
away, if I were a slave."

At first she was disposed to be offended ; but he reasoned
the matter with her, in a quiet and friendly manner, and
they parted on very civil terms. David Tatum often used
to tell this anecdote, after they returned home; and he
generally added, "I never again will travel in a Southern
state with brother Isaac, for I am sure it would be at the
risk of my life."

Isaac Hopper and the Cruel Driver.

He very often mingled with affairs in the street, as he
passed along. One day, when he saw a man beating his
horse brutally, he stepped up to him and said very seriously ;
"Dost thou know that some people think men change into
animals when they die?" The stranger's attention was
arrested by such an unexpected question, and he answered
that he never was acquainted with anybody who had that
belief. "But some people do believe it," rejoined Friend
Hopper, "and they also believe that animals may become
men. Now I am thinking if thou shouldest ever be a horse
and that horse should ever be a man, with such a temper as
thine, the chance is thou wilt get some cruel beatings."
Having thus changed the current of his angry mood, he
proceeded to expostulate with him in a friendly way ; and
the poor beast was reprieved for that time at least.

Quaker Funeral.

Buckingham, in his work on "America," remarks.
" During our stay at Saratoga, we had our house of feast-

ing turned to a house of mourning, by the death of two of its inmates within a few days of each other. The one was an elderly gentleman, whose death, it was believed, if not actually caused, was greatly accelerated by imprudent diet, and an excessive use of the waters. The other was a young Quaker from Providence, here with his parents and brothers and sisters; intended to be married, and his proposed bride daily expecting to meet him. He came here with a slight affection of inflammatory rheumatism, nd was considered to have quite recovered from this affection, when suddenly in the night, he was seized with spasms of the heart and faintness; and before his father could come to his assistance, though sleeping n the next room, he expired. This event, as might be expected, threw sadness and gloom over the inmates of the house in which it occured; and when the funeral of the deceased took place on the day following his death, it was attended by all who were within the dwelling. It was the first Quaker funeral at which I had ever been present; and it affected all very deeply, from the simple and unostentatious solemnit by which it was characterized.

The coffin, of plain mahogany, without the appearance of breast-plate, handles, or escutcheon, was brought from the bed-room by the young men who were his friends and companions in life—and by whom also it was alternately carried to the grave—and placed on a large table, prepared with a clean white linen cloth spread, on which to receive it. It was followed by the parents, relatives, and personal friends, who walked after it in pairs, but in their ordinary dresses, as neither black clothes, nor any outward emblems of mourning, are ever worn by Quakers. They then took their seats on the sofas and chairs around the drawing-room; and soon after this, the remaining space was occupied by nearly 200 persons, living in the house, and some few from the neighbourhood, belonging to the Society of Friends, of which the deceased was a member.

A dead silence prevailed, which continued for more than half-an-hour; and so unbroken and profound was the stillness, that the fall of a pin might be heard if dropped on the floor. There was something indescribably impressive in this spectacle, of a gaily dressed assemblage of persons congregated for pleasure at this focus of gaiety and thought-lessness, sitting in an ordinary drawing-room, with the dead body of one or their own companions, alive and well but two days before, lying in the cold shroud of death in the very midst of them. I do not think, that any spoken discourse, however eloquent, could have more powerfully arrested the feelings, or awakened the attention to the certainty and frequent suddenness of death, and the hourly necessity of preparation for it, than was effected by the silent scene before us : and accordingly many eyes besides those of the friends and relatives of the deceased, were filled with tears.

At length a venerable old Quaker, upwards of 80 years of age, who had come in from the country to attend the funeral, arose, and addressed the assembly. It was unusual, he said, but not unpleasing, to see so many strangers con-gregated together, to witness the departure from among them of one of the members of their Society ; and he felt impelled, by an irresistible impulse, to profit by the occasion, and address a few words to those by whom he was surround-ed. His observations were full of piety, and appropriateness; and there could hardly have been one present, who did not respond to the aspiration with which he concluded, that all might be able to say, in the language of the apostle, " It was good for me to have been here." Another pause of profound silence ensued, which was quite as impressive as before ; and another short address from the same venerable patriarch, the last, he thought it probable he might ever be permitted to utter in the presence of others, made almost every one present weep copiously.

To the pause which succeeded the close of this, followed a most touching scene, when the stepmother of the deceased, who had sat beside her most deeply afflicted husband, and surrounded by her numerous sorrowing children, fell gently on her knees from the place where she sat; and while nearly all the strangers present, instinctively followed her in assuming the same supplicating attitude, she poured forth a prayer so full of eloquence, devotion, sweetness, tenderness, and simple beauty, as to penerate every heart. The evident struggles between her own feelings and her sense of duty, which caused her voice every now and then to falter, and her utterance to become choked, and which shook her husband with deep and convulsive sobs, was so powerful, and so truthful an exhibition of the genuine pathos of unaffected nature under a bereavement with which all could sympathize deeply—that never, perhaps, was there an assembly of the same number of persons so completely absorbed in devotion, awe, and grief combined, as the kneeling mourners (for all had so become by sympathy) which surrounded the corpse of the young and suddenly-snatched flower, fading before their eyes, while the sweetest assents of maternal love, piety, and resignation filled their cars, and penetrated to the utmost recesses of their hearts.

I have seen many funerals in many different lands, and conducted in many different modes—from the "pomps and vanities" which swell the death-pageantry of heroes and kings, to the simple interment of the friendless mariner, who is consigned to a watery grave, without prayer or chaplain, by the hands of his brother shipmates—but I never remember to have witnessed anything half so heart-searching and mind-impressing as this; and I cannot but believe that if so simple, yet purely devotional a mode of interring the dead, were universally adopted by Christian Nations, instead of the "plumed hearse," the hired mourners, the long unmeaning cavalade with scarfs and bands, and sable cloaks, where all within is coldness and indifference—the change would be highly beneficial if the object of accompanying the interment of the dead with any ceremonial at all, be to impress the living with the necessity of preparing to follow them.

THE MAN OF PEACE.

John Tatum, an American Friend, was remarkable for his love of peace; always preferring to suffer wrong rather than dispute. The influence of this pacific disposition upon others was strikingly illustrated in the case of two of his neighbours. They were respectable people in easy circumstances, and the families found much pleasure in frequent intercourse with each other. But after a few years, one of the men deemed that an intentional affront had been offered him by the other. Instead of good-natured frankness on the occasion, he behaved in a sullen manner, which provoked the other, and the result was that eventually neither of them would speak when they met. Their fields joined, and when they were on friendly terms, the boundary was marked by a fence, which they alternately repaired. But when there was a feud between them, neither of them was willing to mend the other's fence. So each one built a fence for himself, leaving a very narrow strip of land between, which in process of time came to be generally known by the name of Devil's Lane in allusion to the bad temper that produced it. A brook formed another portion o the boundary between their farms, and was useful to both of them. But after they became enemies, if a freshet occured, each watched an opportunity to turn the water on the other's land, by which much much damage was mutually done. They were so much occupied with injuring each other in every possible way, that they neglected their farms and grew poorer and poorer. One of them became intemperate, and everything about their premises began to wear an aspect of desolation and decay. At last one of the farms was sold to pay a mortgage, and John Tatum, who was then about to be married, concluded to purchase it. Many people warned him of the trouble he would have with a quarrelsome and intemperate neighbour. But after mature reflection, he concluded to trust to the influence of a peaceful and kind example, and accordingly purchased the farm.

Soon after he removed thither, he proposed to do away with the Devil's Lane by building a new fence on the boundary entirely at his own expense. His neighbour acceded to the proposition in a very surly manner, and for a considerable time seemed determined to find, or make some occasion for quarrel. But the young Quaker met all his provocations with forbearance, and never missed an opportunity to oblige him. Good finally overcomes evil. The turbulent spirit, having nothing to excite it, gradually subsided into calmness. In process of time, he evinced a disposition to be kind and obliging also. Habits of temperance and industry returned, and during the last years of his life he was considered a remarkably good neighbour.

A METHODIST MINISTER FROM THE SOUTH.

In the summer of 1844, Friend Hopper met with a Methodist preacher from Mississippi, who came with his family to New York, to attend a General Conference. Being introduced as a zealous abolitionist, the conversation immediately turned upon slavery. One of the preacher's daughters said " I couldn't possibly get along without slaves, Mr. Hopper,

Why I never dressed or undressed myself, till I came to the North, I wanted very much to bring a slave with me."

"I wish thou hadst," rejoined Friend Hopper.

"And what would you have done, if you had seen her?" she inquired.

He replied, "I would have told her that she was a free woman while she remained here; but if she went back to the South, she would be liable to be sold, like a pig or a sheep."

They laughed at this frank avowal, and when he invited them to com to his house with their father, to take tea, they gladly accepted the invitation. Again the conversation turned toward that subject, which was never forgotten when North and South met. In answer to some remark from Friend Hopper, the preacher said, "Do you think I am not a Christian?"

"I certainly do not regard thee as one," he replied.

"And I suppose you think I cannot get to heaven?" rejoined the slaveholder.

"I will not say that," replied the Friend. "To thy own master thou must stand or fall. But slavery is a great abomination, and no one who is guilty of it can be a Christian, or Christ-like. I would not exclude thee from the kingdom of heaven; but if thou dost enter there, it must be because thou art ignorant of the fact that thou art living in sin."

After a prolonged conversation, mostly on the same topic, the guests rose to depart. The Methodist said, "Well Mr. Hopper, I have never been better treated by any man, than I have been by you. I should be very glad to have you visit us."

"Ah! and thou wouldst lynch me; or at least, thy friends would," he replied, smiling.

"Oh no, we would treat you very well," rejoined the

Southerner. "But how would you talk about slavery if you were there?"

"Just as I do here, to be sure," answered the Quaker. "I would advise the slaves to be honest, industrious, and obedient, and never try to run away from a good master, unless they were pretty sure of escaping; because if they were caught they would fare worse than before. But if they had a safe opportunity, I should advise them to be off as soon as possible." In a more serious tone, he added, "And to thee, who claimest to be a minister of Christ, I would say that thy Master requires thee to give deliverance to the captive, and let the oppressed go free. My friend, hast thou a conscience void of offence? When thou liest down at night, is thy mind always at ease on this subject? After ouring out thy soul in prayer to the Heavenly Father, dost thou not feel the outraged sense of right, like a perpetual motion, restless wit'in thy breast? Dost thou not hear a voice telling thee it is wrong to hold thy fellow men in slavery, with their wives and their little ones?"

The preacher manifested some emotion at this earnest appeal, and confessed that he sometimes had doubts on the subject; though, on the whole, he had concluded that it was right to hold slaves. One of his daughters, who was a widow, seemed to be more deeply touched. She took Friend Hopper's hand, at parting, and said, "I am thankful for the privilege of having seen you. I never talked with an abolitioniat before. You have convinced me that slave holding is sinful in the sight of God. My husband left me several slaves, and I have held them for five years; but when I return, I am resolved to hold a slave no longer."

WILLIAM SAVERY, AN AMERICAN QUAKER, OVERCOMING EVIL WITH GOOD.

But more powerful than all other agencies was the preaching of William Savery. He was a tanner by trade, but

remarked by all who knew him as a man who " walked humbly with his God." One night a quantity of hides were
stolen from his tannery; and he had reason to believe that
the thief was a quarrelsome, drunken neighbour whom I will
call John Smith. The next week the following advertisement
appeared in the county newspaper :—" Whoever stole a lot of
hides on the fifth of the present month is hereby informed
that the owner has a sincere wish to be his friend. If poverty
tempted him to this false step the owner will keep the whole
transaction secret, and will gladly put him in the way of
obtaining money by means more likely to bring him peace of
mind." This singular advertisement attracted considerable
attention ; but the culprit alone knew whence the benevolent
offer came. When he read it his heart melted within him,
and he was filled with contrition for what he had done. A
few nights afterwards, as the tanner's family was about retiring to rest, they heard a timid knock ; and when the door
was opened there stood John Smith, with a load of hides on
his shoulder. Without looking up, he said, " I've brought
these back, Mr. Savery. Where shall I put them?" "Wait
till I can light a lantern, and I will go to the barn with thee,"
he replied : " then perhaps thou wilt come in and tell me
how this happened ; we will see what can be done for thee."
As soon as they were gone out his wife prepared some hot
coffee, and placed pies and meat on the table. When they
returned from the barn she said, "Neighbour Smith, I thought
some hot supper would be good for thee." He turned his
back toward her and would not speak. After leaning against
the fireplace in silence for a moment, he said, in a choked
voice, " It is the first time I ever stole anything, and I have
felt very bad about it. I don't know how it is. I am sure
I didn't think once that I should ever come to be what I
am ; but I took to drinking, and then to quarrelling. Since
I began to go down hill everybody gives me a kick ; you are
K

the first man who has ever offered me a helping hand. My wife is sickly, and my children are starving. You have sent them many a meal, God bless you! and yet I stole the hides from you, meaning to sell them the first chance I could get. But I tell you the truth when I say it is the first time I was ever a thief." "Let it be the last, my friend," replied William Savery: "the secret shall remain between ourselves. Thou art still young, and it is thy power to make up for lost time. Promise me that thou wilt not drink any intoxicating liquor for a year, and I will employ thee tomorrow at good wages. Perhaps we may find some employment for thy family also. The little boy can, at least pick up stones. But eat a bit now, and drink some hot coffee; perhaps it will keep thee from craving anything stronger to-night. Doubtless thou wilt find it hard to abstain at first; but keep up a brave heart, for the sake of thy wife and children, and it will soon become easy. When thou hast need of coffee, tell Mary, and she will soon give it thee." The poor fellow tried to eat and drink, but the food seemed to choke him. After an ineffectual effort to compose his excited feelings, he bowed his head on the table and wept like a child. After a while he ate and drank with good appetite; and his host parted with him for the night with this kindly exhortation, "Try to do well, John; and thou wilt always find a friend in me." He entered his employ the next day, and remained with him a many years, a sober, honest and faithful man. The secret of the theft was kept between them; but after John's death William Savery sometimes told the story, to prove that evil might be overcome with good.

ISAAC HOPPER, THE AMERICAN PHILANTHROPIST, IN AN OMNIBUS.

Until the last few years of his life, Friend Hopper usually walked to and from his office twice a day, making about five

miles in the whole; to which he sometimes added a walk in
the evening, to visit children or friends, or transact some
necessary business. When the weather was very unpleasant
he availed himself of the Haarlem cars. Upon one of these
occasions it chanced that the long ponderous vehicle was
nearly empty. They had not proceeded far, when a very
respectable-looking young woman beckoned for the car to
stop. It did so ; but when she set her foot on the step the
conductor somewhat rudely pushed her back, and she turned
away, evidently much mortified. Friend Hopper started up
and inquired, " Why didst thou push that woman away ? "
" She's coloured," was the laconic reply. " Art thou instructed by the managers of the railroad to proceed in this manner
on such occasions ? " inquired Friend Hopper. The man
answered, " Yes." " Then let me get out," rejoined the
genuine republican ; " it disturbs my conscience to ride in a
public conveyance where any decently behaved person is refused admittance." And though it was raining very fast,
and his house was a mile off, the old veteran of seventy-five
years marched through mud and wet, at a pace somewhat
brisker than his usual energetic step ; for indignation warmed
his honest and kind heart, and set the blood in motion.
The next day he called at the railroad office, and very civilly
inquired of one of the managers whether conductors were instructed to exclude passengers merely on account of complexion.
" Certainly not," was the prompt reply. " They have discretionary power to reject any person who is drunk, or
offensively unclean, or indecent or quarrelsome.". Friend
Hopper then related how a young woman of modest appearance and respectable address was pushed from the step, though
the car was nearly empty, and she was seeking shelter from
a violent rain. " That was wrong," replied the manager :
" we have no reason to complain of coloured people as passengers. They obtrude upon no one, and always have sixpences

in readiness to pay; whereas fashionably dressed white people frequently offer a ten-dollar bill, which they know we cannot change, and thus cheat us out of our rightful dues. Who was the conductor that behaved in the manner you have described? We will turn him away, if he doesn't know better how to use the discretionary power with which he is entrusted." Friend Hopper replied, "I had rather thou wouldst not turn him out of thy employ, unless he repeats the offence after being properly instructed. I have no wish to injure the man. He has become infected with the unjust prejudices of the community, without duly reflecting upon the subject. Friendly conversation with him may suggest wiser thoughts. All I ask of thee is to instruct him that the rights of the meanest citizen are to be respected. I thank thee for having listened to my complaint in such a candid and courteous manner." "And I thank you for having come to inform us of the circumstance," replied the manager. They parted mutually well pleased; and a few days after the same conductor admitted a coloured woman into the cars without making any objection.

ISAAC HOPPER.—A CHEMICAL EXPERIMENT.

When he met a boy with a dirty face or hands, he would stop him, and inquire if he ever studied chemistry. The boy, with a wondering stare, would answer "No." "Well then I will teach thee how to perform a curious chemical experiment," said Friend Hopper. "Go home, take a piece of soap, put it in water, and rub it briskly on thy hands and face. Thou hast no idea what a beautiful froth it will make, and how much whiter thy skin will be. That's a chemical experiment: I advise thee to try it."

ISAAC HOPPER'S WIT.

Sometimes his jests conveyed cutting sarcasms. One day, when he was riding in an omnibus, he opened a port-monnaie lined with red. A man with a very flaming visage, who was somewhat intoxicated and therefore very much inclined to be talkative, said, " Ah, that is a very gay pocket-book for a Quaker to carry !" " Yes, it is very red," replied Friend Hopper ; " but it is not so red as thy nose." The passengers all smiled, and the man seized the first opportunity to escape. A poor woman once entered an omnibus which was nearly full, and stood waiting for some one to make her room. A proud-looking lady sat near Friend Hopper, and he asked her to move a little, to accomodate the new comer. But she looked very glum, and remained motionless. After examining her countenance for an instant he said, " If thy face often looks so I shou.d'nt like to have thee for a neighbour." The passengers exchanged smiles at this rebuke, and the lady frowned still more deeply.

THE UMBRELLA GIRL.

A young girl, the only daughter of a poor widow, removed from the country to Philadelphia to earn her living by covering umbrellas. She was very handsome; with glossy black hair, large beaming eyes, and " lips like wet coral." She was just at that susceptible age when youth is ripening into womanhood, when the soul begins to be pervaded by " that restless principle, which impels poor humans to seek perfection in union."

At a hotel near the store for which she worked, an English traveller, called Lord Henry S———, had taken lodgings. He was a strikingly handsome man, and of princely carriage. As this distinguished stranger passed to and from his hotel, he encountered the umbrella girl, and was attracted by her uncommon beauty. Hs easily traced her to the store, where he soon after went to purchase an umbrella. This was followed up by presents of flowers, chats by the wayside, and invitations to walk or ride all ;

of which were gratefully accepted by the unsuspecting rustic; for she was as ignorant of the dangers of a city as were the squirrels of her native fields. He was merely playing a game for temporary excitement. She, with a head full of romance, and a heart melting under the influence of love, was unconsciously endangering the happiness of her whole life.

Lord Henry invited her to visit the public gardens on the fourth of July. In the simplicity of her heart, she believed all his flattering professions, and considered herself as his bride elect; she therefore accepted the invitation with innocent frankness. But she had no dress fit to appear in on such a public occasion, with a gentleman of high rank, who she vainly supposed to be her destined husband. While these thoughts revolved in her mind, her eye was unfortunately attracted by a beautiful piece of silk, belonging to her employer. Could she not take it without being seen, and pay for it secretly, when she had earned money enough? The temptation conquered her in a moment of weakness. She concealed the silk, and conveyed it to her lodgings. It was the first thing she had ever stolen, and her remorse was painful. She would have carried it back, but she dreaded discovery. She was not sure that her repentance would be met in a spirit of forgiveness.

On the evening of the fourth of July, she came out in her new dress. Lord Henry complimented her upon her elegant appearance, but she was not happy. On their way to the gardens, he talked to her in a manner which she did not comprehend. Perceiving this he spoke more explicitly. The guileless young creature stopped, looked in his face with mournful reproach, and burst into tears. The nobleman took her hand kindly and said, "My dear, are you an innocent girl?"

"I am, I am," she replied, with convulsive sobs. "Oh, what have I ever done, or said, that you should ask me such a question?"

The evident sincerity of her words stirred the deep fountains of his better nature. "If you are innocent," said he, "God forbid, that I should make you otherwise. But you accepted my invitation and presents so readily, that I supposed you understood me."

"What *could* I understand," said she, "except that you intended to make me your wife?"

Though reared amid the proudest distinctions of rank, he felt no inclination to smile. He blushed and was silent. The heartless conventionalities of the world stood rebuked in the presence of affectionate simplicity. He conveyed her to her humble home, and bade her farewell, with a thankful consciousness that he had done no irretrievable injury to her future prospects. The remembrance of her would soon be to him as the recollection of last year's butterflies. With her, the wound was deep. In the solitude of her chamber she wept in bitterness of heart over her ruined air-castles. And that dress, which she had stolen to make an appearance befitting his bride! Oh, what if she should be discovered? And would not the heart of her poor widowed mother break, if she ever knew that her child was a thief?

Alas, her wretched forbodings proved too true. The silk was traced to her; she was arrested on her way to the store and dragged to prison. There she refused all nourishment, and wept incessantly. On the fourth day, the keeper called upon Isaac T. Hopper, and informed him that there was a young girl in prison, who appeared to be utterly friendless, and determined to die by starvation. The kind-hearted Friend immediately went to her assistance. He found her lying on the floor of her cell, with her face buried in her hands, sobbing as if her heart would break. He tried to comfort her, but could obtain no answer.

"Leave us alone," said he to the keeper. "Perhaps she will speak to me, if there is no one to hear." When they were alone together, he put back the hair from her temples, laid his hand kindly on her beautiful head, and said in soothing tones, "My child, consider me as thy father, tell me all thou hast done. If thou hast taken this silk, let me know all about it. I will do for thee as I would for my own daughter; and I doubt not that I can help thee out of this difficulty."

After a long time spent in affectionate entreaty, she sobbed out, "Oh, I wish I was dead. What will my poor mother say, when she knows of my disgrace?"

"Perhaps we can manage that she never shall know it," replied he. Alluring her by this hope, he gradually obtained from her the whole story of her acquaintance with the nobleman. He bade her be comforted, and take nourishment; for he would see that the silk was paid for, and the prosecution withdrawn.

He went immediately to her employer, and told him the story. "This is her first offence," said he. "The girl is young, and she is the only child of a poor widow. Give her a chance to retrieve this one false step, and she may be restored to society, a useful and honoured woman. The man readily agreed to withdraw the prosecution, and said he would have dealt otherwise by the girl, if he had known all the circumstances. "Thou shouldst have inquired into the merits of the case," replied Friend Hopper. "By this kind of thoughtlessness, many a young creature is driven into the downward path, who might easily have been saved."

The kind-hearted man next proceeded to the hotel, and with Quaker simplicity of speech inquired for Henry S ——.

The servant said his lordship had not yet risen, "Tell him my business is of importance," said Friend Hopper. The servant soon returned and conducted him to the chamber. The nobleman appeared surprised that a stranger, in plain Quaker costume, should thus intrude upon his luxurious privacy. When he heard his errand, he blushed deeply, and frankly admitted the truth of the girl's statement. His benevolent visitor took the opportunity to "bear testimony" against the selfishness and sin of profligacy. He did it in such a kind and fatherly manner, that the young man's heart was touched. He excused himself, by saying he would not have tampered with the girl, if he had known her to be virtuous. "I have done many wrong things," said he, "but thank God, no betrayel of confiding innocence weighs on my conscience. I have always esteemed it the basest act of which a man is capable." The imprisonment of the poor girl, and the forlorn situation in which she had been found, distressed him greatly. When Friend Hopper represented that the silk had been stolen for *his* sake, that the girl had thereby lost profitable employment, and was obliged to return to her distant home, to avoid the danger of exposure, he took out a fifty dollar note, and offered it to pay her expenses.

"Nay," said Isaac. "Thou art a very rich man, I presume. I see in thy hand a large roll of such notes. She is the daughter of a poor widow, and thou hast been the means of doing her great injury. Give me another."

Lord Henry handed him another fifty dollar note, and smiled as he said, "You understand your business well. But you have acted nobly, and I reverence you for it. If you ever visit England, come to see me. I will give you a cordial welcome, and treat you like a nobleman."

"Farewell, friend," replied the Quaker. "Though much to blame in this affair thou too hast behaved nobly.

Mayst thou be blessed in domestic life, and trifle no more with the feelings of poor girls; not even with those whom others have betrayed and deserted."

When the girl was arrested, she had sufficient presence of mind to assume a false name, and by that means, her true name was kept out of the newspapers. " I did this," she said, "for my poor mother's sake." With the money given by Lord S——, the silk was paid for, and she was sent home well provided with clothing. Her name and place of residence for ever remained a secret in the breast of her benefactor.

Years after these events transpired, a lady called at Friend Hopper's house, and asked to see him. When he entered the room, he found a handsomely dressed young matron, with a blooming boy of five or six years old. She rose quickly to meet him, and her voice choked as she said, " Friend Hopper, do you know me? " He replied he did not. She fixed her tearful eyes earnestly upon him, and said, "You once helped me when in great distress." But the good missionary of humanity had helped too many in distress, to be able to recollect her without more precise information. With a tremulous voice, she bade her son go into the next room for a few minutes; then dropping on her knees, she hid her face in his lap, and sobbed out, " I am the girl who stole the silk. Oh, where should I now be, if it had not been for you! "

When her emotion was somewhat calmed, she told him that she had married a highly respectable man, a senator of his native state. Being on a visit in Friend Hopper's vicinity, she had again and again passed his dwelling, looking wistfully at the windows to catch a sight of him; but when she attempted to enter, her courage failed.

" But I must return home to morrow," said she, "and I could not go away without once more seeing and thanking him who saved me from ruin." She recalled her little boy, and said to him, "Look at that gentleman, and remember him well; for he was the best friend your mother ever had." With an earnest invitation to visit her happy home, and a fervent "God bless you!" she bade her benefactor farewell.

IN DANGER AT SEA.

Returning from England, the vessel encountered a dense fog, and ran on a sand bank as they approached the Jersey shore. A tremendous sea was rolling, and dashed against the ship with such force, that she seemed every moment in danger of being shattered into fragments. If there had been a violent gale of wind, all must have been inevitably lost. The passengers were generally in a state of extreme terror. Screams and groans were heard in every direction. But Friend Hopper's mind was preserved in a state of great equanimity. He entreated the people to be quiet, and try to keep possession of their faculties, that they might be ready to do whatever was best in case of emergency. Seeing him so calm, they gathered closely round him, as if they thought he had some power to save them. There was a naval officer on board, whose frenzied state of feeling vented itself in blasphemous language. Friend Hopper, who was always disturbed by irreverent use of the name of Deity, was peculiarly shocked by it under these circumstances. He walked up to the officer, put his hand on his shoulder, and looking him in the face, said, "From what I have heard of thy military exploits, I supposed thou wert a brave man ; but here thou art pouring out blasphemies, to keep up the appearance of courage, while thy pale face and quivering lips show thou art in mortal fear. I am ashamed of thee. If thou hast no reverence for Deity thyself, thou shouldst show some regard for the feelings of those who have. The officer ceased swear-

ing, and treated his advisor with marked respect. A
friendship was formed between them, which continued as
long as the captain lived.

A clergyman on board afterwards said to Friend Hopper,
"If any other person had talked to him in that manner, he
would have knocked him down.

An Uncomplimentary Invitation.

A preacher of the Society of friends felt impressed with the
duty of calling a mee ting for vicious people; and Isaac T.
Hopper was appointed to collect an audience. In the course
of this mission, he knocked at the door of a very infamous
house. A gentleman who was acquainted with him was passing by, and he stopped to say, "Friend Hopper, you have
mistaken the house."

"No, I have not," he replied.

"But that is a house of notorious ill fame," said the gentleman.

"I know it," rejoined he; "but nevertheless, I have
business here."

His acquaintance looked surprised, but passed on without
further query. A coloured girl came to the door. To the
inquiry whether her mistress was in, she answered in the
affirmative. "Tell her I wish to see her," said Friend
Hopper. The girl was evidently astonished at a visitor in
Quaker costume, and of such grave demeanour; but she went
and did the errand. A message was returned that her mistress was engaged and could not see any one. "Where is
she?" he inquired. The girl replied that she was upstairs.
"I will go to her," said the importunate messenger.

The mistress of the house heard him, and leaning over the
balustrade of the stairs, she screamed out, "What do you
want with me, sir?"

In very loud tones he answered, "James Simpson, a min-

i-ter of the Society of Friends, has appointed a meeting to be
held this afternoon, in Penrose store, Almond-street. It is
intended for publicans, sinners, and harlots. I want thee to
be there, and bring thy whole household with thee. Wilt
thou come?"

She promised that she would; and he afterwards saw her
at the meeting melted into tears by the direct and affectionate
preaching.

THE TITLE REVEREND.

Isaac T. Hopper, being called upon to give a receipt to
a Catholic priest for some money deposited in his hands, he
simply wrote "Received of John Smith." When the priest
had read it, he handed it back and said, "I am disbursing
other people's money, and shall be obliged to show this
receipt; therefore, I should like to have you write my name,
the Reverend John Smith." "I have conscientious scruples
against using titles," replied Friend Hopper. "However
I will try to oblige thee." He took another slip of paper,
and wrote, "Received of John Smith, who *calls* himself the
Reverend." The priest smiled, and accepted the compro-
mise, being well aware that the pleasantry originated in no
personal or sectarian prejudice.

THE QUAKER AT THE LORD LIEUTENANT'S CASTLE

One day, when Friend Hopper was walking with a lawyer
in Dublin, they passed the Lord Lieutenant's Castle. He
expressed a wish to see the Council Chamber, but was
informed that it was not open to strangers. "I have a
mind to go and try," said he to his companion. "Wilt
thou go with me?"

"No indeed," he replied; "and I would advise you not
to go."

He marched in, however, with his broad beaver on, and found the Lord Lieutenant surrounded by a number of gentlemen. "I am an American," said he. "I have heard a great deal about the Lord Lieutenant's Castle, and if it will give no offence, I should very much like to see it."

His lordship seemed surprised by this unceremonious introduction, but he smiled, and said to a servant, "show this American whatever he wishes to see."

He was conducted into various apartments, where he saw pictures, statues, ancient armour, antique coins, and many other curious articles.

At parting, the master of the mansion was extremely polite, and gave him much interesting information on a variety of topics. When he rejoined his companion who had agreed to wait for him at some appointed place, he was met with the inquiry, "Well, what luck?"

"O, the best luck in the world," he replied. "I was treated with great politeness"

"Well certainly, Mr. Hopper, you are an extraordinary man," responded the lawyer. "I would'nt have ventured to try such an experiment."

A QUAKER'S LETTER.

The following letter from an aged Quaker shows that their system is not opposed to real enjoyment even in old age—"Dear Friend, the days have not yet come, in which I can say I have no pleasure in them. Notwithstanding the stubs against which I hit my toes, the briars and thorns that sometimes annoy me, and the muddy sloughs I am sometimes obliged to wade through, yet after all, the days have *not* come in which I have no enjoyment. In the course of my journey, I find here and there a green spot, by which I can sit down and rest, and pleasant streams, where I sometimes drink, mostly in secret and am refreshed. I often remember the saying of a beloved friend, long since translated from this scene of mutation to a state of eternal beatitude: "I wear my sackcloth on my loins; I don't wish to afflict others by carrying a sorrowful countenance." A wise conclusion. I love to diffuse happiness over all with whom I come in contact. But all this is a kind of accident. I took up my pen to tell thee about our garden. I never saw it half so handsome as it is now. Morning Glories are on both sides of the yard; extending nearly to the second story windows, and they exhibit their glories every morning, in beautiful style. There are Cypress vines, twelve feet high running up on the pillar before the kitchen window, and spreading out each way. They blossom most profusely. The wooden wall is covered with Madeira vines, and the stone wall with Woodbine. The grass-plot is very thrifty, and our borders are beautified with a variety of flowers. How wouldst thou like to look at them!

The Quakeress and her Footman.

Nicholas Waln was a wealthy Friend—a true gentleman, of courtly, pleasing manners, and amusing conversation. Notwithstanding his weight of character, he was so playful with the children, that his visits were always hailed by them, as delightful opportunities for fun and frolic. He looked beneath the surface of society, and had learned to estimate men and things according to their real value, not by a conventional standard. His wife did not regard the pomps and vanities of the world with precisely the same degree of indifference that he did. She thought it would be suitable to their wealth and station to have a footman behind her carriage. This wish being frequently expressed, her husband at last promised to comply with it. Accordingly, the next time the carriage was ordered, for the purpose of making a stylish call, she was gratified to see a footman mounted. When she arrived at her place of destination, the door of the carriage was opened, and the steps let down in a very obsequious manner, by the new servant; and great was her surprise and confusion, to recognize in him her own husband!

FREEDOM FROM PREJUDICE AGAINST COLOUR.

The following very characteristic anecdote shows how completely Isaac Hopper was free from prejudice on account of complexion. It is an unusual thing to see a coloured Quaker; for the African temperament is fervid and impressible, and requires more exciting forms of religion. David Maps and his wife, a very worthy couple, were the only coloured members of the Yearly Meeting to which Isaac Hopper belonged. On the occasion of the annual gathering in Philadelphia, they came with other members of the Society to share the hospitality of his house. A question arose in the family whether Friends of white complexion would object to eating with them. "Leave that to me," said the master of the household. Accordingly when the time arrived, he announced it thus: "Friends, dinner is now ready. David Maps and his wife will come with me; and as I like to have all accommodated, those who object to dining with them can wait till they have done." The guests smiled, and all seated themselves at the table.

THE PROFANE PRINTER.

The conscientiousness of Friend Hopper in his treatment of a coloured printer named Kane, is worthy of record. This man was noted for his profane swearing. Issac had expostulated with him concerning this bad habit, without producing the least effect. One day, he encountered him in the street pouring forth a volley of terrible oaths, enough to make one shudder. Believing him incurable by gentler means, he took him before a magistrate who fined him for blasphemy.

He did not see the man again for a long term; but twenty years afterward, when he was standing at his door, Kane passed by. The Friend's heart was touched by his appearance; for he looked old, feeble, and poor. He stepped out, shook hands with him, and said in kindly tones, "Dost thou remember me, and how I caused thee to be fined for swearing?"

"Yes, indeed I do," he replied. "I remember how many dollars I paid, as well as if it were but yesterday."

"Did it do thee any good," inquired Friend Hopper.

"Never a bit," answered he. "It only made me mad to have my money taken from me."

The poor man was invited to walk into the house. The interest was calculated on the fine, and every cent repaid to him. "I meant it for thy good," said the benevolent Quaker; "and I am sorry that I only provoked thee." Kane's countenance changed at once, and tears began to flow. He took the money with many thanks, and was never again heard to swear.

FRIEND HOPPER AND HIS HAT.

Upon one occasion, Friend Hopper went into the Court of Chancery in Dublin, and kept his hat on, according to Quaker custom. While he was listening to the pleading, he noticed that a person who sat near the Chancellor fixed his eyes upon him with a very stern expression. This attracted the attention of lawyers and spectators, who also began to look at him. Presently an officer tapped him on the shoulder, and said, "Your hat, sir!"

L.

"What's the matter with my hat?" he inquired.

"Take it off!" rejoined the officer. "You are in his Majesty's Court of Chancery."

"That is an honour I reserve for his Majesty's Master," he replied. "Perhaps it is my shoes thou meanest?"

The officer seemed embarrassed, but said no more; and when the Friend had stayed as long as he felt inclined, he quietly withdrew.

While in Bristol, he asked permission to look at the interior of the Cathedral. He had been walking about some little time, when a rough looking man said to him, in a very surly tone, "Take off your hat, sir!"

He replied very courteously, "I have asked permission to enter here to gratify my curiosity as a stranger. I hope it is no offence."

"Take off your hat!" rejoined the man. "If you don't I'll take it off for you."

Friend Hopper leaned on his cane, looked him full in the face, and answered very coolly, "If thou dost, I hope thou wilt send it to my lodgings; for I shall have need of it this afternoon. I lodge at No. 35, Lower Crescent, Clifton." The place designated was about a mile from the Cathedral. The man stared at him, as if puzzled to decide whether he were talking to an insane person, or not. When the imperturbable Quaker had seen all he cared to see, he deliberately walked away.

At Westminster Abbey, he paid the customary fee of two shillings and sixpence, for admission. The doorkeeper followed him, saying, "You must uncover yourself, sir."

"Uncover myself!" exclaimed the Friend, with an affectation of ignorant simplicity. "What dost thou mean? Must I take off my coat?"

"Your coat!" responded the man, smiling. "No indeed. I mean your hat."

"And what should I take off my hat for?" he inquired.
" Because you are in a church, sir," answered the door-keeper.
" I see no church here," rejoined the Quaker. " Perhaps thou meanest the house where the church assembles. I suppose thou art aware that it is the *people*, not the *building*, that constitutes a church ?"

The idea seemed new to the man, but he merely repeated, " You must take off your hat, sir."

But the Friend again inquired, " What for ? On account of these images ? Thou knowest Scripture commands us not to worship graven images."

The man persisted in saying that no person could be permitted to pass through the church without uncovering his head. " Well, Friend," rejoined Isaac, " I have some conscientious scruples on the subject; so give me back my money, and I will go out."

The reverential habits of the door-keeper were not quite strong enough to compel him to that sacrifice, and he walked away without saying anything more on the subject.

A QUAKER IN THE HOUSE OF LORDS.

When Friend Hopper visited the House of Lords, he asked the sergeant-at-arms if he might sit upon the throne' He replied, " No, sir. No one but his majesty sits there.'

" Wherein does his majesty differ from other men?" inquired he. " If his head were cut off, would'nt he die?"

" Certainly he would," replied the officer.

" So would an American," rejoined Friend Hopper. As he spoke, he stepped up to the gilded railing that surrounded the throne, and tried to open the gate. The officer told him it was locked. " Well won't the same key that locked it unlock it?" inquired he. " Is the key hanging here?"

Being informed that it was, he tooked it down and unlocked

the gate. He removed the satin covering from the throne, carefully dusted the railing with his handkerchief, before he hung the satin over it, and then seated himself in the royal chair. "Well," said he, "do I look anything like his majesty?"

"The man seemed embarrassed, but smiled as he answered, "Why, sir, you certainly fill the throne very respectably."

There were several nob'emen in the room, who seemed to be extremely amused by these unusual proceedings.

THE MUSICAL BOY.

One day, when Friend Hopper visited the prison, he found a dark-eyed lad with a very bright expression of countenance, his right side was palsied, so that the arm hung down useless. Attracted by his intelligent face, he entered into conversation with him, and found that he had been palsied from his infancy. He had been sent forth friendless into the world from an alms-house in Maryland. In Philadelphia, he had been committed to prison as a vagrant, because he drew crowds about him in the streets by his wonderful talent of imitating a hand-organ, merely by whistling tunes through his fingers. Friend Hopper, who had imbibed the Quaker idea that music was a useless and frivolous pursuit, said to the boy, 'Didst thou not know it was wrong to spend thy time in that idle manner.

With ready frankness the young prisoner replied, "No, I did not; and I should like to hear how *you* could prove it to be wrong God has given you sound limbs. Half of my body is paralyzed, and it is impossible for me to work as others do. It has pleased God to give me a talent for music. I do no harm with it. It gives pleasure to myself and others, and enables me to gain a few coppers to buy my bread. I should like to have you show me wherein it is wrong."

Without attempting to do so, the Quaker suggested that perhaps he had been committed to prison on account of producing noise and confusion in the streets.

"I make no riot," rejoined the youth. "I try to please people by my tunes; and if the crowd around me begin to be noisy, I quietly walk off."

Struck with the good sense and sincerity of these answers, Friend Hopper said to the jailor, "Thou mayest set this lad at liberty. I will be responsible for it."

The jailor relying on his well-known character, and his intimacy with Robert Wharton, the Mayor did not hesitate to comply with his request. At that moment, the Mayor himself came in sight, and Friend Hopper said to the lad, "Step into the next room, and play some of thy best tunes till I come."

"What's this?" said Mr. Wharton. "Have you got a hand-organ here!"

"Yes," replied Friend Hopper; "and I will show it to thee. It is quite curious."

At first, the Mayor could not believe that the sounds he he had heard were produced by a lad merely whistling through his fingers. He thought them highly agreeable, and asked to have the tunes repeated.

"The lad was committed to prison for no other offence than making that noise, which seems to thee so pleasant," said Friend Hopper. "I dare say thou wouldst like to make it thyself if thou couldst. I have taken the liberty to discharge him."

"Very well," rejoined the Mayor, with a smile. "You have done quite right, Friend Isaac. You may go, my lad. I shall not trouble you. But try not to collect crowds in the streets."

"That I cannot help," replied the youth "The crowds

will come, when I whistle for them; and I get coppers by collecting crowds. But I will promise you I will try to avoid their making any riot or confusion."

Not Thoroughly Baptized.

Upon a certain occasion, a man called on Friend Hopper with a due bill for twenty dollars against an estate he had been employed to settle. Hopper put it away, saying he would examine it and attend to it as soon as he had leisure. The man called again a short time after, and stated that he had need of six dollars, and was willing to give a receipt for the whole if that sum were advanced. This proposition excited suspicion, and the administrator decided in his own mind that he would pay nothing till he had examined the papers of the deceased. Searching carefully among these, he found a receipt for the money, mentioning the identical items, date, and circumstances of the transaction; stating that a due bill had been given and lost, and was to be restored by the creditor when found. When the man called for payment, Isaac said to him, in a quiet way, "Friend Jones, I understand thou hast become pious lately."

He replied in a solemn tone, "Yes, thanks to the Lord Jesus, I have found out the way of salvation.

"And thou hast been dipped, I hear," continued the Quaker. "Dost thou know James Hunter?"

Mr. Jones answered in the affirmative.

"Well, he also was dipped some time ago," rejoined Friend Hopper; "but his neighbours say they didn't get the crown of his head under water. The devil crept into the unbaptized part, and has been busy with him ever since.

I am afraid they didn't get *thee* quite under water. I think thou hadst better be dipped again."

As he spoke, he held up the receipt for twenty dollars. The countenance of the professedly pious man became scarlet,

The Metal Buttons.

Jacob Lindley was a preacher in the Society of Friends, and missed no opportunity, either in public or private, to protest earnestly against slavery. He often cautioned Friends against laying too much stress on their own peculiar forms, while they professed to abjure forms. He said he himself had once received a lesson on this subject, which did him much good. Once when he was seated in meeting, an influential Friend walked in, dressed in a coat with large metal buttons, which he had borrowed in consequence of a drenching rain! He seated himself opposite to Jacob Lindley, who was so much disturbed by the glittering buttons, that "his meeting did him no good." When the congregation rose to depart, he felt constrained to go up to the friend who had so much troubled him, and inquire why he had so greviously departed from the simplicity enjoined upon members of their Society. The good man looked down upon his garments, and quietly replied, "I borrowed the coat because my own was wet; and indeed Jacob, I did not notice what buttons were on it." Jacob shook his hand warmly and said, "Thou art a better christian than I am, and I will learn of thee."

The Ruling Passion Strong in Death.

Elias Hicks, a strong and earnest Quaker preacher, appears to have been a very just and conscientious man, with great reverence for God, and exceedingly little for human authority. Everywhere, in public and in private, he lifted up his voice against the sin of slavery. He would eat no sugar that was made by slaves, and wear no garments which he supposed to have been produced by unpaid labour. In a remarkable manner, he showed this "ruling passion strong in death." A few hours before he departed from this world, his friends, seeing him shiver, placed a comfortable over him. He felt of it with his feeble hands, and made a strong effort to push

it away. When they again drew it over his shoulders, he
manifested the same symptons of abhorrence. One of them
who began to conjecture the cause, inquired, " Dost thou
dislike it because it is made of cotton ? " He was too far
gone to speak, but he moved his head in token of assent.
When they removed the article of slave produce, and sub-
stituted a woollen blanket, he remained quiet, and passed
away in peace.

THE COCKED HAT LOOPED UP WITH A BUTTON.

In old times, when Quakers were accustomed to wear
cocked hats turned up at the sides, a Friend bought a hat of
this description, without observing that it was looped up
with a button. As he sat in meeting with his hat on, as
usual, he observed many eyes directed toward him, and some
with a very sorrowful expression. He could not conjecture
a reason for this, till he happened to take off his hat and lay
it beside him. As soon as he noticed the button, he rose and
said, " Friends, if religion consists in a button, I wouldn't
give a button for it." Having delivered this short and pithy
sermon, he seated himself, and resumed the offending hat
with the utmost composure.

A COMICAL ADVENTURE.

Bernard Barton, the celebrated Quaker Poet in one of
his letters says :—" I met with a comical adventure the
other day, which partly amused, partly piqued me. We
had a religious visit paid to our little meeting here by a
minister of our Society, an entire stranger, I believe, to
every one in the meeting. He gave us some very plain,
honest counsel. After meeting, as is usual, several, indeed
most, Friends stopped to shake hands with our visitor, I
among the rest; and on my name being mentioned to him,
rather officiously I thought, by one standing by, the good

old man said, "Barton?—Barton?—that's a name I don't recollect." I told him it would be rather strange if he did, as we had never seen each other before. Suddenly, when, to my no small gratification, no one was attending to us, he looked rather inquiringly at me, and added, "What art thou the Versifying Man?" On my replying with a gravity, which I really think was heroic, that I was called such, he looked at me again, I thought "more in sorrow than in anger," and observed, "Ah! that's a thing quite out of my way." It was on the tip of my tongue to reply, "I dare say it,"—but, afraid that I could not control my risible faculties much longer, I shook my worthy friend once more by the hand, and bidding him farewell left him.

I dare say the good soul may have since thought of me, if at all, with much the same feelings as if I had been bitten by a mad dog—and I know not but that he may be very right."

STRANGE REQUEST.

A complimentary copy of verses which Bernard Barton had addressed to the author of the "Queen's Wake," (just then coming into notice) brought him long and vehement letters from the Ettrick Shepherd, full of thanks to Barton and praises of himself; and along with this a tragedy "that will astonish the world ten times more than the Queen's Wake has done," a tragedy of so many characters in it of equal importance "that justice cannot be done to it in Edinburgh," and therefore the author confidently intrusts it to Bernard Barton to get it represented in London. Theatres and managers of theatres, being rather out of the Quaker poet's way, he called into council Capel Lofft, with whom he also corresponded, and from whom he also received flying visits in the course of Lofft's attendance at the county sessions. Lofft took the matter into consideration, and promised all assistance, but on the whole dissuaded Hogg from trying London managers; he himself having sent three tragedies of his own; and others by friends of "transcendent merit equal to Miss Baillie's, all of which had fallen on barren ground."

This was not Bernard Barton's nearest approach to theatrical honours. In 1822 (just after the review on him in the Edinburgh,) his niece Elizabeth Hock writes to him, "Aunt Lizzy tells us, that when one of the Sharp's was at Paris some little time ago, there was a party of English actors performing plays. One night he was in the theatre, and an actor of the name of Barton was announced, when the audience called out to inquire if it was the Quaker poet."

Memoir of Bernard Barton.

CHARITABLE JUDGMENT.

It is supposed by many that the Quakers are a very austere and precise class of people, destitute of sympathy with people of a more demonstrative temperament. The following lines by Bernard Barton addressed to a friend by no means sanction the idea. He says "I send thee the annexed little tribute, (A memorial to T. H.) not to challenge any laud for its poetical merits, nor because the character it commemorates had much of what scholars and critics would call poetical in his composition, but simply because *his* had *the elements*, the material of such *in my eye*. He was a hearty old yeoman of about eighty six—had occupied the farm about fifty-five years. Social, hospitable, friendly; a liberal master to his labourers, a kind neighbour, and a right merry companion "within the limits of becoming mirth." In politics, a staunch Whig; in his theological creed, as sturdy a Dissenter; yet with no more party spirit in him than a child. He and I belonged to the same book club for about forty years. He entered it about fifteen years before I came into these parts, and was really a pillar in our literary temple. Not that he greatly cared about books, or was deeply read in them, but he loved to meet his neighbours, and get them round him, on any occasion, or no occasion at all. As a fine specimen of the true English Yeoman, I have met few to equal, hardly any to surpass him, and he looked the character as well as he acted it, til within a very few years, when the strong man was bowed by bodily infirmity. About twenty-six years ago, in his dress costume of a blue coat and yellow buckskins, a finer sample of John Bullism you would rarely see. It was the whole study of his long life to make a few who revolved round him in his little orbit, as happy as he always seemed to be himself; yet I was gravely queried with, when I happened to say that his children had asked me to write a few lines to his memory, whether I could do this in keeping with the general tone of my poetry. The speaker doubted if he was a decidedly pious character. He had at times, in his altitudes, been known to vociferate at the top of his voice, a song of which the chorus was certainly not teetotalish—

"Sing old Rose and burn the bellows,
    Drink and drive dull care away."

I would not deny the vocal impeachment, for I had heard him sing the song myself, though not for the last dozen years. As for his being or not being a decidely pious character, that depended greatly on who might be called on to decide the question. He was not a man of much profession, but he was a most diligent attender of his place of worship and frequently I believe a serious reader of his Bible, and kept an orderly and well-regulated house. In his blither moods I certainly have heard him sing that questionable ditty before referred to, but, as it appeared to me, not under vinous excitement

so much as from an unforced hilarity which habitually found
vent in that explosion; and I think he never in my presence
volunteered that song. It was pretty sure to be asked for once
in a while, by some who liked to hear themselves join in the
chorus. I believe it was his only one, with the exception of
Watt's hymns, which he almost knew by heart, and sang on
Sunday, at meeting, with equal fervour and unction. Take
the good old man for all in all, I look not to see his like again,
for the breed is going out I fear. His fine spirit of humanity
was better, methinks, than much of that which apes the tone
and assumes the form of divinity. So now 1 think 1 have
told thee enough to weary thee, in prose, as well as verse, of
my old neighbour and friend the Suffolk Yeoman.

BERNARD BARTON ON GRAVE-STONES.

Referring to an order he had sent to Carlisle to repair his
grandfather's tomb, he writes in 1846. " Perhaps our good
friend demurs as to the propriety of a Quaker poet having
aught to do with church grave-stones. On this point however, should such be his idea, he is mistaken. I could wish
grave-stones were allowed in our own burial-grounds, a discretionary power being vested in proper quarters as to what
is allowed to be put on them. Confine it, and welcome, to
name, date, and age; rigidly interdict all flattery and folly
But I own it would feel pleasant to me to know the precise
spot where those I have loved lay. I never feel quite sure
which is my Lucy's grave out of the family row. That 1
might have no doubt which was my mother Jesup's, I planted a tree at the foot of it, which is now three times my own
height."

QUAKER-COOKS AND SERVANTS VERY SCARCE.

Bernard Barton in, a letter to a clergyman writes " On behalf
of Ann, who, I am sorry to say, is not well enough to write

herself—I am requested to say that we are quite unable to recommend thee a cook of any kind : as to Quaker cooks, they are so scarce that we Quaker folk are compelled to call in the aid of the daughters of the land to dress our viands, or cook them ourselves, as well as we can. But what, my dear friend, could put it into thy head to think of a Quaker cook of all-nondescripts. * * * * Thou thoughtest we were civil, *cleanly*. quiet, &c., all excellent qualities, doubtless, in women of all kinds, cooks not excluded. But, my dear friend, I should be sorry the reputation of our sect for the posession of these qualities should be exposed to the contingent vexations which culinary mortals are exposed to. "A cook whilst cooking is a sort of fury," says the old poet. Ay! but not a Quaker cook, at least in the favourable and friendly opinion of Adine and thyself:—we are very proud of that good opinion and I would not risk its forfeiture by sending one of our sisterhood to thee as cook. Suppose an avalanche of soot to plump down the chimney the first gala-day— 'twould be cookship versus Quakership, whether the poor body kept her sectarian serenity unruffled; and suppose the beam kicked the wrong way, what would become of all our reputation in the temporary good opinion of Adine and thee? But, all bandiage apart, even in our own Society there are comparatively few who are in the situation of domestic servants, and I never remember but one in the peculiar office referred to. I much doubt whether one could be found at all likely to suit you ; and I have little doubt that you may suit yourselves much better out of our sisterhood than in it.

BERNARD BARTON—NO BIGOT.

It is remarked of the Quaker poet—"that while he had well considered and well approved the pure principles of Quakerism, he was equally liberal in his recognition of other forms of Christianity.   He could attend the *Church* or the *Chapel*, if the *meeting* were not at hand; and once assisted in raising money to build a new *Established Church* in Woodbridge.   And while he was sometimes roused to defend Dissent from the vulgar attacks of High Church and Tory, he could also give the bishops a good word when they were unjustly assailed from another quarter."

Here is a little Epigram showing that the quiet Quaker *could* strike, though he was seldom provoked to do so.

Dr. E———.

> "A bullying, brawling champion of the Church;
> Vain as a parrot screaming on her perch;
> And, like that parrot, screaming out by rote
> The same stale, flat, unprofitable note;
> Still interrupting all discreet debate
> With one eternal cry of Church and State!—
> With all the High Tory's ignorance, increased
> By all the arrogance, that marks the priest;
> One who declares upon his solemn word,
> The voluntary system is absurd:
> He well may say so;—for 'twere hard to tell
> Who would support him, did not law compel."

While duly conforming to the usages of his Society on all proper occasions, he could forget *thee* and *thou* while mixing in social intercourse with people of another vocabulary, and smile at the Reviewer who reproved him for using the heathen name *November* in his Poems.   "I find," he said, "these names of the months the prescriptive dialect of *poetry*, used as such by many members of our Society before me—' *sans peur et sans reproche*;' and I use them accordingly, asking no questions for conscience sake, as to their origin.   Yet while I do this, I can give my cordial tribute of approval to the scruples of our early friends, who advocate a simpler nomenclature.   I can quite understand and respect their simplicity and godly sincerity; and I conceive that I have duly shown my reverence for their scruples in adhering *personally* to their dialect and only using another *poetically*. Ask the British Friend the name of the planet with a belt round it, and he would say, Saturn; at the peril, and on the pain, of excommunication."

A QUAKER'S DEFENCE.

Bernard Barton in 1846 writes:—"And now my dear old friend of about twenty years standing, I have two points on which I must try to right myself in thy good opinion—the swansdown waistcoat, and the bell, with the somewhat unquakerly inscription of "Mr. Barton's bell" graven above the handle thereof. I could not well suppress a smile at both counts of the indictment, for both are true to a certain extent, though I do not know that I should feel at all bound to plead guilty to either in a criminal one. It is true that prior to my birthday, now nearly two years ago, my daughter, without consulting me, did work for me, in worsted work, as they do now-a-days for slippers, a piece of sempstress-ship or needle-craft, forming the forepart of a waistcoat; the pattern of which, being rather larger than I should have chosen, had choice been allowed me, gave it some semblance of the striped or flowered waistcoats which for ought I know may be designated as swansdown; but the colours, drab and chocolate, were so very sober, that I put it on as I found it, thinking no evil, and wore it, first on week-days, all last winter, and may probably through the coming one, at least on week-days. It is cut in my wonted single-breasted fashion; and as my collarless coat, coming pretty forward, allows no great display of it, I had not heard before a word of scandal, or even censure on its unfriendliness. Considering who worked it for me, I am not sure had the royal arms been worked thereon, if in such sober colours, but I might have worn it, and thought it less fine and less fashionable than the velvet and silk ones which I have seen, ere now, in our galleries, and worn by Friends of high standing and undoubted orthodoxy.   But I attach comparatively little importance to dress, while there is enough left in the *tout ensemble* of the costume to give ample evidence that the wearer is a Quaker. So much for the waistcoat; now for the bell!   I live in the back part of the Bank premises, and the approach to the yard leading to my habitat, is by a gate, opening out of the principal street or thoroughfare through our town.   The same gate serving for an approach to my cousin's kitchen door, to a large bar-iron warehouse in the same yard, and I know not what beside.   Under these circumstances some notification was thought to be needful to mark the bell appertaining to our domicile, though I suppose nearly a hundred yards off, and the bell-hanger without consultation with me, and without my knowledge, had put these words over the handle of the bell, in a recess or hole in the wall by the gate-side, and they had stood there unnoticed and unobserved by me for weeks, if not months, before I saw them.   When aware of their being there, having had no concern whatever in their being put there, having given no directions for their inscription, and not having to pay for them, I quietly let them stand; and, until thy letter reached me, I have never heard one word of comment on said inscription as an unquakerly one, for I believe it is well known among all our neighbours that the job of making two houses out of one was done by contract with artizans not of us, who executed their commission according to usual custom, without taking our phraseology into account.   Such my good friend, are the simple facts of the two cases."

RESTITUTION.

Mr. Richards in his Life of Joseph Sturge, remarks, "Two or three years before his death, he took his own children to

Kingley to show them the spot where their father had spent so much of his childhood. Out of that there grew a little incident which strikingly illustrates the tenderness of conscience for which he was remarkable through life. As he passed through the familiar scenes of his early days, amid the crowd of pensive and tender associations that, no doubt, thronged through his mind, there was one of a painful nature, because connected with an act of childish wrongdoing. Walking through the village of Wicksford, in company with Mr. Joseph Bayzand, the present occupant of Kingley, they came to a public-house dignified with the name of the 'Fish Inn,' at the sight of which there flashed through his memory the fact, that, nearly sixty years before, he and a servant-boy of his grandfather's had obtained from the landlady of the house a change in copper for a six-penny piece which they knew to be bad. Trivial as many would be disposed to regard such an offence, Joseph Sturge could not rest satisfied until he had made what atonement he could for this sin of his youth. Accordingly on his return to Birmingham he wrote the following letter to Mr. Bayzand :—

'Esteemed Friend,—The kind attention I received from thee when calling at Kingley with some of my family the summer before last has often induced me to write thee a few lines on a matter which, though it may appear a trifle has, whenever it has passed across my memory, caused me uneasiness. It is now, I believe, nearer sixty than fifty years ago (at the age of about nine years, I think) I was guilty, in conjunction with one of my grandfather's servant boys, of defrauding the landlady of the Fish Inn at Wicksford (Mrs. Haynes) of sixpence, by getting change in copper for a sixpenny piece which we knew not to be a good one. How far I was led into it by the servant boy, who was older than I, I cannot tell, but it would be a satisfaction to

M

me to pay two hundred fold, say £5, to such relatives of the Mrs Haynes we acted so unjustly to, as were she living, she would most wish to assist, if thou could'st kindly put me in the way of doing so. From inquiry I made when with thee at Wicksford, and which thou wilt see was not altogether dictated by curiosity, I think I understood that there was no direct descendant of Mrs. Haynes living; but if thou think'st the money can be satisfactorily appropriated, please to let me know. But perhaps there will be no advantage in letting my motive for giving it be known beyond thyself, though I have no strong objection to it. Hoping thou wilt excuse a stranger for giving thee so much trouble.'

'I am, very respectfully,

Thy obliged friend,

Joseph Sturge.

The inquisition was accordingly made, and it was discovered that there *was* a grandaughter of Mrs. Haynes living at Wicksford, with a large family, in no very flourishing circumstances, to whom the five pounds was given, and proved no doubt a welcome boon.

AN HONOURABLE ACTION.

Mr. Richard writes "A further illustration of the high standard of conscientiousness maintained in their trade transactions by Joseph Sturge and his brother, is furnished by the following circumstance which came accidentally to the knowledge of a friend, by whom it has been communicated to us. The friend was staying at an hotel at Harrogate, and having had occasion to write to Joseph Sturge, laid the letter on the table. A gentleman present observing the address, enquired if he were acquainted with Mr. Sturge, and on being informed that they were intimate friends, he remarked—

He is one of the most honourable and upright men I know. I reside in Ireland, and am in the corn trade, and have had business transactions with Messrs. Sturge. Some years ago a cargo of grain was passing between us, and by some unavoidable circumstances the vessel met with serious detention, entailing very considerable loss. A question arose between us as to the party on whom the loss should devolve; and not being able to settle it ourselves, it was mutually agreed to refer it. The award was given, and the transaction accordingly arranged. A few months afterwards our firm received a letter from Messrs. Sturge, stating that, on deliberate reconsideration of all the circumstances, they had reached the conclusion that the decision of the referee was unduly in their favour, and they therefore enclosed a draft for three hundred pounds, which would be to them an equitable and satisfactory adjustment of the affair."

JOSEPH STURGE'S APOLOGY TO A WORKING MAN.

Mr. Richard remarks "Joseph Sturge spoke of himself, in his school-boy days, as having rather a peppery temper. And bravely as he struggled all through life to conquer it, it seems there were still occasional ebullitions of the old vehemence. And when he had erred, or imagined he had erred in this respect, his penitence was profound, and the amends he made magnanimous. The Rev. J. H. Wilson, who was once associated with Mr. Sturge in some of his labours at Birmingham, tells an anecdote which is beautifully illustrative of this. At one of the stormy political meetings which were often held in the town, in connection with the question of the suffrage, a working-man opposed some proposal of his with a pertinacity and passion which provoked Mr. Sturge to rebuke him, in words which no one else thought particularly harsh or offensive. Still, when the excitement was over, the remembrance of them grieved him deeply. The next morning he sent for Mr. Wilson, and said to him, 'James, thou must find out that working-man to whom I spoke last night, and bring him to me.' 'But I don't know his name, or where he lives,' was the reply. 'It doesn't signify,' answered he, 'he *must* be found; I have not slept all night for thinking of the words I said to him. I can't rest until I have apologised and asked his pardon.' The quest was made, and the man was found and brought to him, and he did apologise with a manly candour and humility that went straight to the poor fellow's heart. From that time he took the man by the hand, and be-friended him for years."

JOSEPH STURGE RETRENCHING EXPENDITURE.

"Twice, at least (says Mr. Pumphrey,) he lost a consid-erable portion of his property, and, with his characteristic decision, he at once reduced his expenditure to his altered circumstances. On one occasion, for three years in success-ion, he limited his expenses to £100 a year, and during that period was known sometimes to deny himself a dinner, that he might have something to bestow on the more necess-itous. On another occasion, rather later in life, but before his marriage, he entirely gave up housekeeping. He often recurred in conversation with intimate friends to the bene-fit he had derived from this resolute course of self-denial, and the satisfaction it afforded him in the retrospect. How rarely do even Christian men in similar circumstances possess the courage necessary to recognise their true position, and, instead of indulging in that perilous casuistry so pre-valent, in our day, that appearances must be kept up or credit will suffer, act on the principle that what is morally wrong cannot be commercialy right."

SUPPLYING THE PROOF.

Mr. Cobden says, " I remember a very graphic description which Lord Brougham gave me in a conversation at his house in Grafton Street, of Joseph Sturge's conduct in the matter of the apprenticeship system, which he adduced as an illustration of our friend's indomitable energy. He told me of Mr. Sturge coming to him to arraign the conduct of the masters in the West Indies for oppressing their apprentices ; how he (Brougham) laughed at him, deriding him in this fashion for proposing to abolish the apprenticeship : ' Why, Joseph Sturge, how can you be such an old woman as to dream that you can revive the anti-slavery agitation to put an end to the apprenticeship?' how the quiet Quaker met him with this reply : 'Lord Brougham, if when Lord Chancellor thou hadst a ward in Chancery who was apprenticed, and his master was violating the terms of indenture, what wouldst thou do?' how he felt this a home-thrust, and replied, 'Why, I should require good proof of the fact, Joseph Sturge, before I did anything : ' how our friend rejoined, 'Then I must supply thee with the proof:' how he packed his portmanteau, and quietly embarked for the West Indies, made a tour of the islands, collected the necessary evidence of the oppression that was being practised on the negro apprentices by their masters the planters : how he returned to England and commenced an agitation throughout the country to abolish the apprenticeship, to accomplish which it was necessary to re-organize all the old Anti-Slavery Societies which had dissolved, or had laid down their arms, happy to be relieved from their long and ardous labours : how he brought them again into the field and attained his object.   This was the narrative of Lord Brougham, and well do I remember the very words in which in conclusion he awarded the whole merit to our friend. ' *Joseph Sturge*,' said he, ' *won the game off his own bat.*' "

LOYALTY TO CONSCIENCE.

Mr Richard in his "Memoirs of Joseph Sturge," says "there were many illustrations of loyalty to conscience exhibited by him in the course of his mercantile career. It is now about twenty five years since the temperance reformation began to attract attention in this country. Mr. Sturge very soon identified himself with that movement. But as forming a regular branch of the corn trade, his firm had at that time, large dealings in malt. No sooner, however, did he become convinced of the duty of total abstinence, than he felt the inconsistency of selling an article directly concerned in the production of intoxicating drinks. He, therefore, relinquished at once that part of his trade, and at the same time declined granting the further use of certain cellars on his business premises to a house that had previously hired them for storing wine and spirits. Nor did he stop there. Further reflection led him to doubt how far he could with a clear conscience take any part whatever in the purchase and sale of barley for distilling or malting purposes. The issue was, that he and his partner gave up that department of their business also, and thereby sacrificed large annual profits. This seems to have called forth expressions of astonishment and remonstrance from some of their commercial connections, to which Mr. Sturge replied in the following quiet and modest circular:—

To C. D. Corn Exchange, London.

Birmingham, 11th month, 5th, 1844.

'Esteemed Friend,—Thy letter of the 4th ultimo has the following remark on the notice contained in our last Monthly Circular:— 'The singular resolution you have come to, as to not selling malting barley, has been much canvassed here to day. I regret it much, and the more so as I can discover no good and sound reason for it.' This observation, and some other circumstances, induce me to give a furthei explanation why this resolution was adopted, believing that thyself and many other of our friends though differing in opinion, will not condemn a course which results from a conviction of duty.

Intemperance produces such an incalculable amount of vice and misery, that I consider it right to use my influence to promote the principles of total abstinence. This I feel the more bound to do, as nearly twenty years personal experience, and much observation in this and other parts of the world, have convinced me that fermented liquors are not necessary to health, and that those who refrain even from what is termed the moderate use of them are in consequence capable of more bodily and mental exertion, and exempt from many maladies which afflict others.

In accordance with these views, our firm has long altogether declined the sale of malt, or the supply of any grain-distilleries and converted to other uses cellars which many years ago we let to wine and spirit merchants. Our continuing to take commissions for the sale and purchase of barley for the purpose of malting, has for years caused me much uneasiness; and I have recently, been so fully convinced that it is wrong to do so, that I must have withdrawn from our concern had it not been relinquished. The belief that we are responsible for the means of acquiring, as well as for the use we make of our property, and that we cannot exercise too rigid a watchfulness over our *own* conduct, is compatible with perfect charity towards those who differ from us in opinion.

I am, respectfully,

Joseph Sturge.'"

RELENTING TENDERNESS.

Mr. Richard in his life of Joseph Sturge remarks:—"We have before us, at this moment, a striking evidence of the relenting tenderness of his nature in reference to a case whose turpitude could scarcely be surpassed. A person who had been long intimately connected in business with the firm of which he was the head, and in whom they had placed unlimited confidence, suddenly decamped to America with a large sum of money, and, what was still worse, leaving behind him many bills to which he had forged the signatures of the firm. At the first discovery of this disgraceful transaction, Mr. Sturge wrote to a friend in America to put the officers of justice on the offender's track. Soon after, however, followed another letter, in which he says, 'With regard to——, though our loss by him was about 50,000 dollars. I am not disposed to take any steps to bring him back to justice.' And when, some months afterwards, the delinquent was apprehended by other agency than that of his firm, it makes one almost smile to hear him say to his friend, though it is a smile assuredly in which there is no bitterness, 'Thou wouldst probably see by the newspapers that——is taken.' This I regret, heavy as our loss has been by him, as, from what I have recently heard, I believe he was suffering even before he was taken for his crimes, perhaps as much as he will by the legal transportation for life which will now probably be his punishment."

THE REFORMATORIES OF JOSEPH STURGE.

He descended by his efforts lower still; he loved and pitied the children in the gaol. It was in the year 1851 he began his efforts especially to rescue the unfortunate. He met with Mr. John Ellis, who had been ten years teaching a ragged school in London, and employing convicted thieves in his trade as a shoemaker. Mr. Sturge arranged with him to come down to Birmingham, to aid him in his efforts there. He took a house in Ryland Road, Edgbaston; he fitted it up, and then went to Mr, Stephens, the superintendent of the police, and said, "Now I want some of the very worst boys you have in Birmingham." Sixteen of the most notorious offenders were chosen; they were leaders of gangs of thieves, regular gaol-birds. The police almost resented the taking of them out of their hands. Twelve months after, one of the magistrates, Mr. Adderley, pronounced the experiment most successful—he was an independent, competent, and impartial witness. From the commencement there had not been a single failure. After this encouraging commencement, the good and glorious man bought an estate at Stoke Prior, near Bromsgrove, sixteen miles from Birmingham, and he devoted it entirely to the work of juvenile reformation. There was a roomy farmhouse, and he built schoolrooms, dormitories, workshops, baths, till accommodation was provided for about sixty boys,—thus he reared his Outcasts' Home, and trained them to habits of industry or agricultural labour, pervading the whole place with Christian love—encouraging them to diligence and thrift. A certain portion of their earnings was laid aside as a reserve fund, and given to them when they left the institution. Suitable situations were provided for them, and even if they lost them, they were taught that the reformatory was still their home. Surely all this was wonderful Christian work: how sad that it should excite so much admiration as it does, showing to us that the very purpose for which Christ gave His gospel to the world, to preach glad tidings to the poor—the opening of prisons to them that are bound, and to proclaim the acceptable year of the Lord, is almost a strange work with us. It was a singular principle upon which he started, to collect, by information from the police, specimens of the very worst of the criminal class of children, and to take the entire responsibility upon himself in conjunction with his brother Charles.—*Eclectic Review* on JOSEPH STURGE.

Mr. Sturge and the Desolation of Finland.

We linger with affection, too, on Mr. Sturge's mission to Finland. When the war broke out, the English Admiral, notwithstanding that the inhabitants of Ullaborg sent out a flag of truce to him as he drew near to the town, and obtained a promise from him not to molest their persons or property, soon threw the whole town in flames. Merchant ships, vast stores of timber and corn, the poor fisherman's boat and nets, the small farmer's sheep and cattle, the scanty furniture of the peasant's hut, they were all plundered by the British soldier and sailor when the flames had done their work. The *Times* of the day said. "One shriek of woe sounds through all Finland "—all was reduced to ruin and ashes. The character of the people—their industry, peacefulness, and seperation from the scenery of the war, excited the heart of Mr. Sturge, and once more he and Thomas Harvey set out upon an excursion of benevolence. They stopped to investigate facts for themselves, and found exasperation and burning indignation everywhere, and the good feeling towards England entirely changed. He writes:—

"On second day morning we saw and examined several cases in which the British had plundered the poor people; but Thomas Harvey has taken down the particulars of these, and you can get a copy of them on our return. One case was particularly touching—that of a poor widow of very interesting appearance, who wept much while she gave her statement, which was that the British had destroyed her husband's little vessel, and also their cargo of wood which was on shore, which included not only the whole of their own small property of about £50, but that of some friends who had helped them to build the vessel. Her husband died two or three months ago, of what would be called a broken heart, and left her with a child of four years of age not only without support but she would have to go through the Bankruptcy Court. This was fully confirmed by others.

Again :—

We must do the persons we examined the justice to say that no disposition was shown to exaggerate their grievences. The merchants did not obtrude their own losses on our notice, and we ascertained them only by direct inquiry. Need it be said that it was evident that the reputation of our country had suffered deeply in the estimation of those simple, honest-hearted people, through the lawless proceedings of our navy? Formerly, no country stood so high in the estimation of the Finn; but now, as one of the poor fishermen said to us, "they can't think of the English as before." The more intelligent, of course, made distinctions, as thus: "The navy is not the nation," and there are rascals in every country," etc. F. Uhden had before remarked to us that the printing of 100,000 copies by the British and Foreign Bible Society, of the New Testament and the Psalms, in their own language, had made a deep impression on the Finnish people; but after the ravages committed on the property of unarmed and unoffending fishermen and peasants, during the war, the cry was "Can these be the English—our friends?" To which he sometimes replied, "The English who send you the Bibles are not the same persons as the English who carry on the war."

Returning home, Joseph Sturge and his brother issued an appeal, in order to raise funds to reimburse the poorest who had been so despoiled—replacing boats, nets, and articles which constituted not only their property but means of subsistence. They headed their appeal with £1000, and eventually raised £9000 ; and with energy and discretion, corn, meal, potatoes, clothing for naked children, and seed for future harvests, and fishing-nets were purchased and distributed among the people, and the curses which were fast gathering on the English nation were exchanged into cries of "God bless the English gentleman!" From the Russian Embassy, also, Mr. Sturge received the following expression of grateful acknowledgment to himself and co-subscribers by the command of the Emperor of Russia :—

Russian Embassy, London, July 13, 1857.

Dear Sir,—In the absence of H.E. Count Chreptowich, I have been instructed, by command of the Emperor, to convey to the subscribers to the fund which has been raised in this country for the purpose of alleviating the calamities of famine in Finland, his Imperial Majesty's thanks for their liberal and charitable donations.

To you, Sir, and your friends to whose generous exertions on behalf of my unfortunate countrymen these thanks are especially due, I address myself in the hope that you will kindly enable me to fulfil the orders I have received, by making known to the numerous subscribers who have responded to your appeal the grateful sense his Imperial Majesty entertains of their conduct.

Believe me, dear sir, to be yours sincerely,

To Joseph Sturge, Esq.   NICOLAY.

When, three years afterwards, the tidings of Mr. Sturge's death reached the shores of the Baltic, there was mourning and tears in the cottages of the Finnish peasants and fishermen, and in lines we cannot quote Mr. Whittier has beautifully commemorated one of the finest sermons on the text, "If thine enemy hunger, feed him : if he thirst, give him drink."—*Eclectic Review on Joseph Sturge*.

QUAKERS AND THE EVANGELICAL ALLIANCE.

When the great Evangelical Alliance met in London and framed its articles, it so framed them that the Quakers could not get in. Only think of an Evangelical Alliance making a creed that should keep the Quakers out! For taking their best men and their best women, they stand in decided contrast with Christians, excelling them in purity, in sweetness, in gentleness, and in whiteness, if I may so say. These qualities have been found to be pre-eminent in that elect, but, I am sorry to say, decaying order of people. We could almost afford to keep the Quakers for the sake of showing what that style of manhood is which has been developed among them. And yet, the Evangelical Alliance went to work and framed a creed that left them out. It was so framed that if a man had a difficulty about any special doctrine in the Christian scheme, although he was a walking saint, he could not come in. A man could come in who had a key of the intellect that he could turn in the lock; but if a man had nothing but the key of love he could not come in.—H. W. Beecher.

The Quaker Wrestler.

Mr. Smiles informs us that George Moore arrived in London the day before Good Friday, 1825. On the following morning all the shops were shut. What was he to do on Good Friday? He knew that all the Cumberland men in London were accustomed to have their annual wrestling match on that day, and he accordingly went to Chelsea to observe the sports.

George Moore found amongst the crowd a young Quaker (a former acquaintance) from Torpenhow, who had won the belt at Keswick, a few years before. It was not with the consent of his family that this young Quaker followed the sport of wrestling. But little boys in the north take to it as ducklings take to water. When the Keswick match, above referred to was about to come off, the young man's mother hid his Sunday clothes to prevent him going to take

part in it. But he had another set of second-best clothes
hid under a berry-bush in the garden; and after he had
donned them, he set off for Keswick, running the whole
way—about sixteen miles—before he had got his breakfast.
Arrived at the toll-bar, outside the town, he went into the
house and bought a penny bun. He could not afford to
buy a breakfast, for he had only a shilling which he had
borrowed for the occasion. In the town he went into a
public house and drank a glass of porter. This made him
terribly sick. He made his way to the wrestling-ground
where he arrived as white as a sheet. Nevertheless his
name had been entered, and when he was called he went
into the ring. He threw the first man that stood against
him. Then he threw another, and another, and another,
all heavier men than himself. He had still four of the best
men to throw—men who had carried off the best prizes in
former years—Armstrong, Frears, Richardson, and Look.
The second last he threw by his *slick at back o' heel*, and the
last by the *outside stroke*. When the last man was thrown,
the victor was taken on the shoulders of the on-lookers and
carried round the ring, with a fiddler and a piper playing
before him. He was then invested with the belt, and after
he had got his prize, he hurried home again.

WHITE QUAKERS.

It was, I think, in the years 1835 and 1836, that a Friend,
named Joshua Jacob, took a very prominent part in the
Dublin Monthly Meeting. His wife also became particularly
efficient in the Women's Meeting. In some respects, like
the modern Puseyites, they were for reviving the obsolete
customs of the early Quakers. To adhere strictly to the
phraseology of George Fox, to imitate his eccentricities—
to throw back the innovations which had crept in, and to
revivify the Society in all its original quaintness—appeared

to be their object. As George Fox had been "inspired by the shining of the light within" to originate, and had been enabled, in "best wisdom," to establish the Society, and, aided by Robert Barclay, William Penn, and some others, who were equally gifted; had published rules, and laws, and bye-laws; and as their teaching was principally directed to exalt the work of the Holy Spirit in the heart of man, in contra-distinction to the great error of the day—an exaltation of the outward forms and ceremonies of religious worship, so these Friends, Jacob and a few others, claimed for themselves the same "inspiration," and the same "best wisdom," with which now to dictate, and to govern.

The Dublin Friends were greatly pleased with what they deemed and called a "New Light which had been vouchsafed to the Society, to preserve it from the degeneracy which for some previous years, had been assimilating them to Christians of other Churches." With deferential submission, they accepted "the leadings and guidings" of those "gifted individuals;" and, at their suggestion, the Yearly Meeting added to the Book of Discipline several stringent rules, which according to the custom of Friends, being once inserted there, must remain until the end.

The Jacobs, mistaking their imaginings for the inspiration of the Holy Spirit, and greatly puffed up in their estimation by the deference conceded to them, yielded very naturally to that inherent desire which man has to assume control over the intellect of his fellow-man, and to bend another to his own opinion. So much of their "best wisdom" having been thus accepted by the Society at large, "fresh guidings" were frequently volunteered, until at last common sense revolted, and reason in some degree resumed her sway.

Jacob had succeeded in convincing the Meeting, that to go "to any place of common worship," to "wear mourning for a deceased relative or Friend," to "allow a musical

instrument inside the door," &c.. &c., were sins of such
enormity, as required that the offender should immediately
be disowned. He now wished to go farther and set an
example for their imitation.

Blue had long been a forbidden colour for Friends to
wear. Jacob declared, that "the simplicity of godliness
required all men and women should array themselves in
white." With untanned shoes, unbleached stockings,
flannel-coloured knee breeches, coat and waistcoat, and a
light drab broad-brimmed hat, he appeared in the Meeting,
accompanied by his wife, who was clad from head to foot
in coarse, unbleached calico. He would not allow anything
to be in his house, except it were white. His walls were
whitewashed, and his doors painted white. His wife united
heart and hand in his "guiding." One morning she
collected every article of china and earthenware in her
house, on which was any colour, or even gilding. She
opened her hall door, and on the door steps smashed them
all to pieces. Her husband applauded her "noble deed,"
as he called it; delighted at such praise from him, she
continued the work of demolition; her looking-glasses were
brought out next and destroyed with a large stone which
she picked up in the street; for this he called her "a noble-
minded woman." His mahogany and rosewood furniture
were replaced with common white wood; and even the
patchwork quilt was banished from his white abode.

The majority of the Friends stoutly resisted these
"leadings and guidings." * * * Jacob and his disciples,
who altogether numbered more than one hundred, finding
they were not allowed to have the entire governing of the
Society, separated from it, and incorporated themselves into
a sect called White Quakers. The original Friends, now
denominated Black Quakers in contra-distinction, disowned
the White Quakers, and they in return, disowned them.

                    Quakerism by Mrs. J. R. GREER.

INWARD PERCEPTION.

Arthur Howell a preacher in the Society of Friends, and also a currier in Philadelphia, was characterized by kindly feelings, and, a very tender conscience. Upon one occasion, he purchased from the captain of a vessel a quantity of oil, which he afterwards sold, at an advanced price. Under these circumstances, he thought the captain had not received so much as he ought to have; and he gave him an additional dollar on every barrel. This man was remarkable for spiritual-mindedness and the gift of prophecy. It was no uncommon thing for him to relate occurrences which were happening at the moment many miles distant, and to foretell the arrival of people, or events, when there appeared to be no external reason on which to ground such expectation.

One Sunday Morning, he was suddenly impelled to proceed to Germantown in haste. As he approached the village, he met a funeral procession. He had no knowledge whatever of the deceased; but it was suddenly revealed to him that the occupant of the coffin before him was a woman whose life had been saddened by the suspicion of a crime, which she never committed. The impression became very strong on his mind that she wished him to make certain statements at her funeral. Accordingly, he followed the procession, and when they arrived at the meeting house, he entered and listened to the prayer offered by her pastor. When the customary services were finished, Arthur Howell rose, and asked permission to speak. "I do not know the deceased, even by name," said he. "But it is given me to say, that she suffered much and unjustly. Her neighbours generally suspected her of a crime, which she did not commit; and in a few weeks from this time, it will be made clearly manifest to the world that she was innocent. A few hours before her death, she talked with the clergyman who attended upon her, and who is now present; and it is given

N

me to declare the communication she made to him upon that occasion."

He then proceeded to relate the particulars of the interview; to which the clergyman listened with evident astonishment. When the communication was finished, he said, "I do not know who this man is, or how he has obtained information on this subject; but certain it is, he has repeated word for word, a conversation which I supposed was known only to myself and the deceased."

The woman in question had gone out in the fields one day, with her infant in her arms, and she returned without it. She said she had laid it down on a heap of dry leaves, while she went to pick a few flowers; and when she returned, the baby was gone. The fields and woods were searched in vain, and neighbours began to whisper that she had committed infanticide. Then rumours arose that she was dissatisfied with her marriage; that her heart remained with a young man to whom she was previously engaged; and that her brain was affected by this secret unhappiness. She was never publicly accused; partly because there was no evidence against her; and partly because it was supposed that if she did commit the crime, it must have been owing to aberration of mind. But she became aware of the whisperings against her, and the consciousness of being an object of suspicion, combined with the mysterious disappearance of her child, cast a heavy cloud over her life, and made her appear more and more unlike her former self. This she confided to her clergyman, in the interview shortly preceding her death; and she likewise told him that the young man, to whom she had been engaged, had never forgiven her for not marrying him.

A few weeks after her decease, this young man confessed that he had stolen the babe. He had followed the mother, unobserved by her, and had seen her lay the sleeping infant on its bed of leaves. As he gazed upon it, a mingled feeling of jealousy and revenge took possession of his soul. In obedience to a sudden impulse, he seized the babe, and carried it off hastily. He subsequently conveyed it to a distant village, and placed it out to nurse, under an assumed name and history. The child was found alive and well, at the place he indicated. Thus the mother's innocence was made clearly manifest to the world, as the Quaker preacher had predicted at her funeral.

A singular case of inward perception likewise occurred in the experience of the mother of Isaac T. Hopper. In her Diary, which is still preserved in the family, she describes a visit to some of her children in Philadelphia, and adds: "Soon after this, the Lord showed me that I should lose a son. It was often told to me, though without sound of words. Nothing could be more intelligible than this still, small voice. It said, Thou wilt lose a son; and he is a pleasant child."

Her son James resided with relatives in Philadelphia, and often went to bathe in the Delaware. On one of these occasions, soon after his mother's visit, a friend who went with him sunk in the water, and James lost his own life by efforts to save him. A messenger was sent to inform his parents, who lived at the distance of eight miles. While he stayed in the house, reluctant to do his mournful errand the mother was seized with sudden dread, and heard the inward voice saying, "James is drowned." She said, abruptly to the messenger, "Thou hast come to tell me that my son James is drowned Oh, how did it happen?" He was much surprised, and asked why she thought so. She could give no explanation of it, except that it had been suddenly revealed to her mind.

"I have heard and read of many such stories of Quakers which seem too well authenticated to admit of doubt. They themselves refer all such cases to "the inward light;" and that phrase, as they understand it, conveys a satisfactory explanation to their minds. I leave psychologists to settle the question as they can."

"Those who are well acquainted with Quaker views, are aware that by "the inward light," they signify something higher and more comprehensive than conscience. They regard it as the voice of God in the soul, which will always guard man from evil, and guide him into truth, if reverently listened to, in the stillness of the passions, and obedience of the will. These strong impressions on individual minds constitute their only call and consecration to the ministry, and have directed them in the application of moral principles to a variety of subjects, such as temperance, war, and slavery. Men and women were impelled by the interior monitor to go about preaching on these topics, until their individual views became what are called "leading testimonies" in the Society."

Jacob Lindley and the Spiritual World.

Once, when Jacob Lindley, a minister in the Society of Friends, was dining with Friend Hopper, the conversation turned upon his religious experiences, and he related a circumstance to which he said he very seldom alluded, and never without feelings of solemnity and awe. Being seized with sudden and severe illness, his soul left the body for several hours, during which time he saw visions of heavenly glory, not to be described. When consciousness began to return, he felt grieved that he was obliged to come back to this state of being, and he was never after able to feel the same interest in terrestrial things, that he had felt before he obtained this glimpse of the spiritual world.

QUAKERS AT FAMILY WORSHIP.

James Backhouse who was accompanied by George Washington Walker on a visit to the Australian Colonies writes in his Journal while staying at Hobart Town, Van Dieman's Land, 5th—4th M., 1837,

At six o'clock we joined the family of W. B——at dinner, and paid them a pleasaut visit. As, on some former occasions, I was requested to read a chapter in the Bible, at the time of their family worship, and to make any addition I might then think proper. This I accepted, again distinctly stating that it was with the understanding that it was with the liberty to keep silence, or to speak, as I might find my duty. After I had read, my mind was calmly stayed upon the Lord, under a comforting sense of his presence, but nothing was impressed for expression. When a seasonable time had been spent in silence I made a movement for separation, which not appearing to be thoroughly understood, I stated that I did not apprehend it to be my duty, at that time, to engage in any vocal labour, such as preaching or prayer: on this W. B——kneeled down with his family and domestics, and repeated some petitions from the prayers of the Episcopal Church, my companion and myself retaining our seats, in testimony to our not recognizing, as being properly prayer, anything not avowedly expressed under the fresh sense of the putting forth of the Divine Spirit. These circumstances, together with the remarks afterwards made by myself, that having now very much finished the work that was given me to do in these colonies, it was rarely I had anything to express in the line of ministry, but rather that I generally found it my place to set an example of silently waiting upon God, gave rise to an explanatory conversation on the subject, elucidating the views and practices of Friends in these respects.

DAVID BARCLAY.

Few men were ever more active than David Barclay, in promoting whatever might ameliorate the condition of man—largely endowed by Providence with the means, he felt it to be his duty to set great examples; and when an argument was set up againsts the emancipation of the negroes from slavery, "that they were too ignorant and too barbarous for freedom," he resolved at his own expense to demonstrate the fallacy of the imputation. Having had an estate in Jamaica fall to him, he determined at the expense of £10,000, to emancipate the whole *yang* (as they were termed) of slaves. He did this with his usual prudence as well as generosity. He sent out an agent to Jamaica, and instructed him to hire a vessel, in which they were all transported to America, where the little community was established in various handicrafts and trades; the Members of it prospered under the blessing of his care, and lived to show that the black skin enclosed hearts as full of gratitude, and minds as capable of improvement, as that of the proudest white.

A QUAKER PREACHING IN THE HALL OF CONGRESS.

Joseph John Gurney writes "The principle object which I now had in view, in visiting Washington, was the holding of a meeting for worship with the officers of government and the members of Congress. My mind was attracted towards these public men, uuder a feeling of religious interest; and far beyond my expectation, did my way open for accomplishing the purpose, Colonel Polk, the Speaker of the representative assembly, granted me the use of the Legislation Hall; the chaplain of the House (a respectable Wesleyan Minister), kindly surrendered his accustomed service for our accommodation; public invitation was give in the newspapers; and when we entered the Hall the following First-day morning, we found it crowded with the members of Congress, their ladies, and many other persons. The President, and other officers of the government, were also of the company. Undoubtedly, it was a highly respectable and intellectual audience; and it was to me a serious and critical occasion. One of my friends sat down with me in the Speaker's rostrum; a feeling of calmness was graciously bestowed upon us; and a silent solemnity overspread the meeting. After a short time, my own mind became impressed with the words of our blessed Redeemer, —' I am the way, the truth, and the life.' Speaking from this text, I was led to describe the main features of orthodox Christianity; to declare that these doctrines had been faithfully held by the Society of Friends, from the first rise to the present day; to dwell on the evidences, both historical and internal, which form the credentials of the Gospel, considered as a message to mankind from the King of heaven and earth; to urge the claims of that message on the world at large, on America in particular—a country so remarkably blessed by Divine Providence,—and, above all, on her statesmen and legislators; to advise the devotional duties of the closet, as a guard against the dangers and temptations of politics; to dwell on the peaceable government of Christ by his Spirit; and, finally, to insist on the perfect law of righteousness, as applying to nations as well as individuals,—to the whole affairs of men, both private and public. A solemn silence again prevailed at the close of the meeting; and after it was concluded, we received the warm greetings of Henry Clay, John Quincey Adams, and many other members, of whom we took leave in the flowing of mutual kindness. Thus was I set free from the heavy burden which had been pressing on me."

WILLIAM HOWITT'S MARRIAGE TOUR.

It was in 1821, not 1823 as the papers have been saying, that the late William Howitt married at Uttoxeter a fair Staffordshire Quakeress, Mary Botham, who has been known to the English speaking world for more than half a century as a writer of the most charming books, both in prose, and verse, for the young. Many have supposed that William and Mary Howitt were brother and sister; whereas they were husband and wife, and to his intimate friends he would proudly say, "My wife is the best poetess and the best wife in England." Their marriage tour was unique. The young couple walked on foot all over the classic scenes in Scotland—actually tramping upwards of 500 miles. The results of this delightful trip were perceptible in many of their books written in after days, and they both cherished the warmest affection for Scotland and its people. Mary Howitt found the motto for one of her first volumes of poetry in Burns; and her husband never wrote a more attractive sketch than his description of a morning walk to the banks of Doon in company with a working man of Ayr. It is included in his "Homes and Haunts of the Poets," one of his best books.—*Nottingham Journal.*

ANECDOTE OF THE QUEEN.

About this time William Allen records—"I accompanied E. J. Fry to Kensington Palace, to meet the Duchess of Kent, and her daughter the Princess Victoria. It was a satisfactory interview. The Princess has much of her father's countenance, and appears exceedingly amiable."

On one of these interviews at Kensington Palace, the following incident occurred, which Mr. Allen used to relate with great interest:—When our present beloved sovereign was a little girl, she was at a window looking out on the crowd of persons in the gardens. Her amiable mother, to whose education this country owes so much, begged her to come from the window, which the little Princess, either did not, or would not, hear. The command was repeated, and when she slowly came away, her mother asked her what was the reason she did not come immediately. With an air of majesty that intimated the future Queen, she replied, "I was surveying my people."

Life of William Allen, by J. SHERMAN.

ABSTAINING FROM THE USE OF SLAVE-GROWN SUGAR.

William Allen met with the Emperor Alexander in Vienna, shortly before the Congress of Verona. After some conversation about the slave trade, the Emperor said, "Will you not take some tea with me?" "I shall be happy," said the Quaker, whereupon the Emperor rings a little silver handbell, and servants appear bearing in the refreshing beverage; but the Quaker, on tasting his cup, discovers it is sweetened with sugar, and sugar he has vowed not to taste for it is in the produce of slave labour, and, therefore he communicates his scruples to the Emperor, who orders a cup to be brought into which the saccharine element has not entered.

Mr. Allen writes in his diary—"Eighth month, 1st, 1834. A day of jubilee. Eight hundred thousand of our fellow creatures released from slavery this day, in our West India Islands! My spirit is clothed with thankfulness. * * * After having for more than forty years abstained from the use of sugar, on account of its being the produce of the labour of slaves, now, that they are declared free by the government I recommenced taking it this day at Peter Bedford's— P. Elout, a judge and celebrated philantrophist at the Hague, was much impressed at this testimony against slavery—he said to Mr. G. W. Alexander, It is to William Allen I attribute all I have felt and done for the cause of the slave. When

he was at the Hague many years since, I was invited, together
with a number of serious individuals, to take tea with him.
I was then quite a youth. He took no sugar with his tea,
which surprised me. I was more surprised for the reason he
gave for this. He told the company that he had long abstained
from the use of it, because he could not, with peace of mind,
partake of that as a gratification, for which thousands of
innocent people were compelled to labour in cruel and hopeless
bondage. I was struck with this example of self-denial, by
so great a man as I thought him to be, in a thing so seemingly
small in itself, and I was led to consider how great must be
the evil of a system which could make so deep and so religious
impression upon his feelings. From that period my own
sentiments have been engaged in the cause of the negro, and
my efforts given to procure their emancipation in the colonies
of Holland."

WILLIAM ALLEN'S KINDNESS TO ANIMALS.

The simplicity and tenderness of Mr. Allen's mind were
evinced on many occasions, especially in his kindness to the
brute creation. When little more than eighteen years of age
we have the following record:—"A day of bitterness and
sorrow, occasioned by the death of my faithful, loving dog,
who was killed by accident in the street. I assuredly bestow
too great a share of affection on the animals I have the care
of. Resolved not to have any more at present."

In one of his journeys with his niece he saw by the road
side an old and worn out horse, around which a number of
boys had gathered, who were teasing the wretched animal.
Mr. Allen stopped his carriage to remonstrate with the boys,
and, finding the poor horse a burthen to itself, ascertained
where the owner lived, went to his house, bought the animal,
and had him shot, and then pursued his journey.

Towards the close of life he had a little Norwegian pony which had been ill for some days. On going to see it, he remarks:—"Poor Pony came up to me to be caressed; I had hopes of his recovery, but in the evening my dear little grandson brought me word that he was dead. I felt low at the loss of this poor animal; it was a beautiful, affectionate, and useful creature: I never had occasion to strike it with the whip in my life. I hope not to repine, but really things which I set my affecteons upon, are taken from me in a remarkable way."

Life of William Allen, by J. Sherman.

Longevity among the Quakers.

Quakers attain great ages. In the obituary of the *Friend* Magazine, 1860, we find the following ages of some deceased members of the Society of Friends:—84, 84, 85, 85, 85, 86, 86, 87, 87, 88, 88, 89, 89, 91, 91, 91, 91, 91, 91, 92, 92, 93, 93, making a total of 2,188 years, with an average for each life of rather more than 88½ years. Fifty lives in the same period give 4,258 with an average of 85 per life The average duration of life in the Society of Friends during 1860 was 58 years and 6 months; but one girl died under 6 months old; five girls and thirteen boys—in all 18 out of 324, or 5½ per cent—did not reach the age of one year.

The Quaker and His Horse.

A man once went to purchase a horse of a Quaker—" Will he draw well?" asked the buyer. " Thee will be pleased to see him draw." The bargain was concluded, and the farmer tried the horse, but he would not stir a step. He returned and said, "That horse will not draw an inch." "I did not tell thee that it would draw, friend, I only remarked that it would please thee to see him draw, so it would me, but he would never gratify me in that respect."

COMPULSORY OBEDIENCE.

A Quakeress informed a friend in reference to the Quaker formula of marriage, "It is true I did not promise to obey when I was married; but I might as well have done so, for I had to do it."

REMONSTRANCE UNAVAILING.

A Quaker maiden of sixty accepted an offer from a Presbyterian elder, and being remonstrated with by a delegation of Friends appointed to wait upon her for marrying out of the meeting, she replied, "Look here I've been waiting just sixty years for the meeting to marry me, and if the meeting don't want me to marry out of it, why don't the meeting bring along it's young men?" The delegation departed in silence.

MAD QUAKERS.

Sydney Smith remarks:—"The Quakers always seem to succeed in any institution which they undertake. The gaol of Philadelphia will remain a lasting monument of their skill and patience; and in the plan of their retreat for the insane, they have evinced the same wisdom and perseverance. The great principle on which it appears to be conducted is that of kindness to the patients. The generosity of the Quakers, and their courage in managing mad people, are placed, by this institution, in a very striking point of view. This cannot be better illustrated than by the two following cases:—

"The superintendent was one day walking in a field adjacent to the house, in company with a patient who was apt to be vindictive on very slight occasions. An exciting circumstance occurred. The maniac retired a few paces, and seized a large stone, which he immediately held up, as in the act of throwing at his companion. The superintendent in no degree ruffled, fixed his eye upon the patient, and in a resolute tone of voice, at the same time advancing, commanded him to lay down the stone. As he approached, the head of the lunatic gradually sank from its threatening posi.ion, and permitted the stone to drop to the ground. He then submitted to be quietly led to his apartment."

"Some years ago, a man, about thirty-four years of age, of almost herculean size and figure, was brought to the house. He had been afflicted several times before; and so constantly, during the present attack, had he been kept chained, that his clothes were contrived to be taken off and put on by means of strings, without removing his manacles. They were, however, taken off when he entered the Retreat, and he was ushered into the apartment where the super-intendents were supping. He was calm; his attention appeared to be arrested by his new situation. He was desired to join in the repast, during which he behaved with tolerable propriety. After it was concluded, the superintendent conducted him to his apartment, and told him the circumstances on which his treatment would depend; that it was his anxious wish to make every-inhabitant of the house as comfortable as possible; and that he sincerely hoped the patient's conduct would render it unnecessary for him to have recourse to coercion. The maniac was sensible of the kindness of his treatment. He promised to restrain himself; and he so completely succeeded that, during his stay, no coercive means were ever employed towards him. This case affords a striking example of the efficacy of mild treatment. The patient was frequently very vociferous, and threatened his attendants, who, in their defence, were very desirous of restraining him by the jacket. The superintendent on these occasions went to his apartment; and though the first sight of him seemed rather to increase the patient's irritation, yet, after sitting some time quietly beside him, the violent excitement subsided, and he would listen with attention to the persuasions and arguments of his friendly visitor. After such conversations, the patient was generally better for some days or a week; and in about four months he was discharged perfectly recovered."

"Can it be doubted that, in this case, the disease had been greatly exasperated by the mode of management? or that the subsequent kind treatment had a great tendency to promote his recovery?"

And yet, in spite of this apparent contempt of danger, for eighteen years not a single accident has happened to the keepers.

THE QUAKER STATESMAN.

The following extracts are taken from an article in 'Truth.' It has been said that eloquence is "reason penetrated and made red hot by passion." Few men illustrate the truth of this definition better than Mr. Bright. He is passionately in earnest; and there is the secret of his strength—for the rest a secret easy enough to divine. Then a circumstance which I have heard Mr. Bright regret, has probably been of some service to him as an orator; he knows no language but our mother-tongue, resembling in this respect the greatest speakers that the world has ever known—those of the Athenian Republic. He has to address Englishmen, and he does so in a perfectly English way, out of an English mind filled with English thoughts (to the exclusion of all others.) His words and sentences too, are pure English, disfigured by no Gallicisms or Teutonicisms, or Hellenisms. He knows nothing of "Solidarity," or of "Geist," and may well have sighed at being obliged to claim "autonomy" for the Bulgarians, while Turkish "hegemony" must have been doubly odious to him.

And how has Mr. Bright acquired his command of nervous English? By almost learning by heart the works of the purest English writers. I remember some one once saying in his presence that it would be difficult to find a man who had read through Milton's "Paradise Regained." "I have read it many times," he said, and then he proceeded to cite several magnificent passages from it.

But few men are so well acquainted as he is with the literature of his own country, not forgetting the Bible or the *Daily News.* The "Fairy Queen" is read through about once in a hundred years. In the eighteenth century Chatham accomplished the feat; in the nineteenth, Mr. Bright. The two men seem sufficiently unlike each other, and yet the fact reminds one of Bulwer Lytton's couplet:—

Let Bright the Minister of England be,
And straight in Bright a Chatham we should see.

No wonder Mr. Bright is an incomprehensible phenomenon to foreign liberals. I remember seeing him and Louis Blanc engaged in a political discussion. The French Radical learnt with amazement and sorrow that his English *confrere* was in favour of shutting up public houses during certain hours on Sundays. "Ah, you have no liberty in England," he remarked bitterly. Mr. Bright rejoined with a polite hope that the immortal principles of '89 might bring the French (in their good time) some greater benefit than that of increased facilities for drunkenness on Sundays.

Mr. Bright himself, by the way, is now a teetotaller, and smokes much less than formerly. In old times he and Lord Stanley (the present Lord Derby) might often be seen in the smoking room of the House of Commons puffing away, according to the elegant expression of a friend, like a couple of chimneys. The two were (and are) fast friends; and, strange as it may seem, there can be little doubt that the

man who recently flung away his chance of becoming a
Tory Prime Minister was the apt pupil of Mr. Bright.
The Quaker statesman very early imbued him with tha.
dislike of war which made him the despair of the Jin~oes.
Mr. Bright's influences, too, contributed to make Lord
Stanley decline a place in the War Cabinet of 1855.

For Mr. Gladstone, his admiration is unbounded. Last
summer, at a garden party, he happened to find himself
amongst a number of ladies and gentlemen who were one
and all speaking with extraordinary bitterness of the
Member for Greenwich. A Princess of the Blood led the
attack, ably seconded by a Dowager of social might.
Mr. Bright said nothing for a while; then quietly turned
to a lady and asked her if her children had ever seen
Mr. Gladstone? "No," she replied. "Then," he remarked,
"You should give them the opportunity of doing so, that
they may be able in after days to say they have seen one of
the greatest men that England ever produced."

Mr. Bright has small respect for the red coat, and scarcely
any more for the blue jacket. In the album of a village
inn he described England as an ass heavily laden with two
packs—the army and navy. Again, he has spoken of our
naval and military expenditure "as a gigantic system of
outdoor relief for the aristocracy." Yet he lived to be a
member of a Cabinet which actually declared war. True,
it was only against the King of Ashantee.

He is a staunch friend and a serviceable one, for in later
years he has developed an extraordinary amount of tact.
They say, indeed of Jacob, that he is John without John's
tact. This is not quite true; but it is certain that John
shows wonderful dexterity in steering clear of all crotchet-
mongers and hobby horses. When there is a Woman's
Rights division he votes with his brother; but is hopelessly
unenthusiastic about the subject. I have heard one of the

tuneful sisterhood denounce him as a "weakling." Higher praise could hardly be accorded him. A Quaker mellowed into a man of the world would not be a bad description of Mr. Bright.

Careful of the public money, Mr. Bright is generous with his own. It is not so well remembered as it deserves to be that during the cotton famine when Mr. Bright's operatives were thrown out of work, he allowed them two-thirds of their regular wages without exacting any sort of return. He is even said to have seriously impaired his fortune by this splendid act of munificence. This is the man whom a Tory paper abused at the time for not subscribing to the Lancashire Relief Fund. He disdained to reply, but the late Lord Derby took care that the fact should be known.

No man is complete without a pet inconsistency. Mr. Bright thinks fox hunting cruel; but cannot be made to look upon salmon fishing (at which he is an adept) in the same light."

THE NONSTRIKING QUAKER.

"I will not strike thee, bad man," said a Quaker one day; "but I will let this billet of wood fall on thee;" and at that precise moment the "bad man was floored by the weight of the walking-stick that the Quaker was known to carry."

A SERMON BY A QUAKERESS.

"My dear friends there are three things I very much wonder at—The first, is that children should be so foolish as to throw stones, clubs, and brick-bats up into fruit trees, to knock down fruit; if they would let it alone it would fall itself. The second is that men should be so foolish, and even so wicked, as to go to war and kill each other; if let alone, they would die themselves. And the third and last thing that I wonder at, is that young men should be so unwise as to go after young women; if they would stay at home, the young women would come after them."

JOHN WESLEY AND THE QUAKERS.

After the sermon, this unbaptized woman, (a Quakeress) abruptly addressing Wesley, asked, "Dost thou think water baptism an ordinance of Christ?" Wesley replied, "What saith Peter? Who can forbid water that these should not be baptized, who have received the Holy Ghost even as we?" Wesley adds: "I spoke but little more, before she cried out, "'Tis right! 'tis right! I will be baptized." And so she was the same hour."

In his wide wanderings, Wesley met with numbers of friendly Quakers, of whom he speaks in terms of commendation; but their system was one which he abhorred, and, in his "Appeal to Men of Reason and Religion," he speaks of the inconsistencies of their community in the most withering terms. "A silent meeting," said he in a letter to a young lady, "was never heard of in the Church of Christ for sixteen hundred years." And, in one of his letters to Archbishop Secker, he remarks: "Between me and the Quakers there is a great gulf fixed. The sacraments of baptism and the Lord's supper keep us at a wide distance from each other; insomuch that, according to the view of things I have now, I should as soon commence deist as Quaker."

Tyerman's *Life and Times of John Wesley.*

CURIOSITY REPROVED.

A lady visiting Newgate with Mrs. Fry says—Being much struck with the appearance of a young female convict, I asked Mrs. Fry the crime for which she was there. Her answer reproved me; for she said, "I never ask their crimes, *for we have all come short.*" Also upon this occasion she rewarded one of the women, who had found a trinket belonging to one of the Ladies in Committee, and had restored it. Mrs. Fry gave her a cotton gown, saying; "Now you *see honesty is* the best policy."

REMARKABLE CIRCUMSTANCE.

Mrs. Fry's *penetration* and *discernment* in prosecuting her benevolent works, were very remarkable. Though charitable in the highest degree, and sometimes, it is probable, imposed upon in her acts of benevolence, she was not often deceived or mistaken in forming an estimate of the real characters of those whom she had even but seldom seen. This may be illustrated by the following remarkable fact:—Walking one morning in Lombard Street with the author, we met a decently dressed female, who yet appeared to be very sorrowful. She asked no relief, nor did she seek to attract attention. But Mrs. Fry, as if prompted or impelled by some superior power, let go his arm, and turned to the woman, saying, "Thou appearest to be in trouble: tell me, I beseech thee, the cause of thy sorrow: perhaps I can assist thee, and afford thee relief." She hesitated; but Mrs. Fry perceiving her burdened spirit, led her to the house of her brother, in the same street; and, by her kind solicitude, obtained a statement of her griefs. She needed no pecuniary assistance; but only the counsels of a judicious and pious friend, whom she had thus most unexpectedly found. And thus this distressed creature was saved from misery and self-destruction; and as she afterwards declared, that when first met by Mrs. Fry, she was on her way to drown herself in the river Thames!

Memoirs of Mrs. Fry, by T. Timpson.

Mrs. Fry's Influence.

Mr. Timpson observes, "One example may illustrate the effect of her Christian influence. On visiting one of the state prisons of the kingdom of——, in 1839, she found many hundred convicts working in chains, sorely burdened and oppressed. In unison with her friend William Allen, she pressed the case, in the absence of the King, on the attention of the Queen and the Crown Prince. Soon afterwards the Queen was seized by her mortal illness, but did not depart from this world, without obtaining the kind promise of her royal consort, that Elizabeth Fry's recommendations, respecting the prisons, should be at once adopted. When the same prison was again visited by her in 1841, not a chain was to be seen on any of the criminals. The were working with comparative ease and freedom. Not one of them, as the governor declared, had made his escape; and great and general was the joy with which they received and welcomed their benefactress."

Thomas Shillitoe's Early Life.

The early life and labours of Thomas Shillitoe are very interesting. Dr. Cunningham writes, "Born in London in 1754, young Shillitoe was educated in the Church of England. but when he was a little more than twenty years of age he forsook the faith of his fathers and joined the Quakers. Through the interest of a Quaker lady, he was now taken from behind the counter in a grocer's shop, and placed in an eminent Quaker Banking establishment in the city. But the raw proselyte soon discovered that his fellow-clerks, notwithstanding their demure looks while at the desk, were as fond of a frolic in the evening as any other young fellows about town. He was shocked at this, and resolved to leave the bank and learn shoemaking, that he might be

able, while ho sat solitarily upon his stool, to commune
with himself, think himself like Fox, who had also started
life as a cobbler. Through time he learned his craft, and
and became a master in it, and, being patronized by his
sect, began to accumulate money. But so soon as he found
himself worth a hundred pounds a year independently of
his trade, he determined to give up his shop-keeping that
he might devote himself entirely to missionary work. And
a most energetic missionary he became, performing most of
his journeys through England and Ireland on foot, with his
coat slung over his arm in hot weather, and preaching with
a stentorian voice and great earnestness wherever he came.
He was one of the first pioneers of the temperance cause,
being not only a total abstainer and vegetarian himself, but
a great enemy of drinking. He made a regular raid upon
the public-houses of Ireland, entering them at all hours,
and remonstrating with their landlords and their drunken
guests."

"Thomas Shillitoe was a dapper little man, with a somewhat remarkable head and face—a prominent brow, deep
set eyes, shaded by shaggy eye-brows, a hooked nose, and
a strong under jaw, which bespoke determination. His
nervous temperament was dangerously morbid. For weeks
together he fancied himself a teapot, and was in dread when
people came near him lest they should break him. In
another fit of hypochondria he would run across London
Bridge, lest it should break down under his weight. His
imagination was so impressed with a shocking murder
which had been committed that he concealed himself for
weeks lest he should be taken for the murderer. The sight
of a mouse would make him take to his bed. He often
went about ' frightened for fear of being frightened,' to use
his own description of his own sad state ; and yet this man
in other circumstances could be as dauntless as a hero. It

it is with such men our asylums are filled, and it it is also out of such men that some of our greatest geniuses and benefactors have been formed. A single hairbreadth to the one side or the other makes all the difference."

THOMAS SHILLITOE THE FAITHFUL ADMONISHER OF THE GREAT.

About the end of the last, and the commencement of the present century, a good man, of humble birth and limited education, a member of the Society of Friends, named Thomas Shillitoe, reflecting upon the vast responsibility which rested upon kings, and the opportunities they possessed for improving the condition of their people, felt it a matter of duty to attempt to obtain audience of some of the rulers of the earth. When Thomas Shillitoe mentioned his desire, or, as he termed it, "his concern," to the members of the denomination he belonged to, they heard him with respect and affection, for such is their wonted manner and feeling, but much encouragement he did not receive, the general impression being, that the attempt, though in itself laudable, was impracticable. However, in the year 1794, Thomas Shillitoe, accompanied by a friend named Stacey, went to Windsor, and having some slight knowledge of a person holding a surbordinate situation in the Castle, they obtained admittance to the part where the royal stables were. The hour was morning, and, as if Providence smiled on the design of the two friends, King George the Third came towards the stables, accompanied by two of his nobles, passed near where they were standing. The king observed them, and came near as if to give them an opportunity of speaking. For an instant the two companions were not prepared to crave the attention of the monarch, and he accordingly turned about, and, though still looking towards them, went into the stable. Thomas Shillitoe feeling compunction that the first opportunity had been lost, proposed to follow the king into the stable. This, however, the attendants would not permit. But the king, hearing their remarks, came out ; when Stacoy said, " This friend of mine hath something to communicate to the king." On which his majesty raised his hat, and, his attendants ranging themselves on his left and right, Thomas Shillitoe advanced in front, saying, "Hear, O King ;" and, in a discourse of about twenty minutes duration, pressed upon the monarch the importance of true religion in persons of exalted station, and the influence and responsibility attached to power. It is to be regretted, that in the quaint but graphic memoirs of Thomas Shillitoe, there is no account kept of the words of this address, a circumstance accounted for by the fact of its being entirely unpremeditated and extemporaneous. Yet we may infer it did not want power by the effect it produced on the royal hearer, who stood with the utmost attention, "the tears trickling down his cheeks."

It is said, that he did not pursue his diversion of hunting that day, but returned to the queen, and informed her of what had passed.

In the year 1813, the same energetic man drew up an impressive religious address to the Prince Regent, in which were plainly set forth his sins, and going down to Brighton, where the prince then was, in defiance of the remonstrances of timid friends, he sought and obtained a personal interview, in a manner seemingly as accidental as that had been with the king, his father, and presented his address. When the inaccessible and ceremonious character of George the Fourth is remembered, such an event seems particularly striking, and evidences that nothing is too difficult for zeal and perseverance to accomplish. Good Quakers tell that the first address had evidently touched the prince's conscience as

after receiving it, he countermanded a great banquet which
had been arranged for the following day; and, on his death-
bed, was heard to mutter, "Oh! that Quaker! that Quaker!"

The Society of Friends, justly appreciating the valuable
qualities of their indefatigable minister, acquiesced in the
wish of the latter to visit the continent of Europe, on a sort
of religious mission, in which he was to do good, as he had
opportunity, to all men. One circumstance, which deeply
and painfully impressed the mind of Thomas Shillitoe, was
the universal desecration of the Lord's-day, which he saw
almost in every continental town. It seemed to him an im-
perative duty to remonstrate with the rulers of the people,
in reference to the general laxity of morals and religion.
Consequently, when he was in Denmark, he determined to
see the king. He had no friend in Copenhagen, either to
advise or aid him in his undertaking; yet, having resolved
on it as a matter of duty, he determined to use every means
to accomplish his object. Accordingly, learning the name of
the prime minister, he went to him and requested his influence
in obtaining him an audience with the king   This bold request, though urged with all the mild self-possesion of native
courtesy, startled the prime minister, who, gazing on the
attire of the person making such a request, said, "You do
not mean to appear before the king in these clothes, do you?"
With the utmost simplicity, Thomas Shillitoe says, in his
journal, " I told him I had no others with me, as it was uncertain I should want my best until summer. I had left
them at Altona, intending to furnish myself with winter
clothes when I reached Norway." The nobleman smiled at
this frank reply, and promised, on the following morning, to
procure the applicant the interview he wished.

Accordingly, the following day Thomas Shillitoe was introduced to the King of Denmark, with whom he faithfully remonstrated on the desecration of the Lord's-day throughout

his dominions, and also took occassion to remark on the sin-
fulness of that species of gambling known by the name of
Lotteries, which the government licensed, and by which many
poor deluded people were reduced to ruin. His communication was heard with indulgent attention, and from this it is
but reasonable to infer that good was done.

In 1824, Thomas Shillitoe was again on the continent,
visiting schools, hospitals, and prisons. When in Prussia,
he felt the same desire as on former occasions to have an
audience with the king; and a most interesting interview
was the result of his endeavours. The audience with the
King of Prussia took place in the garden of the palace of
Berlin. Thomas Shillitoe, in the first place, presented a
petition in reference to the persecution of a member of the
Society of Friends, in consequence of his refusing to serve
as a military man. This the king received graciously, and
promised that no man in his dominions should be persecuted
for conscience sake. After this, the faithful Shillitoe added
a solemn admonition, in reference to the duty of persons in
authority to be "a terror to evil doers and a praise to them
that do well," and to rule their people in righteousness. The
king not only listened with attention, but promised to profit
by the admonition.

In the year 1825, Thomas Shillitoe visited Russia, and
beholding in the city of St. Petersburg the same desecration
of the Sabbath and general laxity of morals, he was induced
to address a circular to all the Protestants inhabiting that
city, remonstrating with them, and showing the necessity
there was for their being more consistent in life and conduct,
so as to be lights in the darkness of an evil world. The opportunity of obtaining an audience of the emperor, to press
upon him also the necessity of this improvement, was not so
difficult as in other instances. Thomas Shillitoe was known
and honoured; the religious body of which he was a member

was highly esteemed by Alexander. There were many of that denomination in Russia. William Allen and Stephen Grellet, eminent members of the Society of Friends, were known to, and esteemed by the emperor. Moreover Alexander was a very superior man, and exhibited in his high and difficult position, many of those virtues which are most uncommon in the atmosphere of a court. On the evening of the twenty-sixth of December, Thomas Shillitoe was received at the back entrance of the palace at Petersburg, and was ushered into the presence of the most absolute monarch in Europe. The venerable messenger of truth—for he was now advanced in years—began boldly to inform the emperor of the abuses and oppressions that existed under his government. The liberty of the press had become so restricted, that the Moravians had been unable to procure the printing of their new-year's hymn; and also that the address, prepared by himself, and before alluded to, could not, under existing restrictions, be translated and printed; and, therefore, he added, "I should not be able faithfully to acquit myself in the Divine sight in this matter, but by giving the address in charge to him whom I was to consider the father of his people; desiring, as I most fervently did, the Divine wisdom would be pleased to direct him to the right disposal of it." On which the emperor cordially received the address. After some further conversation on important religious subjects, the emperor was pleased to give, very pathetically, the following testimony, which, under the circumstances, is an important historical fact in the personal character of Alexander, which is worthy of being far more widely known than it now is :—

"Before I became acquainted with your religious society and its principles, I frequently, from my early life, felt something in myself which, at times gave me clearly to see that I stood in need of further knowledge in Divine things than I was then possessed of." After speaking of the influence of the Holy Spirit in awakening and renewing his soul he added —" My mind is at times brought under great suffering to know how to move along; I see things necessary for me to do, and things necessary for me to refuse complying with, which are expected from me. You have counselled me to an unreserved and well-timed obedience in all things; I clearly see it is my duty; and this is what I want to be brought into the experience of: but, when I try for it, doubts come into my mind, and discouragements prevail; for, although they call me an absolute monarch, it is but little power I have for doing that which I see it to be right for me to do."

Nothing could exceed the condescension of the emperor at this interview: he commanded the humble Friend to sit beside him on the same sofa, and, dismissing his attendants, communed with him as with a friend and equal.

Before Thomas Shillitoe quitted Petersburg, he was favoured with another gracious interview, and experienced similiar tokens of his message being accepted with candour and attention. These instances are very instructive, as evidences of the power of truth, when faithfully uttered, to overleap the barriers which human pride and expediency have raised between man and man, and to bring the humblest and the highest human beings together, as creatures equal in the sight of Him before whose throne " rich and poor meet together," for He " is the maker of them all."

Moral Heroism, by C. L. Balfour.

COURTSHIP AND MARRIAGE OF ISAAC T. HOPPER.

He was as precocious in love, as in other matters. Not far from his home, lived a prosperous and highly respectable Quaker family, named Tatum. There were several sons, but only one daughter; a handsome child, with clear fair complexion, blue eyes, and a profusion of brown curly hair,

She was Isaac's cousin twice removed; for their great-grandfathers were half brothers. When he was only eight years old and she was not yet five, he made up his mind that little Sarah Tatum was his wife. He used to walk a mile and a half every day, on purpose to escort her to school. When they rambled through the woods, in search of berries, it was his delight to sit beside her on some old stump, and twist her glossy bright ringlets over his fingers. A lovely picture they must have made in the green, leafy frame-work of the woods—that fair, blue-eyed girl, and the handsome, vigorous boy! When he was fourteen years old, he wrote to her a love letter. The village schoolmaster taught for very low wages, and was not remarkably qualified for his task; as was generally the case at that early period. Isaac's labour was needed on the farm all the summer; consequently, he was able to attend school only three months during the winter. He was, therefore, so little acquainted with the forms of letter-writing, that he put Sarah's name inside the letter, and his own on the outside. She being an only daughter, and a great pet in her family, had better opportunities for education. She told her young lover that was not the correct way to write a letter, and instructed him how to proceed in future. From that time, they corresponded constantly.

In those days, Isaac did not profess to be a Quaker. He used the customary language of the world, and liked to display his well-proportioned figure in neat and fashionable clothing. The young women of his acquaintance, it is said, looked upon him with rather favourable eyes; but his thoughts never wandered from Sarah Tatum for a single day. Once, when he had a new suit of clothes, and stylish boots, the tops turned down with red, a young man of his acquaintance invited him to go home with him on Saturday evening and spend Sunday. He accepted the invitation, and set out well pleased with the expedition. The young man had a sister, who took it into her head that the visit was intended as an especial compliment to herself. The brother was called out somewhere in the neighbourhood, and as soon as she found herself alone with their guest, she began to specify, in rather significant terms, what she should require of a man who wished to marry her. Her remarks made Isaac rather fidgety; but he replied in general terms, that he thought her ideas on the subject were very correct. "I suppose you think my father will give me considerable money," said she; "but that is a mistake. Whoever takes me must take me for myself alone."

The young man tried to stammer out that he did not come on any such errand; but his wits were bewildered by this unexpected siege, and he could not frame a suitable reply. She mistook his confusion for the natural timidity of love, and went on to express the high opinion she entertained of him. Isaac looked wistfully at the door, in hopes her brother would come to his rescue. But no relief came from that quarter, and fearing he should find himself engaged to be married without his own consent, he caught up his hat and rushed out. It was raining fast, but he splashed through mud and water, without stopping to choose his steps. Crossing the yard in this desperate haste, he encountered the brother, who called out, "Where are you going?"

"I'm going home," he replied.

"Going home!" exclaimed his astonished friend, "Why it is raining hard; and you came to stay all night. What does possess you, Isaac? Come back! Come back, I say!"

"I won't come back!" shouted Isaac from the distance. I am going home." And home he went. His new clothes were well spattered, and his red-top boots loaded with mud; but though he prided himself on keeping his apparel in neat condition, he thought he had got off cheaply on this occasion.

While the experiences of life were deepening and
strengthening his character, the fair child, Sarah Tatum,
was emerging into womanhood. She was a great belle in
her neighbourhood, admired by the young men for her comely
person, and by the old for her good sense and discreet manners.
He had many competitors for her favour. Once, when he
went to invite her to ride to Quaterly Meeting, he found
three Quaker beaux, already there, with horses and sleighs
for the same purpose. But though some of her admirers
abounded in worldly goods, her mind never swerved from
the love of her childhood. The bright affectionate school-
boy, who delighted to sit with her under the shady trees, and
twist her shining curls over her fingers, retained his hold
upon her heart as long as its pulses throbbed.

Her father at first felt some uneasiness, lest his daughter
should marry out of the Society of Friends. But Issac had
been for some time seriously impressed with the principles
they professed, and when he assured the good old gentleman
that he would never take Sarah out of the Society, of which
she was born a member, he was perfectly satisfied to receive
him as a son-in-law.

The letters which passed between him and his betrothed
are rather of a sedate character; but through the unimpassioned
Quaker style gleams the steady warmth of sincere affection.
There is something pleasant in the simplicity with which he
usually closed his epistles to her. "I am, dear Sally, thy
real friend, Isaac."

They were married on the eighteenth of the ninth month
(September) 1795; he being nearly twenty four years of age,
and she about three years younger. The worldly comforts
which a kind Providence bestowed on Isaac and his bride,
were freely imparted to others.

After living most happily together for nearly 27 years the
husband was called to part with the steady friend and pleasant,

companion of his brightest and his darkest hours. She passed
from him into the spiritual world in June 1822, in the forty
seventh year of her age. She left nine children, the youngest
but six years old, to mourn the loss of a most tender, careful,
and self-sacrificing mother.

Time soothes all afflictions; and those who have dearly
loved their first compauions are sometimes more likely than
others to form a second connection; for the simple reason
that they cannot learn to do without the happiness to which
they have been accustomed. There was an intimate friend
of the family, a member of the same religious Society, named
Hannah Attmore. She was a gentle and quiet person, of an
innocent and very pleasing countenance. Her father, a
worthy and tender spirited man, had been an intimate friend
of Issac T. Hopper, and always sympathized with his efforts
for the oppressed. A strong attachment had likewise existed
between her and Friend Hopper's wife; and during frequent
visits to the house, it was her pleasure to volunteer assistance
in the numerous household cares. The fact that his Sarah
had great esteem for her, was doubtless a strong attraction
to the widower. His suit was favourably received, and they
were married in February 1824. She was considerably
younger than her bridegroom; but vigorous health and elastic
spirits had preserved his youthful appearance, while her
sober dress and grave deportment made her seem older than
she really was. See became the mother of four children,
two of whom died in early childhood.

The character of his wife was extremely modest and
reserved; and he took mischievous pleasure in telling
strangers of their courtship in a way that made her blush.
"Dost thou know what Hannah answered, when I asked if
she would marry me?" said he. "I will tell thee how it
was. I was walking home with her one evening, soon after
the death of her mother, and I mentioned to her that as she

was alone now, I supposed she intended to make some change in her mode of living. When she said yes, I told her I had been thinking it would be very pleasant to have her come and live with me. 'That would suit me exactly,' said she. This prompt reply made me suppose she might not have understood my meaning; and I explained that I wanted her to become a member of my family; but she replied again, 'There is nothing I should like better.' "

The real fact was, the quiet and timid Hannah Attmore was not dreaming of such a thing as a proposal of marriage. She supposed he spoke of receiving her as a boarder in his family. When she at last perceived his meaning, she slipped her arm out of his very quickly, and was too much confused to utter a word. But it amused him to represent that she seized the opportunity the moment it was offered.

But clearly above all other things, did he remember every look and tone of his beloved Sarah : even in the days when they trudged to school together, hand in hand. The recollection of the first love, closely intertwined with his first religious impressions, was the only flowery spot of romance in the old gentleman's very practical character. When he was seventy years of age, says Maria Child, he shewed me a piece of writing she had copied for him, when she was a girl of fourteen. It was preserved in the self-same envelope, in which she sent it, and pinned with the same pin, long since blackened by age. I said, "Be careful not to lose that pin."

"Lose it!" he exclaimed. "No money could tempt me to part with it. I loved the very ground she trod upon."

He was never weary of eulogizing her comely looks, beautiful manners, sound principles, and sensible conversation. The worthy companion of his later life never seemed troubled by such remarks. She not only "listened to a sister's praises with unwounded ear," but often added a heartfelt tribute to the virtues of her departed friend.

Leonard Fell and the Highwayman.

It is related of Leonard Fell, that as he was travelling alone, he was once accosted by a highwayman who demanded his money, which he gave him. He next required his horse also, when Leonard Fell dismounted and let him take it. But before the robber rode away, he solemnly warned him against the evil course he was pursuing. The highwayman became enraged; asked him why he preached to him, and threatened "to blow out his brains." But Leonard Fell replied, "Though I would not give my life for my money or my horse, I would give it to save thy soul;" an answer, which so went to the heart of the robber, that he declared, if he were such a man as that, he would have neither his money nor his horse; both of which he returned and went his way, leaving Leonard Fell in the enjoyment of that peace which attends the conscientious discharge of duty.

Biographical Memoirs of Friends.

Early-Rising Friends Far West.

The Western Friends, like their neighbours, have to be very early risers. In summer it is common for them to be up at three a.m., or at the very earliest daybreak. An English Friend, who had just come to one of the rural settlements of Indiana, determined to accommodate himself to the ways of the place, and to rise early with the rest. He woke about five o'clock in the morning, and immediately dressed and joined the family, who were evidently amused at something, and expressed general hopes that he had slept "well," adding, "Why, we've all had breakfast an hour ago." The new comer was astonished to find that five a.m. was about two hours later than the ordinary time for getting up.

Tullack's Friendly Sketches in America.

P

QUAKER'S HOUSE PRESERVED.

A most remarkable case occured at the siege of Copenhagen under Lord Nelson. An officer in the fleet says :—" 1 was particularly impressed with an object which I saw three or four days after the terrific bombardment of the place. For several nights before the surrender, the darkness was ushered in with a tremendous roar of guns and mortars, accompanied by the whizzing of those destructive and burning engines of warfare, Congreve's rockets. The dreadful effects were soon visible in the brilliant lights through the city. The blazing houses of the rich, and the burning cottages of the poor, illuminated the heavens; and the widespreading flames, reflecting on the water, showed a forest of ships assembled round the city for its destruction. This work of conflagration went on for several nights; but the Danes at length surrendered; and on walking some days after among the ruins, consisting of the cottages of the poor, houses of the rich, manufactories, lofty steeples, and humble meeting-houses, I descried, amid this barren field of desolation, a solitary house unharmed; all around it a burnt mass, this alone untouched by the fire, a monument of mercy. 'Whose house is that?' I asked. 'That,' said the interpreter, ' belongs to a Quaker. He would neither fight nor leave his house, but remained in prayer, with his family during the whole bombardment.' Surely, thought I, it *is* well with the righteous God *has* been a shield to thee in battle, a wall of fire round about thee, a very present help in time of need."

ADVICE.

A pretty girl was complaining to a young Quaker, last week, that she was dreadfully troubled by *chaps* on her lips.' "Friend Mary!" replied the Quaker, "thou shouldst not permit the *chaps* to come so near thy lips."

THE QUAKER AND THE OFFICER.

Mr. Dillwayn's son told me that his father in his younger days, was in a stage-coach with a party of military officers. One of them, a pert effiminate dandy, undertook to quiz the plain Quaker, and after some indefinite jokes, asked him at an inn where they stopped to hold his sword for a minute, supposing he would consider it an abomination to touch it. Mr. Dillwayn, however, eyeing the young man from head to foot, said, "As I believe, from its appearance, it has never shed blood, and is not in the least likely to do so, I have not the slightest objection.

A WARNING.

A staid Quaker replied to a fellow who was abusing him, "Have a care, friend, or thee mayest run thy countenance against my fist."

COURTSHIP.

"Martha, dost thou love me?" asked a Quaker youth of one at whose shrine his heart's holiest feelings had been offered up. "Why, Seth," answered she, "we are commanded to love one another, are we not? "Ay, Martha, but does thee regard me with the feeling the world calls love?" "I hardly know what to tell thee, Seth, I have greatly feared that my heart was an erring one. I have tried to bestow my love on all, but I have sometimes thought, perhaps, that thee was getting rather more than thy share."

THE BULLY.

A genuine bully called upon a Friend, avowedly to thrash him. "Friend," remonstrated the Quaker, knocking aside his fists, "before thou proceedeth to chastise me, wilt thou not take some dinner?" The bully was a glutton, and at once accepted, washing down the solids with strong libations of ale. He rose up again to fulfil his original errand. "Friend," said the Quaker, "wilt thou not take some punch?" The bully, now staggering, attempted to thrash his entertainer; but quoth the Quaker, "Friend, wilt thou not take a pipe?" This hospitality was also accepted, but still 'the bully staggered across the room to belabour the Quaker. The latter, opening the door and pulling him towards it, thus addressed him, " Friend, thou camest here not to be pacified, I gave thee a meat-offering, but this did not assuage thy rage; I gave thee a drink-offering, still thou wert beside thyself; I gave thee a burnt-offering, neither did that suffice; now I will try thee with a heave-offering." And with that he tossed him out of the door, and that sufficed.

THE CHURCH ORGAN

"Friend Maltby, I am pleased that thou hast got such a fine organ in thy church." "But," said the clergyman, "I thought you were strongly opposed to having an organ in a church?" "So I am," said Friend Obadiah; "but then if thou wilt worship the Lord by machinery, I would like thee to have a first-rate instrument."

STRANGE TITLE.

A Quaker who was suffering in prison published a book entitled "A Sigh for the Sinners in Zion, coming from a Hole in the Wall, by an Earthen Vessel, known among men as Samuel Fish."

CONSCIENTIOUS LAWYER.

Nicholas Waln was educated in the Society of Friends' in America, but in early life seems to have cared little about their principles. He was then an ambitious, money-loving man, remarkably successful in worldly affairs. But the principles inculcated in childhood probably remained latent within him; for when he was rapidly acquiring wealth and distinction by the practice of law, he suddenly relinquished it, from conscientious motives. This change of feeling is said to have been owing to the following incident. He had charge of an important case, where a large amount of property was at stake. In the progress of the cause, he became more and more aware that right was not on the side of his client; but to desert him in the midst was incompatible with his ideas of honor as a lawyer. This produced a conflict within him, which he could not immediately settle to his own satisfaction. A friend, who met him after the case was decided, inquired what was the result. He replied, " I did the best I could for my client. I have gained the cause for him, and have thereby defrauded an honest man of his just dues." He seemed sad and thoughtful, and would never after plead a cause at the bar. He dismissed his students, and returned to his clients all the money he had received for unfinished cases. For some time afterward, he appeared to take no interest in anything but his own religious state of feeling. He eventually became a preacher, very popular among Friends, and much admired by others. His sermons were usually short and very impressive A contemporary thus describes the effect of his preaching ? The whole assembly seemed to be baptized together, and so covered with solemnity, that when the meeting broke up, no one wished to enter into conversation with another." He was so highly esteemed, that when he entered the court-house, as he occasionally did, to aid the poor or the oppressed in some way, it was not uncommon for judges and lawyers to rise spontaneously in token of respect.

PETER BEDFORD.

We have repeatedly listened to Mr. Bedford's narrative of a remarkable circumstance which first drew his particular at ention to juvenile criminals. He often related it to his visitors, and we here copy the account as given to Mr. Smithies. In the year 1815, in the neighbourhood of Spitalfields, a young man named John Knight was on a certain occasion arrested for stealing a watch. A gentleman living at Hoxton was walking through Whitechapel, and leading a little boy with him. He had to pass through a large concourse of people, who were attending the funeral of a member of an Odd Fellows' Society. Whilst in the crowd, an attempt was made by some one to rob him of his watch. An individual was apprehended for it, and committed to Newgate for trial. Mr. William Crawford (an inspector of prisons) and myself happened to be visiting Newgate together just after that prisoner (named John Knight) had been tried for the above offence, and condemned to death. The ordinary accosted us, and said, "Now, Mr. Bedford, here's a case that ought to claim your attention." "Well, what is it?" said I. He then described Knight's case in detail, and further informed us that, after his arrest on the spot, a rescue had been attempted by his companions,—stones and brickbats thrown, constables wounded; and bloody handkerchiefs had been exhibited at the trial as unmistakable evidence of great violence on the occasion. He added, "This is a case you ought to attend to, though I fear that all the influence that you and your friends can bring to bear upon it will not avail." I replied that we would see about it, and make inquiry. Accordingly, investigations into the matter were set on foot. Whilst they were proceeding, Crawford went down to Brighton, and during his stay there wrote to inform me that the day for Knight's execution was fixed. On the following Saturday I received another letter from Mr. Crawford: "My dear Mr. Bedford, you cannot suffer Knight to be executed without doing all that can be done to have his life spared." Immediately on receipt of this I went to my friends in the City, first to one and then to another, to influential bankers and merchants, but they were all particularly engaged. I then called on Dr. Lushington, and told him I wanted him to go with me to Newgate. He replied, "Well Bedford, if you wish it; I will not say I will go with you with pleasure, but I will go with you." And we went. Knight was now left for execution on the following Wednesday. Previously to our reaching Newgate, I said, "Now, Lushington, it is necessary to take care not to raise any expectations of this poor fellow's life being spared." We reached the prison and obtained the interview. I kept in the background, and left the Doctor to speak with him. After he had addressed him in a very suitable manner on the occasion, the lad turned round to him and said, "Sir, I didn't steal the watch." "Why, what do you mean?" said the Doctor. "Indeed, sir, I didn't steal the watch; it was John Grew, a weaver in Spitalfields; and, sir, there's a boy now in prison that can tell you all about it; his name is Green." The Doctor conferred with me, and I seated myself on the bench by the side of the poor boy Knight, and said to him, "Well, Knight, this is very extraordinary. Why do you attempt to say you are innocent of the crime for which you have been tried and pronounced guilty?" I spoke very kindly to him, but still he persevered in saying, "Indeed, sir, I didn't steal it." I afterwards learned that he did not steal the watch, though he had attempted to do so. It appears that Knight raised the watch in the gentleman's fob, but withdrew without accomplishing his object, believing he was discovered. As he was retreating, another man, named Grew, effected the robbery. Grew, however, eluded the

grasp of the gentleman, who at once seized Knight and held
him, and afterwards, at the trial, swore that he had never
let him go. That was the ground on which Lord Sidmouth
ordered his execution. Well, we talked to Knight about the
awfulness of his situation, and how serious a thing it would
be for him to continue to deny the fact, if it was a fact, and
to die with a lie upon his tongue. With an impression that
he was guilty, the Doctor and I left him. We then saw the
boy Green, who confirmed all that Knight had said. Well,
we met that evening at William Allen's, in Plough Court,
with others of our friends who were interested in the subject
of procuring the rescue and reformation of juvenile
delinquents. It was there fixed that Dr. Lushington should
meet me afterwards at my house, to obtain an interview with
Knight's father. We found the poor man so crushed and
stupified as hardly to be able to give us an answer to any of
our questions. He said he was going into Shoreditch, and
might perhaps be able to bring us some useful information
on the matter. Just after he had gone out, I said to the
Doctor, "Hadn't I better bring him back, and let him take
us to the Virginia Planter?" "Oh, yes, by all means,"
said the Doctor. I then went after the man and brought
him back, and said, "Now, Knight, take us to the Virginia
Planter." This was a public-house at the corner of Thrall
Street, Spitalfields, and a most notorious place of resort for
thieves. When we arrived there we sent Knight in at the
taproom door, and told him to stop everybody in the place.
We went into the bar door, and said we wanted to see the
young folks that were in the bar-room, adding that we had
come about Knight, the prisoner under sentence of death.
We had them invited into a back parlour, and there I met
with a well-known low character, one Bill Horne. We now
stated the anxiety we felt to save the life of poor Knight, if
we could prove his innocence. Bill knew all about it, and

said, "The real thief was John Grew." "Well," we said, "we must have him to-night; for Knight is about to be executed." Bill replied, "You can't have him to-night; we don't know where he is; but you shall know to-morrow." Bill's heart was touched with the kindness of the motive we had in view, and promised he would do the best he could to find him out. We requested that, as soon as any information was obtained, Bill and his companions would come to my house, as I lived in the neighbourhood. But here, again, I was in some difficulty, because I had only two female servants in the house, in which also was a good deal of property. I did not know what might happen with such visitors as I expected; so I deliberated as to what I should do, and whether I should stay at home from going to our usual Friends' meeting for worship. I decided to let everything go on as usual. Just before going to meeting I informed the single servant left at home as to what kind of people might possibly come during my absence, and, should such be the case, requested her to send them on to me. So I went off to meeting, at Devonshire House, Houndsditch, and had been there only about twenty minutes when I saw the door slowly open, and the father of poor Knight enter. I then left my seat and went out with him, and in the yard we found Bill Horne, Grew himself, and the young man that received the watch from his hand, together with some other companions. Grew accosted me, and said, "As soon as I knew, Mr. Bedford, that you were wishing to find me out, I determined I would come to you; and there is the person that received the watch." I said, "Walk with me to my house." And thither I went, escorted by such a company as that. When we reached it, I took them into the parlour, brought out my portable writing-desk, sat down, and recorded, in the form of depositions, all the information I could gain, especially that of the culprit himself. I then fixed for them to be at my house again the next morning at eight o'clock. Meanwhile I sent off to Dr. Lushington, to let him know that at that hour I had appointed an interview with these people, and invited him to be at my house by nine, and also to inform Fowell Buxton of the matter. The Doctor accordingly got his horse, and rode off to Buxton, who also sent information to our Friends Thomas and Edward Foster, of St. Helen's Place. Next day Dr Lushington met the party at my house, and investigated the case most thoroughly, and in consequence became perfectly satisfied that Knight had only made the attempt to steal the watch, but though innocent of the fact, was guilty of being concerned. All our evidence was now complete, except the proof afforded by the watch itself. On inquiry, we ascertained that it had been lodged with a pawnbroker in the Borough for £3. I thought it was most important for us to have the watch, and resolved to obtain it; but as it was stolen property, and I knew it to be such, the Doctor said to me, " Bedford, mind what you are doing." I replied, " Yes, Doctor; I think I do know what I am about." I then took Knight's father aside, and said, "Knight, we *must have* that watch " He replied, "I have not got the money to get it." I answered, "The watch *must* be had." I then talked to him about his son's case for some time. The poor man was extremely distressed. At length I dismissed him—previously, however, putting my hand into my pocket, and giving him £3. Had I not a right to give him £30 if I had liked? And had I not said, " We *must* have the watch ?" We now arranged that all our party were to meet at Edward Foster's, at St. Helen's Place, at ten o'clock. There were there Fowell Buxton, Dr. Lushington, Edward Foster, and myself, and also all those other people, and the watch. Thomas Foster had been sent forward to the Home Office to request an interview with Lord Sidmouth. After going fairly into our plans, two coaches were ordered. We went in one (with the watch), and Knight, Grew, and Horne in the, other. Thomas Foster was waiting at the Home Office for us, and we promptly obtained an interview with Lord Sidmouth. Fowell Buxton on this occasion, took up the subject, stating all the details of the case. Then Dr. Lushington spoke on the awfulness of taking away human life under such circumstances. It was my belief that Lord Sidmouth's political feelings towards the Doctor operated very sadly against poor Knight. He said, "Dr. Lushington, you cause horrible feelings in my mind; but I tell you that if, after investigating the case, or any such case, and giving it the best attention I could, even if I were mistaken, I should think it right, under the circumstances, that the execution should go on; for the person who lost the watch swore positively that he seized the man by the collar, and never let him go." I believe Lord Sidmouth entertained that idea of the case most sincerely; but he was in error. We entreated Lord Sidmouth to see the young man. "No," he replied; "but Mr. So-and-oS at the office will examine him." We went with Grew to the official named, and after his examination, when we got outside the building, Dr. Lushington clapped his hands, and said, "Oh, Bedford, we have saved his life!" But Buxton, who entertained doubts on the subject, answered, "I am not sure of that." I now went into the country, and on the Thursday morning I received a note from Dr. Lushington, saying, "My dear Bedford, I have just seen Mr. Bowler at Newgate, and I find that Knight was executed, declaring his innocence three times when the cap was drawn over his face." On my return to London we called together a number of gentlemen interested in the subject, and their opinion was that there was something further for us to do in the matter, and that we ought to endeavour to meet all the juvenile delinquents in the neighbourhood where Knight had be· n known, and his associates in particular. The proposition was that Dr. Lushington and myself should go down again to the Virginia Planter, and get all the poor creatures together, or as many of them as we could, and then address them. A few days elapsed, and we had meanwhile arranged for a meeting of these juvenile delinquents, and taken measures to have them invited to hear us on the evening of the day on which poor Knight's body was buried. Dr. Lushington called at my house shortly before the time appointed; but before starting with me he took out his pocket-book, a gold watch, and gold snuff-box, all of which I locked up in my desk, and we then walked on arm-in-arm, threading our way through the dirty, narrow streets. As we were going along, the Doctor said, "Well, I don't feel quite as I should like." "Indeed, Doctor," said I; "how is it? What is the cause?" On asking him, further, if he was afraid of anything occurring, "Oh, Bedford," he replied, "if it was that, I would tell you; but I should be ashamed to tell you; it is not on that account." We then walked on in silence, and missed our way. (Perhaps the good Doctor felt a little regret at having divested himself of his property, rather than going forward on his benevolent work in perfect reliance on the Divine protection, if not with complete confidence in the persons he was going amongst) After some time, on a sudden we came upon the place. The Doctor here stood still, and for a few moments was engaged, apparently, in silent prayer. "Now," he said, "I am ready." We went in, and found the room filled; still there were many there who did not like to show themselves, but kept in the passages. Ours was not intended to be a mere matter of talk, but of real usefulness, and we had a proposition to make. At the meeting at Plough Court, £300 had been offered to place us in a position to admit every young delinquent into the Refuge, if willing to enter. Well, the Doctor began, and addressed them most impressively. He said: "Young men, you know that when Mr. Bedford and I were here last we came with a view of saving the life of your associate, if it were possible; *but his character was bad.* You know that he had been living in a course of life that was disreputable, and to that may, in a great measure, be attributed our want of success in endeavouring to save him, though we believe that he was not guilty of the crime for which he suffered However, you know that his life has been forfeited: and I have to tell you, young men, every one of you, that your fate will be similar to that of your poor associate Knight, if you do not forsake the course of life that you are in; or at least you will be transported to another country." The Doctor began upon a low key. but rose as he continued. It was most interesting He then described the horrors of transportation. and concluded by. recommending them to alter their course of life He said: "There are probably some amongst you that would be glad to alter your conduct, but who, very likely. may be so circumstanced that it is impossible for you to maintain yourselves in a respectable manner, having lost your characters, and having departed from the paths of rectitude and honesty. But I have to tell you that some gentlemen have made arrangements for the assistance of any such characters as those who may be sorry for their past wicked course, and who may now repent and wish to alter their mode of living Such may now be put into the way of becoming respectable and reputable members of the community." I then made a few observations, and told them that any further information they might desire on the subject might be obtained on applying to myself, as I should be happy to aid them. It was about ten o'clock at

night when we turned out of this place, and were surrounded
by a crowd of thieves of different ages. One of them said
to me, "Mr. Bedford, are you afraid." "Afraid!" I said,
" what have I to be afraid of?   I am sure that none of you
would hurt me or this gentleman." "No, sir," was the
reply; "if you were covered with jewels, you would not
lose one of them. But if you are at all afraid, we will
form a guard, and see you safe to your own house."
Wishing to inquire about our proposed plan, some of them
came to my house, and I told them of the Refuge for the
Destitute at Hoxton. Several of them went to see it, and
concluded to accept the offer at once. They first went back,
however, having some matters to settle, and fell in with
some of their old companions, who discouraged them from
going to the Refuge.   One young man of their company,
called on me afterwards alone, and, after stating his case,
and learning what I had in view, said, "Oh, sir, can you
do anything for my poor sister?"   He marched up and
down the room in the greatest agony imaginable. I never
saw a poor creature more distressed than he was. I asked
him what was the case of his sister.   Then he described it.
He had placed her on the brink of ruin, as on a precipice,
having introduced her to some of his associates. But she
was a virtuous young woman. I said, "I will try to do
something." I conferred with the clergyman of the parish,
and we got her into an institution; and she proved one of
the best cases they ever had—upright and virtuous, yet
just snatched from destruction. But it was shocking to
witness the agony of the poor fellow. His gratitude
afterwards was very great. The girl subsequently obtained
a good situation. There was a tradesman in Spitalfields
with several sons, one of whom formed an attachment to
her; but before accepting his proposals, she said to his
father, "I cannot listen to any offer until you go and

ascertain from Mr. Bedford all that he knows of the circumstances of my case." Accordingly the tradesman came to my house, and explained to me how the matter stood. I answered that I had only to say that, if it was left to me, I should encourage the young woman to accept of his son. I found that this person had been to my house before. He attended one of the Friends' public meetings, at which a minister from America had preached on some subject in a manner which this man did not understand, and he afterwards called at my house to ask for some explanations. The young couple married, and set up in business not far from London. A year or two afterwards I was passing their shop, and saw the husband behind the counter, and his wife with a nice little child in her arms, and looking so thoroughly happy that I could not muster courage to revive old remembrances, so I passed on without going in.

William Tallack's *Life of Peter Bedford.*

SHOPKEEPER'S TRICK.

An honest rustic went into the shop of a Quaker to buy a hat, for which fifteen shillings was demanded. He offered twelve shillings. "As I live," said the Quaker, "I cannot afford to give it thee at that price." "As you live!" exclaimed the countryman; "then live more moderately, and be hanged to you." "Friend," said the Quaker, "thou shalt have the hat for nothing. I have sold hats for twenty years, and my trick has never been found out till now."

ARIANS CONFOUNDED.

Two of Dr. Priestly's followers, eminent men, once called on an old gentleman of the Society of Friends, to ask him what was *his* opinion of the person of Christ. After a little consideration, he replied:—" The apostle says,

We preach Christ crucified, unto the Jews a stumbling-block, because they expected a *temporal* Messiah; to the Greeks foolishness, because he was crucified as a malefactor; but unto them which are called, both Jews and Greeks, Christ the power of God, and the wisdom of God. Now, if you can separate the power of God from God, and the wisdom of God from God, I will come over to your opinions." They were both struck dumb, and did not attempt to utter a single word in reply.

HUMANITY OF WALKER.

The following anecdote of Dr. Walker, well known as the Director of the London Jennerian and Vaccine Institutions, is extracted from his memoir :

While our troops were using the weapons of destruction, Dr. Walker was busily employed in saving life. His work of vaccination being completed, he attended the sick of the British navy and of the Turkish army. The sense of weariness while engaged in these works of mercy, he seems hardly to have known ; being assisted by his friend General Sir John Doyle, in prosecuting these labours of goodness. The following extract of a letter from that worthy officer speaks volumes. "The general can never forget the impression made upon him by the extraordinary situation in which he first made an acquaintance with that amiable and benevolent individual, Dr. Walker. The day after the action, near Alexandria, where the brave Abercrombie fell, the general was riding over the field of battle, attended by two orderly dragoons, to see if there were any wounded, French or English, who had escaped notice the evening before; when, on turning round a wall by the sea-side, he was struck with an appalling sight of more than a hundred French soldiers, with their officers, huddled together, desperately wounded by grape and cannon shot from an

English ship of war. From being collected in the recess of the wall, they had escaped notice on the previous day of search, and were exposed to the night air, and with undressed wounds. Here the general saw a man, evidently English, in the garb of a Quaker, actively employed in the heavenly task of giving his humane assistance to those poor brave sufferers; giving water to some, dressing the wounds of others, and affording consolation to all. Upon inquiry he found the benevolent individual to be Dr. John Walker, who was himself almost exhausted, having been thus nobly employed from daybreak without intermission."

The Grave Quaker and Miss Landon. (L.E.L.)

William Howitt remarks :—" I recollect meeting her in company at a time there was a strong report that she was actually though secretly married. Mrs. Hofland, on her entering the room, went up to her in her plain, straightforward way, and said, " Ah! my dear, what must I call you, Miss Landon, or whom?" After a well-feigned surprise at the question, Miss Landon began to talk in a tone of merry ridicule at this report, and ended by declaring that as to love or marriage, they were things that she never thought of. " What, then, have you been doing with yourself this last month?"

" O, I have been puzzling my brain to invent a new sleeve; pray, how do you like it?" showing her arm.

" You never think of such a thing as love ! " exclaimed a sentimental young man; " you, who have written so many volumes of poetry upon it !"

" O that's all professional, you know," exclaimed she, with an air of merry scorn.

" Professional! " exclaimed a grave Quaker who stood near; "why dost thou make a difference between what is

c

professional and what is real?   Dost thou write one thing
and think another?   Does not that look very much like
hypocrisy?"

"To this the astonished poetess made no reply, but by a
look of genuine amazement. It was a mode of putting
the matter to which she had evidently never been accustomed. And, in fact, there can be no question that
much of her writing was professional. She had to win a
golden harvest for the comfort of others as dear to herself;
and she felt, like all authors who have to cater for the
public, that she must provide, not so much what she would
of her free-will choice, but what they expected from her."

PHYSIOGNOMY OF FRIENDS.

The serene, placid, peaceful countenances of the people
called Quakers, display, in very striking characters, the
ab-ence of all the turbulent passions   As a sect they excel
all others in the almost perfect command they have over
their passions. They may be denominated a great and
strong people, if it were only from the innocent, perhaps
laudable, ingenuity, which they manifest in concealing
their weaknesses.   Long habits of self-examination, and
its accompanying virtue, self-control have stamped upon
their features a most obvious expression of internal composure and tranquility of soul. Moving in the centre of
their own circumference, and abstracting their thoughts
from the vices and frivolities of the age and country they
live in, all their looks, gestures, and actions bespeak them
persons of one business—bent upon one object—aiming at
one end—and aspiring at perfection in everything they
attempt. In those who are what *ancient Friends* (to use one
of their own terms) would have called true and steady
followers of the light of grace in the heart, the most sober
zeal and piety are painted in the features—mildness and

benevolence beam on the cheek—love and complacency shine through the eye; whilst fortitude and courage characterize their forehead. And even in those *Friends* who ~~who~~ are merely so from birth and education, the same characteristics of perseverance, steadiness, and attention, though directed to worldly pursuits, are strikingly visible.

A Quaker, who is one from conviction and principle, cannot be a morose, vindictive, malicious, or impious character; he who is one from birth only may possibly be all these; but even he will never be accused of indolence or inattention, so long as he preserves the outward forms of the sect to which he belongs. In both cases, the Quakers furnish a demonstrative evidence of the truth of the physiognomical maxim, that habits of mind beget corresponding habits of countenance.

Cooke's View of the Science of Physiognomy.

George III and Hannah Lightfoot.

Although George the Third condemned, with great severity, the first amour of his eldest son with Mrs. Robinson, the youth of the King was not spotless; but he fell into a like derelection himself. The story is variously told; but the following version, written by Sir Richard Phillips, who knew some of the parties, and took great pains to elicit the truth in the *Monthly Magazine*, may be relied on.

About the year 1756, there lived at the corner of Market-street, St. James's-market, a linen draper named Wheeler, a Quaker, who had a beautiful niece, named Hannah Lightfoot, known as "the fair Quakeress," from serving in her uncle's shop. The lady caught the eye of Prince George, in his walks and rides from Leicester House to St. James's Palace, and she soon returned the attentions of such a lover. She is said to have been privately married to the Prince, in Kew Chapel: another story states that the marriage was

celebrated at Curzon-street Chapel, by the Rev. Alexander
Keith, with the Prince's brother, the Duke of York, as a witness; and it is stated that children were born of the marriage,
of whom, a son, was sent, when a child, to the Cape of Good
Hope, with the name of George Rex. This portion of the
story, by Dr. Doran, receives some corroboration, from there
being, in 1830, at the Cape a Mr. George Rex, at the Knysna;
a Correspondent of Notes and Queries, second series, vol. xi.
understood from Rex that he had then (1830) been about
thirty-four years a resident of the country, was about sixty-
eight years of age, of strong, robust appearance, and the exact resemblance in featu.es to George III. This would
bring him to about the time of the Prince's marriage to
Hannah, as stated by Dr. Doran. On Mr. Rex's first arrival
in the colony, he occupied a high situation in the Colonial
Goverment, and received an extensive grant of land at the
Knysna.

We now return to Sir Richard Phillip's version. The
acquaintance alarming the Royal Family, it was contrived to
marry the Quaker to a young grocer and former admirer, of
the name of Oxford, of Ludgate-hill. The Prince, however,
was inconsolable; and a few weeks after, as Oxford was one
evening from home, a royal carriage came to the door, and
the lady was hurried into it by the attendants, and carried off
at full speed. Where she was taken to, or what became of
her, was never known. Some reported that she survived her
lover; others, that she died in 1765, after having had three
sons, since general officers. Her death disturbed the royal
mind. Oxford, broken-hearted, retired to Warminster, set up
a grocer's shop, married again, and had a family : he died in
old age, about 1810, but not without having sought clam-
oursly for information about his wife, at Weymouth and
other places.

                    Timbs " *Century of Anecdote.*"

HAT PROTEST.

Fox, the founder of Quakerism, was in the habit of attending public worship at the established church. When the preacher uttered sentiments of which he disapproved, he would most solemnly put on his broad-brimmed hat, and take it off again whenever a more welcome strain of doctrine occurred. If he had sat long with his hat on, and the ill-sounding propositions or fulminations continued he would rise slowly, and silently walk out. Thus it appears that it was for purposes of habitual protest that the Quakers first learned to sit in places of worship with their hats on.

GEORGE FOX AND HIS HAT.

George Fox and companions were brought before Chief Justice Glynne at the assizes in the early part of 1656. Upon entering the court they stood for some time with their hats on, and the court remaining silent, George Fox was moved to say, "Peace be amongst you."

The judge then asked the gaoler who they were, and on being informed they were prisoners, he said, "Why do you not pull off your hats?"

The Quakers stood silent.

Judge. "Put off your hats." Still they remained silent.

Judge. "The court commands you to put off your hats"

G. Fox: "Where did ever any magistrate, king, or judge from Moses to Daniel, command any to put off their hats, when they came before them in their courts, either among the Jews, (the people of God) or among the heathens? And if the law of England doth command any such thing, show me that law either written or printed."

Judge, angrily "I do not carry my law books upon my back."

G. Fox. "Tell me then, where it is printed in any statute book that I may read it."

Judge. "Take him away, prevaricator,—I'll ferk him!"

They were then removed out of court, and put among the thieves; but presently afterwards were ordered back.

Judge. "Come! where had they any hats from Moses to Daniel? Come, answer me, I have you now fast."

G. Fox. "Thou mayst read in the third of Daniel, that the three children were cast into the fiery furnace by Nebuchadnezzar's command, with their coats, their hose, and their hats on."

This clever reply nonplussed the judge who ordered them to be re-conducted to prison. Afterwards when brought before the same judge, none of the accusations against them being proved, he ordered them back again to prison, and fined them twenty marks a-piece, for not taking off their hats in court, and to be imprisoned till they paid the fine.

REMARKABLE TRIAL OF WILLIAM PENN.

Clarkson in his Life of William Penn writes, On the 1st of September the trial came on; and here I have to express my regret that the limits which I have proposed to this work should prevent me from presenting it at full length to the notice of the reader, because altogether it is a very interesting event in our history, and one of which no part that is recorded ought to be lost to posterity.

The persons who were present on the bench as Justices, on this day, were Sir Samuel Starling, lord mayor; John Howel, recorder; Thomas Bludworth, William Peak, Richard Ford, John Robinson, Joseph Sheldon, aldermen, and Richard Brown, John Smith, and James Edwards, sheriffs.

The jury, who were impanelled, and whose names ought to be handed down to the love and gratitude of posterity, were Thomas Veer, Edward Bushel, John Hammond, Charles Milson, Gregory Walklet, John Brightman, William Plumstead, Henry Henley, James Damask, Henry Michel, William Lever, and John Bailey.

The indictment stated among other falsehoods the prisoners had preached to an unlawful, seditious, and riotous assembly; that they had assembled by agreement made beforehand; and that they had met together with force and arms, and this to the great terror and disturbance of many of his Majesty's liege subjects.

Very little was done on this day. The prisoners were brought to the bar; and having made their observations on several things as they passed, they pleaded not guilty to the indictment. The Court was then adjourned. In the afternoon they were brought to the bar again; but they were afterwards set aside, being made to wait till after the trial of other prisoners.

On the 3rd of September, the trial of those last men tioned being over, William Penn and William Mead were brought again into court. One of the officers, as they entered, pulled off their hats. Upon this the Lord Mayor became furious, and in a stern voice ordered him to put them on again. This being done, the Recorder fined each of the prisoners forty marks, observing that the circumstance of their being covered there amounted to a contempt of Court.

The witnesses were then called in and examined. It appeared, from their testimony, that on the 15th of August between three and four hundred persons were assembled in Gracechurch-street, and that they saw William Penn speaking to the people, but could not distinguish what he said. One, and one only, swore that he heard him preach; but, on further examination, he said that he could not on account of the noise, understand any of the words spoken.

The witnesses h iving finished their testimony, William
Penn acknowledged that both he and his friend were present at the place and time mentioned. Their object in beii g
there was to worship God. "We are so far," says he,
"from recanting, or declining to vindicate the assemblir g
of ourselves to preach, pray, or worship the eternal, holy,
just Gcd, that we declare to all the world, that we do
believe it to be our indispensable duty to meet incessant y
upon so good an account; nor shall all the powers upc n
earth be able to divert us from reverencing and adoring ou r
God, who made us." These words were scarcely pronounced, when Brown, one of the sheriffs, exclaimed, that he
was not there for worshiping God, but for breaking the law.
William Penn replied, that he had broken no law, and desired to know by what law it was that they prosecuted him,
and upon what law it was that they founded the indictment.

The Recorder replied, the common law. William asked,
where that law was. The Recorder did not think it worth
while, he said, to run over all those adjudged cases for so
many years, which they called common law, to satisfy his
curiosity. William Penn thought, if the law were common,
it should not be so hard to produce. He was then asked
to plead to the indictment; but, on delivering his sentiments on this point, he was pronounced a saucy fellow.
The following is a specimen of some of the questions and
answers at full length, which succeeded those now mentioned :—

W. Penn. The question is not, whether I am guilty of
this indictment, but whether this indictment be legal. It
is too general and imperfect an answer to say it is the
common law, unless we know where and what it is; for
where there is no law, there is no transgression; and that
law which is not in being, is so far from being common,
that it is no law at all.

Recorder. You are an impertinent fellow. Will you teach the Court what law is? It is lex non scripta, that which many have studied thirty or forty years to know, and would you have me tell you in a moment?

W. Penn. Certainly, if the common law be so hard to be understood, it is far from being very common; but if the Lord Coke, in his Institutes, be of any consideration, he tells us, that common law is common right, and that common right is the Great Charter privileges confirmed.

Recorder. Sir, you are a troublesome fellow, and it is not to the honour of the Court to suffer you to go on.

W. Penn. I have asked but one question, and you have not answered me, though the rights and privileges of every Englishman are concerned in it.

Recorder. If I should suffer you to ask questions till to-morrow morning, you would never be the wiser.

W. Penn. That is according as the answers are.

Recorder. Sir, we must not stand to hear you talk all night.

W. Penn. I design no affront to the Court, but to be heard in my just plea; and I must plainly tell you, that if you deny me the oyer of that law, which you say I have broken, you do at once deny me an acknowledged right, and evidence to the whole world your resolution to sacrifice the privileges of Englishmen to your arbitrary designs.

Recorder. Take him away. My Lord, if you take not some course with this pestilent fellow to stop his mouth, we shall not be able to do anything to night.

Mayor. Take him away. Take him away. Turn him into the bale-dock.

W. Penn. These are but so many vain exclamations. Is this justice or true judgment? Must I therefore be taken away, because I plead for the fundamental laws of England? However, this I leave upon the consciences of you, who are of the Jury, and my sole Judges, that if these ancient fundamental laws, which relate to liberty and property, and which are not limited to particular persuasions in matters of religion, must not be indispensably maintained and observed, who can say that he hath a right to the coat on his back? Certainly our liberties are to be openly invaded; our wives to be ravished; our children slaved; our families ruined; and our estates led away in triumph by every sturdy beggar, and malicious informer; as their trophies, but our (pretended) forfeits for conscience sake. The Lord of heaven and earth will be Judge between us in this matter.

Recorder. Be silent there.

W. Penn. I am not to be silent in a case where I am so much concerned; and not only myself, but many thousand families besides.

Soon after this they hurried him away, as well as William Mead, who spoke also, towards the bale-dock, a filthy, loathsome dungeon. The Recorder then proceeded to charge the Jury. But William Penn, hearing a part of the charge as he was returning, stopped suddenly, and, raising his voice, exclaimed aloud, "I appeal to the Jury, who are my judges, and this great assembly, whether the proceedings of the Court are not most arbitrary, and void of all law, in endeavouring to give the jury their charge in the absence of the prisoners. I say it is directly opposite to and destructive of the undoubted rights of every English prisoner, as Ooke on the chapter of Magna Charta speaks." Upon this some conversation passed between the parties, who were still distant from each other; after which the two prisoners were forced to their loathsome cells.

But now out of all hearing the Jury were ordered to agree upon their verdict. Four, who appeared visibly to favour the prisoners, were abused and actually threatened by the

Recorder. They were then, all of them sent out of Court. On being brought in again, they delivered their verdict unanimously, which was, "Guilty of speaking in Grace-church-street."

The Magistrates upon the bench now loaded the Jury with reproaches. They refused to take their verdict, and immediately adjourned the Court, sending them away for half an hour to reconsider it.

The time having expired, the Court sat again. The prisoners were then brought to the bar, and the Jury again called in. The latter having taken their place, delivered the same verdict as before, but with this difference, that they then delivered it in writing, with the signature of all their names.

The Magistrates were now more enraged at the Jury, and they did not hesitate to express their indignation at it in terms the most opprobrious in open court. The Recorder then addressed them as follows : " Gentleman, you shall not be dismissed till we have a verdict such as the Court will accept; and you shall be looked up without meat, drink, fire, and tobacco : you shall not think thus to abuse the Court: we will have a verdict by the help of God, or you shall starve for it."

William Penn, upon hearing this address, immediately spoke as follows: " My Jury, who are my judges, ought not to be thus menaced : their verdict should be free, and not compelled : the Bench ought to wait upon them, and not to forestall them. I do desire that justice may be done me, and that the arbitrary resolves of the Bench may not be made the measure of my jury's verdict

Other words passed between them : after which the Court was about to adjourn, and the Jury to be sent to their chamber, and the prisoners to their loathsome hole. when William Penn observed, that the agreement of twelve men was a verdict in law; and such a verdict having been given by the Jury, he required the Clerk of the Peace to record it, as he would answer it at his peril; and, if the Jury brought in another verdict contrary to this, he affirmed that they would be perjured in law. Then, turning to the Jury, he said additionally, "You are Englishmen. Mind youl privilege. Give not away your right."

One of the Jury now pleaded indisposition, and desired to be dismissed. This request, however, was not granted. The Court, on the other hand, swore several persons to keep the Jury all night without meat, drink, fire, tobacco, or any other accomodation whatever, and then adjourned till seven the next morning.

The next morning, which was September the 4th, happened to be Sunday. The Jury were again called in, but they returned the same verdict as before. The Bench now became outrageous, and indulged in the most vulgar and brutal language, such indeed as would be almost incredible if it were not upon record The Jury were again charged, and again sent out of court; again they returned; again they delivered the same verdict; again they were threatend. William Penn having spoken against the injustice of the Court in having menaced the Jury, who were his judges by the Great Charter of England, and in having rejected their verdict, the Lord Mayor exclaimed, "Stop his mouth, jailor, bring fetters, and stake him to the ground." William Penn replied, "Do your pleasure, I matter not your fetters." The Recorder observed, "Till now I never understood the reason of the policy or prudence of the Spaniards in suffering the Inquisition among them; and certainly it will never be well with us till something like the Spanish Inquisition be in England." Upon this the Jury were ordered to withdraw to find another verdict; but they refused, saying, they had already given it, and that they could find no other. The Sheriff then forced them away. Several persons were immediately sworn to keep them without accommodation as b ' ·re, and the court adjourned till seven the next morn

On the 5th of September, the Jury, who had received no refreshment for two days and two nights, were again call·· in, and the business resumed. The Court demanded a pu·· itive answer to these words, " Guilty or not guilty ?" The Foreman of the Jury replied, " Not Guilty." Every Jury-man was then required to repeat this answer separately. This he did to the satisfaction of almost all in Court The following address or conversation then passed. Recorder: Gentlemen of the Jury, I am sorry you have followed your judgments rather than the good advice which was given you. God keep my life out of your hands! But for this the Court fines you forty marks a man, and imprisonment till paid.

W. Penn: I demand my libery, being freed by the jury.

Mayor: No. You are in for your fines.

W. Penn: Fines for what?

Mayor: For contempt of Court.

W. Penn: I ask if it be according to the fundamental laws of England, that any Englishman should be fined or amerced but by the judgment of his peers or jury, since it expressly contradicts the fourteenth and twenty ninth chapters of the Great Charter of England, which says, '· No freeman shall be amerced but by the oath of good and lawful men of the vicinage."

Recorder: Take him away.

W. Penn: I can never urge the fundamental laws of England but you cry, Take him away; but it is no wonder, since the Spanish Inquisition has so great a place in the Recorder's heart God, who is just, will judge you for all these things.

These words were no sooner uttered than William Penn

and his friend William Mead, were forced into the bale-dock, from whence they were sent to Newgate. Every one of the Jury were sent to the latter prison. The plea for this barbarous usage was, that both the prisoners and the Jury refused to pay the fine of forty marks which had been put upon each of them; upon the former, because one of the Mayor's officers had put their hats upon their heads by his own command; and upon the latter because they would not bring in a verdict contrary to their own consciences, in compliance with the wishes of the Bench.

Thomas Ellwood the Friend of John Milton.

A writer in the *Leisure Hour* remarks, Thomas Ellwood was the son of a country gentleman and also related to Lord Wenman. Of this nobleman he says, "I have reason to think I should have received of the lord advantageous preferment, had I not been called into the service of the best and highest Lord, and thereby lost the favour of all my friends, relations and acquaintances of this world." (This loss of favour was caused by his uniting himself with the followers of George Fox.)

Of his introduction to Milton Ellwood gives the following account:—" My friend Isaac Penington had an intimate acquaintance with Dr. Paget, a physician of note in London; and he, with John Milton, a gentleman of great note for learning throughout the learned world for the accurate pieces he had written on various subjects and occasions. This learned person having filled a public station in the former time, now lived a retired life in London; and having lost his sight, kept always one to read to him, who usually was the son of some gentleman of his acquaintance whom in kindness he took to improve him in his learning.

Thus by the mediation of Isaac Penington with Dr.

Paget, and Dr. Paget with John Milton, was, I admitted, to come to him at certain hours, and to read to him what books he should appoint me. At our first meeting he received me courteously, and having inquired divers things of me concerning my former progression in learning, he dismissed me to provide myself with such accommodation as might be suitable to my future studies. I went, therefore, and took myself a lodging as near to his house, which was then in Jewyn Street, as conveniently as I could; and from thenceforth went every day in the afternoon, except on the first day of the week, and sitting by him in his dining-room read to him such books in the Latin tongue as he pleased to hear me read.

"At my first sitting to read to him, observing that I used the English pronunciation he told me, if I would have the full benefit of the Latin tongue, not only to read and understand Latin authors, but also to converse with foreigners either abroad or at home, I must learn the foreign pronunciation. To this I willingly consenting, he instructed me how to sound the vowels, so different from the common pronunciation used by the English that the Latin thus spoken seemed as different from that which was delivered as the English generally speak it, as if it were another language. This change of pronunciation proved a difficulty to me, but my master perceiving with what earnest desire I pursued learning, gave me, not only all the encouragement but all the help he could, for having a sure and curious ear he knew by my tone when I understood what I was reading and when I did not, and accordingly would stop me, examine me, and open the most difficult passages unto me."

After his return from the country where he had been on account of ill-health, Ellwood again pursued his studies with Milton. He observes, "I was very kindly received

by my master, who had conceived so good an opinion of me
that my conversation I found was acceptable unto him; he
seemed heartily glad of my recovery and return, and into
our old method of study we fell again—I reading to him,
and he explaining to me as occasion required."

These agreeable studies were soon to be interrupted—
persecution of the Nonconformi-ts and Quakers again broke
out. Their meetings were disturbed by armed men and
thousands of faithful men were cast into prisons. We quote
Ellwood's description of his imprisonment, as it is full of
incident and may serve to give some idea of the state of
the country in those troublous times.

"I was on the 26th day of the 8th month, 1662, at the
meeting at the Bull and Mouth, by Aldersgate, when on a
sudden a party of soldiers of the trained bands of the City
rushed in with noise and clamour, being led by one called
Major Rosewell. As soon as he was come within the room,
having a file or two of muske'eers at his heels, he commanded his men to present their muskets at us, which they
did. Then he made proclamation that all who were not
Quakers might depart. The soldiers had come so early
that the meeting was not fully gathered when they came;
and when the mixed company had gone out, he that
commanded the party gave us a general charge to come
out of the place, but we having come there at God's
requiring, to worship Him, we stirred not, whereupon he
sent his soldiers among us, with command to drive or drag
us out, which they did roughly enough. When we came
into the street we were received by other soldiers, who,
with pikes holden lengthwise, encompassed us about as
sheep in a pond, and there we stood while they were picking
up more to add to our number, in which work none were
so active and eager as their leader, which I observed stepped
to him as he was passing by me, and asked him if he

intended a massacre, for of that in these troublous times
there was great apprehension. The suddenness of my
question startled him, but recollecting himself he answered,
'No; but I intend to have you all *hanged* by the wholesome
laws of this land.'

" When he had gotten as many as he could, he ordered
the pikes to be opened before us, went at the head of us,
the soldiers with their pikes making a lane to keep us from
scattering; he led us up Martin's and turned down to
Newgate, where I expected he would lodge us, but to my
disappointment he went on through Newgate, and turning
through the Old Bailey brought us into Fleet Street. I was
wholly at a loss whither he would lead us unless it was to
Whitehall, for I knew nothing then of the Old Bridewell,
but on a sudden, turning short, he brought us before the
gate of that prison, where knocking, the wicket was forthwith opened, and the gaoler with his porter ready to receive
us. As soon as I was in, the porter directed me to a fair
pair of stairs, and bade me go up and on till I could go no
further; wherefore following my directions I went up a
storey higher, which brought me into a room which I
perceived to be a court room, and observing the door on the
further side I opened it with intent to go in, but quickly
drew back affrighted at the dismalness of the place, for
besides that the walls were laid with black there stood in
the middle a great whipping post, which was all the furniture
it had.

" In one of those two rooms judgment was given, and in
the other it was execu'ed; it was so contrived that the court
might not only hear but see, if they pleased, their sentence
executed

" A sight so unpleasing gave me no encouragement to
enter, until looking earnestly I espied on the opposte side
a door which led me into one of the fairest rooms that, so

B

far as I remember, I was ever in, and no wonder, for though
it was now put to this mean use it had for many ages past
been the royal seat or palace of the kings' of England until
Cardinal Wolsey built Whitehall, and offered it as a peace-
offering to King Henry VIII, who until that time had kept
his court in this house, and had this, as the people in the
house reported, for his dining-room, by which name it then
went. This room, in length, for I had lived long enough
in it to have time to measure it, was threescore feet, and
had breadth proportionable thereto. In it on the front side
were very large bay windows, in which stood great tables;
other large tables were in it with benches round, and the
floor was covered with rushes. Finding I had now followed
my keeper's direction to the utmost point, beyond which I
could not go, I sat down and considered that rhetorical
saying, 'that the way to heaven lay by the gates of hell,'
the black room through which I passed to this bearing
some resemblance to the latter, as this comparatively might
in some sort be thought to bear to the former; but I was
quickly put out of these thoughts by the flocking in of my
fellow-prisoners. So many Friends having been made
prisoners, great work had the women to run from prison
to prison to find their husbands, fathers, brothers, and
servants; and no less care and pains, when found, to furnish
them with provisions and other needful accommodations.
But an excellent order was practised among the Friends of
that City, by which certain friends of either sex were
appointed to have the oversight of the prisons in every
quarter, and to take care of all Friends, the poor especially,
that should be committed. This prison of Bridewell was
under the care of two grave, discreet, motherly women, both
widows. They provided hot meat and broth, for the
weather was so cold, and ordering their servants to bring it,
with bread, cheese, and beer, came themselves also with it

and having placed it on a table gave notice to us that it was provided for all those that had not others to provide for them or were not able to provide for themselves.

"As for my part *tenpence* was all the money I had about me, and this was a small estate to enter upon imprisonment with, yet was I not discouraged nor had I a murmuring thought. I had known what it was moderately to abound, and if I should now suffer want I knew I ought to be content, and I was so, through the grace of God. I made no doubt that He who sent the ravens to feed Elijah, and who clothes the lilies of the field, would find some means to sustain me with needful food and raiment; and I had learnt by experience the truth of that saying, Nature is content with few things.

"When the evening was far spent, I bethought myself of a lodging. Wherefore, gathering up a good armful of the rushes wherewith the floor was covered, and spreading them under one of the tables, I crept in upon them in my clothes, and, keeping on my hat, laid my head upon the table frame instead of a bolster. My example was followed by the rest. Having a quiet mind, I was soon asleep, and slept till the middle of the night, when awaking cold, I crept out of my cabin to walk about and warm myself, after which I lay down again and rested until morning.

"Next day many who belonged to families had bedding brought them, but I, who had none to look after me, kept to my rushy pallet, and through the merciful goodness of my God towards me, I rested, and slept well, without taking cold, until one William Mucklow (who, through the mediation of his friends with Sir Richard Browne, at that time a great master of misrule in the city, and over Bridewell especially, being with some others released) courteously offered me the use of his hammock. This was a providential accommodation, which I received thankfully, both as from the Lord and from him. Before my tenpence

was spent, Providence, on whom I relied, sent me a fresh
supply, for William Penington, a friend and merchant of
London, came in love to see me, and among other things
asked me how it was· with me as to money. I told him I
could not say I had none (his estate was now reduced to
twopence), whereupon he put twenty shillings into my hand.
I saw a Divine Hand in thus opening his heart towards
me, and I received it as a token of love both from the Lord
and from him. The week following, my affectionate friend,
Mary Penington, sent me forty shillings, and not many
days after I received twenty shillings from my father, who
being then at his house in Oxfordshire, and by letter from
my sister hearing I was a prisoner in Bridewell, sent this
money for my support.

"Now was my pocket from the lowest ebb risen to a full
tide. I was on the brink of want, yet my confidence did
not fail nor my faith stagger, and now I had supplies,
shower upon shower, so that I could in all humility say
'This is the Lord's doing,' and without defrauding any of
the instruments, mine eye looked over and beyond them
unto the Lord, and with a grateful heart I returned thanks-
givings and praises to Him.

And now the chief thing I wanted was occupation, and
many of the company being tradesmen, tailors, etc., I
settled among the tailors and made waistcoats of red and
yellow flannel for a hosier in Cheapside, and so spent those
hours with innocency which want of occupation would have
made tedious, which, indeed, was all the advantage I had
of it. My employer, though he knew not what I had to
subsist on, when I had made dozens of waistcoats, and
bought the thread myself, gave me one crown piece and no
more, but I wanted work more than wages, and took what
he gave me without complaint."

When Thomas Ellwood and his companions had been in

Bridewell more than two months they were brought before Sir John Howell, the Recorder, where, refusing the oath of allegiance (the Friends taking the command of our Lord "Swear not at all" in its strictest sense), the prisoners were committed to Newgate, and ' thrust into the common side." This prison was very full of "Friends and others," and our addition caused a great throng. We had the liberty of the hall, which in the day time was common to all the prisoners on that side, felons as well as others, to walk in, and we had also the liberty of some rooms over that hall to walk in; but in the night we all lodged in one room, which was large and round, having in the middle of it a great oaken pillar, which bore up the chapel that is over it. To this pillar we fastened our hammocks at the one end, and to the opposite wall on the other, quite round the room three stories high, one over the other, so that they who lay in the upper and middle row were obliged to go to bed first, because they climbed to the higher by getting into the lower. And under the lower rank by the wall side were laid beds on the floor, in which the sick and such weak persons as could not get into the hammocks lay. Though the room was large and pretty airy, yet the breath and steam from so many bodies packed so close together was enough to cause sickness amongst us, and I believe did so, for there were many sick, and some very weak, and though we were not long there, yet in that time one of our fellow-prisoners, who lay in one of those pallet beds, died.

"This caused some bustle in the house, for the body of the deceased, being put into a coffin, was carried down and set in the lodge, that the coroner might inquire into the cause and manner of his death, and the manner of their doing it is this: As soon as the coroner is come, the turnkeys run into the street under the gate and seize upon every man that passes by, until they have got enough to make up the coroner's inquest, and so resolute are these rude fellows, that if any man resist or dispute it with them, they drag him in by main force, not regarding what condition he is of.

"It so happened that at that time they lighted on an ancient man, a grave citizen, who was trudging through the gate in great haste, and him they laid hold on, telling him that he must serve upon the coroner's inquest. He besought them to let him go, assuring them he was on urgent business, and that the stopping of him would be greatly to his prejudice, but they were deaf to his entreaties. When they had got their compliment, and were shut in together, the rest of them said to this ancient man, 'Come, father, you are the oldest amongst us, you shall be our foreman;' and when the coroner had sworn them on the jury, the coffin was uncovered that they might look on the body. But the old man said to them, 'To what purpose do you show us a dead body here? You would not have us think, sure, that this man died in this room! How then shall we be able to judge how this man came by his death unless we see the place wherein he died, and wherein he had been kept prisoner? How know we but that the incommodiousness of the place where he was kept may have caused his death? therefore show us the place wherein he died.' This displeased the keepers, who began to banter the old man, thinking to beat him off it. But he stood firmly to them. 'Come, come,' saith he, 'though you have made a fool of me in bringing me in hither, ye shall not find a child in me now I am here. I understood my place and your duty, and I require you to conduct me and my brethren to the place where this man died; refuse it at your peril.' The coroner then told them they must show him the place.

"It was evening when they began this work, and by this time it was bedtime with us, so that we had taken down our hammocks and were undressing, when on a sudden we heard a great noise of tongues and trampling of feet coming up towards us, and one of the turnkeys opening the door cried 'Hold, hold! do not undress yourselves; here is the coroner's inquest coming to see you.' As soon as they came to the door, for within the door there was scarce room for them to come, the foreman, who led them, lifting up his hands, said 'Lord bless me! What a sight is here! I did not think there had been such cruelty in the hearts of Englishmen, to use Englishmen in this manner! We need not now question how this man came by his death, we may rather wonder that they are not all dead. Well, if it please God to spare my life till to-morrow, I will find means to let the King know how his subjects are dealt with."

"Whether he did so or not I cannot tell, but I am apt to think he applied to the Mayor or Sheriffs of London, for the next day one of the Sheriffs came to the press yard, and having ordered the porter of Bridewell to attend him, sent up a turnkey to bid all the Bridewell prisoners come down to him, for they knew us not, but we knew our company. Being come before him, he looked kindly upon us, and spake courteously. 'Gentlemen,' said he, 'I understand the prison is very full, and am very sorry for it. I wish it were in my power to release you; but since I cannot do that, I am willing to do what I can; I would have all you that come from Bridewell return thither again, where will be better accommodation for you; and here is the porter of Bridewell, your old keeper, to attend you thither.'

"We duly acknowledged the favour of the Sheriff, who bidding us farewell the porter of Bridewell came to us and

told us we knew our way to Bridewell without him, and he
could trust us; therefore he would not go with us, but left
us to take our own time, so we were in before bedtime.
Then went we up to our friends in Newgate, and taking a
solemn leave of them made up our packs to be gone, and
taking our bundles on our shoulders walked two and two
through the Old Bailey into Fleet Street, and so to Old
Bridewell; and the shopkeepers and passengers in the way
stopped us to ask us what we were, and whither we were
going; and then we told them we were prisoners going
from one prison to another. ‘ What!’ said they, ‘without
a keeper?’ ‘No,’ said we, ‘our word which we have given
us is our keeper.’ Thereupon some would advise us to go
home, but we told them we could not do so; we could suffer
for our testimony, but could not fly from it.

“When we were come to Bridewell we were not put in
the great room where we were before, but into a room in
another fair court, which had a pump in it, and here we
were not shut up, but had the liberty of the court to walk
in, and indeed we might have gone away if we would, but
both conscience and honour stood engaged for our true
imprisonment. Under this easy restraint we lay until the
court sat at the Old Bailey, and then, whether it was that
the heat of persecution was somewhat abated, or by what
other means Providence wrought it, I know not, we were
called to the bar, and without further question discharged.

“Whereupon we returned to Bridewell, and having
raised some money among us, and therewith gratified the
master and his porter for their kindness to us, we spent
some time in a solemn meeting to return our thankful
acknowledgment to the Lord, both for his preservation of
us in prison, and deliverance of us out of it; and then
taking a solemn farewell of each other departed.”

. We will conclude this notice of Ellwood by quoting what

further he says of Milton in his autobiography:—"Some little time before I went to Aylesbury prison I was desired by my quondam master, Milton, to take a house for him in the neighbourhood where I dwelt, that he might go out of the city for the safety of himself and his family, the pestilence then growing hot in London.

"I took a pretty box for him in Giles Chalfont, a mile from me, of which I gave him notice, and intended to wait for him, and see him well settled in it, but was prevented by that imprisonment. But now being released I soon made a visit to him, to welcome him into the country.

"After some discussion had passed between us, he called for a manuscript of his, which, being brought, he delivered to me, bidding me to take it home and read it at my leisure, and when I had so done return it to him with my judgment thereon.

"When I came home and had set myself to read it, I found it was that excellent poem which he entitled 'Paradise Lost.' After I had with best attention read it through, I made him another visit, and returned him his book with due acknowledgment of the favour he had done me in communicating it to me. He asked me how I liked it, and what I thought of it, which I modestly but freely told him; and after some further discourse I pleasantly said to him, 'Thou hast said much here of *Paradise Lost*, but what hast thou to say of *Paradise Found?* He made me no answer, but sat some time in a muse; then broke off that discourse, and fell upon another subject. After the sickness was over, and the city became safely habitable again, he returned thither. And when afterwards I went to wait on him there, which I seldom failed to do whenever my occasions drew me to London, he showed me his second poem, called 'Paradise Regained,' and in a pleasant tone said to me, 'This is owing to you, for you put it into my

he d by the question you put to me at Chalfont, which
before I had not thought of.' "

MELANCHOLY DEATH.

Barclay in his Memoirs of the Friends in Scotland writes:
" It happened about the year 1666, that James Urquhart, for
his conscientious separation from the National church of the
day, fell under the censure of the Presbytery, and was
excommunicated. The excommunication was sent to one
William Forbes, a minister of the place where Urquhait
lived, with an injunction of the Presbytery for him to publish
it from the pulpit. The minister, conscious in himself of the
honesty and integrity of the person, against whom he was
enjoined to read the sentence, fell under strong convictions,
and great reluctancy of mind against the performance of what
he was commanded. But when he considered, that the
consequence of his disobeying the Presbytery would, in all
probability, issue in the loss of his stipend, covetousness
overcame his convictions; and he publicly pronounced the
sentence against James Urquhart, in direct opposition to the
dictates of his own conscience. This, afterward, gave him
much uneasiness, and his mind became so discomposed, that
he could not, for some time, proceed in performing the usual
offices of his function; until, at length, he publicly and
ingeniously came to confess, that his discomposure was a just
judgment of God upon him, for cursing with his tongue a
person, whom he believed in his own conscience to be a very
honest man. Yet, notwithstanding his convictions were so
clear and overpowering, he again fell into the like error, and
in a way more nearly affecting him. His own daughter,
Jane Forbes, was convinced of the Truth, and joined the
people called Quakers. Church proceedings were carried on
against her to an excommunication, which her father was
required by the Presbytery to pronounce. The poor man's

case, under so difficult a dilemma, was really to be pitied.
Hard was his choice, either to lose his living by disobeying
the Presbytery, or wound his conscience by pronouncing
excommunication against his own daughter, whom he knew
t be a virtuous and religious woman. But alas! both his
conscience and natural affection gave place to the love of
money; so that he was determined to read the excommunication, and had uttered some kind of prayers previous
thereto, when he was suddenly struck by death, at the very
time he had purposed to deliver that sentence. A melancholy and remarkable exit, wherein nature was observed
to sink under the weight and oppression of a conflict
between conscience and self-interest.

REMARKABLE COINCIDENCE.

Barclay remarks, Sir John Keith, who in those days, and
afterward, was very violent against Friends having, in the
year 1667, brought away, under a guard, several of his
people from Inverury, where they had been previously
imprisoned; the magistrates of Aberdeen, to whom they were
delivered, after keeping them in confinement some time,
caused them to be conducted through the streets, with great
contempt and reproach, to the Bow bridge, where a guard
was provided to conduct them southward to Edinburgh, from
shire to shire, as the worst of malefactors. When they had
proceeded a little way out of the town, one of the prisoners,
William Gellie, a man of very weakly and infirm habit, sat
down; and the rest of the Friends followed his example,
refusing to go further, unless horses were provided. Alexander,
who attended, in order to see them set out, was much
enraged, commanding William Gellie to rise and go forward
on foot; and because of his refusal he struck him piteously.
Friends, however, continued to sit still; upon which, the
magistrate with all his train, not being able to prevail in their

purpose, returned to Aberdeen, and the Friends to their respective dwelling places. But, what was remarkable, the first object that presented itself to this persecutor on reaching his own house, was his son, who had by a fall broken his arm, and in the very same time that the father had been using his arm to strike the harmless servant of the Lord; which circumstances, thus coinciding, so awakened the conscience of this person, that he said, (and afterwards told it to some Friends,) *he should never strike a Quaker again.*

RUDE TREATMENT OF QUAKERS.

An occurence in 1662, took place which affords a specimen of the kind of rude treatment to which the Quakers were subjected at their religious meetings, even from people of the higher classes. An Ambassador in company with an Irish Colonel and some other riotous officers, came one day to the meeting at Pall Mall, with the intention of disturbing the meeting and dispersing the Friends. But the meeting having broken up just before their arrival, George Fox had stepped into an adjoining room, from which, however, he was soon brought back again by the great disturbance and uproar that suddenly burst forth. Upon re-entering the meeting-house, he found the Colonel storming and threatening, "that he would kill all the Quakers," upon which George Fox relates, "he was moved of the Lord to speak to him, and to tell him, that the old law enjoined, 'an eye for an eye, and a tooth for a tooth;' but thou threatenest to kill all the Quakers, although they have done thee no hurt." He then said, "But here is gospel for thee, here is my hair, here is my cheek, here is my shoulder;" and suiting the action to the word, he turned his cheek and back to the smiter, which took so sudden an effect upon him and his companions, that they stood gazing with amazement; and the Colonel at last said, "If that is your principle, and you act thereby, we

never met with such men before." George Fox replied,
" What he was in words, he was the same in life." They
then entered upon an explanatory discourse, which ended in
a mutual good understanding, and they parted on friendly
terms; "for," he continues, "the truth came over them, and
the colonel as well as the ambassador carried themselves very
lovingly towards the Friends, the Lord's power being over
all."

PERSECUTION.

Sewell observes that in 1674. One Robert Tillett, in
Buckingham, sick of a consumption, and believing his death
to be nigh at hand, desired some of his friends to visit him.
At this invitation some came to his house, yet not above the
number of fourteen persons; and two informers went and
acquainted a justice of the peace thereof, who recorded this
small assembly as a seditious meeting, and fined the sick man
twenty pounds for this pretended transgression; and so his
goods were seized, and six cows taken from him. And one
Robert Smith, being overheard by the informers to have
spoken five or six words, was fined also twenty pounds as a
preacher; which fine was afterwards extorted from some
others then present.

In Norfolk in 1675, the rage of the persecutors was such,
that some having been bereaved of all, were obliged, even in
winter-time (as among the rest, Joseph Harrison, with his
wife and children) to lie on straw; and yet they, unwearied,
did not leave frequenting their religious meeting: nay, even
the dead were not suffered to rest, for outrageous barbarity
came to that pitch, that Mary, the wife of Francis Larder,
being dead and buried, was, by order of Thomas Bretland,
dug up again, whereby the coffin was broken, which they
tied together, and carrying it away, exposed the corpse in
the market-place. Thus this deceased woman was no more
suffered to lie quiet in her grave, than in her sick-bed, when

the day before her death she had been threatened by order
of one Christopher Bedingfield to have her bed taken away
from under her while living.   Now the reason of this taking
up the corpse was, that though her husband was one of those
called Quakers, yet she not being properly a member of that
society, it was taken ill that she had been buried in a plain
way, without paying to the priest his pretended due, for the
ordinary service over the dead.

PERSECUTIONS IN MASSACHUSETTS.

The first settlers of the New England states, as is pretty
well known, were men who fled from civil and religious persecution in England in the early part of the seventeenth
century.   As they had felt in their own persons and fortunes
the sorrows of oppression for conscience sake, it might naturally be expected that they would have had some sympathy
for others in like circumstances.   In this respect, however,
the Pilgrim Fathers, as they have been termed, were no
better than the men before whom they had fled.   A volume
might be written of their doings in the way of intolerance;
but the following short chapter may suffice.

In the year 1656, when the colonists of Massachusetts
were complacently congratulating themselves on having established a vigorous system of uniformity in religious matters, ·
and expressing great thankfulness for having escaped from
the troubles which had lately agitated England, they were
very much surprised to learn that two women of the sect
which had begun to be called Quakers were arrived in Boston
from Barbadoes.   There was no law in the colony against
such persons; but that was considered unimportant; it was
easy to make a little law for the occasion, or easier still to act
without any law at all.   This alternative was adopted.   The
two unfortunate women, against whose character there was
no reproach, were seized and put in prison; a few books.

found in their trunks were burnt by the hangman; and after suffering various indignities, they were turned out of the country. Persecution requires only a little spark to kindle, it into a great flame. It would almost seem as if the mis-usage of the two women caused a flocking of Quakers from all the points of the compass to Boston, only for the sake of getting ill treated. In a short time eight made their appearance, and they in a like manner were imprisoned and banished. Thinking it now time to get a little law to regulate proceedings, a local court passed an enactment, declaring that any Quakers who should hereafter arrive in the colony should be severely whipped, and confined at hard labour in the house of correction. Immediately afterwards several came, were whipped, confined, and dismissed; and others took their place. It was evident the law was too lenient, so a fresh enactment was passed. Fines were imposed on every person who gave house-room to Quakers, or who attended their meetings, or otherwise sanctioned their pernicious opinions. Every Quaker, after the first conviction, if a man, was to lose one ear, and the second time the other; if a woman, she was each time to be severely whipped; and for the third offence, both men and women were to have their tongues bored through with a red-hot iron.

Quakers now arrived in the colony in great numbers. Glorying in their sufferings, the more they were persecuted, the more they came to testify their sincerity in their belief. Whippings, confinement, hard labour, fines, cutting off the ears, and boring the tongue being thus found ineffectual, a new law was passed in 1658, declaring that in future all Quakers who intruded themselves into Massachusetts should be banished on pain of death. Three Quakers forthwith offered themselves as the first victims; they had returned from banishment. Their names were Mary Dyer, Marmaduke Stephenson, and William Robinson. From their defence at

their trial, nothing is more plain than that they were persons
in a state of frenzy: their general argument was, that by
means of visions they had been induced to come to Massachusetts and brave the worst that could be done to them. On
the 19th of October 1659, they were condemned to die as
malefactors; and three days later they were led out to execution. Mary Dyer saw her two brethren die before her eyes;
and she was on the point of meeting the same dreadful doom,
the rope being already round her neck, when a faint shout
was heard in the distance, which grew stronger and stronger,
and was soon caught and repeated by a hundred willing
hearts. "A reprieve, a reprieve!" was the cry, and the
execution was stopped; but she, whose mind was intently
fastened on another world, cried out, that she desired to suffer
with her brethren, unless the magistrates would repeal their
wicked law.

She was saved by the intercession of her son, but on the
express condition that she should be carried to the place of
execution, and stand upon the gallows with a rope about her
neck, and then be carried out of the colony. She was accordingly taken home to Rhode Island; but her resolution was
still unshaken, and she was again moved to return to the
"bloody town of Boston," where she arrived in the year 1660.
This determination of a feeble and aged woman, to brave all
the terrors of their laws, might well fill the magistrates with
astonishment; but the pride of consistency had already involved them in acts of extreme cruelty, and they thought it
impossible now to recede. The other executions were considered acts of stern necessity, and caused much discontent;
a hope was entertained till the last moment that the condemned would consent to depart from the jurisdiction; and
when Mary Dyer was sent for by the court, after her second
return, Govenor Endicott said, "Are you the same Mary
Dyer that was here before?" giving her an opportunity to

escape by a denial of the fact, there having been another of the name returned from England. But she would make no evasion. "I am the same Mary Dyer that was here the last general court." "You will own yourself a Quaker will you not?" "I own myself to be reproachfully called so;" and she was sentenced to be hanged on the morning of the next day. "This is no more than thou saidst before," was her intrepid reply, when the sentence of death was pronounced. "But now," said the governor, "it is to be executed; therefore prepare yourself, for to-morrow at nine o'clock you die." "I came," was the reply, "in obedience to the will of God, the last general court, desiring you to repeal your unrighteous laws of banishment on pain of death; and the same is my work now, and earnest request, although I told you if you refused to repeal them, the Lord would send others of his servants to witness against them."

At the set time on the next day she was brought forth, and with a band of soldiers led through the town, about a mile to the place of execution. the drums beating before and behind her the whole way. When she was upon the gallows, it was told her that if she would return home she might come down and save her life; to which she replied, "Nay, I cannot, for in obedience to the will of the Lord I came, and in his will I abide faithful unto death." Another said that she had been there before; she had the sentence of banishment upon pain of death, and had broken the law in coming again now, and therefore she was guilty of her own blood. "Nay," she answered, "I came to keep blood-guiltiness from you, desiring you to repeal the unrighteous and unjust law of banishment upon pain of death, made against the innocent servants of the Lord; therefore my blood will be required at your hands, who wilfully do it; but for those who do it in the simplicity of their hearts, I desire the Lord to forgive them; I came to do the will of

my Father, and in obedience to his will I stand even to death "
A minister who was present then said, "Mary Dyer, repent,
oh repent, and be not so deluded and carried away by the
deceit of the devil!" But she answered, "Nay man, I am
not now to repent." She was then asked to have the elders
pray for her; but she said, "I know never an elder here."
"Perhaps," said one scoffingly, "she thinks there is none
here." Then looking round she said, "I know but few
here." Being again asked to have one of the elders pray
for her, she said, "Nay, first a child, then a young man,
then a strong man, before an elder in Christ Jesus." She
spoke of the other world and of the eternal happiness into
which she was about to enter; and "in this well-disposed
condition was turned off, and died a martyr of Christ, being
twice led to death, which the first time she expected with
undaunted courage, and now she suffered with Christian
fortitude." "She hangs as a flag for others to take example by," said a member of the court, as the lifeless body
hung suspended from the gallows.

Instead of being a warning, her death was only an encouragement. Another Quaker, named William Leddra,
soon made his appearance, and after a tedious imprisonment, during which he was chained to a log of wood, he
was brought to trial on the usual charge of returning from
banishment. There was a dash of the ludicrous in the proceedings. One of the charges against him was that he refused to take off his hat in court, and another was that he
persevered in saying "thee" and "thou." "Will you put
me to death," he asked, "for speaking good English; and
for not putting off my clothes?" "A man may speak treason in good English," was the reply. "Is it treason to say
thee and thou to a single person?" No good rejoinder
could here be made by the judges, and while they were
trying to stop his mouth by a few more questions, to their

exceeding dismay another Quaker, named Winlock Christison, who had also returned from banishment, entered the court and placed himself beside the prisoner. The case of Leddra was first dispatched, by condemning him to be executed, and this atrocity was committed on the 14th of March. Christison, at a second appearance before the court, received a like sentence, but leaving him choice of voluntary banishment, and this latter alternative he appears to have embraced. The next culprits of the same class were Judah Browne and Peter Pierson, who, for no offence that we can perceive but that of being Quakers, were condemned to be tied to a cart's tail and whipped through several towns in the colony. Immediately after, as appears from the records of the court, a day of thanksgiving was appointed to be kept in acknowledgment of the many mercies enjoyed for years past " in this remote wilderness."

According to Mr. Chandler, from whose interesting work we have derived these melancholy details, the persecutions in Massachusetts gave offence to Charles II., who had other reasons to be dissatisfied with the colonists. He therefore enjoined all the governors of New England to proceed no farther with corporal punishment against Quakers, but to send them to England, with their respective crimes specifically set forth, in order that they might be disposed of according to law. The Quakers in London immediately chartered a vessel, and the mandamus being committed to Samuel Shattock, who had been banished from Massachusetts on pain of death, he arrived in the harbour of Boston in six weeks. The king's messenger and the commander of the ship landed on the day after their arrival, and proceeded directly to the governor's house. Admitted to his presence, he ordered Shattock's hat to be removed, but after perusing the letters, restored it and took off his own. After consultation with the deputy governor, he informed the messenger that they should obey the king's command. In the evening the passengers of the ship came on shore, and, with their friends in the town, held a meeting, "where they returned praises to God for his mercy, manifested in their wonderful deliverance."

Chambers's Journal.

SUFFERINGS OF FRIENDS.

When James came to the throne, there were in the prisons of his kingdom about 1,400 Quakers, more than 200 of them women, unoffending people, forced by the very tenets of that faith for which they suffered to be loyal subjects and peaceable citizens, whose sole alleged crime was their obedience to the voice of conscience. For this obedience, from the time that they had first gathered together as a sect, each religious party, as it gained political sway, had measured its power by their persecution. As Penn said, when stating their wrongs to the Parliament of 1679, they had been as the "common whipping-stock of the kingdom; all laws had been let loose upon them, as if the design had been, not to reform, but to destroy them." More than 320 Quakers had died in confinement between 1660 and James' accession; at that very time many "were tending towards their destruction;" and very shortly before "several poor innocent tradesmen had been so suffocated by the closeness of Newgate, that they had been taken out sick of a malignant fever, and had died in a few days." Nor were their sufferings restricted to imprisonment; their meetings for worship were dispersed, their wives and daughters ill-treated, their goods spoiled, often "not a bed left to rest upon;" informers—hardened wretches, their own consciences being seared in sin—were set upon them, encouraged to turn their consciences to profit, to make merchandise of their misery. These bloodhounds of the law were the missionaries—sanguinary enactments were the arguments employed in the conversion of the Quaker alike by cavalier parson and puritan preacher.

Few persecutions, indeed, have been more cruel or severe than that endured by the first generation of the "Friends," and in none have the patience and faithfulness of its victims been exceeded. History records no instance in which they, any one of them, denied or concealed their principles, or attempted to retaliate on their oppressors. Thus long and fiercely had the storm of bigotry raged against Penn's fellow-religionists, nor had he fled from its fury. Bravely had he borne up against it. Four times he had been imprisoned, twice sent to the Tower; once at the instigation of the Bishop of London, he had for writing a book in defence of his faith, been immured there in close confinement, none of his friends allowed access to him: his father, the old Admiral, whose distaste for enthusiasm was almost equal to Mr. Macaulay's, then managed to inform him "that the Bishop was resolved he should either publicly recant or die a prisoner." "Tell my father," he replied, "that my prison shall be my grave before I will budge a jot, for I owe my conscience to no mortal man. I have no need to fear. God will make amends for all!"

W. E. Forster's Preface to *Clarkson's Life of William Penn*.

Rev. Titus Wendney's Troubles.

The above named clergyman in the diocese of London had among his parishioners some Quakers who occasioned him much trouble by their refusal to pay tithes, Easter offerings, and marriage fees. Their grievances, prosecutions, and imprisonment were printed in the early part of the last century. The Incumbent was much annoyed at his conduct being publicly called in question, and he endeavoured by means of the press to vindicate the course he had pursued "The three following reasons induced me in the year 1721," he says, to file a Bill against four Quakers (two of which immediately comply'd in the Exchequer.)

FIRST REASON.

The Justices refused to act, saying, They would not be troubled every year with such complaints. So that then I had no other remedy, but to apply to the Honourable Court of Exchequer. It was not matter of choice, but necessity that forced me to that expedient; unless I would give up my right and lose my just dues. It was by their obstinacy and management, six years in the Exchequer, before I could obtain a Decree. During that time, one of them sold his estate, and made over all that he had, on purpose, as he boasted, to cheat me of my tithes, and then went to gaol. I at last obtained a Decree for £59 13s. 4d. of which I received of the two Quakers but £44 10s. including costs and tithes, and my Attorney's bill came to £92 6s. 3d., so that I was out of pocket £47 16s. 3d., and it cost them according to their own accounts, David Chapman £29 3s, James Rawlins £24 9s., so that I am apparently the greatest sufferer

SECOND REASON.

I found myself yearly cheated and defrauded of my tithes by the Quakers, who would never inform me of their tithes, if I charged them too little, as I often did; nor would they rectify any such mistakes; but if I made the least mistake on the other hand, they were very clamorous and abusive. Besides, it is next to an impossibility to come to the truth of small tithes; and the Exchequer being a Court of Equity as well as Law, where the Farmer is bound by oath or solemn affirmation to set forth the quantity and quality of their tithes, small as well as great; it was the chief inducement to me, and I believe is to the Clergy in

general the chief reason, why they so often apply to the
Honourable Court of Exchequer for relief in case of tithes,
and not because (as has been suggested by the Quakers)
that it is an expensive Court.

THIRD REASON.

I have, after many years experience, found a very ill use
made of taking tithes by a Justice's Warrant. *First*, the
Quakers have thereby grown very abusive, saying, I was
afraid to sue them in the Exchequer, &c. They have also
stopt and insulted me on the road with the most approbrious
language, even on a Sunday as coming from doing my duty.
Nay, I have had threatening notes thrown into my yard,
viz., *Remember Cæsar's Fate*, &c. Secondly, I have found
that method of proceeding by a Justice's Warrant very
prejudicial to my own interest; for the Justices rarely gave
me above four or five shillings cost, and I am forced to
give their clerks six shillings, and to ride about 60 miles
backwards and forwards with an *Evidence*, before I can
obtain a Warrant of Distress. Besides, and what adds
still to my expense, the Quakers use all their endeavours
to hinder my selling the goods (corn or cattle) taken by
Distress, to any of the neighbours; for they persuade the
people, the *goods are stolen;* so that I am forced to send 12
miles to a Market. Further yet; more than once, the
officer who made the Distress, and had the goods in his
custody hath *failed*, so that I have lost my Trouble, Tithes,
and Charges.

It may be asserted, without breach of truth—that there
has been but one Prosecution carried on to Effect; meaning
by that expression—that there has been but one Cause carried
on against the Quakers, so as to obtain a Decree. There
was indeed a Bill filed 1719, against three Quakers, but it
was soon ended, and they were not at the expense of putting
in an Answer. The same was done in 1735, against John

Jasper, for one year's Tithe for £6 6s. (and not four years) and two other Quakers; but this suit also was soon ended, and without putting in an Answer.

I may add further, that there has been no Prosecution in the Ecclesiastical Court, that could deserve that name. The case was this. In 1719, John Foster married his maid servant, for which I demanded the usual Fee of 10s. (not of £7 1s. as he sets forth) for the recovery of which, I applied to the Justices, but they made such mistakes in their order and warrant of distress, that I could not make use of them, without involving myself in a tedious and expensive law suit. For the said John Foster did keep in his house a whole day a certain Attorney, to be ready to take all advantages of us, if we made a Distress; but the Attorney finding that we did not come, in the evening he called at my house, and threatened me, that if I had made a Distress, he would have ruined me; then boasted, how good clients the Quakers were; for let him bring in never such extravagant or exorbitant Bills, they made no defalcations, no abatements, but paid him to the utmost farthing; for they gloried in spending their money to oppose the Priests, and to make the recovery of their dues as chargeable to them as possible; for they had a fund to support them.

After this, I did apply to the Ecclesiastical Court, for the recovery of the marriage-fee, and John Foster did appear there once by his Attorney, but was put to no expense by the Court, that I ever heard of; for the cause was immediately dropt. The Fee is unpaid to this day, notwithstanding the saving clause in the Act of Toleration; "That nothing therein contained, shall be construed to exempt any of the Persons tolerated from paying Tythes, or other Parochial Dues, or any other Duties to the Church or Minister, or from any Prosecution in any Ecclesiastical Court, or elsewhere, for the same." And I do solemnly declare, that the said John Foster was never prosecuted by me at Common Law for a marriage-fee, or upon any other account, but as before mentioned.

INTERVIEWS WITH THE EMPEROR OF RUSSIA AND THE KING OF PRUSSIA.

Mr. Sherman in his Life of William Allen remarks "During the year 1814, the Emperor of Russia and the King of Prussia, with many of the foreign nobility, visited London· Mr. Allen took advantage of the opportunity to seek an interview, in order to plead with them on behalf of peace and education. As Clerk of the meeting, he wrote two addresses, which the Friends adopted. That to the King of Prussia, besides congratulating him on his arrival, and expressing desires for his welfare, solicited the continuance of his kind protection to members of their own persuasion who had been sufferers on account of their peculiar opinions, and faithfully tells him,—'Our conviction, O King! is, that the regard of a monarch to his conscientious subjects is a sure means of promoting the best ends of government, as well as the drawing down upon himself the favour of Almighty God!'

That to the Emperor of Russia, after stating their peculiarities, and the religious freedom they now enjoyed, continues:—'The Lord has put it into thy heart to promote the circulation of the Holy Scriptures among thy subjects; may he bless the endeavour to promote their general improvement, and as religious enquiry is now widely spreading among the nations, and many pious persons are searching for themselves into the things pertaining to salvation, we entreat thee, great Prince, to continue to be an indulgent protector of such upright, and conscientious subjects wheresoever found in thy extensive empire.'

Luke Howard and William Allen called upon Baron Jacobi, the ambassador from the king of Prussia, and showed him the address, which he seemed to approve, and promised to show it to the king. On the 16th of June Mr. Allen reports :

"Stephen Grellet, John Wilkinson, Luke Howard, and I, attended at James' Palace according to appointment with Baron Jacobi, to present the address to the king of Prussia ; after waiting some time, we were told that the king had been up all night, and was much hurried, and that the only chance we had of seeing him, was by standing in the passage through which he was to pass to his carriage. When he came up, Baron Jacobi directed the king's attention to us, and the address, together with some books, was presented ; S. Grellet had only time to say a few words in French, and on adverting to some of our society in his dominions, and to the Society's testimony against war, the king observed, that they were excellent people ; but without waiting for the conclusion of the sentence, said, ' war was necessary to procure peace ' "

The interview with the Emperor of Russia was so pleasing and is so graphically written, that it will be best told in Mr. Allen's language. He had previously obtained an introductory letter from the Marquis of Tavistock to Count Lieven, the Russian Ambassador.

" 18th.—This morning Luke Howard accompanied me to Count Lieven's, Harley-street. I first made an apology to him for not taking off my hat, on the ground of our religious scruple in this particular, which he received in a very affable manner. We then explained the nature of our mission, and gave him a copy of the address from our religious society to the Emperor Alexander, in English. He appeared to read every word with the most marked attention, and very deliberately ; I watched his countenance, and observed that his mind was considerably affected by it. He assured us that he would lay it before the Emperor, and take his pleasure upon it. He requested me to attend at the Pulteney Hotel that evening at nine o'clock, which I did, but the Emperor not arriving, I left at between twelve and one, and arrived at Plough-court about half-past one."

"The next day I went up to Count Lieven's. Soon after eleven, one of the servants came into the room, and said that the Count was at the door in his carriage, and requested me to go to him; he smiled, and made me get into the carriage, and, driving off immediately, informed me that the Emperor wished to attend one of our meetings, and that there was no other time for it but the present. I replied, then it was plain we must go to the nearest, which was Westminster, and lose no time, otherwise it might be broken up. We were soon in the midst of a crowd of carriages and people, I think at Count Nesselrode's, Curzon-street, Mayfair. My mind was much exercised for the honour of the Truth, and my secret petitions were put up to the alone Source of Divine help. The Count was dressed in his regimentals, gold epauletts, stars, crosses, &c., with a large hat and feathers, sword, &c. On entering the house I was shown into a parlour on the left hand, the steps, passage, &c., being lined with people. I suggested, that to prevent annoyance from the mob, the Emperor had better go as privately as possible. The Emperor and Duchess soon came down, the former in a plain dress· I was introduced to them, and then gave the coachman di‑ rections where to drive. The Emperor and Duchess, with the two Dukes, went in one carriage, and Count Lieven took me in his. The plan was for the Emperor's carriage to follow us, but in the crowd we lost each other; however, we met much about the same time at Martin's-lane. A number of persons had collected, but not one of them had gone up the court. The Emperor alighted, and the Count, taking me by the arm, made way through the crowd. I went, at a respect‑ ful distance, before the Emperor, and had just time to beckon out four Friends who sat near the door. I desired them to get behind the Emperor and keep the crowd back, which they managed exceedingly well. I showed the Emperor, the two Dukes, and the Count, to a seat fronting the meeting; the Duchess preferred the first cross form on the women's side. I sat opposite the Emperor on the first cross form.

"The Emperor and the whole party conducted themselves with great seriousness. The meeting remained in silence about a quarter of an hour. Richard Phillips then stood up with a short but acceptable address to the meeting, and soon after John Wilkinson was engaged in explaining the effects of vital religion, and the nature of true worship, beautifully applying the text, ' He is their strength and their shield.' After he sat down, John Bell uttered a few sentences, and John Wilkinson sweetly concluded in supplication. I think I may say, Friends were evidently owned in this their strait, and that nothing could have answered better, if it had been ever so well contrived. After meeting, the Emperor and his companions, with the Grand Duchess also, very kindly shook hands with the Friends about them, and a passage being made through the meeting, I went before them to the carriage, they continuing to shake hands with the Friends as they passed. At the step of the carriage, the Emperor, in French, appointed the 21st, at ten o'clock, for Friends to to meet him at the Poulteney Hotel, limiting the deputation to me and the person who spoke second, which was John Wilkinson."

"21st.—We took up the address; the Emperor having been engaged till six o'clock that morning, was not up when we arrived, and we had to wait about two hours and a half. At last a message came for us, and Stephen Grellett, John Wilkinson, and I, were introduced into an apartment where the Emperor stood to receive us; he was quite alone, and dressed in a plain suit of clothes, and, with a look of benignity, seemed to receive us as friends, rather than as strangers.

I put the address into his hands, which, as he had seen the copy, he did not open, and then on behalf of the Society, presented him with some books. He looked into each of them, but seemed desirous of employing all the time in conversation, which was carried on partly in English, which he pronouced very well, and partly in French. His questions were chiefly in reference to the doctrine and practices of our Society, and evidently showed that he was acquainted with the operation of the Holy Spirit in the soul, and considered forms and external observances but of secondary importance. On the subject of worship, he said, he agreed entirely with Friends, that it was an internal and spiritual thing; he said that he himself was in the habit of daily prayer; that at first he employed a form of words, but at length grew uneasy with them, as not always applicable to the present state of his mind, and that *now* the subject of his prayer was according to the impression he felt of his wants at the time, and in this exercise he felt sweet peace.

" He was desirous of knowing whether any among us were set apart for the ministry, and whether we had any particular form on such occasions, or appointed any to preach at particular times. We stated the principles of Friends, which drew from the Emperor many interesting and feeling expressions. He remarked that Divine woaship consisted not in outward ceremonies or repetitions of words, which the wicked and the hypercrite might easily adopt, but in having the mind prostrate before the Lord.

" In conversation with S. Grellet in French, the Emperor feelingly remarked upon the importance of the trust committed to him—the many temptations to which he was surrounded, and the few to whom he could open his heart upon such subjects, saying that it would be a profanation of holy things to speak of them to persons in general Our dear friend S. Grellet, under the impression of gospel love, addressed a few sentences to him in French : the Emperor, pressing S. Grellet's hands, with both of his, was much contrited, and with tears in his eyes, said, ' These, your words, are a sweet cordial to my soul, they will long be engraved upon my heart,' indeed, several times during the opportunity, he took one or other of us by the hand, and to John Wilkinson he expressed how fully his spirit united with him in prayer, at the meeting, on first-day. He said he desired to have this opportunity, apprehending that he was in sentiment with us and though, from his peculiar situation, his practice must be different, yet the religion of Chirst being one, and his worship spiritual, he believed that in this we might all unite.

" He stated how the Lord had made him acquainted with spiritual religion, after which he had much sought it, and that herein he found strength and consolation; adding, that he, and all of us, were only placed in this life to glorify God, and be useful to one another, and that we ought to strive to be prepared for another life.

" He expressed how much he was disgusted with the practice which prevailed in this country, of sitting several hours after dinner, saying it was a waste of that time which might be employed for the good of our fellow creatures.

" On S. G. congratulating him with having such a sister as the Duchess of Oldenburg, who appeared to be one in religious sentiment with him, he said it was a great favour that they could freely converse together on such subjects, and profit by each other's experience.

" S. G. having directed his attention to suffering Africa, the Emperor went into the subject with warmth of feeling, saying that the Africans were men, and objects of redeeming love as well as ourselves; and that when the articles of peace were framing, he had done all he could for them, and from what passed, it appeared very plain, that if the cause of Africa were given up in the treaty, it was no fault of the Emperor's.

"I then addressed him on the subject of establishments for training the poorest of the people in habits of morality and virtue, and in useful knowledge. and respectfully remin(?)d him that he possessed the power, in a greater degree than any other person now in existence, for doing incalculable good in this way. I briefly stated the plans now pursued in this country, and the preference claimed by the British and Foreign School Society, and that it was well calculated to assist Bible Societies: the Emperor listened with marke(?) attention, and said, 'It is indeed a subject of great importance.'

"The interview lasted about an hour, and the Emperor stood during all that time; his conduct throughout, though familiar and affectionate, was dignified, and he said, 'If any of your Friends should visit Petersburg on a religious account, let them not wait for any introduction, but come direct to me, and I will do everything to promote your views.' He remarked that he should never forget this opportunity, and. as we withdrew, he took each of us by the hand, and said, 'I part from you as from friends and brethren.'"

The Emperor, when at Portsmouth, expressed an inclination to "visit a family of the persuasion of Friends, and stop for half an hour to have a little friendly conversation." Lord Sidmouth signified the Emperor's desire, and arrangements were accordingly made for John Glaisyer to receive him: but when he reached Brighton, the crowd was so great, that he passed on without fulfilling his intention. Mr. Glaisyer, however, writes to Mr. Allen :—

"I think thou will be pleased to learn that the Emperor was not willing readily to give up his wish to see a Friend's family. My cousin, Nathaniel Rickman, and his wife, were standing at their own gate last first-day afternoon, to see the Emperor pass; he, seeing they had the appearance of Friends, desired the driver to stop, when he alighted, and asked N. R.

if they were not of the people called Quakers. Being answered in the affirmative, he requested liberty to go into the house, which, of course, was most willingly granted The Duchess then alighted, and they all went together shortly afterwards the Duchess asked if they might go over the house, and they were accordingly conducted into the principal apartments, the neatness of which they praised; On returning to the parlour they were invited to take some refreshments, which they did, and seemed much pleased with the attention. On finding that the family had not heard of the Emperor having had any communication with Friends in London, he gave them an account of his having been at meeting, and also of the conversation he had had with some members of the Society, in an interview *out of meeting*. They seemed unwilling to take leave, but said, two or three times, that they had to go as far as Dover that night, and they wished to know whether they should pass any more Friends houses on the road; they said they had intended to go to one at Brighton. but could not get there for the crowd; they wished to be remembered to Friends generally, said it was not likely they should see each other again, but they hoped they should not be forgotten. On parting, the Emperor kissed Mary Rickman's hand, and the Duchess kissed her; they shook hands cordially with N. R., saying 'Farewell.' They stayed about twenty minutes, and, during their conver. sation, the Emperor spoke in praise of the Friends he had seen in London, and behaved throughout in the most free and affable manner possible."

Who, after reading this touching narrative, is not ready to exclaim, May all future Emperors of Russia resemble the good Emperor Alexander, and all the uneducated poor children in his vast dominions have as earnest and disinterested a friend to plead on their behalf as William Allen!

MODERN PERSECUTION OF QUAKERS.

A writer in a well established journal remarks:—
The record now lies before us in *A Narrative of the Cruelties inflicted upon Friends during the years* 1861 *to* 1865, *in consequence of their faithfulness to the Christian View of the Unlawfulness of War;* and a very remarkable narrative it is. The statements, says its preface, may be accepted as literally true, taken down in most instances from the lips of the sufferers themselves; and the pamphlet is issued by direction and on behalf of the representatives of the North Carolina yearly meeting of Friends, in July 1868.

At the breaking out of the civil war in America, if the Quakers were unpopular with the North as being non-combatants, they were doubly odious in the South, on account of their hostility to slavery. Upon that subject, they were far in advance of their southern fellow-countrymen. In 1740, this same North Carolina Meeting contented itself with pronouncing an 'advice' that all slaves be well used; but thirty years later, it declared the importation of negroes from Africa to be iniquitous; and in 1776, the practice of slaveholding was formally condemned. For more than thirty years after, there were 'Friends' who were not fully convinced of this evil, or were so involved in it as to make their extrication difficult; but in 1818, slaveholding was abolished in the Society, and the brief record of the yearly meeting ran thus: 'None held slaves.'

To begin with, therefore, the Friends had placed themselves in antagonism with the people of the Southern States, and, when hostilities commenced, the ill-feeling towards them took a practical shape, and increased with the duration of the contest. By the passage of the Conscription Act in the Confederate Congress in 1862, every man between eighteen and thirty-five years of age was required to enter the army; in

T

1863, it was made to include all between eighteen and forty-five; and in 1864, all between seventeen and fifty. The Friends petitioned Congress for relief; and in the first instance, obtained exemption on the payment of one hundred dollars each, which tax however, was raised a few months later to five hundred dollars. As the war proceeded, and the necessities of the Southeners increased, the Quakers were more and more severely treated. Rude arrests, short but uncertain imprisonments, and violent menaces, were at first, the lot of those who were drafted and refused to fight. Some escaped to the West; others felt at liberty to engage in the state salt-works, though not a few of the latter, finding their work too closely connected with war (probably the making of gun-powder), relinquished it. Then the Southern gentry began to use sharpness, and to hang up Quakers by the thumbs. Here is one instance out of many. 'In the spring of 1865 about forty men, professing to be in the search of conscripts, came to a mill belonging to J. D., of Cane Creek, Chatham Co.' The miller was first hung up by a rope three times, to force him to betray his sons, who were hidden. Upon hearing the screams of the miller's wife and children, J. D. went out to the crowd. The same information was demanded of him, but he assured them of his entire ignorance as to their retreat. He was at once seized and carried into the barn. A rope was tied around his neck, and thrown over a beam, while he was mounted on a box. Then, beginning to tighten the rope, they said: "You are a Quaker, and your people, by refusing to fight, and keeping so many out of the army, have caused the defeat of the South;" adding, that if he had any prayers to offer, he must be quick, as he had only five minutes to live. J. D. only replied that he was innocent, and could adopt the language, "Father, forgive them; they know not what they do." They then said they would not hang him just then but proceeded to rob him ; then ordered him under a horse-trough, threatening to shoot him if he looked up. While lying there he could hear them hanging up the miller three different times, till the sound of stiangling began. After finally extorting a prom.se from him to find his sons, they left, charging T D. to lie still till they came back with some others to hang. They did not return, however, but went on to one of his Methodist neighbours, whom they hung until unconscious, and then left him in that state ; and the next night they found one of the missing conscripts, whom they hung until dead.

This was not a mere ebullition of anger on the part of a pressgang. The officers of the Southern army were instructed to carry out these precautions ; at all events, they did so. On their refusal to take a gun, the unfortunate Friends were subjected by the military authorities to something very like torture. Not only were guns tied to the arms of these non-combatants, and straps round their necks, by which they were dragged about, but they were married to a sort of Scavenger's Daughter. 'S. F.,' for instance, was subjected for two hours to the brutal punishment known as Bucking, in which the person is placed in a stooping position, the wrists firmly tied and brought in front of the knees, with a pole thrust between the elbows and the knees, thus keeping the body in a painful and perfectly helpless positi n. After this, he was made to carry a pole for two or three hours, and then tied during the night. The next morning, he was tied up by the hands for two hours. The same afternoon, a gun was tied to his right arm, and a piece of timber to his neck. Unable longer to endure the weight of it, he sat down, in order to support the end of it upon the ground, when he was pierced by a bayonet. Then they bucked him down again, and gagged him with a bayonet for the rest of the day. Enraged at the meekness with which these cruelties and indignities were borne, the captain began to swear at him. telling him it was useless to contend further; he must now take a gun or die.   As the captain proceeded to tie the gun upon his arm, S. F. answered quietly, "If it is thy duty to inflict this punishment on me, do it cheerfully—don't get angry about it."   The captain then left him, saying to his men, "If any of *you* can make him fight, do it—I cannot."   Two young men now appeared with their guns, telling him they were going to take him off and shoot him.   "It is the Sabbath," he replied, "and as good a day to die as any." The next day, the Bucking was again resorted to.

There are, in fact, so many examples given of this practice, that Bucking a Quaker seems to have been an amusement as popular with the Southern army as the game called 'fighting-cocks' is with schoolboys.   Friend H. M. H. suffered a still more severe punishment.   "At three different times, he was suspended by his thumbs, with his feet barely touching the ground upon the toes, and kept in this excruciating position for nearly two hours each time. They next tried the bayonet: their orders were, they said, to thrust them in four inches deep; but, though much scarred and pierced, it was not so severely done as they had threatened.   One of the men, after thus wounding him came back to entreat his forgiveness."

If the 'four inches deep' strikes the reader as a little exaggerated in the martyr's recital, this mention of entreating his forgiveness must be set down *per contra*.   It seems to us, indeed, that Friend H. M. H. was not only a martyr, but a fanatic, since he declined to make use of such means of relief as Providence placed within his reach, though with what precise object, unless, through extra suffering, to increase the subsequent spiritual penalties of his persecutors, does not appear.   His story runs as follows

"In the Spring of 1862, two brothers, H. M. H. and J. D. H., were drafted, arrested, and taken to Raleigh. Being allowed to return home for ten days, they faithfully reappeared. They were soon sent to Welden, where they were required to drill, and were warned of their liability to be shot if they proved refractory. They were, however, only kept in close custody in the guardhouse, and the next month were discharged, and sent home. About a year after this, they were included in the conscription. They were assigned to an artillery company at Kinston, and after various threats, were sent to Gen. R——, who declared that his orders should be carried out at all hazards. They were now confined in an upper room without food or drink. Various persons were allowed to converse with them, and, as day after day passed on, so far from sinking under the suffering, they used their little remaining strength gladly in explaining their testimony, and telling of their inward consolation. They felt that, in this time of fiery trial, this did indeed turn to them for a testimony, and that they knew the promise fulfilled : " It shall be given in that same hour what ye shall speak." Their sufferings from thirst were the most acute. On the third night, the brothers were wakened from a peaceful sleep by the sound of rain. A little cup had been left in their room, and from the open window they could soon have refreshed themselves. The first thought of each was to do so. They were in nowise bound to concur in this inhuman punishment; *yet an impression was clearly made upon their minds, before consulting each other*, that they must withhold, and they scarcely felt the copious showers tempt them. The next morning several officers entered the room and questioned them closely: they claimed it to be impossible for them to retain so much strength without any food, and charged them with secretly having obtained it. They then, in much simplicity, told

them of their feeling not easy to take even the rain that
fell. This evidently touched the hearts of the officers.
Soon after the end of four and a half days' abstinence, a
little water was allowed, and about the end of five days
their rations were furnished again.

MARRIAGES.

It has been observed, "Among other matters ordered
in the monthly meetings were marriages. No Quaker might
dare under the impulse of any sudden affection to solic.t the
hand of a maiden without the previous consent of his or her
parents, nor might he woo any but a Quakeress, for no allowance was made for the erratic tendencies of love. The consent of the parents and the daughter being obtained, the
matter was propounded in a meeting of the Friends, lest any
might have something to object. This done, at the next
monthly meeting the parties appeared, and, if no hindrance
arose, they publicly took each other, as husband and wife,
and promised, with God's assistance, to be loving and faithful in that relation till death should seperate them. A record
of this was entered in the register of the meeting, to which
the couple attached their names, and there the matter ended.

The Quakers had aimed at being a distinct people, but
eventually under the pressure of modern ideas that was no
longer possible. The marriage-law of the Society was felt
to be a grievance—no Quaker could marry out of his
Society without being expelled; no Quaker could allow a
clergyman or magistrate to marry him without subjecting
himself to the censures of his Society. Now, it so happened
that Quakers, having their eyes wide open, sometimes saw
women who were beautiful to look upon though they did
not dress in drab or grey; and, sometimes even when their
furtive glances were returned, such a commotion was raised
in their heart that love became stronger than religion, and

they resolved to abandon the Friends that they might get a wife after their own heart. So the Society lost some of its members who were otherwise good and true. The quarterly meeting for Yorkshire was the first to feel that allowance must be made for human frailty, and that under certain restrictions, the Friends might wed with the daughters of the land. The subject was debated three several years, and then referred to a conference of three hundred sages of the Society, who met in London, in November, 1858, and by whom, after much talk and some wrath, it was finally allowed. So the marriage-law of the Quakers was altered, and Friends allowed to look upon a maid, though she was not a Quakeress, provided only she sometimes came to their meetings, and had some sympathy with Quaker ways—a thing to be easily supposed, if her heart was set upon a Quaker husband."

The Quakers " by Dr. Cunningham.

A GREAT CHANGE.

A writer in Fraser's Magazine, October, 1878, remarks, " Those whose lot it may have been to live near a Quaker's meeting-house thirty years ago, and to revisit the same neighbourhood lately, must have been struck by the transformation which a generation has produced. Among the elders the old costume, picturesqly simple in form but often costly in material, may still be seen, but it is thrown into an insignificant minority by the younger folk, who, as far as outward appearance goes, might be the congregation of a Ritualistic church, while as to dialect it is doubtful if a young member of the Society would not be floored by Macaulay's famous "divinity" question which he is recorded to have set a niece ambitious of being examined. " Translate the following passage into the Quakeric dialect : You and Sir Edward Ryan breakfasted with me on Friday the eleventh of December."

THE QUAKER MAYOR OF LEEDS AND ASSIZE SUNDAY.

Two amusing circulars have just (Jan., 1880) been issued to the members of the Leeds Corporation. Mr. Alderman Tatham, a Quaker and a Teetotaller, who has no wine on his table, even when the Judges dine with him, is the present Mayor of Leeds. It is customary for the Mayor to go to Church with the Judges, arrayed in his insignia of office, and accompanied by the Corporation. Alderman Tatham has informed the members of the Corporation by circular that next Sunday the Judges and himself will be present at the Parish Church in the morning, and at the Friends' Meeting House in the evening. He says:—
" Divine worship being the most solemn act in which a human being can engage, display and parade appear to me to be out of harmony with the occasion. I therefore propose to meet at the respective places without any official gathering or insignia, as private worshippers, with the object of obtaining all the spiritual good that can be derived from the service." The pleasant novelty of a Quaker Mayor going to Church, and the Judges on circuit going to a Quaker Meeting House, has not been allowed to pass without a kind of indirect protest. Three past Mayors of Leeds have issued another circular, in which they invite the other members of the Corporation to meet at the Town Hall on Sunday morning, " in order to robe and proceed to the Parish Church in the usual manner."

Echo.

THE END.